Becoming Doctor Robinson

DON STARK

DEDICATION

This book is dedicated to all those lovely people who encouraged me to write it, mainly friends and family. Particularly impressive as most of you know that for every fifty projects I start. I generally only finish one or two. So, I suppose I should also dedicate it to all those other tryers in the world too: Keep going, you're nearly there.

DS

Contents

It is my firm belief that 'Doctor' is the highest calling to which a human being can aspire, though my other daughter insists that 'Maths Teacher' comes a very close second.

Don Stark

Chapter 1 – The Incident

The sun shone rather more than usual in the summer of eighteen fifty-seven and Its warm glow easily caressed the young faces of Emily and Spencely. As they walked over the fields towards the duck pond a pony and trap clattered swiftly along the tree lined driveway leading from the Big House to the road. "Farewell Father," yelled Emily at the top of her voice as she waved excitedly. The gentleman in the trap, the one in the top hat, waved enthusiastically back nearly knocking off the driver's hat. "I think he's going to Falkirk, to catch a train to Glasgow," she explained.

"Your father must have a very important job Emily," confided the seven-year-old Spencely.

"He doesn't have a job silly, he's The Laird." Somehow, she seemed to infer that by being a Laird you didn't need to work. Yet how, without a job, could anyone get to own a very big house full of treasures, and own all of the local land, the houses on it, and even the people in them?

"How do you get to be a Laird then Emily?" he asked, "...because I'd like to be a Laird one day." Emily often knew the answers to difficult questions; after all, she was nine so nearly a grown-up, at least in Spencely's eyes. But Emily thought that was a silly question.

"Well, you get to be Laird because your father was the Laird, but you haven't even got a father Spen, so you can never be a Laird." He stopped suddenly and let go of Emily's hand. Her words had shocked him, and he felt as if all his insides had been suddenly nettled. Although deep down he knew that he was never likely to be a Laird, hearing Emily tell him that he didn't even have a father really had a salty sting somehow. He'd never thought that she'd even noticed before. Until then, Spen didn't think he'd missed having a father, hardly even noticed it himself really, but at that moment he suddenly felt how nice it would be to have a father he could call his own.

Emily looked into Spen's face as the tears rolled silently down his cheeks. "Oh, sorry, did I say something?" She honestly didn't know why he'd instantly become sad. She tried hugging him because she couldn't think of anything to say. But Spen just stood loosely upright not making any attempt to hold onto her. She pulled out her handkerchief from some recess in her dress and began mopping his face. She saw the dirt come off onto the clean cotton. Oh dear, that would be another telling off from Mrs Wilding; 'kerchiefs were for carrying, not for using,' she'd say.

Then a pang of guilt at having upset her best friend caused her to recall someone once telling her 'If you can't say something nice, don't say anything at all.' She'd not known what the phrase had meant until then. She searched her mind desperately trying to think of something kind to say to him. "You're mother is lovely, much nicer than my mother." Spen thought about what she'd just said.

"I think that's actually true Emily," he said quietly, "but you never call your mother 'mother' do you, always mamar?" Then it was Emily's turn to be pensive.

"No, I don't, none of us do." Then, after a short silence, "I've never thought about that before... but you're right, we don't." After another, longer silence Emily suggested that they were equals once again. Spen's mother was lovely, Emily's father was lovely. Emily didn't have any brothers; he didn't have any sisters. Actually, Spencely didn't have any brothers either, but that fact didn't seem to figure in the young girl's logic.

"I'll be your brother Emily" said Spen trying to repair the hole of quietness which had opened up between them. "So long as I don't have to be brother to Mary and Catherine too."

"No, you can be excused that Spencely, I'll just keep you as my own, personal secret brother." They smiled and turned to continue walking across the field. She took his hand again.

They heard shouting in front of them, not of anger, but of horror. They broke into a trot, then a sprint. Once over the rise in the field a cottage came into view. By that time Spen was a long way in front of Emily, and he ran straight towards the cottage by the duck pond. The front door was open, and a woman's voice was screaming in horror from inside the tiny building. He ran straight in. Mr. Bell was laying down but only the back of his head and the backs of his heals touched the stone floor. His whole body was arching upwards, a most unusual pose for one so old. Spen felt shocked, he never knew that Mr. Bell had that much strength in him. He rolled sideways and crashed down onto the floor roughly, though he was still in the same backward arched position. The poor man was rigid. Mrs. Bell bent over him and offered him some soothing kind words, But Mr. Bell was not listening to her. His face looked angry and tortured; every muscle in it tensed up. She spotted Spen looking, then Emily too as she reached the open doorway breathing very heavily. "Spencely, please run and fetch Doctor Snoddy, as quick as you can laddie."

He barged past Emily in the doorway and headed for town. It would be a long run, and Mrs. Bell knew that Spen was only seven, but she couldn't think of anything else to do. She felt Doctor Snoddy was her only hope of saving her aging husband. Another neighbour had heard the shouting and had hurried across from some nearby farm buildings. Mrs. Grant was quite surprised to see the Laird's daughter in all her finery standing at the doorway of the small stone hovel. "Be off with you Miss Emily," she told her as she went inside to help Mrs. Bell. The old man had relaxed from his muscle spasm and Emily was relieved to see the improvement. However, she was not used to being spoken to in such a manner by one of her father's estate workers. She made a mental promise that she would tell her mother about it. Then she wondered if she should stay or go, Spencely would be another hour and she obviously wasn't wanted there. So she decided to walk back alone. She felt a little guilty again, the second time that day, this time for leaving. But there was nothing she could do, and she felt it was impolite to stand and stare whilst someone suffered. She also didn't want to hang around to watch an old man die.

* * *

Luckily, a fine gentleman on horseback asked Spencely why he was running along the road to Falkirk? He tried to explain about the affliction poor Mr. Bell was suffering, and his need for Doctor Snoddy. The gentleman forced him to stop and explain properly, once he'd caught his breath and calmed down. Then the gentleman told him that he was heading for Doctor Snoddy's surgery that very afternoon and would accompany him back out to Sir William Forbes' estate. He instructed Spen to return to the main entrance of the estate and wait for him and Doctor Snoddy there. They would arrive on the trap in due course but would need guiding to whichever cottage on the estate poor Mr. Bell occupied.

Once back at the stone arch into the estate, Spen wondered how long the pony and trap with the two gentlemen on it would be. He wondered about poor Mr. Bell. He'd never seen anyone arch their back so strongly before. It was even more surprising from a man in his sixties. He wanted to run across the fields and see how he was doing, but it was one thing to see how someone was, and quite another thing to be able to help them improve. Or even to cure them. Maybe, if Spen couldn't ever be a Laird, perhaps he could become a doctor. Surely you could become a doctor even if your father wasn't a doctor, or even if you didn't quite have a father.

The trap eventually hove into view and Spen jumped to his feet. He waved furiously but the pony was already at a good canter. He could see the unmistakable figure of Doctor Snoddy, hat on head, whip in hand, on the bench seat in the front of the trap. Next to him was the second gentleman who didn't look at all comfortable to be riding on such rough country lanes on this most basic of carriages. It must be the young gentleman he'd met on the road. As the two neared the archway he waved again and turned to run inside the estate grounds. He headed across the fields but was soon caught by the pony pulling the trap with the gentlemen on it. It drew up in front of him and he followed their instructions to clamber aboard, then they were off again. He stood in the back being careful not to damage the two leather Gladstone bags on the wooden deck. He saw the two bags were nearly identical, though one was much older than the other. The young gentleman turned and noticed how Spen was standing up in the rear, not even holding onto anything, whilst he, sitting on the bench seat, was holding on tightly with both hands as they bounced across the field. Spen saw him smile.

At the cottage he jumped down, took hold of the two heavy bags from the trap and ran for the open door. The young gentleman was close behind, but the elderly doctor was still extricating himself from the footstep of the trap.

Mr Bell was still on the floor but looked much more at ease. The young gentleman took some sort of listening tube from the newer of the two bags and pressed it between some buttons to the old man's chest. He bent down and put his ear to the end of the trumpet. "The heart rate is very elevated" he said to the old man as he arrived. "Breathing's too quick." Spen watched the young man lean away and carefully look at old Mr. Bell from his head to his toes.

"More light, Misses Bell if you please" said the old doctor as he stood over the young man, himself blocking some of the light from the doorway.

"Will he be alright Doctor?" murmured the old crooked lady.

"The neck scarf, does he usually wear it?" asked the young man. He'd spotted a mark on the patients neck which the scarf wasn't quite covering and had begun undoing the knot.

"What's wrong with him Doctor?" asked Mrs. Bell in a very worried tone. She hadn't answered the young man's question but simply asked the old man for answers.

"No sir, not usually" said Spen. He'd been paying attention. The scarf was gently removed revealing a large scratch, maybe even a cut, on Mr. Bell's neck. But the scratch was bright red and leaking yellow goo.

"Possibly Tetanus?" suggested the young gentleman.

"Aye, Possibly," agreed Doctor Snoddy.

Spen watched Doctor Snoddy and thought how he looked even older than poor old Mr. Bell on the floor. But at that moment Mr. Bell convulsed again into another tortured arched back pose. His forearms came up and his hands clenched tightly. Mrs. Bell yelped a little in fright. "There's your answer Doctor Cameron," said the old Doctor. 'Ah' thought Spen, so the young gentleman was a doctor too; Doctor Cameron. "I'll prepare a tincture of opium to relax the muscles," said Snoddy as he turned to carry his bag into the light by the door. "Get out of the way woman," he scornfully addressed the neighbour standing in the open doorway blocking the precious light.

"May we try Potassium Bromide first Doctor?" Spen listened to the two gentlemen discussing what treatment to give the old man. Snoddy was definitely old school, Cameron full of new ideas. "If you wish Cameron, you prepare that, and I'll prepare to let some blood."

"You're going to BLEED HIM?" Doctor Cameron struggled not to make his voice sound exasperated.

But Dr. Snoddy calmly replied, "Aye, his blood pressure is high, as is the speed of his heart." To Snoddy, it seemed a perfectly reasonable thing to do, he did it for a lot of his patients. It was what most of them expected. He reasoned that as neither of them had a cure for the illness, the least they could do was relieve some of the symptoms. Spen realised that the doctors were of totally opposing views, but noticed how the younger gentleman graciously deferred to the elder one with the line "He's your patient sir…"

As Mr. Bell relaxed again Cameron lifted his head and tried to persuade him to take some of the Potassium Bromide salt which he'd had Mrs. Bell mix into a small glass of water. He then began cleaning his neck wound with some liquid on a clean rag. Meanwhile Snoddy took a device from his bag, wiped its sharp projections, then somehow seemed to prime a spring in it. He then pressed it against a particular place on old Mr. Bell's forearm. When he pressed some kind of trigger the thing clicked causing Mr. Bell to jump. As Doctor Snoddy was in the way and blocking their view Spen, Mrs. Bell and the neighbour Mrs. Grant leant forward to see the scarlet trickle come from Mr. Bell's forearm. Spen could just make out that there seemed to be four small cuts each about a quarter of an inch long which Doctor Snoddy's device had made. Spen noticed that the only person not looking was the young doctor. He was still carefully bandaging Mr. Bell's neck. He handed the old scarf to Mrs. Bell and told her to burn it.

It was only at that moment Spen realised that Emily had gone. He wondered what had happened to her. He supposed that she must have got bored waiting and gone home. So, after wishing Mrs. Bell "Good day," and thanking the two gentlemen (which was the right way to take your leave from company) he turned to go. Just as he reached the doorway the young gentleman turned and spoke to him, "Hey, boy, you did well today, what's your name?"

"Spencely sir, Spencely Robinson," he replied proudly.

Chapter 2 – There Are No Rules

The next six winters were harsh, but Spencely and his mother Dorothy not only survived, but indeed, flourished. Spen always made sure that his mother had plenty of wood for the stove. He even took the sawmill offcuts to Mrs. Bell by the duckpond. His mother would sometimes make her a pie or a cake, and they'd take it to her after church on Sunday. She'd been on her own for nearly six years now. Dr. Snoddy had said that the old man had died eventually from poisoning of the blood, which was quite usual, rather than from the Tetanus which he must got from working near the cesspit. Doctor Snoddy had long since retired but unfortunately the nice Doctor Cameron hadn't taken over his practice. Dorothy told her son that she'd heard someone saying that Doctor Cameron's housekeeper had mentioned that the young doctor could learn little from Snoddy, and so he'd moved on after only a week of helping in the old man's surgery. Meanwhile Mrs. Bell, though not a well woman, had made it through another winter.

Spen still harboured thoughts that one day he might become a doctor, though that would mean the expense of going to a medical school, and that would cost money. He didn't have money. No amount of wood chopping and delivering in the evenings would gain him enough to be able to do that. So his dream had faded a little. And his hopes of ever becoming a laird had been laid to rest long ago by Mrs. Campbell, his teacher, who'd told him not to be so stupid.

But though she was probably right about him having no prospect of ever becoming a laird, she was definitely wrong about him being stupid. He'd slowly realised that he wasn't stupid at all. It was just that she spoke to everyone in that same derogatory manner. Emily's teacher however, was a much kinder lady. They didn't actually call her a teacher though; she was known as a Governess. She was even kind enough to let Spen join Emily in the library on Saturday mornings. She read them poetry, which seemed to Spen merely a way of complicating what you wanted to say. He would often just pull out his favourite book, the new one on Human Anatomy, written by Henry Gray, with beautiful, though sometimes grotesque drawings by Henry Carter. But he was always careful to not have it open at the pages showing anything that a young gentleman shouldn't be looking at, when Miss Fowler, or worse, Lady Sarah, came into the library. But Lady Sarah seldom came in, or even took much interest in anything in those days. Even her own three daughters.

Emily was still two years older than him, and at fifteen she was definitely shaped like a grown-up woman. Not quite like the slender elegant figures of her sisters, but more like one of the farm worker ladies on the estate. He had to admit that Emily had grown sideways a little more than her sisters, and upwards a little less. But she felt nice and soft, and squashy when he cuddled her. He'd even told her that she felt nice and squashy once, but Emily didn't seem to appreciate the compliment. Apparently, she'd not eaten cake for a full week afterwards.

He was still good at school but found himself asking more and more questions which Miss Campbell was becoming less and less able to answer. Could she explain the difference between Dogmatic and Pragmatic please? She'd answered that they were the same thing, but he strongly suspected they weren't. So, the Saturday morning afterwards he'd found one of the Laird's fine English Dictionaries and got the proper definitions. Even then, he had to put the answer into his own words so that he was comfortable with his understanding: Dogmatism was where you concentrate on one task or issue, and shake it like a terrier with a rat, striving through all problems to achieve your aim. Pragmatism was to see the full picture, take the wider view. After all, every argument had an opposing view which was equally valid to another person. One man's up, there in Scotland, was another man's down, in Australia. The world is round you see. A freedom fighter to the people is often a terrorist to the government. But this new understanding only led him to more questions; what actually *was* the truth? Yes, the view of the hill changed depending on where abouts you stood in the valley. Hmmm, being a grown up was going to be complicated. By the way, that was called an analogy (or was it an allergy?)

After school he would snare rabbits up on the sandy warren, or even try hitting a pheasant or two with his catapult. The more rabbits and pheasants he brought home, the more his mother seemed to enjoy the meat. She never used to like rabbit, or pheasant or even cow or pig meat when he was younger. She would always insist on giving it to him. But somehow, as meat got more plentiful, she seemed to enjoy it more. Odd that, he thought. They even had enough for old Mrs. Bell sometimes. She was always grateful, but strangely, often in tears.

The sawmill underwent a very large change that year. Last summer the stream had nearly dried up so there wasn't enough flow to turn the water wheel. At that point the Laird decided to invest in a new steam engine to drive the saw blade. September saw the arrival of some large iron castings and a huge boiler. One casting was called an engine and this was to take the steam, which the boiler made, and use it to turn the saw blade. Five men with funny voices (they called themselves Lancastrians) arrived with the ironwork to fix it in place and make it work.

They all stood around, with many of the estate workers too, on the day they first set a fire inside the boiler. It roared softly but after an hour or so began to hiss. Then one of the men shouted that they were 'up to pressure.' Rather marvellously, when a second man unscrewed some sort of tap in the pipework the mighty saw blade started to spin. It looked like nothing on earth would stop it. The estate workers smiled and gasped as the blade spun and parts of the engine pumped back and forth making a chuffing noise each time. Everyone smiled and some of the women even started to jig along in time with the engine.

At first Spen felt a little sorry for the stream as it would no longer be needed to turn the waterwheel, but then he realised that streams didn't have feelings. It wouldn't mind not being used; it was probably happy just continuing on its sweet way. No, streams can't feel either happiness or disappointment. That was just poetic tosh. Yes, the tosh of poets. Streams were inanimate objects, (yesterday's word of the day), even though they did actually move. Even so, Spen was just a little bit pleased when one of the men told him that the stream would indeed still be useful as the engine needed a regular drink of clean water for the boiler and some cold water for the condenser. Unfortunately, it needed a large amount of wood too. Spen thought that the off-cuts and the bark which he had been allowed to take for his firewood enterprise would all be consumed in the boiler's fire. Hence poor Mrs. Bell and perhaps his own mother too might go cold in the coming winter. But what actually happened, was that the new steam engine worked so much harder and produced so many more offcuts that he ended up with more wood than he could carry away on the hand cart.

Soon Harry, that's the Lancastrian who'd stayed, had told him that Spen's Laird was now having logs carted in from other estates, sawing them up, and sending them to Glasgow. *Lucrative*, became one of the words of the day.

* * *

One day, another lad joined his village school. Eric was a year older than Spen but quite a bit bigger. He was quiet when he first arrived, even friendly. But after a week or two he started being horrible to some of the girls. A couple of Spen's friends became more friendly with Eric and a little less friendly towards him. Eric wasn't very good at sums, but he was good with his fists. A combination Spen had noticed a number of

11

times before. He saw eric take a bread bun from Mags and when she'd tried to snatch it back, he'd hit her in the face. Spen was incensed and went up to defend Mags. But Eric hit Spen, several times, knocking him to the ground. The worst bit wasn't the physical hurt, but the way Mags came and stood over him blocking Eric from continuing the beating. Saved by a girl. Oh, that was terrible. She didn't even seem grateful either. Eric gained a few more friends that day, which Spen thought was unfair. Not right. Things didn't always go right in the world.

On his way home from school that day Matthew Carter went past him along one of the estate roads. He stopped and had a word. He even got down from his horse when he noticed Spen had blood on his shirt, and a swollen eyelid. He made him explain what happened and told him to come to his residence later that evening. Spen considered not going as he thought he might be in for another telling off. He'd had about as much telling off that day as any thirteen-year-old could stand. But his mother said that he should go.

So, after his evening meal, called 'tea' by the estate workers and 'dinner' by the estate owners, he went along to the Estate manager's rather grand house, which Mr. Carter referred to as his 'residence.' He came out of the rear door onto the lawn and was initially quite friendly towards Spen. But then, rather oddly, the man ordered Spen to "Hit me Spencely, as hard as you can."

"But sir…" Spen objected, "that would be wrong of me, totally wrong."

"It's alright, I want to show you something." Spen worried that as soon as he struck Mr. Carter, Mr. Carter would strike him back, and his nose already hurt, and his left eye was starting to close. But the estate manager insisted. So, Spen pretended to hit him, gently in the chest.

"No," bawled Mr. Carter, which made him jump. "I said HIT ME." So Spen obediently raised his left fist, pulled back his arm and threw it towards Mr. Carter as quickly as he could, whilst at the same time worrying about the consequences. But though the man's chest was definitely in front of Spen when he'd launched his punch, his fist struck only fresh air. "Again" shouted Mr. Carter. But though Spencely's arms flailed and windmilled round as he moved forwards towards Mr. Carter, he never struck him once. Mr. Carter eventually caught hold of Spen's left fist and his right forearm, and laughed as he held on, bringing the tirade to a halt.

That evening, Spen learnt many rules of fighting. 1/ There were no rules in a fight, only in boxing. 2/ Boxing was a sport, fighting was a battle. 3/ Mr. Carter had been able to dodge out of the way because Spen had made it obvious what punch he was going to throw, and when. 4/ There are three types of punch: Jab, Hook and Upper cut. They should all be used in combination, never just one. 5/ A punch is thrown from the shoulder, even the waist, not just the arm.

Mr. Carter taught Spen the delicate balancing art of dodging. Then how to block, how to keep moving, Mr. Carter called it 'Bob and Weave.' Spen never considered just how little he knew about fisty-cuffs before that evening on the lawn.

Mr. Carter ended the lesson by asking Spen to show him what he'd learnt. He then fended off Spen's punches with his open hands, shouting "good," and slapping him on the face a couple of times as they danced about. The lesson ended by Mr. Carter catching his fists again. But this time he skillfully spun him round and kicked Spen's rear end causing him to fall on all fours on the grass. Spen was incensed (again). He jumped up and ran towards Matthew Carter, but this time Mr. Carter came towards Spen and held him in a bear hug. It really surprised the thirteen-year-old. "Rules One and Two Spencely?"

"No rules, sir. It's not boxing, it's just fighting."

"And rule six is 'control your anger' Spencely, think calmly, don't be a hot head."

Spen held onto Mr. Carter perhaps a little longer than he perhaps should have done. He'd never hugged a man before, or even one of his mates at school. Only ever Emily, and his mother of course. It felt good.

But Mr. Carter had already loosened his grip and Spen realised he should probably do the same. He thanked Mr. Carter for his valuable lessons and politely took his leave, as he'd been taught. But that evening was full of surprises; As he made to go, Mr. Carter took a step closer to Spen and held out his hand. Spen cautiously stepped towards the estate manager and took his hand. Mr. Carter had a firm handshake, so Spen squeezed hard. "Good Lad" said Carter warmly, "You'll be fine young Spencely." The way he said, 'You'll be fine' sounded like Mr. Carter was somehow saying 'goodbye.'

The following day at school Spen was accused by Eric of having been saved by a girl on the previous occasion they'd met, and some of the boys laughed. Spen's blood started to boil. Then he remembered Rule six from Mr. Carter; 'Control your anger.' But Eric strolled up to Spen full of bravado and came within what Spen considered to be punching distance. As Eric smirked and flicked his eyes to one of his new friends Spen took the opportunity to catapult his left fist straight into Eric's face. It caught Eric, and everyone watching by total surprise. Spen was rather surprised too. But Eric looked back towards Spen as a trickle of blood started to run from his nose.

Spen raised his right fist in front of him to join his left, which Eric took as a challenge to fight. Spen moved his feet into the position which Mr. Carter had shown him. In a flash Eric launched two punches at Spen. The first, from Erics 'right' he avoided by 'bobbing' out of the way. The second Eric put all his might behind, but again Spen managed to jinx out of the way leaving his foot for Eric to trip over as the big lad lunged forward. Spen gave him a seriously good left hook to the side of his head as he fell over. It looked for all the world that Eric had been knocked to the floor by Spen, but Spen knew that the truth was really that he'd mostly tripped.

But the real victory came a moment later when Mags stepped forward over the crumpled Eric and asked him "Shall I protect *you* today Eric?"

and everyone laughed. Everyone except Eric that is. But then that day turned a little sour too. "Spencely Robinson, my room, NOW," shouted Miss Campbell.

Spen received a whacking from Miss Campbell's cane and was nearly brought to tears. The sting started from the moment the cane first whooshed through the air and didn't stop until at least a week later. His mother was in tears too over the issue. Mr. Carter told him he was very proud but had suggested a rule seven; that fighting was not to be a means of getting your own way, nor even of extracting retribution, but merely of defending the weak, the innocent, and the right. Retribution became a word of the day.

Eric was surprisingly tolerant of him after that. He even showed a little sympathy for Spen having taken a whacking from Miss Campbell's cane over the issue. They weren't exactly good friends after that, but they weren't any trouble to each other either.

* * *

The summer passed with a good harvest and full barns. The sawmill chuffed for twelve hours a day and it seemed that Glasgow had no end to its hunger for the wood. The laird had started sending bags of coal to each of his estate worker's cottages from one of his new mines. Spen also noticed that fewer canal barges were loaded with loose piles of white limestone, but of white sacks of something instead, perhaps baked, or cooked limestone. Spen discovered that, at the quarry there was now a new lime burning kiln, to make limestone into, well, just lime. That's what they called it.

Spen decided to make lime burning the topic for his Saturday morning study in the library. He'd asked Miss Campbell about lime burning but she'd told him that she couldn't be expected to know everything, and, anyway, he didn't need to know about that sort of thing.

Spen discovered that if you pack limestone into a container and heat it up, it changes somehow into Lime. And if water is added to the lime it changes again, even giving off heat in what is called an exo-thermic reaction. Exo meaning outside, and thermic, meaning heat. Wow!! This made Slaked lime which can react with something called Carbon Dioxide to set hard, used for joining bricks or stones together. Spen tried to explain to Emily that everything, absolutely everything was made up of only a few elements. He didn't fully understand what elements were, but they could join together in different patterns and could make thousands of different things, from Chickens to Gold candlesticks. Emily tried to converse wisely with Spen, explaining that she had been taught that elements were things like Earth, Air, sea, and fire. "Well, they aren't elements themselves, they are 'the' elements, but they're made up of elements." Emily glazed over a little when Spen talked to her about it. But Spen was even more engrossed when he discovered that each element was given a letter (sometimes two) and these letters were joined together to make things that weren't elements, but they were substances. Things like Limestone.

The Laird strolled into the library un-noticed by Spen, though Emily and Catherine had both seen him, and sat up from their studies. He gestured to them to stay quiet as he crept up behind Spen to observe what he was studying this week. "Ah, the Lime cycle Spencely." Spen sat up with a start.

"Hello Sir, sorry, I didn't see you there," said Spen as he pushed back his chair and moved to stand up. But the chair spell hit the Laird in the leg, and he groaned and acted as if his leg was broken "Oh, Sir, I'm desperately sorry, I didn't mean to..." But the girls, and Miss Fowler began to giggle. But then the Laird continued to hold his leg and hop about the floor.

"No, I think it *is* broken." He uttered painfully. At this the giggling stopped and the girls both stood up, ashamed of themselves for laughing in the face of their poor father's plight. Poor Spen didn't know what to do. But relief was brought quickly as the tall, elegant gentleman couldn't continue any further with his pretence and started roaring with laughter.

"Oh, Daddy, you're wicked," remonstrated the girls gently pushing and slapping him. Even Spen saw the funny side.

"So, Spencely, tell me about the Lime cycle" he asked. Spen stood to attention with his shoulders back. He took a deep breath. He was well used to being tested in such a way, though no-one else in his class ever seemed to undergo the ordeal.

"Well sir," he began. "Limestone is Calcium Carbonate, sea ay, sea oh, three, and by heating it above fifteen hundred and seventy degrees …"

"Centigrade or Fahrenheit?" the laird asked butting in.

"Oh, Fahrenheit sir."

"Please continue Spencely" commanded Sir William, (the three women were all listening intently at that point too).

"Well sir, by heating the limestone so, it is caused to chemically change into Calcium Oxide, sea ay oh, by giving off Carbon Dioxide; sea, oh two, into the atmosphere. This is also known as Quicklime. This can be transported in sacks in barges or carts to the buildings being constructed whereupon it is mixed with water to make slaked lime, which is sea, ay, oh, aitch, I think, and is quite slippery. This is Calcium Hoxide."

"Calcium Hydroxide Spencely, but that's near enough." Interjected the Laird. "What happens next?"

"This is an exothermic reaction. Which means it gives off heat when the water is added. It's mixed with mud or aggregate to form mortar or screed, and possibly something else, I forget that bit, then once it's dried out and cooled down it slowly reacts with the Carbon Dioxide, sea, oh, two in the atmosphere and sets hard again."

The three ladies all sharply turned their heads from Spen back to Sir William, as he asked, "And will that be the same Carbon Dioxide which it gave off earlier I wonder?" The three women's gaze flicked back from the Laird to Spen.

"Oh, I doubt it sir, that will all be miles away by now, I should imagine," he said with a victorious giggle.

"Bravo Spencely, marvellous," said Sir William as he smiled and graciously gave Spen a small clap. The three women clapped him too, but much more enthusiastically. He smiled and took a small bow.

"So tell us Young Spencely, when you grow up do you want to be a chemist, or perhaps an engineer?" As he spoke, the Laird suddenly realized that Young Spencely would probably make an ideal Estate Manager for him some day.

But Spen took no time in considering his answer and said, "I'd like to be a doctor one day sir." But then after a thoughtful moment he continued, "But I don't suppose that will ever happen..." He looked slightly wistful and forlorn, quite pathetic even.

Spen thought the conversation was at an end, but the Laird asked him, "Why a *Doctor* Spencely?"

Spen looked up into the face of the gentleman and said, "Because I believe it's the highest calling of mankind sir."

"Hmm, is it indeed," and it was the Laird's turn to be pensive. "Yes, young Master Robinson, I suppose it is."

* * *

Lady Mary (the eldest of the three sisters) had not joined them in the library on Saturday mornings for many months by then. She had grown too old to be governed by a Governess. Spen calculated that she was twenty-one years old, hence her learning was all done. Catherine and Emily told him that she spent most of her days riding horses, reading silly stories or doing needlepoint with her mother in the Morning Room. When Spen took time to consider Lady Mary he realised how she'd changed over these last few years. She had become more, well, 'snooty' was the word. She didn't treat him as a friend anymore, but as a youth, a mere boy, or even worse, just one of the oiyks from the farm.

When, on one of their long walks together Spen had mentioned Lady Mary to Emily, she'd told him of a gentleman caller, probably a suitor, who visited on a regular basis. It seems that Lady Mary was quite infatuated with the young man. 'Infatuated' became the word of the day. It meant 'possessed with an intense admiration.' Emily thought the relationship looked serious and Mary might one day be whisked away to England by the young man. Emily would miss her. Spen didn't think that he would.

Spen actually met the gentleman only a few days after learning about him. He and Sir William were driving along in the trap. Spen had seen them both a number of times that morning, perhaps the Laird was showing the young gentleman round his estate. Emily and Spen heard the trap rattle up behind them and Emily quickly let go of Spen's Hand. The trap slowed and stopped next to them as they turned and stood back a little. "Good morning to you Spencely," said the Laird, though rather formally, not in his usual friendly manner. Spen presumed that Sir William had already breakfasted with Emily that morning, and that must be reason he didn't greet her too. "Spencely Robinson, may I introduce Mr. Charles Richardson-Eames." Spen moved forward and began to offer his hand to greet Mr. Richardson-Eames, as he'd been taught. The Laird smiled. But rather oddly, Mr. Richardson-Eames didn't offer his hand back towards Spen. Sir William had whispered something to Charles about 'Estate Manager,' which seemed to quell any friendly feelings which the young gentleman may have had towards Spen. Spen read the situation well, he thought, and stopped short of the trap, stood to attention and bowed slightly from the hip.

"Good morning Sir William, how do you do Mr. Richardson-Eames."

"Morning Robinson" was the terse reply. Spen thought that the young gentleman was a little off handed in his manner. He put it down to him having noticed Spen's clothing, clean but not at all fine. As the Laird flicked the reins Spen stepped back, and the pony jerked forwards. But one of the leather straps joining the horse's collar to the trap snapped.

"Woooh" shouted Sir William quickly and the trap came to a halt again. Spen ran up and immediately detected the problem. The Laird and his guest jumped down to see the broken strap. It was the end of the trace running from the breast collar back to the left side of the singletree. Spen backed up the pony and re-threaded the worn end of the trace through the metal ring on the end of the singletree. He doubled it round and threaded it through again. He would have tied a knot in it but there wasn't enough length, and the leather was much too stiff. So, he picked up a small stick from under the hedge and pushed the narrow end of it through the ring jamming the leather strap tightly in place.

"Hopefully, that should get you home sir," said Spen to Sir William."

"Thank you, dear boy, I'm sure that will suffice," said the Laird as he climbed back aboard the trap. Mr. Richardson-Eames didn't smile or even offer any acknowledgement, let alone any degree of thanks for his assistance.

As they continued with their walk Emily told Spen that the second gentleman, Mr. Richardson-Eames, was the man who was visiting Lady Mary. He was visiting more and more these days. Catherine and Emily had both agreed that, although they originally had liked Charles, their kind regard for him had worn a little thin. Spen didn't enquire why, he deemed it impolite to do so. But at that first meeting Spen hadn't particularly warmed to hm either.

But neither had Charles formed a favourable opinion of Spen, it seemed: As Sir William and Charles returned to the mansion, having curtailed their tour due to the broken trace, Sir William expanded on his thoughts regarding Spencely possibly becoming the Estate Manager some years hence. But Charles had asked The Laird if he had noticed the teenagers holding hands upon their approach. He had but considered their relationship a mere dalliance. They were just good friends. Surely Spencely knew he could never have Emily's hand. "Yes sir, quite so, but Emily sir; as she matures will she not have an affection which would cause her heart to break when she finds her path of true love barred?"

Charles did have a point. Perhaps the Laird should find a way to send Spencely Robinson away. Get him out of Emily's future. Just for a time, until she was married off. Well, that's how he explained it to Charles Richardson-Eames.

* * *

From that day forward, Spen found his schoolteacher was surprisingly more helpful in her tuition. Miss Fowler too had started to take more of an interest in him on Saturday mornings. She set him all sorts of new work. She even taught him French and a little Latin. But Spen didn't see the point in Latin as no-one spoke it anymore. It was occasionally slightly interesting though to discover that an island in Latin is an Insula, giving us the English term insulation and isolated. Janus or rather Ianus, as there were no J's in Latin, was a door, and this was the root of the word January, the door of the year, obviously. But many of our English nouns which ended in 'um' or even 'orum' like arboritum or decorum had a Latin root, which the Romans brought to our shores. Greek was the other heavy influence on the English language, and perhaps the Vikings from Denmark too. But he thought he might leave those lessons for another day.

Surprisingly, his mother didn't mind that he was spending less time working around the estate and more time with his nose in a book. He still had time for fencing, walling, lambing and helping Matthew Carter on the farms, and Harry to fix that unreliable steam engine at the mill.

But for every benefit gained, it seemed there must be a cost. As he became more educated, he realised that he was slowly outgrowing many of his friends. He became tired of helping them with their maths as it just seemed so simple. He just couldn't understand why they didn't get it.

It was soon obvious to Miss Fowler the governess, and to Miss Campbell his teacher, that Spencely was actually, really quite bright, but more importantly he was still very eager to learn. However, he also had the skills and abilities which would make him of great utility to any company or organisation one day. The Laird would be sorry to lose him. He was torn between the self-interest of keeping Spencely on the estate and giving him more responsibility, perhaps eventually as Estate Manager, or having the lad educated at a proper university and thereby fulfilling his obvious potential. But then, sending him away would certainly alleviate the problem of Emily falling for someone of low birth.

There was however another problem which had been developing. And it was a delicate matter. Sir William had agreed to the union of Lady Mary and Mr. Charles Richardson-Eames. But it was beginning to look increasing like Charles had no intention of taking his bride back to Surrey, but instead was intent on staying North of the border. It was considered much less of a problem that he and Lady Sarah had not met Charles' parents, nor even that there was any prospect in plan for that to happen; Charles was obviously a gentleman of breeding, and he believed every word of Charles' reports of his family estate in Surrey and his education at Kings college in Oxford. No, Sir William's problem in prospect was 'what did he *do* with Mr. Richardson-Eames,' and more to the point where did he put him on the estate? He couldn't afford to build them a new large house as he was already committed to spending a lot of money that year: digging a new canal basin for the wood mill, buying a pair of ploughing engines. And that offer of another fifty-three acres of a deceased neighbour's land was simply too good to turn down. Hence, he considered it imprudent to build another house for Charles and Lady Mary that year, or even next. He was sure Charles would understand. But before the year was out the problem would seem to have resolved itself.

* * *

Just before the summer ended, when all the wheat, barley and oats were cut, threshed and stored, Spen took a walk over the fields to the sawmill one evening. He was glad to see Mr Matthew Carter arrive there at about the same time. He liked Mr. Carter, despite his gruff exterior, and had great respect for him. He might even consider himself a friend to Mr. Carter, ever since he had taught him how to throw a punch. And, upon further consideration, also for giving him back his respect amongst his school friends. Mr. Carter dismounted his horse and passed the time of day with Spen as they neared the sawmill.

As they drew closer, Spen saw one of the men tap his mate on the back and point to Mr. Carter obviously warning him that the Estate Manager had arrived. The two men used to be top dog and underdog in the time long ago, when some of the wood was sawn by hand. They'd been given the job of managing the mill. The second man came over and ran up the short steep embankment to where Mr. Carter stood with his young protégée. "Just getting the third cart loaded now sir, it should be all set by nightfall," said the man.

"But the engine is still going at full steam Barnes," observed Mr. Carter.

"Aye, sir, we've another three wagon loads to cut for tomorrow, so we thought while we had the light we'd get some in hand." But Mr. Carter didn't seem to know anything about those six loads of Timber being sawn and sent out. The usual daily quota for timber was one load per day with possibly two on Saturday.

"On who's instruction was this Barnes?" asked Carter.

"Why Mr. Eames sir, he said you'd approved it," answered Barnes.

"Did he now?" Replied a slightly disgruntled Mr. Carter. He turned to go, but then turned back and spoke to Mr. Barnes again. "Will there be any further extra-ordinary loads to your knowledge Barnes?"

"No sir" replied Barnes, "None beyond next Tuesday's three and of course the Tuesday after." Then, as an afterthought, or was it an attempt at humiliating poor Mr. Carter, he added, "But I'm sure you know about those sir." Spen could tell that Mr. Carter didn't know about them and was quietly fuming with anger. At that point he must have decided that he'd passed enough time of day talking to Spen and

Barnes, and without another word he mounted his horse and galloped off.

Spen stayed a little longer watching the sawblade effortlessly slice the logs thinner. He enjoyed listening to the rhythm of the engine. The first two carts must have departed earlier but he recognised the one being loaded. Or, more precisely, he recognised the grey horses pulling it. He didn't know the name of the wagoner but was sure that he was the regular man. He was the one who came every day, though usually at a much earlier hour.

On his walk home he thought how good it was that the sawmill was doing so well. Three times the amount of work that they had been doing for most of the summer. But he thought again about the estate manager having no knowledge of the extra purchases of wood. Seemingly so anyway. Spen felt a little uneasy too at the prospect of Mary's new husband giving orders to the sawmill workers over the head of Mr. Carter. 'Getting his feet under the table,' this was called. Indeed Mr. Richardson-Eames seemed to be taking an interest in many aspects of running the estate lately. Spen remembered that too had a name: It was known as 'learning the ropes.' But Spen had a mild suspicion that Mr. Richardson-Eames' motives weren't entirely innocent.

Chapter 3 – What's Matriculation?

It was around mid-winter a few years after when Spen walked up the lane to his home late one afternoon. It was dusk and the light wasn't good, but he saw a figure on horseback riding off from behind the cottage as he approached. From the upright style of the rider, it looked a little like the Laird. But Spen thought that it couldn't be him, as the Laird hadn't taken to the saddle much since his fall. Once inside, he was surprised to find his dear mother silently sobbing.

After his attempt at comfort using the powers of embrace, kind words and the making of tea, she had finally composed herself sufficiently to tell him the good news. "Spencely, I'm unsure about the details but you have won the opportunity to matriculate at the University of Edinburgh." She made it sound like it was a punishment, but Spen only heard three words; Won, Opportunity and University. "You would be the first person on this estate ever to go to a University Spen." But was his mother sobbing happy tears or ones of sadness? He wasn't sure how to react. "I don't understand mother" he said softly, "What does matriculate mean? And how has this come about?"

Dorothy sat next to Spencely as she threw more crescent sectioned logs onto the fire. "It's a wonderful opportunity Spen, one you *must* take."

"I don't want to leave you mother," said the young man gently, but quite firmly. "How will you manage on your own?" But Dorothy was quick to dispel any problems that might get in the way of her son advancing. Especially with a degree from a fine university.

Spen had been all too aware of the changes taking place on the estate in the past couple of years. Sometime before that day, he had spotted two wagons piled high with possessions on the track. The shock of seeing that the man driving the second wagon was the estate manager Mr. Carter still cut him to the quick. He was leaving and would probably never be coming back. Spen could not imagine an offense so vile that would make Sir William send his loyal estate manager off in such a humiliating way. Spen always imagined that Mr. Carter would die and be buried on the Stannet-Forbes estate, a loyal servant to the end. He could still picture the look on Mr. Carters face and remembered well the helpless feeling of emptiness and anguish it gave him. On that occasion Carter could hardly bring himself to speak to Spen when he'd run up and tried to ask the old man for an explanation. He'd simply told Spen that not all his enemies would come from in front of him. Spen had been quick to hold out his hand to Mr. Carter and even intended to give him a hug, should the moment be right. But it wasn't. Matthew Carter just shook Spen's hand and offered his final words of advice, which were "Watch your back son, watch your back."

His mother continued with her talk. Matriculation was a set of examinations which Spen would be asked to sit. If he passed, then he could go to the university. If he failed, then he couldn't. It was as clear cut as that. Spen sat and stared into space for a moment. Medical School, at Edinburgh. This meant Spen could maybe one day actually become 'Doctor Spencely Robinson'. He couldn't believe it. His mind raced. What would he have to do to pass the entry exams? Where would he live in Edinburgh, how would he even get there, how would he find where he was going (he'd never been to Edinburgh before), who would buy his books? In fact, who would pay for his food, and his lodgings, his school fees? Oh, this was simply impossible. His mother couldn't begin to make enough money to support him, not even if there were a thousand harvests a year. "But," he asked "who is going to pay for it all mother dear?"

'Scholarship' became the word for that day. She said that the Laird had put him forward for a Scholarship and had written a letter in his support. It had obviously worked. He had visited only moments before Spen arrived home to tell her the good news. But he thought the news would be better coming from his mother, rather than from himself.

* * *

The next months passed in a whirl of reading, guidance and learning for Spen. Word got round the estate that Spencely Robinson was going to be a doctor. Everyone knew that he was a bright lad, but to be a doctor was to be elevated to another world above threshing wheat and herding sheep. Folks even started to doff caps and tug at their forelocks in a show of mock respect when he arrived, or when they passed him in the lane. At first, he started responding by trying to explain about matriculation being exams that he would have to pass even before he would be allowed to commence training as a doctor. He might (very easily) fall at the first hurdle. But he quickly realized that no-one was listening to his lengthy explanations., Moreover, none of them truly expected a lad that they knew personally, had grown up with, had lived next door to, could ever, ever, become a real doctor.

He studied hard, harder than he'd ever studied before. He stopped looking at things simply because they were interesting. If he didn't have to know about something for the exams, it didn't get time spent on it. 'Syllabus' became a word for the day. He learnt Calculus, the area under the graph, a reducing size of increments, differentiation, integration. He practiced it until he fell asleep, until he knew it backwards, well, differentiation was only integration going backwards, after all. He started again at the very beginning of Latin; Bo Bis, Bit, Bimus, Bitis, Bunt. Brilliant, but what did it mean again? English; he confirmed in his mind the difference between adjectives and adverbs. He tried never to end a sentence with a preposition. So, (or was it 'henceforth') he stopped asking his friends 'What are you up to?' and asked them instead 'To what are you up?' But that just sounded silly. To so many rules there were so many exceptions in the English language. And he felt he needed to know every one of them.

He sat long hours in the Laird's Library, then in his own front room, by candlelight, long into the evenings. Over the next three months his legs and arms seemed to lose weight, but his stomach definitely looked like it had gained some, to him at least.

Emily got less of his time, but she gladly supported him in his endeavours, though she felt secretly that it might all be in vain. Sometimes he would call for her, and sometimes they'd meet by the wood at the bottom end of Ten Acre. But increasingly she would come to call on him. Often, when she did, Dorothy would invite Emily to come and sit with her in their parlour. They'd talk, sometimes for the best part of an hour, until Spencely had finished his chapter or the exercise he was doing. Dorothy enjoyed talking to Emily, particularly about her two sisters Mary and Catherine. Emily was surprised to find out how well Dorothy knew the little quirks and foibles of them both. They laughed a lot together.

Once or twice Spen, working in the next room, had finished his chapter, but as he got up to join Emily he'd hear her in excited conversation or sometimes giggling with his mother. At that point he would start studying again, just for another ten minutes or so.

Spen and Emily still walked miles together, sometimes hand in hand, sometimes slightly apart. They were too old now to play tag and chase across the fields, though Emily would still try and tease and tickle Spen when they stopped to sit when the weather was sufficiently clement. They both secretly liked it when their heads, especially their faces, became very close to each other. Emily particularly liked it when she felt Spen's breath on her cheek. Once, when this had happened, they both went quiet, and Emily's smile changed to a much more serious look. She softly said to him "Spen, I think I love you." Then she quickly sat up and turned away.

"Well, that's good," replied Spen after a moment, "...because I think I love you too Emily." Then it was his turn to look serious. But almost straight away she smiled and lunged at him, holding him in a bear hug and forcing them both to roll over, twice. The smiles returned but Spen was suddenly horrified to see that they'd rolled over a mole hill and Emily's dress had got brown and green patches all over it. "Mrs. Wilding will be furious," said Spen.

But Emily replied, "I don't care, this is the happiest day of my life Spen." She was kneeling on the grass in front of him and started to move slowly towards him. Spen half expected another tickling attack, or a bear-hug roll all the way down the hill. But instead, she softly kissed his lips.

* * *

A week after that (very memorable) incident, they were walking along by the same stream and Emily asked Spen a question; "Spen?" she began, "did you know that your mother used to be Governess to Mary and Catherine?" This was indeed a revelation to him. He had always assumed that his mother lived on the estate because his father had worked for Sir William. But it turned out that it was his mother Dorothy who was the employee, and his father was simply found a job in the fields, apparently accommodated by Mr Carter. "How do you know?" asked Spen. "Catherine told me, and she should know Spencely. She was my governess too, after the wet nurse, but I can't remember her, I was only little."

"So why did she stop being your Governess then?" he asked. But Emily stopped and gave Spen a questioning look. "Well, maybe, just maybe, she had a baby of her own..."

"Ohhhhhhh" said Spen. It was obvious when he thought about it. Well, that was interesting. It maybe also accounted for his mother being rather bright for a woman who lived in an estate cottage. He realised also that he must indeed have a father, somewhere. He must have been there, well, at the start. What had happened to him, he'd love to know where he went? Where he is now. Spen wondered about all the other knowledge in the world that he didn't yet know. He hoped it would always be interesting and never too shocking when he discovered it.

* * *

A couple of years before then, the wedding day had dawned bright and beautiful. Everyone was happy. Many wealthy guests were invited to the reception at the 'Big House' in the evening and most of the estate workers helped with their many carriages and then feeding their horsemen and horses. Some of Spen's friends were given jobs in the kitchen, his mother was even asked to be a silver service waitress and reported back on how the speeches had gone, and who had danced with who afterwards. Charles and Lady Mary looked very grand in their finery. Lady Mary looked every inch the fully matured woman, her dress was very long, white and very beautiful. Spen thought that there was rather a lot of it, but the sight of it made the old ladies of the estate bill and coo as if they were trying to sound like pigeons.

On the night Spen had hoped that Emily might have been able to sneak out of the big house to see him. He'd have liked to see her in the party dress which she had told him about (several times), but either she had forgotten about him for the night, or he had simply got his timing wrong. He did have a good time in the big barn though. Earlier in the day he'd helped some of the other men to clear the floor and decorate the rafters with paper bunting. They'd set up trestle tables and the Laird had kindly organised a Hog-Roast and several crates of ale and lemonade for the estate workers. Spen wasn't sure he liked the taste of beer, but the older men kept encouraging him to keep taking swigs from his tankard, and before long he could feel his heart gladdening and his head starting to spin.

One of the sizeable men's sizeable wives grabbed him and took him for a jig around the dance floor. He'd never danced before and so didn't perform quite like the others. But the ale had convinced him that it was the spirit of the dance which was important rather than the exactitude of feet placement and timing. Yes, most of the others were indeed all doing the same movements together, generally at the same time. He would have liked to, and the large lady with whom he was dancing would have preferred it that way, but it mostly didn't happen. People smiled and pointed, and at the end of each dance yet another over-confident wench would come up and say, "Pass 'im here," to his previous owner, and off they'd gallop again. By the end he was puce and glowing, but he had to admit, dancing was fun.

As he looked back on those good and simple times, he remembered how he'd slept really well that night. And how the next day had been a big clear up. And how at noon they all had to appear along the driveway from the big house, to politely clap as Charles and Lady Mary drove past as they left for their honeymoon. Even then he remembered hearing one or two of the men suggesting quietly that the longer they were gone the better they'd like it.

In the month they were on honeymoon the estate seemed to run just as efficiently as it ever had. But more than that, there seemed to be a calmer air about the place. Emily reported the same was true up at the Big House too. The staff there were smiling more than usual. People seemed more relaxed, friendlier somehow.

However, one morning The Laird had gathered all the kitchen staff, the chamber maids and the footmen in the hall and told them all that Lady Mary and Charles wouldn't be returning to live in the Mansion but would be going to live in the Estate managers Residence instead. There was a gentle but spontaneous round of applause for the happy couple. But then, when Sir William had asked for volunteers to go and staff at their new home only one person volunteered. It was Elizabeth McFael, who was Lady Mary's chambermaid. Her hand shot up. Everyone seemed quite surprised as no one else had any inclination to transfer, but perhaps she had a sense of loyalty towards Lady Mary. The others hadn't volunteered as the thought of going to work for Charles filled no-one with glee.

"Oh, come, come now. Robbins, they'll need a good footman," suggested Sir William.

"If you wish Sir..." said the reluctant Robbins slowly raising his hand. All the positions were eventually filled though Sir William was glad that neither his butler nor his cook had volunteered to leave. He noted how all the staff (bar one) were reticent about moving across to the other house but had decided to think of it as loyalty to himself and Lady Sarah, rather than any lack of desire on their part. Even so, he really didn't like to press-gang people against their will.

When Emily explained all of this to Spen, he wasn't very surprised. He didn't know of anyone on the estate who had a good word to say for Mr. Charles Richardson-Eames. He just didn't have the 'touch' that Mat Carter had had. Their opinions were reinforced when, two weeks after the 'Happy Couple's return, he and his mother visited old Mrs. Bell with a Blackberry and Apple pie and found her packing her trinkets and belongings into boxes. They asked her what she was doing and where she was going? She had a sister in Kirkintilloch and was going to live with her. But with a little further questioning to clarify his understanding, Spen confirmed that she had only one sister, the one she couldn't abide. "Then why go Mrs Bell?" he asked innocently.

"Needs must where the devil drives," was her poetic reply. Spen didn't really follow that as a reason, but when he considered the situation further it all became clear.

"Which devil is driving you out Mrs. Bell?" he asked. The old woman stopped what she was doing and looked up to Spen.

"Oh, there's only one Devil around these parts Spencely." It was a shock to him. It was certainly a shock to poor old Mrs. Bell. Spen decided that this could only be Charles' doing. He obviously wanted her house so that he wouldn't have to pay lodging expenses to some of the new workers at the Sawmill. Mrs. Bell hadn't been a productive soul for many years, and indeed she looked like she might go on for a few years yet occupying that big cottage on her own. But the Laird would never have done that. Indeed, Spen wondered if the Laird even knew about it.

So, the following Saturday morning when the Laird came wondering into the library, Spen mentioned to him that he was… "Surprised to hear that old Mrs. Bell was leaving."

"Leaving Spencely, where is she going?" Ah, so the Laird didn't know.

"I'm not sure sir, I don't even know if *she* does." The Laid turned to leave the room, even though he'd just arrived. Spen heard him shout for a horse to be saddled immediately.

But when Sir William arrived at the Bell's cottage it was empty, not just of life, but of all evidence of life. He stood in the hovel for a moment with his hands on his hips considering the problem, which it seems he had created for himself. His situation was difficult. He couldn't on the one hand ask Charles to run the estate, and then on the other go counter-manding every instruction he gave. That would be grave interference and show a total lack of trust in the man. He just whished that Charles would talk to him a little more about his plans before executing them.

It was a fine day too when Sir William decided to ride over to the sawmill. He stopped his horse on the hillside above the mill. Down in the dip the engine chugged away rhythmically as usual. He could see two wagons, one nearly full of timber, one empty. He walked on and as he neared the shed the full wagon moved off and the empty one pulled forward into its place. The full one was Hargreaves' wagon, the usual man, with his two grey heavy horses. But Sir William didn't recognise the second wagon, nor its driver. So, he waited for it to be loaded. As it moved off, he slowly, surreptitiously, followed it. At a good distance. It went all the way to a merchant's yard on the outskirts of Falkirk. Before the wagon could go in, it waited until another one came out. Sir William suspected that it was the same as the first one to leave his mill. Was that one Hargreaves? He couldn't be sure from that distance, not with his failing eyesight. But by Sir William's understanding all the wood should have gone to their new canal wharf and on to Glasgow that day.

At the merchant's yard the men doing the unloading couldn't throw any light on this new arrangement and told the fine gentleman on horseback that he must return on Monday and ask the yard owner, a Mr. Perkins.

Upon his return home the Laird was aching from his journey, even though it was only quite a short one. Since Lady Mary and Charles had moved out into their new home he didn't see much of Charles anymore. Perhaps, he considered, Charles had got his feet under the table just a little too far. Sir William decided to check the accounts incoming ledger. As he studied the columns he was disappointed to find there were no entries which he didn't recognise. Certainly nothing with the name 'Perkins' or even any reference to Falkirk. There seemed to be forty-six wagonloads of timber in the last forty-nine days. Six per week, two on some Saturdays. Exactly what he expected.

He sat back in his chair and remembered that awfully embarrassing conversation with Matthew Carter when he'd inferred fraudulent trade of wood from the sawmill. That was a couple of years ago now. How Mr. Carter had stood before him and was the closest he'd ever come to being rude to Sir William. The Laird covered his face with his hands in embarrassment when he recalled how Carter had told him that he had no wish to remain in the employ of a man who no longer trusted him. Sure, wasn't it Carter himself who had come to Sir William to tell him of his suspicions about the un-documented trade, though only after Charles had already warned him and planted the seed of suspicion in his mind? He felt very foolish. More than that; he felt the bitterness of treating a valued friend with unwarranted suspicion, and it really stung him.

And here it was happening again. Perhaps not 'again,' the word he was looking for was 'still.' He vowed to ask Charles about this new arrangement with the yard in Falkirk, the next time he was over.

Chapter 4 – A Chance Too Good

Interestingly, six or seven months after starting work at Charles and Mary's 'Residence,' Robbins, the press-ganged footman had sought employment elsewhere and left, giving very short notice.

On one of their walks Spen asked Emily if she knew why Matthew Carter had left, just before Lady Mary was married. She didn't know any details but thought that Charles had uncovered a private arrangement which she believed was to do with the wood yard. Spen asked Emily to explain. It meant somehow that he had been cheating the estate and making money 'on the side' whatever that meant. Mr. Carter had protested his innocence, but then he would do that if he was guilty, wouldn't he. But as she expounded on the topic of Charles, Spen realised that Emily too didn't much care for him. He'd been disrespectful to her on a number of occasions, even in her own home. She'd also heard him shouting at the staff at the Hall, and even at Lady Mary herself. He shouted at Mary a lot in their own home too. Often it happened in the evening when Charles had been at the decanter. Spen asked how Emily knew all this? Oddly, she told Spen that this information had come from Lady Mary herself. Mary had even suggested that Charles was showing more interest in Elizabeth McFael, her chamber maid, than he did in her.

Spen was sorry to be going away from the estate just as things seemed to be in turmoil. He had a nagging worry that what had happened to poor old Mrs. Bell, might possibly happen to his mother too. Things were changing. But Dorothy told Spen not to worry about her. He must simply concentrate on his studies and make sure he passed those matriculation exams to gain a place at Edinburgh University. At her behest, seasoned with the responsibility of needing to provide for his mother one day, Spen redoubled his efforts with his studies.

* * *

When the eighteenth of October, Eighteen-sixty-nine came, Mr. Bateman arrived outside their cottage in a trap which carried a bag and a new footman. Spen was quite privileged to ride on the front seat with Sir William's butler and have the younger man, though a little older than himself, be told to ride in the back. Not much older, but probably a little higher in status than himself, he imagined. Mags and one or two others from his old school stood on fences along their route or waved from fields as Spen went by. They'd never seen him ride in the front of a trap before, unless he was driving it for someone else. It seemed to be quite an occasion, not just for Spen but for all those who knew about his exams. They waved and shouted their best wishes; "Good luck Doctor Robinson," being typical. Mr. Bateman was moderately surprised to see how well Spen was regarded by the folks of the community. Bateman himself didn't really do emotion though.

Once at the station the footman left in the trap. Bateman bought tickets at the ticket office for the two of them, and they walked through onto the platform. 'Platform 1 – Eastbound,' said the sign. Spen was very excited; he'd never been on a train before. When one arrived in all its mechanical grandeur, he followed Mr. Bateman into a compartment whereupon they sat opposite an old lady and her grandson. Spen thought that Falkirk railway station was big and complex, but it was nothing when compared with the mighty and very new Waverley station in the centre of Edinburgh. When their train jolted to a halt there, everyone stood up and crowded to the doors. They all seemed to know exactly where they were going and what they were doing. People were everywhere. Spen felt just a little intimidated. He stood and gauped at the scene. He even noticed Mr. Bateman briefly standing, gazing about him too.

Surprisingly, they couldn't just walk off the train and out through the station building, but had to find a foot bridge, climb many steps and cross many more tracks before climbing again next to the station terminal building. Things were much bigger in Edinburgh; buildings, streets, carts and carriages. People on horseback and people on foot. So many on foot, from proper gentlemen to oiyks. Everyone seemed to have a purpose, a destination or a meeting which they were late for. No, he meant 'for which they were late.' This was important, never more so than here and now.

Edinburgh seemed to be built in a valley with the station at the lowest point. As Spen looked around he spotted a magnificent castle on the other side. Its mighty walls stood atop a sheer rock face. His mouth fell open in awe again. Mr. Bateman caught sight of him and smiled, but they were quickly brought back to the present by the driver of a wagon shouting for them to, "shift or be crushed." The two leapt out of the way but were nearly straight under the large wheels of a handsome carriage. Spen had never seen Mr. Bateman giggle before but when the two of them reached the paving they confirmed that they were glad to make it all the way across Princes Street and yet still be alive.

Spen carried the bag and followed Mr. B as he studied a note from his pocket, then looked up at the street names on the corners of the magnificent stone buildings. He went down a side street, then up an alley, through a little portal and in through a door marked 'The Durham Lodging House.' Spen was surprised to find that he didn't have to share a room with the old man but was given one all to himself. It had gas lighting and three beds in it, and he could choose which one he wanted. He excitedly had a peep out of the window, but was instantly disappointed as the view was of a dingey yard and the backs of other buildings.

There was a knock at the door; Mr. Bateman had somehow found two cold meat pies and a couple of slabs of bread. He told Spen that tonight they would take a walk out and identify where they were to present themselves in the morning. They couldn't risk turning up late through misidentification or poor navigation. That would be a dereliction of duty to Mr. Bateman, and Mr. Bateman took his duties very seriously indeed.

The city was a bit less busy in the evening, or was Spen's perception getting a little more attuned to the hubbub, he wondered? They went back towards the station, but this time crossed the huge three arched North bridge over the station as well as all the tracks. They continued along an elevated section of road known as South Bridge. Or was it an actual bridge, just a very long one? Spen wasn't sure. He observed and concluded that 'South Bridge' was indeed a bridge of perhaps twenty or so arches, though the city was so concentrated that the buildings on either side were built up to such a degree that they had a second frontage onto the top of the bridge, upon which they were strolling. This made it look much less like a bridge crossing and more like a normal everyday street. Spen was surprised and even a little delighted to see just how many parks and gardens had been built into the plan of Edinburgh.

Building after building imposed themselves upon his eyes, his mind, his very being. A building which looked for all the world like it might be The Royal Bank of Scotland stood atop massive stone steps away to his right. Through one of the arch-way entrances he could see a large grass square within, and grand stone buildings on the other three sides. Bateman told him that it was no bank but was in fact the university, the one which Spen was attempting to join. At that moment Spen thought that flying to the moon would be an easier task. It all looked very grand. Certainly, too grand for a lowly estate worker like him. The thought that he might one day soon be starting his training there was way past overwhelming. He wondered if there were different levels of 'overwhelmingness.' If so, his would be just above the very highest level of overwhelming possible.

Then, a little further along, Surgeon's Hall stood to his left, proud and stately. Even if it had been some fancy royal palace it couldn't have looked more impressive. They walked up to the first grandiose entrance archway then stopped. Mr. Bateman checked his note and compared it to the shining brass plate adjacent to the black wrought iron gate. Two ladies, one mid-twenties, one a good number of years older (he'd been taught never to assume or guess the age of a lady) came and stood next to them. They seemed to be admiring the brass plate too. Spen was going to burst unless he could tell someone about coming back tomorrow for the exam. So, in a somewhat out of character moment he proudly told the young woman "I'm coming here tomorrow to begin sitting the exams," even though he shouldn't be talking to a total stranger without the formality of an introduction first.

She smiled at him. And in an educated English accent she replied, "Yes, me too." Oh, a fellow student in prospect, how exciting, thought Spen.

But Mr. Bateman opened his mouth and put his foot in it with, "No miss, Young Robinson is here to take the matriculation exams for the Medical School."

"Yes," said the young woman once more, rather more seriously, "me too."

"Oh but, I didn't think there were any lady doctors," said Bateman to her.

"There aren't," she replied, "not yet." Then, turning back to Spen she asked, "But there's no earthly reason why there shouldn't be, wouldn't you agree Master Robinson?"

"I can't think of a single reason why not," he answered. Then, holding out his hand he said, "I wish you good fortune in the examinations tomorrow Miss."

She took his hand, shook it gently but firmly, and said, "I'm Edith, Edith Pechey." Spen had been unsure of whether he should kiss her gloved hand or not but decided just to shake it firmly without crushing it.

"My name is "Spencely Robinson. How do you do Miss Pechey."

"Yes, I feel we all need a little luck on our side" she said with a warm smile. Spen liked Miss Pechey.

"A demain" she said with a very convincing French accent. Spen's glance to Mr. Bateman caught him furrowing his brow and silently questioning what she'd said, and why she would suddenly start speaking French in the middle of the Capital of Scotland? Spen ignored him and returned his gaze to the lovely Miss Pechey saying, "Yes, until tomorrow." Mr. Bateman rolled his eyes ever so slightly at the older woman, but she just smiled back at him, obviously full of pride and admiration for the youth of today.

Spen hardly slept a wink that night. He was half bursting with excitement and half going over maths formulas and Chemical reactions in his mind. Mr. Bateman had to knock very loudly and repeatedly to waken him from his slumbers in the morning. But once awake he sprang into action and washed, dried and dressed before running down the stairs and finding Mr. Bateman at a table in the dining room. Others milled about the place. Spen noticed how Mr. Bateman was a little brusque with the serving staff perhaps enjoying his role reversal. Spen was gracious and polite, always remembering to smile and thank the waiter and waitress. He asked them politely and patiently for the things he needed. Bateman just seemed to order people about. But old Mrs. Bell had once said something about a Leopard never changing its spots. He realised that she must have been talking about Mr. Bateman at that very moment.

The first exam was Mathematics. It seemed easier than he was expecting. But after that, it was Latin. That one was hard, and he put a lot of answers down that he merely hoped were right. He'd always felt his Latin was a little feint. Indeed, he couldn't even remember what the Latin for 'feint' was.

English in the afternoon, that went well enough, he thought. But bringing that very statement to mind took him back to his school days when once, after a test, he and some of the other brighter pupils in the class discussed the questions. They agreed that it was tough and that they'd all probably failed. But one or two, particularly those who weren't quite so bright (Eric was one), confidently broadcast how well they thought they'd done. The following day the results were announced and all those who thought they had done well had failed, and those who had worried about failing had all passed. He hoped that the same would be true in Edinburgh, but only for his Latin exam. Not for his Maths and English exams, obviously.

The second night he slept much more soundly; he was so tired. Not from physical labour, but from mental exhaustion. Before slumber Spen reviewed his day and thought how he'd not caught sight of Miss Pechey at the Surgeon's Hall, though he had noticed three or four other young ladies sitting the exam.

On day two of exams, he went along the South Bridge with Mr. Bateman again, and as they walked, he recognised a young gentleman called Andrew, who he had sat next to in the exam room some twenty hours earlier. They discussed how the previous days testing had gone and wondered what would befall them today. Andrew had a funny accent and continually sounded like he was about to break into song. He was from the English Midlands.

The second day's exams were Chemistry, then a choice of subjects. Spen had opted for French, and Further Maths. Andrew had chosen Philosophy and Logic, arguing that any answer given in a Philosophy exam couldn't be wrong, so long as you could justify your answer. At the Hall, they shook hands and went their separate ways, wishing success on each other. Whilst he waited, Mr. Bateman considered taking a turn around the castle, but instead repaired to the same quiet café in Niddry Street which he had patronised on the previous day. He wrote a card to his sister in Falkirk and stuck the penny red to the corner of the envelope, making sure he'd post it in Edinburgh's fine city, so that she might see the stamp's cancellation location.

The whole experience filled Spen with wonder. Edinburgh was where he wanted to be, mixing with all these bright and witty people from far and wide. His opinion of the well-educated classes had been rather poor until that moment. As an estate worker he had always been talked down to, generally in derogatory tones, though the Laird stood out head and shoulders above this group as he had never treated Spencely, nor any of his staff or workers, with anything other than kindness and consideration. But most of the Big House's visitors had generally cast him off as a mere means to an end, to acquire something they wanted, or to get something done. But in Edinburgh he felt a warm glow inside. These people didn't need to swear to express themselves adequately, no, they used a cornucopia of warm toned eloquence instead. They easily and readily conversed bringing new ideas, without strongly held opinions ingrained by a dull and dreary life. They were funny, and so entertaining to be with. He desperately wanted to stay, or at least return there as quickly as possible. If he failed today, he vowed to try again at the earliest possible opportunity.

Mr. Bateman didn't ask how the exams had gone; he didn't really do small talk. But in the quiet of the railway carriage on their return, when tiredness had overtaken them both, Spen thought he could broach a subject that was on his mind. He asked Mr. B if he knew how the opportunity of him maybe going to university had come about? In short, he didn't, but knew that only the Laird could have arranged such a thing, perhaps through an old school tie network. His Lordship had not deemed it necessary to enlighten his butler with the name of the Scholarship which might be supporting him. The only thing which Mr. B could tell him was that his bills and allowance would be arranged through the solicitors C Brader & Sons of Edinburgh. They hadn't travelled to visit them and make contact on that occasion, as, well, the need had not yet arisen; To wit: Spen had not yet passed the entry exams.

At Falkirk Station the same footman had brought the trap and awaited their arrival. As the two emerged from the building he sat on the bench seat holding the reigns ready for Mr. Bateman to climb up, and (presumably) for Spen to clamber up into the rear. But Mr. B told the 'Lad' to put the bag in the back and to jump in after it. He looked a tad 'crestfallen.' Somehow, Spen felt that Mr. Bateman was thus treating him with an increased respect.

* * *

His mother was almost overwhelmed to see her son back. Two whole nights he'd been away, longer than ever before. She welcomed him back as if he'd been to the ends of the earth, and she kept referring to him as Doctor Robinson. They both knew the title was a lot too premature, but they enjoyed hearing the term, and saying it too. Emily arrived and Dorothy held her by the hand and brought her through into the living room, clearing a seat of a tea towel and an old newspaper. But before she sat down she grabbed Spen physically, though gently, and gave him a hug. Dorothy was somewhat taken aback. Spen too, was a little embarrassed, but nonetheless, politely asked her to sit. "From, the start" she asked, "what have I missed so far?" Once more he recounted every detail of the whole two days from start to finish. Dorothy really didn't mind hearing the whole thing for a second time.

Spen rather hoped that after all the build-up of interest and often hollow encouragement locally, the news from Edinburgh (someday soon), would be good. He shared his doubts and concerns with Emily as they walked across the fields as night fell. Everyone in Edinburgh seemed to be so confident, not in the exam answers, but somehow within themselves, in life. They came across as so much more than he felt himself to be. He genuinely didn't think that he was as good as the other candidates. Emily became pensive too. As Spen walked her towards her stately home he could detect a slight tremble in her voice. "But if you do pass the exams, it means that you'll leave, and never come back, and you'll find some fine lady in Edinburgh and you'll marry

44

her and live happily ever after." That all sounded very well to him, very well indeed, but then he realised what she was really saying. He stopped, turned to face her, gently took both of her hands and looked into her eyes.

"But I've already found you Emily, you are the one for me." She smiled, even though she knew that his confession was merely the paper of true love which couldn't begin to conceal the cracks of yawning class divide existing between them. A daughter of Sir William Stannet Forbes would never be allowed to marry a common estate worker. But even so, a feint flicker of hope dawned deep within Spencely's mind that day. Perhaps, this was why the Laird had organised for his education to happen; to make him into a Doctor, a gentleman. Or, on the other hand, and just as likely, so that he would meet someone else and leave his daughter free to fall in love with some proper society Beau. Hmm, he wondered which of the two was more likely.

He left Emily near her door, kissed her warmly and said goodbye. As he turned and walked slowly home, it crossed his mind that he may just have kissed goodbye to a romantic relationship with his life-long friend. He hoped not.

* * *

A week later he and Dorothy were summoned to the Big House and there they were shown into the withdrawing room. Lady Sarah greeted them briefly but left them almost immediately. A footman attended them asking that they be seated, then offered refreshment. They politely declined both. Spen recognised the footman as the one who had accompanied them to the station and then collected them two days later.

Emily poked her head around the door, but said nothing, she just smiled at them and fluttered a little wave of her hand. No hug this time thought Dorothy. Her own initial fears that they had been summoned to be told they must leave their cottage and find another home were slowly evaporating. Surely that news would come via the estate office, not in the 'drawing room of the Big House, and wouldn't have involved the offer of seats, or refreshments. "Thank you, Clarke," said the Laird as he pushed open a door behind them. They turned to see Sir William enter with Mr. Bateman three paces behind him. Clarke, the footman, left after a small bow to the Laird. Sir William smiled at them both and formally bade them a good morning. He asked them to sit, which they did, whereupon he pulled a letter from his inside pocket, then a pair of pince-nez, which he clipped onto his nose. He looked funny, neither of them knew that Sir William wore glasses. "I have received a letter from Professor Sir Robert Christison, head of admissions for Edinburgh University Medical School and Spencely..."

"Yes sir?" answered Spen.

"...he invites you to attend on the second of November to sign the Matriculation Roll."

"That's very gracious of him sir, but what does that mean?" asked a baffled Spen. His mother started to smile.

"It means, dear chap, you're in..." the Laird said with a beaming smile.

"What, I've got a place?" shouted a disbelieving Spen, springing to his feet again. At that point, as the Laird strode forward with his hand outstretched his mother grabbed him and squeezed him so hard, he thought his eyes would pop. Then Sir William shook his hand vigorously and even compounded the action by adding on his other hand too. Mr. Bateman, almost un-noticed by the Laird until then, strode forward and offered his hand too.

"May I be permitted to add my deepest felicitations and congratulations Master Spencely." They all beamed.

"Thankyou Mr. Bateman, that's jolly decent of you to say sir."

"Now perhaps you *will* take tea Mrs. Robinson?" asked Sir William, but before she'd had time to consider a reply, he'd shouted for Clarke and ordered tea, with cakes, for this was a fine day. Mr. Bateman bowed, un-noticed by Sir William, and politely took his leave.

The Laird explained all that he knew, which wasn't much, telling Spen where he was to report, and at what time. Clarke brought in the tea and Dorothy had a flush of confidence and began to pour it herself. Spen was a little surprised at how the Laird was perfectly accepting of this, as if it was somehow a totally natural occurrence. Then came a little more of what Spen would need to take with him, and where he was to stay. He wouldn't need much equipment as the Laird was sure Spencely wouldn't be allowed to touch or even go near real patients initially. He certainly wouldn't be allowed to poke them or stick needles into them. "But" said Sir William, "when you do need a listening tube or indeed perhaps one of those new-fangled stethoscopes, then Edinburgh would be the best place to find it."

When it was time to leave, Sir William offered his pony and trap to return them home, but they'd decided to walk, and talk, and laugh, and smile and sing all the way back together. On the way out of the drawing room Clarke was still standing there like a statue. Spen caught his eye, gave him a wink and softly said "Thank you Mr. Clarke." Clarke smiled. The remark made his day.

They left by the front door.

Emily came round that evening, but it was too wet to go for a pleasant walk. They sat in the living room by the fire as Emily's wet clothing steamed a little in the heat. They couldn't talk intimately about what this would mean for their relationship. Their words stayed on the polite side of shallow because Dorothy was only in the next room, sometimes the kitchen. All three of them felt a little gooseberry-ish. Spen finally saw Emily to the door of the cottage, moved to say farewell, but then, as it was still raining heavily, he dashed back inside and grabbed his hat and coat. He should really show Emily safely to her door. That's what a gentleman should do.

Unfortunately, the cold heavy rain was about as conducive to intimacy as having one's mother in the next room, so the nearest they got to closeness was a quick parting kiss on the lips at the end of the ornamental garden. He ran home.

Chapter 5 – Edinburgh

On the first day of November 1869 the eighteen-year-old Mr. Spencely Robinson stepped off the Falkirk train in the middle of Edinburgh station, which was in the middle of Edinburgh, which was in the middle of the medical universe. He stood for a moment with his bag in one hand and his hat in the other. He just breathed in the cold air. As his fellow passengers scurried off, and others got on his train behind him he remained in the shaft of low afternoon sunlight which bathed him warmly. He was awakened by a man asking him "Carry your bag sir?" What, a man was asking *him* if he could carry *his* bag? And even calling him 'Sir!' Spen smiled at the gentleman, thanked him, and told him that he could manage perfectly well, but thanked him again for his kind offer.

Outside the building Spen saw another man dressed just the same, seemingly a railway worker's uniform. He was carrying three bags and walking behind a well-dressed portly gentleman up to a large carriage. As Mr. Porter, for that was the name on his hat, put down the bags for the driver to load, the gentleman flipped a coin up into the air which Mr. Porter caught. 'Aah,' realised Spen, 'he wasn't just being kind, he was trying to earn a living.'

Spen consulted a wall map and found Waverley station. The clue was in red at the top saying "You Are Here," and then followed the index to find Grassmarket and Candlemakers Row.

He walked Southwards across The Waverley Bridge and over a road called Market Street, along the curving Cockburn Street a little then up a passageway with a lot of steps and through a narrow opening onto High

Street. As he emerged the mighty Saint Giles Cathedral with its magnificent crown of stone appeared straight before him. Then Right along High Street as if towards the castle for a short way. He remembered from the map that after Parliament Square, he needed to turn left onto George Street and go South a little. Spen was very surprised to find that the junction with The Cowgate wasn't a junction at all, but another bridge, with no access down onto the other road. There were lots of men digging up the middle of George Street which was causing all sorts of mess and confusion. He saw how the men were hacking away at the cobbles and fitting tram tracks down the centre of it. Spen wondered about the wisdom of putting a tramway system into a city built on such a collection of steep hills as Edinburgh was. But he surmised that the city council knew what they were doing.

He was quite surprised to see so many street urchins flitting about. They looked genuinely poorer than poor and made him feel like a gentleman, a real toff. But then there were other true gentlemen about who, by their bearing alone made him feel like a mere street urchin himself.

In this older part of town the number of pedestrians had reduced though there was still plenty of road traffic trotting along the cobbles, though perhaps not so many Palomino drawn glossy varnished carriages. There were a lot more hand carts too, he noticed. He asked a fellow pedestrian if he knew the way to Candlemakers Row, and was surprised at the reply of "Aye, yer rayght fe the Greyfriars." Ah yes, Greyfriars Church he remembered. It backed onto his lodging house. Or at least its graveyard did.

The door to 2A Candlemakers Row was straight onto the pavement with no step in front of it. The rather understated red door had a fox's head knocker. Spen gingerly lifted the large brass ring and then aided its return. It made a loud metallic bang but brought no response. He wondered how long he should wait. A young gentleman ran up behind him and pushed past. "Go straight in dear Chap, they won't come to you," he said as he pressed on the handle and heaved open the door. As it swung, he went through and held it slightly ajar to give Spen time to pick up his bag and follow him in.

"Thank you," began Spen, "I'm Spencely Rob..." But the young man had gone, sprinting up the stairs shouting,

"Sorry, Old Man, can't stop, busting for a pee." Spen smiled to himself and wondered briefly what he should do next. A dull green door to his right said 'Private' on it, and a little further to the right was a push button mounted on the wall. Adjacent was a small placard which read 'Ring for Reception.' Spen wondered if they'd missed off the word 'Please' somewhere. He pressed it.

The tired green door creaked open and an ill looking overweight woman with a half-smoked cigarette in the corner of her mouth came out. Spen lifted his hat, though strictly speaking he should no longer be wearing it, as he was indoors. "Good afternoon, Madam, I'm looking for Mrs. Moffatt," he said to her. Without removing the cigarette, she replied,

"You've found her, Name?"

Moments later, after having been relieved of three pounds in exchange for a key he was climbing the stairs to the third floor to find room number thirty-two. He considered how the house didn't look large enough to have over thirty guest rooms, but as he ascended he observed that the rooms on the first floor were numbered eleven to fourteen, on the second, twenty-one to twenty-four and on the third thirty-one to thirty-three. He presumed (rightly) that the first digit represented the number of the floor. The stairs finished at the third floor.

He fitted his new key into the door lock, but it refused to turn the full circle. He tried again, but much to his surprise the door opened for him, pulled by someone inside the room. Spen was quite shocked to discover that 'his' room was to be shared by another young gentleman. John was less surprised and warned Spen that, as there were three beds in the room, there would likely be yet another person joining them.

 John was also starting his training in the morning for a degree in Medicine. He was a pleasant fellow, quite short but stockily built. He spoke with an educated far northern Scottish accent, Spen guessed Shetland, as his words were not flowing but rather staccato. His forbears were definitely Viking. John showed himself to be a practical man, somewhat devoid of passion, either for or against anything. He was a scientist through and through and he knew more of how things worked even than Spen himself did.

 The room was quite dingey, and a little smelly. The walls used to be a light brown but over the many years since they had last been painted that colour (the only time they had ever been painted that colour), the many occupants' cigarette smoke had turned the tops of the walls an even darker shade of brown. The ceiling was a similar grimy brown colour too. No pictures adorned the walls. Spen dropped his bag by his chosen bed and walked to the single window to look out upon the Greyfriars graveyard. A small black terrier trotted past a new looking grave and gave it a sniff. The glass to the window was quite filthy, but Spen considered the difficulty of cleaning the outside of windows so high off the ground.

 That evening he took a stroll out to identify two locations. First of all, was tomorrow's initial appointment to sign the Matriculation Register at the college building. Then back the other way along Lauriston Place heading for the Professional quarter to identify a lawyer's premises. John joined him for the walk and asked, 'did he want just any lawyer, or was he wanting a specific lawyer?' Spen explained to John about him having won some sort of scholarship which would be administered by Messrs C. Brader and Sons on Rutland Court to the West of the Castle. "What? Someone's paying you to come to Med School?" asked a dumbfounded John.

"Yes, I think so," replied a slightly embarrassed Spen, but then quickly countered with, "Why, who's paying your fees?"

"No-one of course," huffed John, but then, having realised how ridiculous that sounded added, "Well, my father, I suppose."

"So, neither of us are paying for ourselves then," said Spen with a disarming smile. John gave him an acknowledging nod. As they walked Spen explained about his upbringing on the Stannet-Forbes estate, which was owned by the fifth Earl of Callander, of how he didn't have a father, or if he did have one somewhere, he'd never known him. And how the Laird had sort of taken him under his wing. In fact, there was a suggestion that Spen might have become estate manager one day. But that was before Sir William's eldest daughter Mary had married a man who had then sort of cuckoo'd his way into the estate manager's job.

"But the Lairds' loss is your gain Spen," said John, "As here we are at Doctoring School." The two looked at each other with a momentary crazed laugh. It was at that moment they knew that they shared an almost disbelief in their miraculous good fortune at being at the Edinburgh University Medical School.

They identified the Solicitors' building just as a very smart female figure was locking the gleaming black front door to the offices. As she turned around, she nearly descended straight into them. "Oh, I do beg your pardon gentlemen," she said as she jerked to a halt. The two young men almost competed to be first to lift their hats.

"No, no, it was our fault entirely," said John quickly, and smiled broadly.

Then she moved her gaze from John to Spen, and he could only agree with his new friend, "Yes, indeed, it was his fault entirely miss." At which the three of them laughed. She was beautiful, not just in a pretty way, no, she was really beautiful. A little older than them. They stood there for a moment, the young lady on the lowest step, and the two young men on the paving, still blocking her way. Their heads were approximately at the same height, with John's a little lower.

"Well, if you'll excuse me please gentlemen…" The two came to their senses and shuffled apart to let the lady through.

"Erm… Brader and Sons" mumbled Spen.

"Yes," said the epitome of marbled perfection, "that's us." She'd stopped and turned back to them.

"Erm, you're the solicitors with whom I have to make contact, regarding… I'm Spencely Robinson." He stuttered as he began to offer her his hand.

"I'm very pleased to make your acquaintance Mr. Robinson, perhaps we'll meet again during office hours." She offered no hand, simply turned and walked away up the road in a westerly direction. They stayed, frozen to the spot once more, watching her diminutive but perfect form walk off. Her satin black dress hugged her tiny waist tightly, then it curved outwards to huddle her perfectly defined hips and the small of her back before becoming loose and voluminous around her legs. It ended exactly two inches from the ground all the way round the hem.

"Wow," said John quietly, "I wish she was *my* solicitor too."

In the morning the two young men returned to the College building and found the room where first year students were to sign the matriculation papers plus a small collection of forms and other paperwork, many of which were regarding finances. Spen's paperwork was a little different to a lot of the other students, as his seemed to mention his solicitors quite a lot. Obviously, it must be for his scholarship. The paperwork filling was very tedious but when Spen spotted Miss Pechey talking to some other young ladies in the room he was determined to renew their acquaintance. He hurried over and waited for Miss Pechey to notice him. He stood a short while before the woman who seemed to be in charge stopped speaking and pointed with her eyes to him. All five young ladies turned to look at him and the two who had their backs to him parted to let him forward. He stepped up, rather bravely he thought, into the huddle and held out his hand towards Miss Pechey saying "Congratulations Miss Pechey, we made it through then." She took his hand gingerly but gave him a look which said, 'I don't know you' "Two weeks ago, in the evening... outside Surgeons Hall. We met at the door," he continued.

"Oh, yes, of course, I remember, you were with your butler."

"NO," choked Spen, "Well, yes, he was, is, a butler, but he's not *my* butler."

"Ah, impersonating a man-with-butler eh?" said the leader of the lionesses, and all the ladies laughed.

Spen felt a little like he was making a fool of himself. So, he smiled at Miss Pechey, nodded at the other ladies and parted company from them with a final "Congratulations once again Miss Pechey." Edith returned his smile, but as soon as he'd finished speaking the head lioness began speaking again and all the women gave her their full attention. The two moved back into position to re-form their defensive circle.

As he left the group, he felt a tap on his shoulder and turned to see Andrew once more. Spen felt grateful for this rescue as even in this crowd he'd suddenly felt very alone. "We got through then?" he said with dancing tones and a heartfelt smile. "Yes indeed, I still can't really believe it," confirmed Spen. The two talked and Spen shared with him that he'd been lucky to get away with his head still on his shoulders after speaking to the group of ladies over in the corner. "What," said Andrew, "they're all medical students too?" he asked with a look of incredulity.

They talked at length as more young gentlemen came into the hall and were guided to the tables for signing the register and filling out the forms. Then a man wearing a black gown, probably one of the professors shouted, "Would all those who have already completed their legalities please move along. The introductory assembly will commence in the main lecture theatre at two, post meridian."

"I think we're being told to sling our hook," said Andrew.

Spen confirmed, "It *is* getting a little crowded in here." So the two young men moved with the crowd, but before reaching the doorway Andrew diverted to the wall and picked up two travel bags. He explained how he'd stayed over in a hotel on the previous night as he hadn't found anywhere permanent to stay yet. Spen told him about his room at the lodging house having three beds but only two occupants so far, and thought he'd make the ideal third occupant. Before exiting he searched the room for John but didn't see him anywhere, so the two decided to trek back along to 2A and ask Mrs. Moffatt if Andrew could be their third roommate.

On the way they got to know each other a little better. Andrew was the son of a Rector and had lived nearly all his life in a Rectory on the outskirts of Coventry. This accounted for his singing English accent. He was a gentle soul, always considerate. He kept saying "Thank the Lord" and vehemently believed that he should, everywhere, in all things. He tried to live a life of purity and honesty, being charitable whenever he saw the need. Oddly, he wouldn't let Spen help carry either of his bags on the journey along South College Street, Lothian Street and Bristo Port.

They found John just as they reached the lodging house and he readily agreed to Andrew joining them, though Spen detected a little reticence once he'd discovered that Andrew was a devout Christian. Mrs. Moffatt answered her bell to the three young men and joined them in the scruffy entrance hall of the building. Initially she said that the room was already taken by a young gentleman who had just ascended to the top floor. He was at that very moment verifying its suitability. But Spen told the woman courteously that if Andrew couldn't join them, they might consider looking for another establishment after their initial rental period had run its course. "Wouldn't we John?" John was a little less than convincing in his confirmation. Mrs. Moffatt appeared unthreatened.

But as the three of them stood there negotiating with the old woman the sound of a bag being humped down individual steps grabbed their attention. The noise of breathing too was even louder than its accompanying heavy footsteps. As they all looked, a short but very over-weight young gentleman jerked his heavy suitcase over the last steps and came towards them. As he did so he heaved up his case with both hands and struggled towards them uttering the phrase, "Not for me… sorry to bother…" Andrew lunged to open the door as the men parted, and the bright red sweating figure exited into the daylight. Spen, Andrew and John turned to look at Mrs. Moffatt without saying a word. She continued in much the same tone as before saying, "It's your lucky day, that'll be three pounds if you will young sir," and she held out her hand towards Andrew. As he reached for his wallet John picked both of his bags off the floor and carried them up taking the steps two at once.

Soon after one o'clock the three strolled along the newly finished Chambers Street and were very much looking forward to their initial gathering as students of Medicine. The main lecture theatre was filled with arcing rows of steeply banked tiers of wooden seating, each with a tiny desk area in front of it. The lime-lights were somehow being focussed onto a decoratively carved wooden lectern on the stage. The chaps compared the room to a real theatre, but Spen told them he'd never even been in a real theatre before and certainly never a lecture theatre. After the place had filled up, the doors were closed and at least ten minutes then passed as the crowd chatted excitedly. Spen spotted the group of lady students, all sitting together, in the middle at the front.

A whitehaired gentleman slowly walked, almost un-noticed, to the lectern but before he reached his destination a clatter of chairs folding up alerted everyone to have 'eyes front.' Soon everyone had risen to their feet. The old gentleman stood there a moment holding their gaze. As quietness was finally achieved, he said, "Please be seated."

For the next ninety minutes the gentleman spoke without reference to any notes. He held onto the sides of the lectern only letting go occasionally to gesticulate and confirm the importance of some point he was making. And he made a lot of points. "Intellect," he began, "Is not measured in the number of your qualifications, nor the number of years spent within the bowels of Academia. But quite simply in one's proven ability to change one's mind. Old dogs really must learn new tricks lest they be eaten up by the ravages of tradition, convention, and hence putrefaction. For to change one's mind is the very essence of learning. Gentlemen..." at this the chief lioness on the front row coughed rather pointedly, "Ladies and Gentlemen, we are at the very cusp of a medical revolution. Each week we hear of a new disease countered, a new instrument invented, or improved beyond all recognition. A new treatment or technique or another means of organising our army of defences against the hitherto victorious illness. But, gentlemen..." He quickly glanced to the chief Lioness again "...and Ladies" which brought a ripple of laughter, "be in no doubt that as we travel further down this path of national industrialisation, where our population swells and concentrates together, the epidemics will gather anew at our door." He stopped to take a sip from his glass. Everyone in the room hung on his every utterance. "Though we may have outgrown Hippocrates, and Galen with his Miasma, progressed from the endless though pointless extraction from our patients their Bile, Phlegm and Blood, we still do not have all the answers. And I give you all this warning: Be very, very careful of consigning traditional wisdom to the fire. Yes, we may gladly allow our mistakes to disappear into the oblivion of the past, which, indeed is where they belong, but much of wisdom has often been gained over many years. Discount tradition at your peril. We must move forward slowly, thoroughly, majestically but most of all scientifically. Though we may be able to treat the symptoms of Malaria, Cholera, Typhus and a dozen other ravaging diseases we still don't know what causes them. And I... probably never will. But you, you indeed will. You must. You are my hope for the future. And in your lifetimes will come many more of the answers, God willing. Though you now be blessed beyond the blessings of any men before you. Or women, for that matter…" Again, a small ripple of laughter, though Spen could see that his continual omissions were starting to cause the ladies offence. "…you will never, I can confidently assure you… know all of the answers either. There will often be times when you are overwhelmed, at wits-end, even heart-broken by your inability to bring healing or even benefit to some of your patients. So, may I leave you with my final thought for this day. Be aware, be very aware, that as you change your thinking, yes always opting for the science led answer, be careful that you do not throw out the baby with the bathwater. As doctors you will find yourselves to be far more than the mere relievers of pain, bringers of cure, and healers of sickness. You will find yourselves being asked advice, your counsel sought on a myriad of subjects about which we cannot teach you here. You will be a friend to the friendless, the voice of reason to those in turmoil and a mediator of hope to those whose lives are broken. In short you will be the personification of wisdom. So, may I beseech you to always act with kindness, consideration, good temper, patience and tenderness. For if you do, then you will always be considered to be a good doctor."

At the end, the hall took to its feet again and clapped the old gentleman for over two minutes. For they all knew that if they lived another hundred years, they were unlikely to witness such wisdom again.

Only Spen sat down again at the end of the ovation. Everyone else moved towards the doors, but he just sat back, drinking in what had happened to him within the last hour and a half. He felt reborn. He wished he could hear all that again. He hadn't even caught the name of the gentleman but was convinced that he would see him again. He certainly hoped so. Every fibre of Spen's soul tingled.

He felt he had to write to his mother that evening about what had happened to him. Oh, how he was in the right place, travelling the right course in life. He'd never felt so certain of who he was or what he wanted to become. He felt so lucky. He thought he should write to Emily also, but unfortunately, when the time came he was much too tired, and considered that it would best be done the following day.

The following day came all too quickly, and they were led into a much smaller hall, more akin to a classroom. The lecture his first ever, was entitled "Observe and Deduce." He found this one too to be remarkably interesting, though perhaps not quite as sensational as the previous day's talk, which, he'd discovered was by the Medical School's principal, who's name he'd already forgotten.

He was told how he must observe objectively. The lecturer explained that human beings tend to conclude first, then simply look for signs of confirmation. What they were being exalted to do was to remain open, observe first, and having observed, to weigh all the evidence, and then deduce secondly. Then to test their conclusions. 'Always, always, always try and test your hypothesis,' the lecturer had said. He continued with 'And this is the most important piece of *scientific* advice you will ever be given, and hence it is the most important piece of *advice* which you will ever be given: Never try and prove your hypothesis right. For that is what the world does. Always, always try and prove your hypothesis wrong. For that is what the scientist does. Whilst the small audience was still trying to understand what was being said the lecturer continued, "And always remember that an experiment can never fail." This statement too brought a number of disagreeing furrowed brows. "You will hear politicians and journalists talk of a failed experiment here or a failed experiment there. When you hear these words, know that the speaker doesn't have the bearing or training of a scientist." He could see that the audience needed some clarification. "You see, an experiment, be it social, chemical or physical, is simply a test to see what happens. Mix acid with salt, add weights to a spring or put a hundred carpenters on an island growing only grass. You add together the components and observe what happens. That's it. That's an experiment. And the results are simply that, *results*. And though the results might be predictable, they are never assured. If the result is not what you imagined it would be, then it is surely your imagination which is at fault, but never, never the fault nor especially the failure of the experiment itself." The room breathed a collective sigh of understanding and all agreed that they had broadened their minds that day.

The afternoon brought a lesson in which they all had to roll up their sleeves and touch something. All who entered the room were awestruck by the fine array of identical brass microscopes, but were again a little disappointed to only be peering at butterfly's wings or bed bugs. They realised that before equipment could be used to detect disease or a thousand other things, it's proper use must first be mastered: slide preparation with dyes, focus, lighting, aberrations. cleanliness.

Other lessons would follow in the use of the new Bunsen/Desaga burner, listening tubes and even a new stethoscope. Luckily, their new glass hypodermic syringes were used only to inject apples. (None of the apples survived).

Lessons on ethics, philosophy, chemistry, and anatomy followed and fell into a repetitious weekly pattern. They even gathered in a real operating theatre once but were all disappointed to be standing around for over two hours watching some professor slice into the body of a pig and bring out the offal, identifying which organs they were and what purpose they had served for the pig. Spen had seen the guts of a pig many times before so found a seat at the top of the room and read more on chemical testing. He still had to endure the smell though. And the sound of the occasional student being sick. Spen concluded that the major distinction between Physicians and Surgeons was probably that Physicians still had a working sense of smell.

Over dinner the three agreed that they had really enjoyed their lectures so far that year, and indeed had gained broad understanding. But they each admitted to a little frustration that so far no-one had talked about real body parts or even real bodies. (Apart from the pig).

One Friday morning brought a talk on terms and descriptions and what the three called 'medispeak.' They noted that Superior was higher, not a surprise to anyone, and inferior was below or beneath (ditto), as in the superior and inferior Vena Cava. That Medial meant central, Distal, further away, Anterior was frontal and Posterior was, "Oh that beautiful vision of the disappearing woman in black as she walked away from us on our first meeting Spen, do you remember?" said Andrew pretending to be in a trance. Spen laughed because the image outside Brader's was etched on his mind too. Andrew looked slightly hurt as the other two had obviously shared something rather special together and he had missed out. But graciously, John agreed to take Andrew with them during their self-study free afternoon later that day. Spen readily agreed as he really needed to contact Messers. Brader and sons (during office hours). He also thought that it was cute how John had offered to take Andrew on Spen's trek to the solicitors. In Johns mind it was a foregone conclusion that he himself would be going with Spen, but he'd so kindly thought of giving Andrew the treat of meeting the beauty in black too. Spen really needed to go as he was running out of money; life in Edinburgh had been quite expensive thus far.

When one o'clock that afternoon arrived, john was urging them both to gulp down their lunch more speedily as they didn't have a moment to lose. Then he strode out in front of the other two on their way to Rutland Court. Spen and Andrew were nearly breaking into a trot trying to keep up with him. Andrew confided, "Quite quick for one with such short legs isn't he."

At the offices John galloped up the front steps, forcibly opened the door and went through. Spen stepped back and allowed Andrew through before him.

The tiny front office suddenly looked crowded as Andrew spoke to the expected young lady bidding her a fine afternoon and announcing that Mr, Spencely Robinson, soon to be Doctor Spencely Robinson, was here to make contact with Messrs Brady and Sons. "It's Brader and sons Mr. Robinson," said the voice at the desk. At that point Spen had not set eyes on the woman as John took centre stage and Andrew wasn't far behind him. "Oh no," spluttered John, "I'm John, John McFarlane." The young lady turned to look at Andrew and began addressing him before he too reluctantly felt he should confess that he wasn't Spen either. At this charade the young lady was beginning to show signs of tension. Spen shuffled himself past the crowd of two and began speaking to her. She was even more beautiful than he remembered. On the previous occasion she'd worn a hat, but this time her long golden hair made her into a rather fine impression of Venus de Milo. "I do apologise, they both insisted on coming with me to see you miss." She was a little surprised at Spen's honesty, though not untouched by it. She stood up behind her desk and held forward her hand. "And I'm Moira Beaty Mr. Robinson, I'm honoured to meet you, sir."

"Delighted" replied Spen, "I'm here about..." But she swiftly held up her hand to stop him speaking. It worked perfectly. It usually did. She addressed Andrew and John with "And now that they have seen me perhaps you would be good enough to wait in the other room while we discuss our business gentlemen."
"Oh, we don't mind," blurted Andrew, "You continue miss please."
"Well, I would but that would give me a teensy problem with our new client confidentiality sir, which we at Brader and Sons take very seriously, very seriously indeed." And she slowly held out her hand towards a door marked 'waiting room.' They both obediently went through and sat down. "This way Mr. Robinson please." She moved in the opposite direction and went through a large door marked C. Brader Snr. Spen followed her in fully expecting to find an old man sitting

behind the large green leather covered desk which looked like it would need an earthquake to move it. Much to Spen's surprise the room was devoid of people. Its back wall was lined with files holding papers loosely bound with scarlet or blue silk ribbons. She turned and pulled one off the middle shelf and as she did so Spen took another lingering look at her hourglass figure. He inwardly smirked that the other two hadn't been afforded that particular privilege. "Please take a seat sir," said Miss Beaty, again gesticulating with her delicate hand. Spen was sure that Miss Beaty could have been or indeed still was a ballerina. She sat in Old Mr. Braders chair and Spen noticed that there was still a lot of room either side of her once she had done so. She delicately pulled at the bow holding the file closed. It fell open and there in front of them was a large sheaf of bank notes on top of some papers. "I'm afraid I can't tell you much about the Homfultum Scholarship Mr. Robinson..."

"Oh, please call me Spen," interjected Spen.

"I'm afraid I can't tell you much about the Homfultum Scholarship Mr. Robinson, partly because I don't know much about the prize, and certain things which I do know, I'm not allowed to tell you."

"I'm sure I would tell you Miss Beaty, if I knew," said Spen with a smile," but again she ignored him and continued.

"Only that it's enough to cover all course fees and tutelage at the university, which have been and will be paid directly to the Organisation, plus a living expense of one hundred and twenty pounds a year directly to you so long as you are in training at the Edinburgh Medical School..."

"Wowww" said Spen loudly, "That's a king's ransom."

"And it's for a maximum of Four years. The money is to be paid quarterly, by us, either in cash or through a bank. Do you have an account at a bank Mr, Robinson?"

"A bank account. Me?" said Spen "No, I've never felt the need, Miss Beaty. I keep all of my investments firmly in the top of my sock." She stared at him, without expression and patiently waited for him to stop waffling.

"Then please forgive my presumption, but I've taken the liberty of commissioning you one sir, it's across the road, at Willy Glyn's, I'm sorry, William and Glyn. I've put one pound in there and taken the opportunity to copy down the account number so that you won't need to return here to collect your money in the future. Just go to the bank and draw it out there sir." Spen immediately felt a little disappointment, both for himself and for the two in the waiting room, that this would be their only meeting. She continued, "The remaining twenty-nine pounds are here, if you'd care to count it please Mr. Robinson."

"Oh, I don't think I need to do that Miss Beaty, if you say there are twenty-nine pounds here then…" But she had already begun to count out the notes in front of him. But rather than be mesmerized by looking at the money, he just watched her lips move as she quickly counted out the money onto the desk top. He was mesmerized, non-the-less.

"Please sign here Mr. Robinson, it's a receipt for the money." Then she swapped the receipt for another three sheets which she also asked him to sign. "And here please; one is your acquiescence to be bound by the agreement, one is a contract of employ between us and you for this transaction and the third is your agreement to confidentiality, any questions sir?"

"Yes, I do have one actually," said Spen, with a half-smile. She looked straight at him, said nothing and raised her eyebrows that suggested he might let her know what that question might actually be? "Do you mean to say that I have signed to agree to accept the money from this scholarship, for four years, at one hundred and twenty pounds per year…"

"Plus tutelage." She added.

"Yes indeed, plus tutelage. And to agree not to tell anyone about it, nor ask you any questions about it either? My question is, Miss Beaty, is there some sort of punishment upon me should I fail to keep our little secret…" He was desperate to form some sort of an emotional connection between himself and the marvellous Miss Beaty.

"You mean 'are there any penalty clauses,' and, by the way that was two questions?"

"My mistake Miss Beaty, my question is 'Are there any penalty clauses please?" he asked, still trying to maintain composure.

"No sir, none, as far as I can see," she replied. He continued to sit despite the transaction obviously being complete. "Do you not want the money Mr. Robinson?" she asked him wryly. Spen laughed openly as he picked up the three piles of bank notes from her desk, he put them together and folded them over roughly. He crumpled them into his inside pocket and stood up. But she didn't laugh, in fact she was still showing no hint of emotion. Maybe it hadn't been a joke. "Will there be anything else sir?" she asked also standing up slowly.

He decided to grab the bull by the horns: "Only one thing; may I take you to dinner Miss Beaty, you see I've just come into rather a lot of money and I've no-one to spoil with it, so I wondered if..." but she cut him off with the raising of her hand again. "No, Mr. Robinson, we have a professional relationship only, I'm your solicitor, you've just signed the agreement to accept that sir."

"Yes but..." He tried to cut her off with an interjection of his own, but failed miserably. "... and anyway, I don't think my husband would agree to that sir." At this point he noticed that she was holding up her left hand this time, and the third finger was banded with gold.

"Ah, well," accepted Spen solemnly, "that would seem to rather make such an occasion problematic."

At that they both shook hands again. She left the file on the desk, walked round it and opened the door for him. He tried to offer her through first, but she remained firmly rooted to the spot; immoveable.

As Spen stepped off the last step onto the pavement John said, "Just carry on without me for a minute, I've just forgotten something." And with that he turned and leapt up all three steps and went back through the door again.

"John, I wouldn't..." said Spen, but he was too late. John was through the door closing it behind him after twinkling a smile at them both. Spen turned to Andrew and said, "She's married."

Only seconds later the large shiny door opened rather more slowly this time, and John returned to them down the steps. "She's married," he said to the other two.

"We know," said Andrew.

"Let's find an Ale house and do a little more Self-Study," suggested Spen. So Spen put his arm around the shoulder of John from his right, and Andrew did the same from his left. They sauntered over towards Grassmarket talking of more fish in the sea, and of lucky husbands. Her loss.

In the alehouse Spen offered to treat his friends to a flagon of best and a steaming bowl of Pottage. Luckily, the place was still nearly empty when Spen pulled the collection of notes from his pocket, and a few fluttered to the floor. Unfortunately though, Andrew shrieked in surprise at the amount of cash Spen suddenly had on him, and the shout attracted the attention of a thirty something year old woman standing at the bar next to a much older man. He was slumped heavily on a barstool and half sprawled on the counter; he must have been in there all day. She noticed the profusion of cash. She'd never seen such an amount, and the boys were so young.

"Put it away man," said Andrew in his well modulated voice. But the woman had already started to come across to them. She was quite pretty, but rough looking, somewhat dishevelled with lots of black curly hair. Certainly not ugly, quite shapely (for an older woman). What she had, she was making the best of, and was displaying it as best she could. As she came over Spen noticed that she adjusted her neckline downwards a little more. But when she arrived John pushed back his chair an inch or two, and leant forwards and sideways. His left shoulder gently leant into the woman's grubby tight skirt as she stood to greet them. She spoke something about fine gentlemen and not having been in there before, but John ignored her and leant against her thigh rather more heavily. Andrew gave him a look of disapproval.

"Och, cheeky, very forward sir." She pretended to be affronted at the young gentleman's shoulder leaning against her body but smiled at him all the same time. As she moved a little sideways John sat up again having picked a bank note from under the lady's foot.

He flicked it onto the table towards Spen, saying, "Missed one." Neither Andrew nor Spen had noticed the girl standing on it. "Ooooh," said the woman, "I'd do anything for that." And she leant forwards across the table towards Spen trying to show him her ample cleavage. John looked at her face for the first time. She made a grab for the note on the table, but Spen was quicker and slid it across the table towards himself. From behind her, John asked, "And what exactly *would* you do for it madam?" Having failed with Spen, she twisted around and leant forward towards John pushing her shapely rear as close to poor Andrew's face as she dared. To her John suddenly seemed to be a better prospect for business. "Oooh, I'd do anything sir, absolutely anything," she said to him, narrowing her eyes seductively.

John pointedly took a long stare at her chest and said, "Do you know I can see your navel from here?" and the three men burst out laughing. She stood up and mockingly hit him on the shoulder. Poor Andrew nearly choked on his ale. John took two shillings from his pocket and said, "As you're willing to do anything, perhaps you could furnish us with three more Ales and bring me the change." She took the money and huffily went to the bar. Spen spotted the innkeeper smiling.

As she returned with the ale the three men were more polite and thanked her properly. "Remember my offer gentlemen. You can usually find me here. Ask for Mary-Ann." As the three looked at her she flung back her curly black hair and revealed a large brown birthmark between the base of her neck and her right collar bone.

"Clavicle" said Andrew, reminding them all that they were now respectable *medical* men.

In those winter evening sessions Andrew was generally the responsible one, thinking of the consequences, preparing for the future and mostly taking care of the other two. Particularly when they'd spent too long in the ale house.

On one occasion they were walking home through one of the backstreets of the old town when they heard shouting. It was a young girl's voice. Down one of the alleyways a young teenage girl was being held by two men, who were treating her very roughly indeed. She was screaming and trying to break free. The three of them ran to her rescue, but as they drew close, they were spotted and one man, the larger of the two, stepped in front of the second who was left still holding the squirming girl. She must only have been twelve or thirteen thought Spen. He quickly observed where the gas lighting was, it shone dimly into the big man's face for it was behind his own head at the entrance to the alleyway. That's good, thought Spen. The second man, who wore a high fronted peaked cap, freed up one arm by gathering together the girl's long straggly hair and holding it in one fist. "I'll deal with these three Mac" said the larger one threateningly. Spen stood there with his back to the light slightly in front of his two friends. Andrew had started talking in appeasing tones, but Spen quickly realised that mere reason would carry no weight in the alley that night. The man lashed out at Spen, but he saw it coming and managed to dodge out of the way in plenty of time. Spen raised his fists. A second punch was thrown by the thug. Again, he missed, but this time Spen countered with a straight left jab in return, and it landed squarely on the brute's nose. But much to Spen's surprise he hardly flinched. Again, the ruffian tried throwing the same predictable punch, but again Spen dodged it successfully moving the other way, and gave him a perfect left hook in return. It connected crisply with the side of his jaw. He followed that up with an uppercut to compound the fracture, hopefully. The man started to fall forward so Spen danced back a little and kicked him in the face as he went down.

"Ooh," said John and Andrew in unison. Once on the floor Spen stood on the man's arm with his boots, meaning only to pin him down. But unfortunately for the thug, his arm had landed between the cobbles and a kerbstone unseen in a dark shadows. As Spen trod, the three men heard two distinct clicks in quick succession. The man yelled out in pain. Andrew grabbed Spen to stop him doing any further damage to the villain, even though he'd realised that no more was required. As the three stood over the groaning body they looked again at the second man holding the girl. He gave them a worried look, let go of the girl's hair and ran off further into the alley disappearing into the shadows. At this the girl ran towards them. They were half expecting a grateful hug, but she gave no thanks, nor indeed anything else, and kept on running past them off into the night. Andrew murmured laconically something about "Well, I'm glad we sorted that out," and moved his hands as if he was brushing off soil or baking flour from them.

As they walked the rest of the way back to 2A, Spen was asked where he'd learnt to fight like that? "On the lawn of Mr. Carter's residence," he told them.

"But that wasn't boxing Spen, that was thuggery," said Andrew. He was obviously referring to the way Spen had kicked the man in the face and stamped on his arm. "Spen, is there something you're not telling us?" asked John.

But Spen simply replied "Rule 1, John, rule 1." Further questioning meant he had to recount the time when he was Seven, the Eric incident, and the evening which followed. The one on the lawn when Mr. Carter had taken him under his wing. Rule one was that in fighting there were no rules, that was boxing. And there was very little similarity between the two, and tonight required fighting skills. The Marquis of Queensbury didn't get a look-in.

Chapter 6 – The Naked Headless Woman

Christmas break back on the estate was a total delight. Perhaps because he'd been away for a number of months everyone looked to Spen just a little older, greyer, perhaps slightly more weather-beaten. But everyone was still warm and friendly. They all wanted to hear Spen's stories, especially the gory bits. It was obvious to all that he was becoming a fine young gentleman, one who loved life and was very self-assured. But from Spen's own point of view he found that he was having less and less of a two-way conversation with folks and was delivering far more of his entertaining monologues. His company was sought by everyone on the estate. Though he loved to talk with the farm hands and sawmill workers, he realized that he was slowly outgrowing his old life. In fact, he couldn't wait to get back to Edinburgh. He dared to share these thoughts with his dear mother but far from being disappointed, she was very pleased for him, at least, that's what she said. The real truth was that it confirmed her worst fears.

Back in Edinburgh the second term's timetable of events made his first term look like he had been on holiday. There would be exams at the end of March. The three chaps in room thirty-two agreed that they must knuckle down and not have quite so many late nights, nor drink so much alcohol as they had done previously. They set up Andrew's father's microscope in the corner and clubbed together to buy a bookshelf. Whoever had paid for the book had first refusal for its use, but if it wasn't being used, either of the other two could borrow it. They re-arranged the room slightly so that the chair had light from the window for reading; the beds didn't need light. And anyway, natural light was so much kinder on the eyes than gas lighting. They clubbed together to buy a syringe and agreed that they would save for a stethoscope. They pinned up a copy of the timetable on the wall so that they could prepare adequately for the lessons or lectures of the next day. Soon the far wall was adorned with descriptions and lists. The descriptions defined Haematology (blood science), Cardiology (heart), Neurology (brains and nerves), Phrenology (Character traits, though probably to be dropped from the syllabus next year), Rheumatology (obviously the study of rumours?)... that sort of thing, then lists of bodily fluids (blood, saliva, gastric acid, aqueous and vitreous humour, urine, mucus, etc.), Then lists of bones, muscles ligaments, tendons and cartilages. And a few notes were appended here and there: "Never confuse Vitreous Humour with Vitriol (One is innocuous, one is 96% Sulphuric acid!!!). They took self-study periods much more seriously and tested each other at the end. In short, they made a good learning team. Sometimes they were even consulted by fellow students for both their knowledge and their learning techniques.

They all got a little stronger in the leg and smaller in the belly from all that running up the stairs and skipping meals.

A dissection had just been posted and it was a female, so John had bought three tickets, "You each owe me three bob," said John excitedly one Wednesday dinnertime. Extra-mural dissections had become quite the fashion. Although it was only executed criminals who didn't have the choice whether or not their bodies were dissected and gazed upon by dozens of young men, the required number of anatomy sessions had increased alarmingly of late. The syllabus dictated so many sessions were to be undertaken by each student, and the requirement simply didn't match the number of executions at the prison. The Anatomy act which they'd all heard about became law after the Burke and Hare fiasco, and was meant to provide many more bodies for study. Even so, everyone suspected that there probably still weren't quite enough waifs, strays and unclaimed workhouse deaths to go round. And even after the small number of philanthropic types willing to have their kind hearts cut out for the world to see, were added, there still probably wouldn't be enough. And criminals, on the whole, were men. Dissections of ladies' bodies were still a rarity. This would be their first. Saturday was also John's birthday; it would be a real treat for him said Andrew; a trip to the theatre.

When Saturday morning arrived, they gathered in a large house on the Northern end of Graham Street as it turned the corner into Keir Street. They were shown into a newly built operating theatre and the three chaps descended through the gallery to stand one step up from the lowest tier, which was the front row. Though the room itself was square, the stepped flooring was in a series of concentric horseshoes with the lowest tier nearest the centre. At the open end of the oval floor (the stage), was a wall with a door at the centre and two small tables, one either side. The solid wooden operating table was directly in front of them, and central to the whole room.

The room filled up quickly with young and old gentlemen and also two young ladies. A man came in through the stage door and began pottering away at the centre of the room. He wore a heavy cotton apron down to below his knees and had his shirt cuffs rolled back. He went to the narrow central table and moved the leather straps off the top and buckled them together underneath out of the way. He then went to the end and swung up a slight extension which had been hanging loosely. The table was quite old looking, much older than the room. It had saw marks in the top surface, obviously where some crazed surgeon must have forgotten to stop sawing. It looked moist, though Spen suspected that it wasn't from water but from formaldehyde or perhaps just bodily fluids. There were plenty of dull red stains about the table and even the floorboards beneath it. The reality of surgery for any poor soul being operated on made Spen gulp with dread. How traumatic it must have been for those only a few years ago who had to undergo the trauma with no anaesthetic, just a belly full of alcohol, if they could afford it.

The attendant left through the same door but within a minute it swung open again and he backed into the room holding one end of a stretcher. The crowd became quieter as everyone paid attention and leant forwards against their rails. The corpse, covered in a white sheet, was unceremoniously dumped on the table still atop its canvas stretcher. The carrying poles were slid out, though a member of the audience had to move slightly to allow the extraction. As the attendant pulled on the pole a naked arm fell from under the sheet on the opposite side of the table. it swung limply down. One of the attendants tucked it back underneath but it fell again, and the audience laughed as if witnessing some music hall jape. The second attendant clumsily carried the two poles away clattering them on the lintel of the small door. He returned immediately with a wooden box setting it down on the theatre floor just in front of Andrew and John. He returned to the door, peeped through, nodded and then turned and addressed the room. (He'd obviously already noticed the two young ladies present.) "Ladies and Gentlemen, welcome to Professor Davies' Saturday morning Dissections, please be aware that, God willing, there will be a regular dissection of bodies or major parts thereof at ten AM every Saturday for the foreseeable future, bodies allowing." There was a slight laugh at the notion that the bodies had a choice in the matter. "May I present to you, possibly Edinburgh's greatest surgeon, Professor A. I. Davies." There was a spontaneous round of genuine applause despite no-one having actually heard of the professor before. Their eyes were on the stage door. But as the applause rose further a distinguished looking gentleman entered the room through the door at the top of the gallery, the same door where everyone else had entered. Many quickly spotted him and turned to face the professor as he grandly descended the steps. Spen suspected that only the 'first timers' like him had been watching the door at the bottom of the room, as others were obviously expecting his lofty, grandiose and rather theatrical entrance. Three men on the front row of the steps parted and he swung open a small gate in the wooden rail. As he entered the stage, he grandly walked around the corpse on the table eyeing the audience. There were probably sixty people in the room. He stopped, eyed the room, took a silver cigarette case from his pocket as one of the assistants picked up a lit candle. The professor waved his cigarette at the crowd and grandly announced, "We have no need for Ether to stop this patient moving about today gentlemen." The crowd laughed. He put the cigarette in his mouth and the assistant held the candle up to light it. Spen turned to Andrew with a questioning look. Andrew leant in towards him and whispered, "Ether's very flammable."

The crowd were transfixed as the professor took a large knife from his tool-chest in front of Andrew, stood up, and with a flourish removed the sheet from the body almost like a matador whirling a cape, and threw it over the assistant. There was a slight, but perceptible gasp from the crowd. The young woman's body was totally naked. It also had no head. Spen had never seen a naked woman before. He suddenly felt that he might be staring a little too intensely and that possibly someone would notice him. He glanced up at the crowd on the other side of the theatre, but they all seemed to be staring too, He assumed that it was the first time many of them had set eyes on a naked woman too. The professor told the crowd that the head had been severed and kept for this afternoon's tutorial, for which there were unfortunately no more seats available, as the topic there would be 'The Complexities of the Ear.'

He leant over the body and announced "I make an incision just above the right clavicle as it joins the shoulder and cut, thus, across, all the way, to the top of the left clavicle ditto." And as he spoke, he made a deep wound across the base of her neck. Spen was surprised that no blood oozed out. Then the gentleman surgeon moved positions ready to make the next cut and Spen caught sight of the woman's neck. He couldn't be sure, but there looked to be a brown birthmark at the base of her neck running across to the clavicle. He thought he'd seen the mark somewhere before but couldn't remember where. Was it possibly on one of his fellow students he wondered, though think as he might, he couldn't place it? "See the birthmark on her neck Andrew," he said quietly, "recognise it?" Andrew moved his gaze up to her neck from where it had been focussed, saw the mark and said, "Stone me!" Others heard the remark and looked at him. The surgeon didn't, but his assistant did, and he looked across to where Spen and Andrew were gazing. He didn't draw too much of the audience's attention though because someone in the gallery behind them had feinted as the surgeon had made the first cut.

Speedily, a long cut down the centreline was made, followed by a little 'filleting,' and he had the skin pared front the front of the woman's thorax and abdomen. The sub-cutaneous, and a little visceral fat were removed next, which suddenly revealed all her bodies marvellous though gory workings. Starting near the groin he sliced with his blood covered knife down into the body and lifted out, "The bladder." Next came the Uterus, and he held it up to the crowd as if it were some kind of trophy. The ovaries were still attached to its top corners by the Fallopian tubes, though it didn't much resemble the pictures in Gray's Anatomy as the professor was holding it upside down. He announced how the ovaries were the female gonads producing the egg, though not as often as the male gonads produced their half of the bargain. This brought another guff-haw from the crowd. An embarrassed Spen flicked his eyes up to the two ladies in the audience, as did a number of others, and noticed that they were not laughing at the professor's misogynistic remarks.

Next came the large colon, starting at its junction with the ileum on the lower right side, up the ascending colon, across the transverse colon and down the descending colon towards the lower left. As he talked, he pulled out the organ in all its glory. He further explained that it was thus arranged to aid its function to extract moisture from the faeces before passing them along the short sigmoid and into the rectal cavity. "And then, on out, back into daylight again." Once more the crowd gave a giddy laugh. This man was plainly enjoying his work. "Quite the entertainer isn't he," said Andrew in Spen's ear.

As the assistant took the weight of the colon the professor sliced it from the junction with the Cecum, then the Sigmoid at its other end. Next, having sliced inside the abdomen at what Spen presumed to be nerves, blood vessels and various other connective tissues, the gentleman surgeon pulled up the end of the ileum. He explained that the direction of travel for the ingested food was opposite to today's direction of dissection, "Blind Cecum with its ileocecal valve, sometimes referred to as the Tulip Valve." He kept pulling. "Then between seven and ten feet of ileum, third section of the small intestine. He pulled more, "The Jejunum..." he kept pulling, and seemed to delight in his assistant's inability to keep a hold of the slippery entrails, letting some fall to the floor. He was carried away by his own entertaining verve and kept piling the hose of twisted ileum into the arms of his assistant, even purposely slapping the poor man in the face with it at one point. This of course brought a roar of laughter from the crowd. At this the assistant, who, Spen started to suspect, was part of the act, dropped the whole lot on the floor in mock frustration. Again, the crowd loved it.

The professor picked his half-smoked cigarette from the ashtray and let the audience calm down a touch as he placed it in his mouth. In doing so he left grim red stains on his white beard and moustache from his bloody hands. He announced that the ever-growing pile of organs on the side bench would be for sale to students wishing to dissect parts for themselves after the event. Spen leaned back and gently pulled his two roommates to him "How much shall we bid for the heart?" he asked them quietly.

Next, as the professor moved up the abdominal cavity the pancreas, bile ducts, gall bladder and stomach, with its pyloric and cardiac sphincters were identified, and removed. The stomach came out with the short rubbery curve of the duodenum attached, "A bonus for the purchaser of the stomach," he proclaimed to all. He shuffled a little lower again and extracted the kidneys telling the assistant loudly that he should give them to his cook as he might have one of them for his lunch;

they were after all in perfect order and disease free. Again, a laugh emanated from the crowd, though not everyone was convinced he was joking.

Spen was surprised how big the woman's liver was, and how much it obviously weighed, from the way the assistant was carrying it to the second of the two smaller tables.

"And finally, for today at least, we come to the thorax" said the professor. At this Spen wondered how the professor was going to saw through the ribs as the adjacent ribs would obviously hinder the reciprocation of a saw; Spen could see the professors bow saw below him at Andrew's feet. He surmised that if he were to saw vertically with the end of the saw going into the lungs then the tissue would be pounded and pulped to a state of unrecognizability. But he hadn't noticed that the assistant had left through the stage door and was returning with what looked to Spen like a pair of gardener's branch loppers. Having handed them to the professor he then pulled back the layers of skin and fat as far away from the breastbone as he could. The surgeon held up the loppers and placed the blades either side of the lowest rib on her left side. He deftly slid his hands up to the handles and forced them together. There was a grisly crunch as the bone severed. He continued to the next one, and to the next one, and each time there was the same sickening crunch. "As we are separating this poor unfortunate into her component parts for the purposes of anatomical exploration, and won't be reassembling her, we can afford a little expediency," announced Professor Davies. Spen assumed that to mean that if he'd had to remove ribs from a live patient another method would be used, though he couldn't think what that might be.

After further similar crunches the surgeon handed over his loppers to the ever-attendant assistant and lifted up the breastbone with what looked like a nightmarish collection of shortened lobster legs emanating from it. "Sternum," he announced, as he held it to the crowd. Spen looked again at the brown birthmark on the neck and tried hard to remember where he'd seen this woman before.

Even after nearly two hours of standing the crowd were still very attentive. In went the knife again "I cut through the pulmonary arteries which join the right ventricle to the lungs sending dark blood there to be relieved of its carbon dioxide waste and to collect precious oxygen." He continued slicing. "Whereupon it returns via the pulmonary veins to the left atrium. Note, gentlemen, that the pulmonary vein is the only vein in the body to carry light blood and the Pulmonary artery the only artery to carry dark blood in the whole of the body." He obviously still hadn't spotted the two ladies in the audience, despite looking up to the crowd's faces a number of times during the morning. "You will notice that the left lung has two lobes and is slightly smaller than the right, which has three. The lungs were pulled out with a slight slurping noise after Davies had further severed joins to the windpipe branches. "This is because the heart sits to one side of the centreline to facilitate plumbing betwixt heart and lungs."

The knife went in again and Davies worked it up and down a little to cut the major vessels. "I cut the upper and lower Vena Cavae..."

"Superior and Inferior," uttered John quietly, though not too quietly that the surgeon and some of the crowd couldn't hear him. "Quite so, quite so. And the Aortal arch feeding into the..." at this point the surgeon stopped and turned round to look at John behind him and paused for him to continue the sentence. "Brachiocephalic and subclavian arteries sir?" offered John, much to Spen's, Andrew's and many of the crowd's surprise."

"Yes, indeed, Mr...?"

"McFarlane sir," said John confidently.
But then Professor Davies addressed the crowd and asked, "And which one has Mr. McFarlane missed?" There were at least a dozen murmurs

from the crowd of "Common Carotid." John felt a tad crestfallen, though was a little pleased to have had the attention of the gathering for at least a few seconds. "I then make sure the Aorta, which is relatively thick walled, is separated and remove the heart.... Unless Mr. McFarlane would like to take over the demonstration of course." And as he spoke he looked up at the crowd before him, and the wall of faces laughed and looked directly at John; whose moment of glory had degenerated into mere embarrassment. Spen smiled at him and in full view of the crowd ruffled his hair to show him he still had at least two friends in the room.

Much to Spen, John and Andrew's disappointment the young woman's heart went straight into a large clear glass jar half full of liquid, presumably formaldehyde and Davies announced that it would be the object of yet another tutorial, for which some seats were still available. The assistant confirmed with a quietly respectful "Yes sir, correct." He carried the jar away as the professor stood up straight, put his hands on his hips and arched his back, giving it a good stretch. "What more can I tell you all. Perhaps only from a pathology viewpoint the young lady probably wasn't a manual labourer..." As he spoke, he lifted her right hand and inspected the palm and fingers. "No callouses, you see. So probably didn't use her hands to earn a living." And with that there was a mumbled remark from somewhere in the audience quickly followed by a localized group of giggles and some open laughter. Spen could only imagine at the allusion being made as to which part of her body she *had* used to make a living. But as he looked up, he noticed the two ladies turning to leave. "Perhaps we should leave it there and go for a light lunch gentleman. Thank you all for coming, thank you for your attention." A round of appreciative applause filled the room, and the professor took a small bow of thanks.

On his way out of the theatre Spen and his friends mingled a little with the others and discussed the event, and quality of the entertainment. One of the two ladies who had been present came and stood next to

Spen, presumably waiting for an audience. A number of the other gentlemen had watched her approach from behind, and he was alerted by their focussed gaze. He turned and greeted both ladies in the manner he'd been taught. "Good day Ladies, did you learn anything from the event this morning?"

The nearest, youngest and prettiest one answered with a slightly serious look, "You mean other than how bigoted, chauvinistic and misogynistic Professor Davies is?"

"Yes," Spen replied with a pitying smile, "I mean other than about Professor Davies' unfortunate attitude to the fairer sex, miss…?"

"Chaplin, Matilda Chaplin Mr. Robinson." She said confidently.

"Oh, you know my name?" said Spen in genuine surprise.

But John as always quick to join the conversation when there were ladies involved blurted, "He's Spencely, Spen to his friends, and I'm John."

"Yes Mr. McFarlane, I think everyone knows your name after this morning," said Miss Chaplin with a smile. Her companion smiled too, she must have been approximately ten or twelve years older than Miss Chaplin and had been the other female figure at the dissection of the corpse that morning. "May I introduce Mrs. Isobel Thorne, Mr. Robinson." Spen held out his hand to Mrs. Thorne too. The very fact that she was being referred to as 'Mrs.' anything meant John had immediately lost interest in the woman.

"And this is my other friend," said Spen, but before he'd had time to make a proper introduction Andrew stepped forward, held out his hand and said,

"Hello, I'm Andrew, very pleased to meet you both.

"How may we help you ladies?" asked Spen politely.

"Well, we were just wanting to come and apologise on behalf of our friend Sophia, she can be a little cutting, she doesn't mean to be, she just comes out with it and tramples on a lot of feelings," explained Miss Chaplin.

Then, as if to throw more light on the topic, Mrs Thorne added, "She's lovely really, just a little on edge sometimes." But poor Spen didn't have a clue what the two ladies were talking about, nor why.

"I'm sorry ladies, I'm not following?"

"You came to congratulate Edith on her success with the matriculation exams on the first day, and Sophia, she's sort of our group leader, was a little less than gracious to you Mr. Robinson." Spen still couldn't remember though now realised that they must have been talking about something that happened nearly four months ago. Miss Chaplin continued, "She accused you of fraudulently pretending to have a butler or something like that." And with that the penny dropped.

"Ohhhh, yes, I remember, oh please don't feel the need to apologise Miss Chaplin, I took no offence," said Spen in a warm friendly tone.

"Well, that's good then" said Miss Chaplin, hovering for a moment wondering what to say next. Spen tried desperately to think of some witty line with which to entertain the ladies and continue the intercourse, but none came. And at that moment, just as John was about to ask Miss Chaplin if she might like to join them for a spot of luncheon, another student came up and, ignoring the three chaps, grabbed her by the arm and tried to get her to leave.

"Come on Tilly, we'll be late for my father." The three parted and lifted their hats to Miss Chaplin and Mrs Thorne as they were sped away by the young man.

She tried to complain at him by saying, "Oh Bill, let him wait, we're supposed to be five minutes late at the very least..." The three watched as they walked off. Mrs. Thorne hurriedly walked behind them struggling to get enough length of step in her tight skirts. She at least looked back briefly with an apologetic smile.

Before long, Andrew said, "If I were a betting man, which I'm not, then I'd guess at 'Edgbaston.'" But John and Spen exchanged quizzical looks confirming that neither of them knew what Andrew was talking about.

"Bit of a day for bizarre statements from strange people eh Spen?" commented John.

"Who are you calling strange?" asked Andrew pretending to be offended. As they drifted off Andrew made it clear that Miss Chaplin had probably been raised not far from his home in Coventry. Probably less than twenty miles away. The other two simply agreed more out of a need to move the conversation on than anything else.

Over lunch the three talked first of the morning's dissection and how the internals of the body didn't seem as clear cut and straight forward as their copy of Gray's had suggested it was. Then to the food. It was un-noteworthy. Then Spen brought up the question of the identity of the body. "Did you see the mark on the poor woman's neck today?" asked Spen.

John nonchalantly asked, "Oh, was the body female, I never noticed?" Andrew and Spen exchanged a silly grin. John had seen the mark on the young woman that morning but didn't think he'd seen it anywhere before, though it was quite distinctive. Andrew tended to agree with Spen that they had indeed witnessed such a mark before, but he couldn't place it either. There were one or two people in Edinburgh after all.

* * *

It was pitch black outside, and the rain pelted angrily against their window. Spen guessed that it must be getting near five, but Saint Giles' bell stopped tolling after only three chimes. Moments later Saint Columba's bell did the same, though more quietly. The wind must be in the North East again, thought Spen. He was wide awake, though the other two were soundly asleep. Spen wondered if they would even wake up if the building suddenly burst into flames? Probably not.

Although he'd forgotten all about the topic, he suddenly remembered where he'd seen that young woman before, the one with the birthmark. It was the alehouse, with the money, the pottage, she was the woman who tried to conceal the fallen note under her foot. It was her. Then his mind drifted to the much more memorable event earlier that same day;

his meeting with the lovely Moira Beaty. He forced himself back towards thinking of the alehouse woman again. Probably a prostitute, scraping a living as she could, from tips, cinder gathering, or more likely selling her body. *She* was the one on the dissecting table last Saturday. Spen was convinced of it. He lain there as quietly as he could shuffling from one side to the other then back again, listening to the other two taking it in turns to snore, then snort loudly, wake themselves up, turn over and soon enough, begin snoring again. Saint Giles chimed four, as did Saint Columba's, then five. He was slowly falling out with Saint Giles. As soon as one of the bodies moved quietly without snoring, Spen concluded that he was probably awake and whispered, "I've remembered where we saw her."

But Andrew's voice came from deep within the darkness of the room, sounding like he was still more asleep than awake, "Your eyes are very heavy... you feel sleepy, you are floating in a warm bath, go to sleep... go to sleeeeep...."

Then from the other side of the room a northern Scots voice joined in with, "I'm trying but you two moooorons keep talking." Spen and Andrew chuckled a little and Spen sat up.

"She was the prozzie, who stud on my note, and you spotted it, and gave her two bob and asked her for drink and change..." Spen leapt out of bed and poked and stoked the fire back into life. He was wide awake so he felt the other two should be too.

Fifteen hours later the three were trekking along Bread Street and up The Lothian Road past Caledonian's old Lothian Road Station. On they went towards Caledonia's new station, being referred to by locals as 'The Shanty.' They found the public house where they'd gone before Christmas after their meeting at Brader and Sons. But this time they noticed the name on the front of the pub; "The Spurtle," it was called. Andrew asked what in the name of the Almighty was a *Spurtle* when it was at home? John explained that it was a special stick to stir the pot of porridge. "A bit like a spoon then?" Andrew asked. The two Scotsmen agreed that it probably was, though not quite as useful.

At the bar they waited for the attention of the innkeeper, but a barmaid came up to them and asked them their pleasure. Andrew put his hand over John's mouth before he could utter any attempt at wit, and asked her, "We're looking for a particular young woman with a birthmark, maybe you can help us please miss."

But before she could answer, the innkeeper stopped what he was doing and came over saying "Alright Beth, I'll serve these three gentlemen." And Beth moved along the bar to serve someone else. "We serve grog and Ale here gentleman, not information." They obediently ordered Ale, and tried again, but the innkeeper avoided answering a second time by asking a question of his own. "Who wants to know?"

"We just want to be sure that she's alright, does she still work here please?" asked Spen in his most reasonable tone, which, it must be said, was very reasonable indeed.

"No" said the man and went off to check that another of his customers didn't need serving. He didn't, so the three students shuffled along the bar to where the innkeeper remained. (Only John dragged his ale with him).

"Did she leave on good terms?" they asked, adding that they were concerned for the woman's safety, and may have some information to exchange. The innkeeper strolled back to the far end of the bar. The three side-stepped back again and joined him there. It wasn't a long shuffle, only a couple of paces, but it was getting tedious, though rather comic to a couple of the regulars.

"Will you three keep your voices down." Said the publican glancing over to the man whose company he'd just left. "Why, what do you know?" he asked quietly, leaning across the bar.

At this point John leant forward and said, "We asked first. Just if she doesn't still work here, did she leave on good terms?" The three were able to extract that Mary-Ann (Yes, that was her name) had never actually been in his employ but had indeed suddenly stopped coming into that public house a week or ten days before. He hadn't seen her since. Furthermore, he didn't know where she was. "Well, we think we have seen a body at the university on a dissecting slab, with a brown birthmark which looked just like hers." said John. (They hadn't had any instruction thus far on breaking bad news to relatives and friends). The man stood up straight, gasped a little and went white. He leant back against the shelves of bottles and glasses behind him and appeared for a moment as if he was about to feint. One of the glasses rocked and fell to the floor smashing into fragments. He ignored it and wobbled to the far end of the bar leaving the poor barmaid to sweep up the shards.

The three took their tankards and went to sit at a small table in the corner of the room. "I think we can say that it's the same woman," said Spen. All agreed that it probably was, but John and Andrew couldn't see why that mattered.

"What have we gained?" asked John.

"And where does that lead us?" asked Andrew. Spen hypothesised that it was only criminals' who's bodies could be dissected at the university, Or waifs, strays, unclaimed paupers and work house deaths. and Mary-Ann had been living a normal (for the old town) life of prostitution and part time villainy. Worthy of the work-house perhaps or maybe even prison, but certainly not a hanging offense surely?

Much to the three's surprise, ten minutes after sitting down at the table the innkeeper came and joined them. He brought four pewter tankards containing ale which were noticeably fuller than the ones they'd paid for earlier. He was much more friendly then. The three apologised to the man for breaking the news so roughly, as she'd obviously meant something to him. He neither confirmed nor denied it, but by the way he'd reacted earlier he didn't have to. They told him what they knew, and he was horrified. Not so much by her sudden disappearance, he always suspected Mary-Ann would meet an untimely end, but by the way her naked body had been publicly viewed and mutilated in the name of science. He told them of what he knew which was only that she rented a room by some warehouses on the canal wharf, the rough quarter, where the rats lived. And that she had no known relatives. As he talked, he couldn't stop himself looking over at a man by the bar. It wasn't an innocent glance either, no, definitely suspicious, worrying even. "And I'll tell you another thing, she's not the only disappearance lately."

No one spoke, but they all exchanged glances across the table still wondering what they should do with these nuggets of information. Who would want to know? Spen looked around at the man sitting at the bar, the one the barman had kept glancing towards. Again, he thought he'd seen him before somewhere. It wasn't so much his face as his hat that he seemed to recognise; he wore it at a jaunty angle, the same way as the man in the alley, the one holding the young girl's hair. John recalled the incident too. The girl had run off into the night, without stopping to say thank you.

"Did the man at the bar have a friend who came in here with him, perhaps one who had broken his arm lately?" asked Spen quietly. The innkeeper certainly knew he had a friend, a bigger man who, yes, used to come in with him, but he hadn't seen him lately. He didn't seem to know anything about him having a broken arm, but said he'd not been in for three weeks or more. Then he reasoned that these people were always falling out then falling back in love. Their relationships would best be described as 'fluid.'

Andrew suggested, "I wonder if it was broken by some brute masquerading as a medical student." But the innkeeper didn't follow. "An honest mistake," added Andrew kindly.

Spen realised that they'd got all of the information that was available from the innkeeper, and the conversation had turned to mere consolation. The man was quite happy to supply them with more ale if they would only sit there listening, and John at least was keen for that to happen, purely to somehow emotionally benefit the poor innkeeper's soul. But Spen noticed the man at the bar, the suspicious one, quaff his last drop from his tankard then get up to leave. He waited until he'd got to the alehouse door, noticed which way he went, then stood up abruptly. "Come on, we're going," he said sharply, almost rudely.

John belched a "Thanks for the beer, sorry for your loss," before they both hauled themselves to their feet and followed Spen out.

"Thank you for your time," said Andrew.

"And the ale," added John. But Spen was out the door and following the darkened figure with the high peaked hat. In a quick paced and rather spread-out line the four figures went South down the Lothian Road and jinxed right onto Morrison Street. The Dark loom of the Hopetoun Basin revealed itself occasionally behind the warehouses and offices on their Left. It wasn't long before the figure dived left onto Semple Street. Spen presumed that the drawbridge over the canal at its other end must be open for pedestrians. But the figure had disappeared.

Spen reasoned that he must have gone into a warehouse or maybe down one of the dark alleyways onto the wharf between the Hopetoun and Hamilton Basins. He went into the first alley, between the lofty buildings, even though it was pitch black. Slowly he emerged, being careful not to be jumped on. He found himself in some sort of loading yard. No barges, just the backs of warehouses on four sides with plenty of lifting derricks and high doors under winch huts. He stopped and looked around. Stacks of square sawn timber were arrayed along one wall of a warehouse. He could just make out 'Perkins of Falkirk" as the moon momentarily appeared from behind the clouds. The name was stencilled along the outside edge of the fine wood. Just like the ones that the Stannet-Forbes estate produced, thought Spen. Through a large archway he could see the side of a barge moored along the wharf side. It had a dull light shining against a curtained window of the living quarters, and a curl of smoke rising lazily from the short chimney tube.

* * *

Spen wondered what the pain in his cheek was. He lifted his head and the pain ceased, or at least dramatically reduced. He tried to lift himself off the ground a little. His head pounded, and as he got to all-fours the stone unstuck itself from his cheek and fell the few inches or so to the ground. Slowly he realized that he had been lying on his front, by the canal. "There you are," said a voice he recognised as friendly. "He's over here John," Andrew shouted. As the two hauled Spen to his feet he reached up to the back of his head, from where the other (even more severe) pain was now emanating. Grit from the cinder paving was still on his fingers as he felt the lump there. He also felt blood. They held him up and the three staggered in unison back onto the street. They went down towards the drawbridge over the canal and found some light. Under a gaslamp the friends inspected the cut and diagnosed very professionally that it was probably hurting. Spen struggled to congratulate them on their medical brilliance and suggested they take him home.

Andrew and John considered themselves lucky to have amassed carbolic soap in their embryonic doctor's tool kit back at 2A. Spen, was rather less impressed though as it stung like the very devil when they tended to his wound with it.

As Spen slept Andrew and John talked about who the woman was and how she came to be on the dissecting table so soon after being a healthy free woman, supposedly unwanted by the law. They concluded that the next logical step in their amateur sleuthing should perhaps be to return to the large house in Graham Street and ask the professor how he came by the body.

The following morning Spen's head throbbed, and his pillow had a few bloodstains. He decided against allowing his friends further access to his headwound or indeed to the contents of their collective medical bag. The strips of old blue and white striped sheeting pretending to be bandage made him look like something from an Egyptian horror story.

He was simply not comfortable with it. He had to tell them so, he opted for a hat instead.

They agreed to visit Professor Davies of Graham Street as soon as they could, but first they needed to attend tutorials on Ethics, Chemistry and Optics. They were also greatly looking forward to the lecture the week after by the famous Joseph Lister on Antisepsis in Surgery too.

On the rainy dark Thursday evening the three knocked on the rear door of the large residence of Professor Davies in Graham Street. His man answered, asking "Good evening gentlemen, are you buying or selling?" An odd welcome thought the three, but the ever-confident John glossed over the question and asked, "Good, evening, may we have a brief audience with the professor please, McFarlane, Robinson, and Lewis?" But far from obediently inviting them in or asking them to wait he said, "That would be professor…?"

"Professor Davies of course, this is his residence is it not?" asked Andrew rather impatiently.

"No, sir, it is not, I believe that professor lives near Bruntsfield, shall I find his address for you sir?" Having confirmed their need for the address the three had the door gently shut in their faces and they waited a minute in the rain wondering how they could have made such an error. Presently the door opened a little again and the servant handed out a notelet with an address in Bruntsfield on it, bidding them, "Good evening gentlemen," and then shutting the door again somewhat more abruptly.

As they trekked back the way they'd come, but in a rather more frustrated mood, Andrew announced that the servant who answered the door was one of the chaps who had assisted at the dissection. Not the main assistant, but the one who had lit the prof's cigarette. He was the one who had tucked the arm back up under the sheet, not the one who struggled to get the stretcher handles back through the stage door. Spen agreed that it probably *was* the man. John couldn't confirm or deny as, given a choice between looking at a young woman's naked body or the faces of old men didn't leave him with much choice.

They found a rather smaller residence in Bruntsfield. And much to everyone's surprise an old gentleman with white whiskers answered the door. It was Professor Davies. The three greeted the man respectfully and he readily invited them in. His living area was small but tastefully furnished. He had no servants present, at least at that time of the day, nor even a wife, from what the three could see. The professor offered them a sherry and poured himself a rather large one. They suspected that it wasn't his first that day.

The old man remembered McFarlane and even apologised for any embarrassment that he may have caused him on that occasion at the Graham Street dissection. In fact, the professor privately was a lot less ebullient and loud than his public persona had suggested. He shared with them that in a room of sixty gentlemen watching his every move for two hours he had to be the entertainer, in order to be asked back. When the three enquired about what he meant by the phrase, 'asked back,' he described in detail the politics of how the extra-mural dissection and anatomy circus worked. They were all ears though Spen was keen to ask his question regarding Mary-Ann. In the end, he didn't have to.

In order to give teaching in anatomy, each professor, a few years ago, needed to have his own room, sell his own tickets, source his own corpses. Then they started to group together, through the university, to share facilities. But as the numbers of students continued to grow the process had been rather uniformalised, and unfortunately, somewhat taken over. One man, the professor thought he was probably Greek by his name, had been rather efficient at streamlining the whole process and helping everyone to make rather more money, much more easily. Especially himself. His name was Mr. Voithos Rotuida, and he lived in the large house in Graham Street. When the chaps exclaimed that they had just come from there he smiled sympathetically and poured himself more sherry. "Are you sure you won't?" he asked the three as he held up the decanter. "May we sir, if it's not too much bother" said John before the others could politely refuse again.

"You seemed to be under the impression, that my assistant worked for me gentlemen?" The three nodded. "No, it was I who worked for him. At least on Saturdays."

"Good Lord above," uttered Andrew expressing the sentiments of them all. As they sipped their sherry, they listened to the stories of how Mr. Rotuida had a circle of physicians and surgeons who he could rotate through his operating theatres. Yes, plural. He had few rules but always insisted that they should announce the date of the next dissection, and also that they should offer the body parts to the audience afterwards, for a price of course. They would get a percentage of the sales. All very gentlemanly. Good business you see. He went on to say how the room was used for genuine operations during the week, either with surgeons requesting its hire, or sometimes by families asking Rotuida to provide the means for the treatment of a family member. He would then provide the room and an appropriate surgeon (usually the cheapest). He would also arrange the sale of tickets if the family would allow an audience, or simply charge extra if they didn't. If they allowed interested spectators, then he sold tickets to the event in the usual way, from which they would get a cut. An unfortunate term in the circumstances. Sometimes he sold the room twice per day charging extra if the first patient didn't turn up on time or the surgeon over-ran. He'd really elevated himself from being a mere dealer in bodies and parts, to being the hub of a quickly spinning, money-making wheel. The three were amazed at the almost industrialisation of medical learning and indeed medical treatment. There was obviously a lot of money changing hands.

Spen moved onto where the bodies came from. "A number of sources," said the old man, "some convicts, though they are mostly taken directly to the University, a few from the poor house who's relatives can't afford to bury them, waifs, strays, the usual and..." The professor took a sip from his ornate glass but didn't continue speaking afterwards. The three watched as he sat back and stared at the wall light flickering.

"And, sir...?" asked Spen.

"Well, I think it's safe to say that not all bodies are honestly sourced, particularly those, like your young woman, who are presented with no identifying features or paperwork. I'm sure you realise that with so much money at stake paperwork can always be, erm, *found* for Her Majesty's Inspector of Anatomy. You only have to look back to the 'Daft Jamie Wilson' episode with his gammy leg..." John looked across at Spen and shrugged his shoulders slightly to share the silent question.

Andrew explained, "Burke and Hare's last but one victim, a popular lad, though simple, used to beg on the main streets, and run errands for the college. Huh, *run*; he had a gammy leg, and because of it was recognised by some students when he appeared on the slab."

The Professor chimed in again, "It not only brought an end to the life of Mr. Burke but also to the career of Professor Knox too." Spen noted that poor Jamie Wilson's life wasn't considered.

What Spen, Andrew and John had just picked up was that Mary-Ann's corpse was probably illegally sourced. Meaning she was probably murdered. At that moment Andrew realised why the man who answered the door at Graham Street had greeted them the way he did. He'd asked, 'Were they buying or selling?' Obviously, it wasn't tickets, it was bodies. Meanwhile John had somewhat glazed over and fallen asleep. Then, as the professor took another sip and stared into nothingness he spoke, almost thinking out loud, "What worries me more than anything, is how the bodies all seem to be quite fresh, in such good condition." Spen and Andrew looked at each other across the room, there was only one simple answer to that question.

* * *

The whole of the next week it rained. No-one wanted to venture out, so they restricted themselves to doing only what they must, and not bothering with anything if they didn't have to. One of the major lectures that week was to be by the new Professor Cameron, who had returned to Scotland from a two year spell in Paris and Berlin. He was to talk on the latest Germ Theory. Germ Theory, whatever that was, was where the future lay and the three felt they must attend. Any revision days for their coming exams also went on the 'Must Do' list. So, their pet mystery took only second priority that week behind studying to be a doctor and honouring all that money being spent on their education.

Chemistry was still Spen's best subject if not his favourite one. But he didn't want to become an apothecary or even a laboratory scientist, he wanted to be a doctor and help people. He was good with people, he had the right manner, which, apparently couldn't be taught, though it could be learnt. All the Physicians told him so. He had the right manner, even with the poorer patients.

The highlight of the first quarter of the year was to have been hearing from the great Doctor Joseph Lister, revolutioniser of surgery: in that his new Antiseptic treatments had made surgery far more survivable. But unfortunately, the good doctor had to cancel at the last minute and another eminent Professor had to stand in his stead. Rather disappointing.

Professor Cameron's talk on Germ Theory, was most interesting; he spoke of how improvements in the optics of microscopes had increased useable magnification and allowed scientists in Germany and France to prove that different diseases were in fact caused by different germs. The common cold, and various other ailments like poliomyelitis, still eluded their search for a reason for the infection, but so many others could be identified from their microscopic in-dwellers of the body.

It was becoming obvious, said Cameron, and it was likely to be proved in the coming years that it was not 'Strong Passions' which caused the troublesome lesions of Phthisis, but a germ of some sort. "In time, and not too far away we will show that a trip to the seaside, though a delight, is no more efficacious than a trip to the countryside, or any other means of extracting the patient from the circumstances of squaller and poverty in the city. For squaller and poverty were the breeding ground for the germs of disease. Open sewers, or even no sewers at all were the paradise of Eden for germs, and it was presently the best defence against them to cut off their breeding grounds. That's what Doctor Snow had proved at Broad Street in Soho, and it worked." But as he looked out into his audience Cameron could see a few blank faces. "It will be the scientific battle against the germ by doctors and scientists which would eventually cure the world of its ills."

But it was not going to be easy; even Plague, the black death, always thought to have been the fault of the brown rat, might now be being understood more deeply. Yes, rats were a factor, but seemingly not the whole story. Perhaps it was their faeces or their bite which propagated and transmitted the germs. But perhaps there was some other reason that rats were involved, Their fleas perhaps? Were the rats merely carrying the carriers which carried the germs? After all, germs are very small, microscopic even, as we have now seen. Quite literally. Small, but ferocious little buggers. He was confident that in themselves, rats weren't the complete answer to Bubonic Plague. In the same way Galen's miasmas were possibly involved with disease but again, not the whole story. Simply smelling a foul odour would not in itself kill, infect or even harm anyone. BUT, modern thinking was that the cause of the odour would very likely turn out to be those self-same germs. The bad smell was merely a by-product of the germ's putrefying work. For whom amongst them had not endured the stench from the rotting flesh of a corpse, as it was slowly eaten away by those germs?

He turned back again to the famous figure of whom (most of) the audience knew well, and even held in high esteem. Doctor John Snow of London, who Cameron had already mentioned, had developed his theory of the faecal to mouth transmission of Cholera. He reported on how he'd had the opportunity to test that hypothesis in Soho. There was a drinking well, topped by a pump, which was later shown to have been sunk into an old cess pit and subterranean course of sewage transfer. Snow had plotted on a map the homes of Cholera victims. They were concentrated around that pump. So, by having the council simply remove the handle from the Broad Street pump, preventing its use, the outbreak died out. Cameron did, in all fairness though, explain that even Doctor Snow had suggested that the outbreak in Soho was already on the wane before the removal of the pump's handle; so the evidence wasn't watertight, so to speak. Cameron further told of more work by the good Doctor Snow regarding his large-scale test to extract drinking water from the mighty Thames upstream of London's city and count the numbers of Cholera infections in the recipients. Then he compared this against those who were drinking water extracted from the river on the downstream side of the city. The numbers were conclusive, even predictable; consuming the sewage, even in miniscule amounts which had already been through Cholera victim's bodies' would re-infected more.

Cameron even broached the revolutionary notion that 'Fever' was not a disease in itself at all, but rather a symptom of many other different diseases. Elevated temperature, sweating, nausea, the shakes, not only happened for Malaria, but for typhoid, diphtheria and for Cholera too. All separate diseases but with similar symptoms. It was part of the body's own fight against the invading germs. He explained how not only the numbers of particular germs were innumerable, but also the variety of different species of germs. And not all germs were our enemies. Yeast was probably his favourite, as it not only had a hand in the production of bread, but also of Ale. The Alimentary tract of all animals, including ourselves probably, utilised the germ as a means of breaking down that same bread and beer once inside us. This allowed us to extract the salient chemical parts and allow us to absorb their support for life. Though some germs were vicious little buggers, other types were indeed clever, helpful little buggers.

Doctor Cameron's talk went on longer than scheduled, but not one soul in the audience minded. He received a standing ovation at the end, and he stood smiling and gazing out at the crowd of probably a hundred faces before him. As his eyes fell upon Spen he seemed to wave at him. Andrew asked, "Did the Prof just wave at us Spen?" Spen denied it but then, for the first time since the talk began, he thought there was something about Professor Cameron which was familiar. Perhaps Cameron had thought the same about Spen. But from that distance it could easily have been John or Andrew that he'd waved at.

As the crowd jostled towards the doors at the rear of the hall, the young men of room thirty-two went forward to congratulate the Professor and to thank him for his scintillating talk. "Do you still run?" he asked Spen with a smile. Spen was confused, even though the question was simple. But before confirming or denying, the professor continued, "you don't remember me do you?" Spen didn't. "I don't recall your name, but I do remember that you stood up not holding onto anything in the back of that jig as we raced across the fields, I remember admiring your balance. It was to a patient on some country estate near Falkirk. Fourteen years ago, it would be, I'd be twenty six," said Cameron with a smile. Spen remembered the incident and smiled broadly.

"Ah, yes indeed sir, I was seven. You spent some time with Doctor Snoddy, I remember. Robinson sir, I'm Robinson."

"*Spencely* Robinson, yes I remember." All three of them were surprised at the professor's powers of recall. Spen had even forgotten that he'd told Doctor Cameron what his name was on that day.

"Tell me, is the old fool still around?" asked Cameron.

"I believe he's still alive sir though he retired many years ago."

"Good, good. And the patient, sorry, the names gone, there have been so many. It was tetanus though. Typical arched back, as I remember," he said.

"Mr. Bell died a few weeks after that sir. Survived the Tetanus..."

"But died from the cure no doubt," added the Professor.

"Probably the bleeding with a lancet full of germs, I shouldn't wonder," said Spen sympathetically.

"Hmmm, the shock of scepsis, I'm sure of it."

'Well, what a surprise, one of the newest and brightest rising stars of the medical world being on first name terms with our Spen,' ribbed the boys on the trek back to 2A. They further pulled his leg about being one who seemed to attract good fortune. They hoped some of it might rub off on them, especially for tomorrow's exams. They decided not to go out for the evening, but stay in and test each other on ester, ethane, ethene, the ethyls and the ethylenes, et cetera.

Their exams went rather well, which, as Spen explained, was a worry in itself. But maybe all that mutual assistance combined with their organised system of learning and testing had worked. There were one or two tears in the examination hall but, from what Spen could see, none from any of the seven ladies who also took the exams. Thus far they hadn't been allowed to join the same lectures or Tutorial gatherings as the men throughout the year, though they could attend any extra-mural teaching by the same professors, just not so within the grounds of the university. The men had also heard a rumour that the ladies were even being charged higher course fees.

At the close of the final Friday exam (Chemistry) Spen went straight to Waverley and embarked on the next Train to Falkirk.

Chapter 7 – A Difficult Offer to Refuse

Apart from his dear mother, increasingly it was only Emily who brought him back to the estate. She still had that impish grin and, and though she was always full of irreverent fun, she'd somehow become more sophisticated. He'd noticed that she was even a little narrower in the waist. He wondered if he should tell her, hmm, safer not to. She still felt good to hold though, and they held each other very closely quite often, whenever they could. They still went for long walks over the fields, even laying sometimes in the meadow looking up at the blue sky. Spen tentatively asked about her future. He wondered if her father had tried to pair her off with anyone. "No, but Charles has though," she said. Spen sat up at this remark and got suddenly serious.

"Really?" he asked, "How?" Emily told him of the half dozen attempts at finding Emily and Catherine a suitor by arranging parties at the residence for his friends. "What, his college chums?" suggested Spen, but from what Emily could tell they were more like gambling friends or gentleman's club type chums. She didn't think they had the intellect to attend a college. And they certainly hadn't been gentlemen; they'd generally got drunk and started being suggestive and lude beyond the point which she and Catherine found acceptable. The second half of the last two parties she and Catherine had gone into Mary's room and left the men and one or two of their 'lady friends' to continue partying downstairs. She had grown to hate the parties and thought that if Sir William really knew what went on, he'd put a stop to it jolly quickly. "Then why don't you tell him Em?" asked Spen, which to him seemed to be the obvious thing to do. "Because Mary made us promise not to. Charles would be horrible to her again if we did."

But as they lazed away that particular day, Emily seemed rather keen to move the subject onto Catherine, as she had a slight concern regarding her middle sister. Again, she held Spen's attention fully captive. The only thing good to have come from any of Charles' parties was a new friend for Catherine. "Well, that's good surely, Catherine doesn't have many friends Em."

"That's true, none of us have," said Emily sorrowfully. The words came as a bit of a revelation to Spen, but when he considered it, from what he knew of the family, he realized it was true.

"She's never had a gentleman friend. Ever,"

"so this new boyfriend then, what's he like?"

She continued, "in fact..." Spen leant over her as she stared up at the clouds, "He's a she...she has a girl-friend. One of Charles' friends', friends."

"What's wrong with that?" asked Spen, not really getting Emily's point.

"Lottie comes on the train some weekends, from Glasgow, and they walk over the fields, hand in hand... Together, just like we do," she continued.

"And?..." asked Spen, "Your point is?"

"Oh Spen, they sleep in the same bed and if Daddy found out he'd be furious." But Spen just tried to defend Lady Catherine saying that it was not uncommon for two girls to share a bed, even in their mid-twenties. "But they spend the whole night giggling like schoolgirls... and sometimes ooh-ing and aarh-ing. I've heard them Spen; they're only in the next room." Spen was listening and as he did so, the light was slowly percolating through his misty understanding.

"You mean, she doesn't even like men? Oooh, I see. Well, why didn't you say." 'Finally,' thought Emily.

"But she'll rot in hell Spen," couldn't he see? And Emily really didn't want that.

"Then sit up and pay attention Miss Stannet-Forbes," he'd told her. Spen lectured Emily from his superior (which meant higher) Doctor's understanding on the topic of God and two girls being in the same partnership. Point one was that if Catherine and her friend liked girls more than boys, then God the all-powerful creator, had created them (all-powerfully) that way, because that's what He wanted. Secondly, If God was the god of anything, even before he was the god of Love, he had to be the god of Truth. So, Catherine must be true to her feelings, true to herself, otherwise she was slapping God in the face by living a lie. No-one should have to go through life pretending to be someone they're not. It was not up to pompous self-righteous individuals, always men, to dictate to other folks how to be. All they had the right to do was offer advice on God's love, and their interpretation of how it was shown to His people. So many priests weren't even married so how could they possibly know what they were talking about when it came to women of the opposite sex? I ask you?" Spen had managed to work himself up into quite a steam.

But Emily, as ever, smiled and said, "Thank you for your kind words and your wise wisdom Doctor Robinson," and then kissed him.

"Everyone has the right to be happy Em, do what they want, so long as it's not illegal, immoral or going to hurt anyone else."

"Well said doctor," smiled Emily again, somewhat relieved. He laid down next to her again and continued looking at the clouds rolling across the sky. "One other thing..." she said slowly.

"Yearrrrse, Miss Stannet-Forbes? Come on, spit it out, my next patient is waiting," he said in mock ill temper.

"Well Doctor, I will admit to being a little jealous of Catherine..."

"Em, are you saying that you prefer girls too?" That would indeed have been a real revelation for Spen.

"No, silly." She answered.

"What then?" asked a curious Spen, "tell me."

"It's just that the ooh-ing and Aah-ing, late of an evening."

"Yes?"

"Well, it sounds quite fun." And she rolled over, on top of Spen, then sat up, with her legs doubled back either side of him. She took his hands from his sides and placed them gently on her breasts. "You see Doctor, I think I've grown up... Don't you Doctor?" she said coyly. Spen hadn't expected that! He didn't know quite how to respond. Did he grab her passionately as his heart was yelling at him to do? Or did he remove his hands and talk to the young woman like a grown up, as his head reasoned. So, because he was a male, he compromised; leaving his hands where they were, for the moment, and suggested that they should talk. He admitted to her that there was nothing in the world that he wanted to do more than make love to Emily right there and then, truly. But if that were to happen, then everything would change for her, and probably not for the better. He carefully explained, as gently as he could that if they did make love, from that point onwards, she would no longer be pure in body, untouched. At that point in the conversation Emily couldn't see a problem. It certainly wasn't illegal, immoral and (probably) wouldn't hurt anyone. But, didn't she see, that it would mean that she would no longer make a good prospect as a bride for a gentleman?

The conversation went downhill a little after that. Though they were both happy to settle down and be married to each other, to make love all night long and then in the meadow all the next day, the reality was still, that she was the daughter of an Earl, and he was the son of a penniless estate worker. And never the twain could meet. Emily said that perhaps Spen didn't really want her, now that he lived in the metropolis. But Spen couldn't convince her that although *he* had nothing to lose by the action, she had everything.

They both went quiet. He walked her home, though she didn't seem to want to hold hands. But she didn't want him to stop writing though; she so enjoyed his letters. They were the only thing that kept her going each week. She said it almost as if their relationship was at an end.

As they still had a way to go back to the Big House Spen asked about the sawmill. He couldn't think of anything else to say. "That Steam engine was the best investment daddy ever made," she told him.

"Glasgow can't get enough wood these days. It all goes there, and they would buy more if we had it." A man from the agent's came quite often and urged her father to sell them all the wood they cut, and he promised to beat anyone else's prices. But her father was already selling everything to them. Apparently, the steam engine and boiler had already paid for themselves twice over. Spen wanted to bring the conversation back to them, but somehow that moment had passed. And they were suddenly outside the house.

That evening, he shared the day with his mother, well, perhaps not quite all of it, and she told him that he mustn't worry. Given time all things would work themselves out. The truth probably was that a fine gentleman with lands of his own would come riding along one day and sweep Emily off her feet. And that, Spen too shouldn't look to tie himself down, because when he was a doctor, he would be able to have the pick of the crop. He didn't really want the pick of the crop, he just wanted Emily. Though he could see that all the signs were indeed still pointing him the other way, blocking his path. But he held on to hope, for hope was rather more comforting than any realistic prospects.

* * *

Back in Edinburgh Spen, Andrew and John greeted each other warmly and decided they should go out to celebrate them all passing the pre-holiday examinations. To no one's surprise Spen had scored in the top decile of the Chemistry results. That was Academia-talk for the top ten percent. But, somewhat to everyone's surprise the ladies had scored much better than everyone had expected, and every one of them was in the top decile too. More to the point perhaps, many of the students, and even some of the professors were rather disappointed that mere woman had scored more successfully than they had hoped. The highest two scorers in the exam were gentlemen both of whom were re-sitting the test after a previously dismal showing, but then all the other male candidates had been beaten by at least one of the ladies, and most of them were beaten by all of the ladies. "The Hope Scholarship awards will be interesting then," said Andrew, as John went to the bar for more ale.

John had no real news to report from Shetland, apart from the horrendous three-day journey he'd had once more from Lerwick, via Aberdeen and Perth to Edinburgh. "What have you to report," he asked Spen, "how's the lovely Emily?" And Spen felt he should briefly report to his friends on his near sexual encounter. John thought Spen had done the wrong thing by resisting, he would have torn her clothes off and leapt on top of her.

"Very romantic John," said Andrew. Andrew himself was proud of Spen for waiting until they were married, as that was the right and proper thing to do. God's way was best.

"But they're never going to be married Andrew, haven't you heard?" said an exasperated John.

"Well, that's all the more reason for her to abstain, isn't it," Andrew insisted.

"But not if her future husband is out there now, sowing his wild oats into every filly he meets," exploded John, "why should it be alright for him to be out there … 'sowing,' whilst she is expected to live the life of purity and chastity waiting for the right man to come along? And then, even when it does happen, the poor girl can't marry him anyway?" But Andrew insisted that God's way wasn't John's way. At least the three agreed on something.

The conversation moved on from marriage and women to God. It often did. Why were the Israelites God's chosen people, and why not the Scots? More to the point, why weren't all nation's God's people, as He's not supposed to have favourites, right? Andrew offered the notion that it wasn't up to mere mortals like them to ask God the Almighty to justify His ways. All Spen could bring to the conversation was the section he knew of in first book of Samuel (or was it Exodus) when God had instructed the Israelites to go into the land of the Amalekites (or was it the Midianites), and murder all the men, women and children then their sheep, goats, cattle and camels, and take nothing out. Something which the Israelites failed to do, which upset The Almighty. There it was in the bible (somewhere) and he'd like Andrew's take on the purpose behind it. Bit tough on the sheep and goats at the very least. And another thing, surely if God was the God of all, then why wasn't He the God of the Amalekites, Amorites, who-ever, which would suggest that God was having his own people murdered? How can that be? Spen was just wanting to know, he genuinely wanted to know.

As the conversation drew to a close, Spen realised that Andrew and John were both replete with answers, though on opposing sides. Each was totally convinced that they were right. Yes, they were both full of answers, Spen felt himself to be only full of questions.

The big excitement for their first week was to be a talk on Anaesthetics, their use and application. But before that there were to be the awards of the various prizes, scholarships and medals of achievement at a grand assembly. Everyone was required to attend. Most of the awards were usually for the fourth years who were nearing the end of their training. The main award for first years (which Spen nearly won) was the Hope Scholarships for Chemistry. But there were three awards and four ladies had finish above him in the table of results. The two students finishing above them would be excluded as they were both second timers at the exam.

On the way into the gathering, the topic of conversation was all about the women taking kudos away from the men in the recent run of achievements. Spen and his friends couldn't see a problem, as they had won fair and square. But they were very aware of an undercurrent which had pervaded the university for some weeks up to that meeting.

Once inside the hall, Spen was sat in the middle of a row of seats in the central block about a third of the way back from the stage. He could just see the backs of the heads of the seven lady students who were close to the front. The ordeal was long and boring with many speeches by the good and the great about the young and the bright. None of the ladies had won any of the prizes by the time they neared the end. Spen was very surprized at that, after all, they were very bright. But when the Hope Scholarships were announced he knew that they would have their moment of glory. It turned out to be their moment of fury.

"And the Hope Scholarships for Chemistry have been won by Robert Kinman, Kevin McKay and Spencely Robinson." Spen's jaw dropped as he sat in his seat. Not so much because he heard his name announced, but because the prizes should have gone to three of the women. His friends nudged and lifted him to his feet. He then excused himself as he shuffled sideways along the long row of seated well-wishers. Those who weren't clapping him were patting him on the back as he went by them. As he climbed the steps to the stage, he caught the eye of one or two of the ladies, none of whom were clapping. Sophia (the ringleader) Jex-Blake looked daggers at him. Seated to her right was Miss Edith Pechey and he looked at her whilst shrugging his shoulders in a rather forlorn attempt at apology. He knew that it should be her up on the stage and him sat in the audience. Doctor Crum-Brown shook his hand warmly and smiled into his face willing him to be happier than he must have appeared. He couldn't smile, he felt like he'd cheated his way to the prize. He looked out at the sea of faces, all smiling, all except seven people on the second row that was. He felt that the whole audience must have seen the result of the chemistry exam and known that the ladies were due the prizes. They all must have known that he'd won the prize unfairly, so why were they clapping?

As everyone crowded to leave the Grand Hall Spen tried to catch up with Miss Pechey to apologise to her in person. But as he got closer, he noticed that a number of students around the ladies were being un-necessarily rough in their jostling towards the door. Spen was ashamed of them; they weren't on the rugby field now but were in the Great Hall of one of the finest universities in the world. That kind of behaviour was inexcusable. Outside, the ladies had all left to return to their lodgings before Spen could get through the exit. He decided to try again to speak to them at a later juncture.

***

The issue of Mary-Ann's death and subsequent dissection had largely gone away. The three friends had only discussed her demise once since re-joining together for the new term. They'd decided that she'd probably been murdered, and someone had probably gained by selling her body to *The Assistant*. They all said that he was undoubtedly at the centre somehow of an illicit trade, but they didn't know any details. Neither had they one jot of proof against him. They didn't even know *who* he was. But one thing they had done was taken a vow not to return to the canal side near the wharfs and warehouses between the Hamilton and Hopetoun basins. At least not at night-time and certainly not alone.

The next exciting event that week was to be the introduction of Chloroform into the syllabus. For Spen and the chaps it got even better when they discovered their tutor was to be none other than Doctor Arthur Cameron again.

The three were early for his lecture despite the lesson being attended by only a few people. So they were on the front row, Cameron liked his pupils t to get up close and personal. He came into the room with no announcement and brought with him a bottle of clear liquid which had a glass stopper in the top. He also brought four or five muslin facemasks which looked quilted, probably with layers of lamb's fleece, and were shaped to go over the nose and mouth of the patient. They were thick to aid absorption and spread the drops which were to be poured onto them. He put the bottle on the front desk and passed the masks into the audience for them all to feel and inspect, even to try them on for size.

"Chloroform is 'Trichloromethane' and has a distinctive and not unpleasant smell," began Cameron. He walked to the first row of seats swooshing the liquid round inside the bottle. As he reached its end, he removed the stopper and walked along the row holding it up for the students to take a sniff as it went by. He was right, it was distinctive. One or two students were a little timid at putting their nose into something which might knock them out, but Cameron kept the bottle moving and never allowed anyone to overindulge. Even students on the second row could detect the odour. As he moved, he spoke, "It has two major advantages over Ether in that it is much quicker acting for the patient, and is not flammable, which is of benefit to everyone. Ether has been responsible for many a fire in surgeries and theatres these last dozen years; gas lighting, candles and cigars do not mix well with ether." The audience gave an appreciative grown of amusement.

He got more serious in his tone, "There is a fine line to be drawn, by the doctor applying the anaesthetic. On first applying the liquid, the patient begins to worry that he is losing control and going into a state where he is powerless to respond. Which of course, he is. Next, the eyes close and the dark curtain of sleep, painless sleep is brought upon the patient. His nervous system is dulled, his muscles relax. This is the state we aim to achieve and maintain." Cameron held the room's absolute and total attention. "However! There is always an 'however,' it does not take the same rate of application of chloroform drops to maintain unconsciousness as it does to bring it about. And this is where the skill of the anaesthiologist is paramount. For if the same rate of application of the chloroform is maintained, then the same *rate* of 'increasing relaxation' of the patient is also produced. That is to say, the patient continues to sink past sleep and into oblivion. After the nervous system is dulled and the arms and legs are totally unusable, then by continuing to apply that same amount of chloroform, the diaphragm too will soon be made to relax, rendering the lungs inoperable and therefore useless. The patient stops breathing. Next, the heart will detect the reduction in blood quality and will attempt to pump faster, for a moment at least, until it too enters into that same state of perfect relaxation, which is better known gentlemen," he looked up, "as death." A small murmur of amusement rippled across the audience again. "So this, gentlemen, is why I, and an increasing number of my peers today, use a second person, other than the theatre assistant, to apply the chloroform. This way I can give my full concentration to the job in hand, and I do not have to divide my attention between curing my patient on the one hand, and not killing him with the Chloroform on the other. They are both very important jobs, but quite distinct, I feel."

Cameron talked too of the consequences of applying any volatile liquid to the lungs via a mask, such that common air might be totally displaced. Air is needed for survival, even when asleep, or in a coma. "Make sure you still allow the vital air into the patients lungs." He explained how ether fed through a close-fitting mask had led sometimes to the exclusion of atmospheric air and brought about the demise of many a patient in the early days of Anaesthetics.

Appreciative applause went around the room as some of the students expected that this last statement was the conclusion of the lecture. But Doctor Cameron looked them all in the eye. "But, gentlemen, theory is all well and good, but what about the practical?" he said clearing the desk at the front of the room. He lifted off its few books and folders and placed them on the floor underneath. "Do I have a volunteer please?" he asked as he moved the chair from behind the desk to its end. He looked at the audience. Everyone averted their gaze, and no-one volunteered as they all rightly expected what was coming next. "Thank you, Mister Robinson, if you'd be so kind." He looked at Spen with a small grin and beckoned him towards the front of the room. All eyes were on Spen. Poor Spen could do nothing other than stand up and step onto the platform in front of him and join Doctor Cameron. He moved towards sitting himself in the chair. "On the desk please Mr. Robinson, no need to be a shrinking violet." The audience had all sat up in their chairs and were gripped by what was about to happen. A man at the end of the back row stood to his feet to get a better look. Others joined him.

Spen laid on the desktop. His feet and lower legs hung down over the end. "Next time we should have a longer desk," observed Cameron.

"Or perhaps a shorter volunteer sir?" added Spen wittily, to which the audience and Cameron laughed giddily.

Cameron addressed the audience with a smile, "Do we have a shorter volunteer please?" No-one offered and they all willed Cameron to anaesthetise Spen. "No offers Robinson, but they all asked me to assure you of their complete support." The crowd laughed more out of relief for themselves than anything else, as Cameron sat in the chair and leant forward over Spen. With his left hand he scooped Spen's neck upwards causing his head to rotate back towards himself a little. "Raise the chin to keep the airway patent and make sure the tongue hasn't fallen back into the snoring position. Are you comfortable Mister Robinson?" he asked.

"Not really sir," Spen replied, much to the delight of the class.

"Good, good," answered Cameron which brought an even louder laugh, though from some it sounded a little hysterical now. "One last thing, before you di... before you go to sleep..." Spen joined the audience as they laughed at Cameron's humour, the truth was that Spen trusted this man completely. "What's thirteen squared, do you know?"

"A hundred and sixty-nine sir," answered Spen after just a moment's thought. No-one, not even Spen knew why thirteen squared mattered. Then Cameron placed the mask over Spen's nose and mouth holding it between his left thumb and forefinger. His little finger was hooked under Spen's chin holding his head back and his mouth closed. With his right-hand Cameron lifted the dropper bottle and deftly loosened but retained the stopper in it. He made a point of beathing in heavily and then holding his breath as he tilted the bottle over the mask. A tiny trickle of the clear chloroform came out and fell onto the mask and he moved the bottle around spreading out the first few drops. "It's important to re-assure your patient with kind words spoken softly as you administer the drops. Breathe through your nose or mouth Mr. Robinson, you're quite safe," though a quick face pulled by Cameron to the audience brought another laugh. "Please stand your left forearm upright from the elbow, and balance it on the desk please," requested Cameron, leaning forward to place Spen's Arm where he wanted it, which was to stand it up like a miniature totem pole. He returned his hand gently back to holding the mask. He then put down the bottle and placed his flat palm three inches above Spen's chest. As his chest rose slightly, he raised his hand. Then as Spen breathed out he lowered it, but his left hand lifted the mask from Spen's face at the same time. His chest rose, the right-hand rose, as the mask returned. "I recommend the technique of holding the mask tightly to the face when the chest is rising..." they all watched Spen breath in, "And lifting the mask slightly when he exhales. Thus, the patient gets the anaesthetic, and he doesn't blow it into the room putting the surgeon and the audience to sleep too." The audience were transfixed. They were loving the demonstration. "How are you feeling Mr. Robinson?" asked Cameron as he momentarily lifted the mask.

"Fine, thank you sir..." answered Spen, though he'd begun sounding quite drunk by then. The audience held their collective breath for the next ten seconds or so as the Doctor replaced the mask and added three more drops to it.

"I watch for the breathing to slow, as it is doing, and at this stage I could listen for the heart rate to slow too. Though hopefully not too much" he said, again eliciting a slight giggle from the excited crowd. Spen's arm began to fall over but he quickly corrected it to its vertical position. But it fell over again almost straight away flopping onto the table with a limp slap. There was a slight gasp from the audience. "One drop every thirty seconds should maintain this state, but be aware that larger patients need more, smaller ones less. Be aware too that different dropper bottles with different size stoppers give a different size of drop." He looked round to the audience to emphasize his point. Once Spen was fast asleep, Cameron asked him. "What is two plus one Mr. Robinson?" There was no answer, just a slight murmur of realisation from the room. Ah, that was why he'd asked the thirteen squared question.

Cameron rose from his chair, placed the stopper more firmly in his bottle and walked forward to gather the remaining masks from the audience. "Well, that's all for today gentlemen, good day," and he turned to leave. Only half a dozen of the young gentlemen began to clap. The remainder all stared at poor Spen still lying fast asleep on the table. They were open mouthed at the audacity of the professor about to leave him in that state. How long would he be like that, they wondered? They were totally aghast at the prospect of a professor from the university anaesthetising one of their own then leaving without further ado, hoping *perhaps*, that his patient might recover. As Cameron reached the door, he stopped and turned round. He had the most enormous smile on his face. "Oh yes, and one last thing, gentlemen. Recovery. He placed the masks and bottle by the door and walked back to Spen on the desk. He looked down at him, then to a student standing at the back he said, "Open the door would you, there's a good chap, and you sir, the tall one, maybe you could open a window or two please?" He looked down at Spen as the cool blast of fresh air circulated within the room. "Come on Mister Robinson, kindly get your sorry back-side off ma-desk." Spen's arm raised first, then he sat up. "Sit there a moment if you will Spencely, let your blood circulate a little. How do you feel?" Cameron turned and addressed the audience. "The point I am making gentlemen is that your patient is still your patient until he has regained his own wits and is capable of rational thought once more." He turned to Spen and asked, "Are you capable of rational thought Mr. Robinson?" Spen rubbed his eyes, "Only as much as I ever was, I'm afraid sir." The audience gave a little cheer, both at his recovery and his admission of humility, and of course, at the point well made by the professor about patient recovery and the anaesthesiologist's responsibility.

"That Lecture was Brilliant!" said John on the return to 2A, "Shame you missed half of it Spen," laughed Andrew.
"We must get some Chloroform and give it a go" John added enthusiastically.

That evening they took a walk to the park called 'The Meadows' and discussed the stupefying effects of Chloroform and how it compared to Ether. Andrew mentioned that there had been such things as Ether parties in London where everyone 'gives it a go' and compares the benefits to alcohol. Apparently Nitrous oxide was the best when it came to having fun though, it was even starting to be known as 'the laughing gas.' "So why don't we use that?" Asked John. But Spen, who had already read about these things, said that it was only of use for relieving pain and wouldn't completely knock the patient out. Although it had knocked one or two out, when the mask had fitted rather too well and been used for prolonged periods. It had caused the patient to asphyxiate and had 'killed them to death' apparently.
"So why don't they mix nitrous oxide with air?" asked John. It was, to him, an obvious solution.

They walked by a group of some other students lazing in the evening sun and stretching out on the grass. They were asking themselves why there had been so few people attending the talk by Doctor Cameron. "Hey, Robinson!" came a shout from behind them. The three looked round. It was Rob Kinman, so they stopped to spend a few moments with him. After a minute or two he suggested that they should sit on the grass and enjoy the last of the evening sun together. Kinman, who was one of the other Hope Foundation prize winners, told of where he and a lot of the other students had been that day. During Dr. Cameron's Chloroform lecture. They had been attending another discourse on Mesmerism, now more commonly being known as Hypnosis. "We actually saw someone being Hypnotised, before our very eyes," he said excitedly.

"Yeah, but could you have sawn his arm off when he was under?" asked Andrew referring to the spectacle of Spen having been anaesthetised at their own lecture.

Kinman glossed straight over Andrew's remark and continued, "Because there was one subject, a groom ex of Falkirk I think he said, who mentioned the Stannet-Forbes estate, and I remember you saying something about you having been there once Spen."

"Yes, I went there once for about nineteen years, I grew up there, what was his name?" asked Spen.

"Dunno," replied Kinman, "no-one was very keen to know much about him to be honest, bit of a grumpy sod. Not one you'd want to socialise with."

"That's all very interesting, but there must have been hundreds of people through that estate," said Spen in a non-committal sort of way.

"You'll see him tomorrow, won't you?" asked Kinman picking up a four leafed clover from the grass. Spen looked puzzled by what he'd just said.

But John explained, "We have their lecture and they do ours tomorrow. But probably won't be the same subjects there though.

That night Spen's letter to Emily included all the exciting details of being anaesthetised by Doctor Cameron. It also included the topic of the grumpy groom from Sir William's estate. He wrote that he might be able to throw a little more light on that though in his next letter, as he was to be in the same room as the chap the following day.

* * *

When the time came for the Hypnosis lecture to begin, Spen sat as near to the front as he could, though they weren't particularly early that day and the front three rows had already been filled. Andrew sat next to him, and John was just behind them on the next row. There were already three rather rough looking people sat in chairs on the stage, two men, approximately fifty years of age, though they both looked rather older, and a young lady. The young lady, perhaps in her early twenties, continually tried to make eyes at the gentlemen students as they gathered in the audience. She smiled regularly and even ventured an occasional shy wave at some students who had waved at her. Spen guessed that they were just playing boyish games by teasing her affections. John leant forward in his seat and put his head between Andrew and Spen's. They leant closer in to catch John's whisper. "I'm guessing, from a pure psychology viewpoint, that the two men are here to get beer money, but the woman, hmm, she's a mystery, I'm really undecided..." Andrew and Spen both chuckled at John as it was obvious to everyone in the room that she was there to try and find a husband with good prospects.

Doctor Choudhary, from India, was to give the lecture but the audience were somewhat disappointed to see a typical Victorian gentleman walk in and step onto the platform. He was wearing typically ordinary Eighteen Seventies clothes, though upon consideration, they did look perhaps more like eighteen fifties to the young trendy gentlemen in the audience. Cravats had gone out months ago, had nobody told him? The good doctor wore no colourful head dress, as many had hoped. He even wore a pair of very British looking circular spectacles. But his face, and most certainly his accent were undoubtedly Indian in origin. Terribly exotic. And the fact that he was from the East added to the mystic quality of the event. He asked for the curtains to be drawn over the windows and the subdued atmosphere brought a further element of theatre.

Choudhury stepped forward to address the audience, though most of the returning glances were going straight past him to the young lady sat on the stage. Choudhury spoke of Hypnosis not being able to help with ailments of the body, but of the mind. How it could take a person into their deep unconsciousness, back into the recesses of their history, which they thought they had forgotten. The purpose of this was to reveal anything which might possibly be the root cause of their continual mental insufficiency in the present. The more Choudhury droned on, the more Spen lost interest. It sounded like guff, the stuff of music hall entertainment. He looked at the two men on the stage and wondered which one had been on the Stannet-Forbes estate. He didn't recognise either of them. They were both relaxed, sitting back slumped in their chairs behind Choudhury. They each had their legs stretched out and crossed in front of them. Spen suspected they were both glad to be there, doing nothing yet obviously being paid for their time. As Spen watched them, one slowly closed his eyes. As Choudhury continued in his monotone the man snored once but it was loud enough for the whole room to hear, and a dis-respectful murmur of amusement swept the audience. Choudhury looked over his shoulder at the man, but he'd already woken himself up and was shuffling to a more upright position in his seat.

John leant forward again to whisper to them. "Looks pretty relaxed already to me ..." Andrew and Spen smiled again but said nothing.

Finally, it came to the point in the talk where Choudhury was to mesmerize the three victims, or were they subjects? Patients perhaps? Yes, he called them patients. As they were being paid for their complicity, Spen had no trust in anything they were about to say under *hypnosis*. He'd already concluded that there was no possible way anyone could be persuaded to fall asleep purely by the power of speech and then be able to answer questions sensibly about things in their un-remembered past. It was definitely guff. Choudhury took out his pocket watch, held it by the chain and swung it backwards and forwards. It swung quite swiftly, but as the three on stage were listening to his words and watching the watch, Choudhury lengthened the chain in his hand and the swing slowed a little. "Your bodies are very heavy, your arms are made of lead, your eyelids too are closing under the weight." At this the young lady and the middle gent closed their eyes and the woman's head slumped back against the cushion. The man on the end still watched the chain, but he was somehow staring, looking straight through it, not blinking. He seemed to be in a different world. Spen thought that he must be a very good actor, probably from the Theatre Royal, yes, probably an out of work actor. Spen and Andrew heard a soft purring sound which they both recognised. They heard it most nights in their room, just after lights out. They turned to look behind them at their dear friend in a totally relaxed sleep. John's neighbours turned to look at him too. They all thought he was fooling around but, once his joke had been appreciated, he stayed there, emitting the same contented purr. He was genuinely asleep. One or two others looked up and down the row of faces and were surprised to see John wasn't the only one asleep.

Choudhury continued, "You can only hear my voice, no other sounds exist. If I touch you on the shoulder, then I am talking to you, and only you," He spoke as he walked around the back of the victims. Though everyone was fully expecting Choudhury to touch one of the sleepers on the shoulder, he surprised them all by touching the man who was still awake and staring. "What is your occupation?" he asked. And in a very relaxed tone, the man slowly said

"Groom and Farrier."

"Have you a family?" Asked the doctor softly,

"No sir."

"Married?" There was a distinct pause before the answer, but Choudhury didn't prompt.

"Don't think so sir," said the man.

"And why do you work with horses?" asked Choudhury, this was not a very revealing question at all, thought Spen, though the answer was slightly more-so.

"They're reliable sir, 'don't let you down." The Doctor waited to see if the man might add anything to the statement, and for a while, it looked as if he might.

But when it became obvious that he wasn't going to, Choudhury moved next behind the young woman and said, "Whoever I touch on the hand I am talking to. He touched the young woman's hand. "And you my dear, what is your name?"

"Betsy, sir" she said confidently, as if she was wide awake.

"And Betsy, are you married?"

"Oh no sir, I'll never marry." Spen, and most others saw how her answers were very different in style to the groom's.

"And who do you live with Betsy?"

"My dear mother sir. She's ever so old." Choudhury could tell that the audience too were unconvinced.

"Betsy, do you have any brothers or sisters?" he asked kindly. To this Betsy didn't answer confidently nor immediately. Instead she quietly began to sob.

"Betsy…?" prompted Choudhury,

"Did have sir. Died." She sobbed again. This was a much better performance.

"How did he die Betsy?".

At this Andrew leant across to Spen and whispered very quietly. "He? How do we know it's a *he*?" Good point thought Spen.

"He dived in and saved me sir…but he drowned."

"Don't worry dear one, you're safe now, and, also, he is safe too. He's fine." Choudhury walked behind the man in the middle of the three and grandly said, "The person I touch on the knee I am addressing next. And he walked between the two men and touched the middle gentleman on the leg as he came past. And you sir, you are eight years old, it is mid-winter, it is very dark. Where are you?" There were a few moments before this man answered, he was obviously better primed than Betsy, thought Spen. Quietly, the man answered but hardly anyone could hear him, many in the room were losing interest. It seemed that Spen wasn't the only one to think that they were wasting their time there. "Where man, speak up?" said Choudhury a little more loudly.

"In the cupboard."

"In the cupboard, why are you in the cupboard?" This was more interesting, at least it was a good story.

"Locked in" uttered the man.

"By whom? Do you know who locked you in there?"

"Mammy." This had the room's attention though; because a fifty year old rough handed dock labourer (as Spen presumed him to be) wouldn't have referred to his mother as 'mammy', though an eight year old boy might well have done.

"Are you in the cupboard with anyone else?"

But a voice from near the back of the room broke the mood for a moment with "Betsy perhaps?" which raised a slight laugh.

"Hamish" said the man suddenly.

"Who's Hamish?" asked the Doc giving an evil look to the back of the room in an attempt to get the crowd to be serious.

"Brother." He replied.

"And what was the reason your mammy locked you and Hamish in that cupboard? Do you know?" The man didn't answer, so after a short wait the prof asked another question. "What can you hear?"

"Shouting, mammy's shouting…, and screaming… Dadda's hurting her again." And the man started to breath much quicker. This was a very good performance indeed.

"It's alright, your mamma is safe, Hamish is safe, and you're safe." The man calmed his breathing down again, Spen noticed that he was sweating profusely. How would an actor do that, he wondered? Then the meeting took an unusual turn. Doctor Choudhury faced the audience and asked, "Would any of the audience like me to ask any questions of our sitters?" Spen looked at the three seated individuals still on the stage who were still in basically the same pose as half an hour ago before Choudhury had 'Put them under' as he'd called it. They were all very relaxed, apart from the stare from the first one, the groom.

A man stood up at the back, Spen suspected it was the heckler from earlier, "Betsey," he began, have you ever had carnal knowledge of a man?" The class of young men looked forward to Betsy with a smile and watched her with great concentration. She said nothing.

After a long wait where Betsy's expression didn't change, Choudhury asked, "Betsy, have you ever had a gentleman lover?"

"Ooh no sir, I'm saving myself 'til I'm married." Replied Betsy. Spen remembered that she'd previously said that she'd never get married.

Choudhury thought that was enough of an answer for the impertinent questioner. Spen stood to his feet and was surprised to find that he was the only one standing. "Could you ask the groom if he ever met Sir William please." The question baffled everyone else in the room, but Spen nodded to the gentleman Doctor and stayed on his feet. He moved behind the first man again and touched him on the shoulder, then softly asked "Tell me, did you ever meet Sir William?" The crowd waited for an answer to this obviously fabricated and bizarre question.

But the answer seemed to be quite clear. "Not personally sir, though I saw him from afar many times." A jolly woolly answer thought the crowd. The doctor looked to Spen and his expression seemed to question whether the man's answer satisfied him?

"Does anyone else have a question?" asked Choudhury, but Spen stayed on his feet and although the doctor didn't want to allow a second question for the groom, the crowd seemed to be quite keen for him to do so, as his first question had been very creative. Spen thought to himself that he was taking a bit of a chance asking this second question, but thought it was worth it; he must obviously be the man from the Forbes estate. "Please ask the gentleman 'what is the name' of his wife, if you will Doctor."

"But he has already stated that he doesn't know if he was married." Answered Choudhury to Spen. But Spen stood there implacably and gesticulated towards the groom. With a sigh of acquiescence Choudhury turned to the seated man again and asked, "What was the name of your wife?" Spen was instantly furious; he'd said *is* and not *was* to Choudhury. But as he seethed the man mumbled a single syllable and put his hands to his face. Finally, he closed his eyes. "Speak up man if you will, what was the name of your wife if you please?" But the man blew into and sucked air back through his cupped hands.

After a few breaths he took his hands away and said "Dot, her name was Dot." Spen felt a cold shiver go through his body as he starred at the man. Though he'd only attempted to find through which family on the estate he might have known him, he never thought that the answer would be, 'his own.' He knew the whole room had switched their gaze and were looking at him. Some wondered what marvellous question Spen might dream up next, others watched to see what he'd actually *do* next. They could see Spen was affected by the answer though no-one, not even Andrew or John knew why. Spen flopped to his chair. Andrew put his arm around Spen and asked if he was alright. He wasn't, but there was nothing Andrew could do about it.

Spen wasn't really paying attention when Doctor Choudhury brought the three sitters out of their hypnotic trance, if indeed they had ever been in one. The Doctor dismissed the three and they stood up and began leaving. He addressed the class again telling them that by searching out and uncovering traumatic events in someone's past, then medical science might help them recover from the psychological scaring which it had left. But Spen rather rudely stood up and excused himself along the row in an attempt to catch the 'groom' before he left forever. Andrew asked if he should come too, but Spen told him to please stay and take notes so that he didn't miss anything important.

As Spen left the classroom and went into the corridor, the person he was attempting to catch had somehow disappeared. He saw the billowing skirts of Betsy though, so he rushed to her and asked as politely as he could where the other man had gone? "Who, Smithy? she asked. But Betsy was more interested in spending a little time with Spen than talking about the other person on stage with her; Spen was after all a fine gentleman, he would nicely fulfil her needs. But reluctantly she pointed back the way he'd come. He waved his thanks and ran off, hoping he would be in time to catch Smith. At least it was daylight this time and he knew where he was going, unlike the last time he went chasing dubious characters through the streets of Edinburgh. He blundered through a door straight into a Classics lesson whereupon a dozen young men all turned to witness his interruption. He apologised profusely but as he did so, he saw through their window a man hurriedly shuffling across the grass outside. It was him. He pulled the door closed rather noisily, (shouting another apology again through it) and ran down to the exit door. Once through he spotted Smith again and ran up behind him, slowing to a speedy walk before reaching him so as not to scare him off. Smith didn't seem to hear him come. "Mr. Smith" he said from behind, but the man didn't respond, he just kept on walking. He went up alongside and Smith did eventually notice him. "That was interesting Mr. Smith, very interesting indeed."

"Was it sir, I'm glad you enjoyed it." Answered the man curtly.

"Tell me, how much did Doctor Choudhury pay you please sir." Smith stopped in his tracks. This was indeed more interesting, a fine gentleman calling *him* 'sir' and wanting to talk about money.

"Two shillin's sir, why do you ask may I ask, might there be more university work sir?" Spen had always found the Edinburgh underclass to be bold and straight to the point 'What's in it for me?' was their single motivation. Spen tried to tell the man that he wasn't needing him as an object of display for one of his classes but just wanted to ask him some questions, to talk to him. The man began walking again. He was heading towards the canal, not Spen's favourite part of town. But he'd quickly made it plain that if the fine gentleman in his fine clothing and his educated accent wanted to have some of his time, then it was going to cost him, as time was money. That's one thing he'd learnt from the world.

But Spen didn't know what to offer the man, he couldn't come right out and tell him that Spen thought that he might be his son. He'd have to go in much more gently, pull a little wool over the man's eyes.

Deceitful yes, but his best strategy. Spen hurried after him and talked at him as he walked along. "I'm doing some research and I'm looking for help. And I realise I'll have to pay." Smith stopped dead again. The mention or even the mere thought of money seemed to have an arresting effect on this man. He looked up at Spen.

"Two shillin' fe half a day." And held out his hand.

"Done" said Spen striking his hand on Smith's hand to seal the deal. Smith realised that he could probably have asked for more, but two shillings was more than a day's wage not half a day.

"And you buy the Ale," he added as a subclause to their contract. Spen smiled and pointed to a public house across the road.

"There's no-one waiting for you at home then Mr. Smith?" asked Spen to begin some groundwork.

"Only Bonny, Prince and Charlie ma three terriers," said Smith with a smile.

At the door of the ale house he stopped before entering. "Perhaps we'd best complete our business before going in, eh?"

"Oh yes," said Spen remembering the time in The Spurtle when Mary-Ann had tried to conceal one of his pound notes. So, he removed two shiny coins from the purse section of his wallet (he was learning fast in Edinburgh), then snapped it shut and pushed the wallet into his coat pocket at his hip. He gave the two coins to Smith, for whom it was becoming a good day. But because they were blocking the doorway a man pushed between the two of them rather abruptly with no word of apology and entered the building. Smith went through after him into the dingey interior and Spen followed him in.

Smith pointed to an empty bench seat by the wall and said, "Just there aye?" Spen obediently took his seat on the bench but noticed that Smith was suddenly no longer with him. He'd gone a little further into the bar-room and straight up to a table with one man sat by it. It was the man who'd just pushed between them through the doorway. Spen was shocked to see Smith throw his open hand into the man's neck and force him back against the wall. He suddenly wondered if he'd done the right thing getting into business with this sort of character. He watched as Smith spoke with true venom straight into the man's face, spluttering some of his own saliva into his mouth as it gasped for air, "Unless you want me to tear your heed arf its scrawny neck and force it sideways up your skinny earse, then you'll be givin' this fayne gentlemen back his wallet." The man shook as he reached inside his filthy coat to its poacher's pocket and pulled out two wallets.

Spen recognised his and said, "The light brown one Mr. Smith if you please." Smith brought the two wallets across the room and handed the brown one to Spen. The scoundrel left through the same door even quicker than he'd come in.

"Well, if you're harvin' the brown een, I'll be harvin' this black een." This was indeed a very good day.

But Spen thought he recognised the second wallet too. "May I," he requested as he held out his hand. Smith reluctantly handed over the second wallet too and Spen looked inside it. A gold inscription read 'Robert Kinman. Reginald Road, Crosby, Shire of Lincoln.' It's Rob Kinman's, he's a friend of mine. Would you mind if I returned it to him?" Smith didn't reply, instead he asked himself 'would the fine gentleman he was sat with be a good long-term earner or, should he make a quick shillin' now and perhaps risk killing the goose which might possibly lay him a few more golden eggs. But before he could give his answer, the matter was settled; Spen had taken one of the two ten shilling notes from inside Kinman's wallet and given it to him, placing the wallet in an inside pocket along with his own. Spen was surprised how little money Kinman had on his person.

The men sat and drank for an hour or two and Spen made up some cock and bull story about societal imbalance and general health of the poorer stratum of the urban population. His plan worked; Smith hadn't followed a word of what he'd just said but had nodded politely as if he had done. His nodding fooled no-one though, including himself. Spen hoped that this ploy would allow him to ask about Smith's past without alerting him to the real reasons for his questioning. He asked first about horses. Smith ran a makeshift stable by the canal tending to the horses that worked the tow path from Glasgow along the Union and the Forth and Clyde Navigations. He would feed them, groom them and make sure they were safe and rested up, before their return journey. He made a bit on the side sometimes sourcing food stuffs and Ale for the bargees on a quick turn-around. When things got quiet, he would sometimes help in the warehouses as a general labourer, but he wasn't as fit as he used to be, and heavy loads made his back hurt now. Just lately he had discovered the work at the university, which paid well, at least better than his usual day job, and there was much less pain.

Spen made arrangements with the man to meet him in the same place next week for another sponsored drinking session, but before they parted Spen thought he'd try one more question. "Have you always gone under the name 'Smith'" he asked? But Smith looked a little suspiciously at him, how could this question be relevant to anything? Was this fine young gentleman working for the peelers perhaps?

He bade Smith a farewell and offered his hand, but Smith just nodded, moved to dough his cap slightly, turned and went. Spen was left standing there not really knowing if he would ever see Smith again. He concluded that the chances of the erstwhile Mr. Smith being his real father were probably quite high.

Though it was late, Spen diverted his route back to 2A to visit Kinman in Tantallon Place. Rob was quite surprised when Spen offered him his wallet back. Rob thought he must be some incredible stage magician as he reached round to his rear pocket. It wasn't there. "I took it off a man who wrenched it from the man who picked it from your pocket."

"Oh, that's awfully decent of you dear chap, here, have something for your trouble," he said opening the wallet and sliding out the remaining note.

"No need Old Man, I already gave him one of your notes, which I thought was jolly decent of me, don't you think? Rob smiled and agreed, then shook Spen by the hand. He was a good egg.

* * *

It must only have been a week after Spen had been anaesthetised by Doctor Cameron when he arrived back at 2A one evening to find a notelet had been pushed under the door of room 32. It read 'Would like to talk about Anaesthesiology post. Join me at my college rooms before weekend if you please." And it was signed A Cameron (Dr.). Spen was honoured to have received a communication from Doc Cameron but saddened by the thought that he might only be used again as the object of some demonstration. Even so, he thought he should go along, more out of duty and respect, rather than hope of any benefit.

The following morning, he set off earlier than usual from his room and crossed the Forrest Road then walked along Bristo Place towards Bristo Square. He considered the possible questions that Cameron might want to ask him. He went through a few possibilities and thought how he might respond to each one. He found the college staircase and climbed to the hallowed first floor where only the elite were allowed; it certainly wasn't the stomping ground of second year students like him. He found the room and much to his surprise the door was answered by a pretty young lady. She was probably just over thirty, so a good ten years older than himself. She wore a loose fitting underdress, or was it even a night dress perhaps? Before he could speak, she asked, "Spencely Robinson?" Her accent was as beautiful as her face, though it took a little while before Spen could place it. "Yes, miss." He quickly concluded by her bearing and the exotic tone of her voice that she was no temporary lady of the night. She turned out to be "Mrs Cameron, of some eleven years now," she stated with a friendly smile. French, he thought, she was French.

"Congratulations Mistress Cameron, I had no idea..." She showed him into a beautiful room tastefully furnished without too many of the usual skeletons, microscopes and books on anatomy which he imagined adorned most of the professor's rooms (from what he knew). Instead, there were ornaments and figurines from Europe; Paris and Berlin, and artistic drapes and tapestries. It showed the tasteful touch of a lady of class.

Cameron breezed in and lunged towards Spen with his arm outstretched. "Thank you for coming, I see you have already met Yvonne, my wife." At this point, after shaking Cameron's hand he turned to face Mrs. Cameron and again held out his hand. At this she smiled and graciously held forward her right hand face down. As it wasn't gloved, Spen wondered if he should kiss it or merely shake it. He took the liberty and kissed it.

"Enchanté Madame."

"Come on you two, settle down." Smiled Cameron. "Spen, I hope you don't mind me calling you Spen?"

"Not at all sir." Spen was most flattered, but he didn't assume that it was an invitation for familiarity on his part. He wouldn't have addressed Doctor Cameron any other way than 'Sir'.

"I want you to consider helping me please." He looked at Spen with his hands on his hips. Spen thought, 'here it comes, I'd like to anaesthetise you again.' But instead, in the next instant, his day just got a hundred times better. "My usual anaesthiologist chappy has gone and got an operation of his own and so can't help me on Saturday. I wondered if you might..."

"Yes, absolutely sir, I'd be honoured," said Spen in a rush, wearing a grin from ear to ear.

"I'll supervise of course, 'don't suppose you've done it before eh?"

"No sir, I'm afraid not. I have undergone the procedure before but only as a recipient." Spen tried to infer humility and a readiness to learn, but it came out as a little negative he thought. Cameron was throwing on his coat and pushing papers into his briefcase, then gesticulating that Spen should move towards his door.

"Might even be a little money in it for you, let's talk about it on the way." He kissed Yvonne on the lips and grabbed the door handle holding it open for Spen.

"Thank you sir, I don't know what to say. Good day Mrs. Cameron, lovely to meet you, I'm honoured sir, thank you. And I have no need of payment certainly, in fact I'd be prepared to pay you for the privilege, the experience. Saturday, where?" Spen was speaking quickly and hurrying along the corridor in true medical professional style now that he too was suddenly one of the elite.

"Number Ten Graham Street, you know it?" asked Cameron.

"I do sir, what time?"

"Ten A.M. don't spend all the previous night in the public house and don't be late. The patient is rich but miserable, he has a necrotic foot due to infection caused by his chronic gout. No circulation to the right lower limb, hasn't had for months. It has to come off. 'Confirm arrangements for Saturday in room three at five on Friday, got that? Make sure the patient hasn't died before we can kill him." The men glanced at each other and Cameron had a grin. He veered off down one of the many corridors of the college with a wave and farewell of "Friday at five, room three." Spen was ecstatic.

Spen's next lecture on the 'The Liver, it's Function and Fallibilities,' felt a little flat after the way the day had begun. He found it difficult to concentrate properly, which was unusual for him. He took copious notes on Hepatic this and Pancreatic that and made a pact to read them all later when his excitement had calmed a little.

A quick lunch in the refectory, then back at it into another room for 'Skeletal disfunction of the lower limbs.' Spen decided to go to the room early and find a corner to just close his eyes and clear his mind. But as he went into the room a single seated figure turned to look at him. He was sat on a stool with a board balanced on one folded knee. "Oh, sorry, I didn't think there'd be anyone in here, do you mind if I join you sir, I won't be a bother?" Spen pointed to the far corner of the room and continued, "Please don't let me disturb you sir." The gentleman stopped what he was doing and spun round on his stool to look at Spen. He spoke with an English accent, though his vocabulary showed that he'd been in Edinburgh for a number of years. There was a hint of the Irish lilt too, or was it slight inebriation? A pleasant sort though, and as Spen got nearer he observed that he was sketching a mounted section of skeleton; a Fibula and Tibia were held vertically on a small wooden base and the bones of the ankle and foot were arranged correctly beneath them. As Spen came closer he could see the sketch more clearly, "That's exquisite Mr…."

"Doyle sir, Charles Altamont Doyle, known as Cad, the draughtsman sir. Nearly finished, I'll be out soon."

"Please don't hurry on my account Mr. Doyle, it is I who shouldn't be in here. Tell me, are you employed by the University?" asked Spen, as Doyle resumed his position and started shading with his pencil again.

"Not permanently, I just do illustrations under contract for some of the professors, you know; one or two books and some pamphlet covers as well." At this he stopped again and began flicking back through some of the previous pages in his large sketch book. The earlier three drawings were of the same lower human leg bones, though from differing angles. But as he turned back another page it revealed a beautiful pastel watercolour of two fairies. One sitting in a buttercup and the other hovering close by, causing some blades of grass to be deflected by the draught from her wings.

"Not just medical illustrations I see, Mr. Doyle. You obviously have a liking for the mysterious sir. That one is beautiful." Doyle was obviously pleased to have his work so warmly appreciated.

"Would you like it sir?" asked Doyle glancing up at Spen.

"Oh, thank you, but I couldn't Mr. Doyle." He turned back more pages. A ribcage, a sternum with collar bones, then a goblin and some bizarre horned animal. A third fantasy one, then…Mary-Ann's severed Head! Spen reeled back a little un-noticed above Doyle's shoulder. Doyle kept leafing back through his sketch book as Spen gathered his wits. "And who is the foot drawing for sir?" asked Spen shakily having regained some of his composure.

"Doctor Arthur Cameron sir, do you know him?" asked Doyle looking up at Spen. Yes, there was definitely more than a hint of alcohol in Doyle's breath.

"I do, Mr. Doyle, in fact I was with him earlier today. Actually, I'm working for him too, or at least I hope to be doing so, soon."

"Ah, Doctor Cameron is a lovely man, a fine gentleman, you'll not go wrong working for Professor Cameron. Same name as my boy."

"What, *Cameron*?" asked Spen before thinking.

But Doyle laughed at what he thought was the young gentleman's joke. "No sir, Arthur, Arthur Doyle. Though he too has a liking for the mysterious, he says he'll call himself by one of those fancy double barrel names when he's older, make himself sound much more wind-swept." He smiled as he brought to mind the image of his own son.

"Sounds like a bright lad your Arthur. What will he call himself?" asked Spen. He wasn't quite prepared for the answer.

"He intends using his mother's name," explained Doyle.

Oh, maybe not so bright then; why would any young lad want to saddle himself with a woman's name, thought Spen? Doyle noticed Spen had a look of confusion. "Then what's her name Mr. Doyle?" He was expecting to hear some sort of androgynous christian name.

"*Mrs. Conan* sir. Arthur says that by calling himself Conan-Doyle he'll go far. But I'll be happy if he could just become a doctor. Like you sir."

Spen glossed over where this conversation was taking them and, realising that Doyle might not be too attached to his work asked to look at that picture of the woman's head again. Doyle leafed forwards through his book and there she was. It was definitely her, just as he remembered her; tight black curls, a slight moon-shaped scar beneath her right eye. She looked much more peaceful in the picture though. "A fine looking woman, I always wonder what some of these fine ladies did in their lives," mused Doyle, but Spen offered no answer to that question.

"How much for that beautiful drawing Mr. Doyle?" But Doyle was already beginning to tear the page from the book.

"Ah, it's nice to have my work appreciated by such a fine gentleman as yourself sir," and he handed the image to Spen, who put it on the table and reached inside his coat for his wallet.

"I insist Mr. Doyle, you're a professional, and a good one sir. And you make a living by selling your work, so you must take money for it. Ten shillings, would that cover it?"

"Oh, thank you sir, Mrs Conan will be over the moon with that sir." Spen glossed over the fact that Doyle didn't have the same surname as his son's mother. He simply presumed that they weren't married. Or maybe he'd had an affair. That might make young Arthur even more mysterious. He rolled up the drawing and shook Doyle's hand before he left the room.

The other students started filing in through the door ready for their tutorial. He looked at the image again and wondered indeed what sort of life Mary-Ann had lived, and perhaps more importantly, how she'd died.

Chapter 8 – The Operation

Saturday morning arrived and instead of going in through the front door of the house on the West side Graham Street, Spen, Andrew and John took themselves around the back again. They reasoned that the usual Dissection spectators would be going in through the front door, but they were attending a different operating theatre, at a much more select event. They followed a sign which simply said 'Trade.' They presumed it meant 'Tradesman's Entrance.' Down the side of the house was a narrow path with stone slab paving and a shoulder height wall topped with thick hedging. A blackbird was startled into flight as they went by. At the back corner of the house, they turned sharp left and went through a latched full-height gate set in a solid wooden fence. It was somewhat less intimidating in the daylight. The sounds of cattle bellowing and men shouting came from the cattle market the other side of the wall. Once through the gate the pathway opened up to a small yard containing three barrels stood on end. None of them remembered any of this from the last time they were there. But then it was dark then. In the far corner of the yard was a narrow handcart with two open topped tea chests on it. Each one was half full of kitchen waste and the occasional newspaper. Andrew bent down and sniffed at one of the barrels. He recognised the odour; "Formaldehyde," he announced quietly. On the top of the first one was an address label stuck over a second note. He peeled it back to reveal what this more official looking Label said. The word FORMALIN was stamped on it. They presumed the other two barrels contained the same. "Someone's doing a lot of preserving," he said softly. "Cheaper than Whisky and Brandy though," added John. Spen didn't follow, so flashed an enquiring look at the other two. Andrew filled him in; "They sent Nelson's body home from

Trafalgar in a barrel of brandy." Spen nodded his understanding.

Next to the large door Spen pulled down on a brass handle. They thought they heard a bell ring deep inside the large house. Presently a middle-aged bald man wearing a high collar and an apron opened the door and looked at them. "I'm the anaesthiologist for Doctor Cameron at this morning's operation," Spen grandly announced (perhaps a little too grandly). The man looked blankly back at him, and said "Front door please gentleman," then shut the door without ceremony. They trekked back through the tall wooden gate giving the three barrels a last look. Andrew tried to press the address label down flat again. It didn't stick.

They joined the queue of four or five young men at the front door. They recognised all of them as being students on the same course as themselves. They exchanged a nod as a greeting. None of them seemed to notice that they'd come from the side of the house rather than from along the street.

The man at the front door was different to the man at the rear. When he asked to see their tickets Spen announced (rather more humbly this time) that they were there for Doctor Cameron's operation and not the dissection. The man told them that Dr. Cameron's medical event wasn't open to the public. "We aren't the public, we are here to take part, as members of the team," said Spen in a somewhat frustrated manner.

"In that case, one moment please gentlemen." The emotionless employee disappeared down a corridor returning a few minutes later and asked Spen, "Your name please sir?"

"S. Robinson."

"Ah yes, Doctor Robinson, one moment please sir." The man then gravely addressed Andrew and John saying "I'm sorry gentlemen but I can only allow Doctor Robinson into Mr. Cameron's event."

"Well, we'll have tickets for the Davies mutilation then please," requested John with as much authority as he could muster.

"I'm sorry sir, all tickets have been sold for Doctor Davies' dissection this morning but I'm sure there'll be another one next week." He looked to Spen again and said, "This way please Doctor," and lead him off down the corridor into a small operating room. Spen wondered what Andrew and John would do with themselves since their morning plans had been scuppered.

The tiny room had a central narrow wooden bench, a side table, and a kitchen sink built onto the wall at one end. Cameron's bag was on the floor next to a wooden box and what looked like a gardener's rose spraying can. The lighting wasn't as good as Spen was expecting as there were no outside windows. As he entered, he was hit by the undeniable stench of necrosis. Dr. Cameron greeted him warmly, shook his hand and introduced him to Mr. Andrews who was seated.

"Forgive me for not getting up doctor," he said hoarsely. Spen was about to correct Mr. Andrews saying that he was not a doctor, only a medical student but quickly realised how that might have been received by a man about to have his leg removed. He went instead for simple reassurance, with a little flattery thrown in.

"Mr. Andrews, you must be a very wealthy man to be able to afford the best of surgeons," indicating Dr. Cameron. He noticed the nurse smile and realised she was Yvonne Cameron. "Bonjour encore Madame," he smiled.

She nodded politely and said, "Good morning to you Spencely."

Cameron took charge, "Now, Mr. Andrews, you have had your bath this morning as requested?" (He had), "Let's get you up and onto our workbench please. Andrews lifted up his arms and Spen and Cameron each manoeuvred themselves under his armpits and together heaved Mr. Andrews out of the chair. "Head this end," directed Cameron. Yvonne helped lift his swollen black leg onto the end of the bench as the two men laid the large patient down in the right position. Cameron did all the talking; mainly words of reassurance to the worried patient. "I promise you won't feel a thing Mr. Andrews." Spen really hoped he was right, because if he did, then it would be his fault. Yvonne was already pouring water from the jug into a wash basin that was inside the sink. She scrubbed her hands with a stiff brush and used a new block of unpleasant pink soap. "Jacket off, sleeves up," said Cameron. Spen realised that it was he who was being spoken to, and quickly obeyed. He went to the sink to wash his hands next to Cameron. "You'll be awake within the hour, then home for tea, Mister Andrews."

After passing the towel back to Yvonne, Cameron grabbed the chair which the patient had been sitting on and moved it speedily to the head of the table. He nodded to Spen that he should sit down on it. At least this end of the patient he would be furthest from the black and deadened foul smelling lower limb. He'd been told a number of times that the smell of necrosis was the worst of all smells. Right at that moment he felt it to be the strongest smell too. He swallowed hard to stop himself being sick. Looking down the table Yvonne showed no reaction in her face to the horror in front of her. Very professional. She bent down and opened the Gladstone bag on the floor. She took out a muslin mask which she handed to her husband. Then she bent down to the bag again. Meanwhile, Cameron handed the mask to Spen saying, "Here you are doctor." Spen took the mask from him and placed it slowly over the man's mouth and nose. It didn't fit particularly well over his whiskers. Yvonne passed Cameron the dropper bottle, who again, handed it straight to Spen. Spen made a hash of partly loosening the stopper but retaining it in place. He tilted the bottle over the mask and spoke to Mr. Andrews.

"This will make you feel sleepy sir, it's not too unpleasant I hope." Nothing came out. Spen let go of the mask momentarily as he needed both hands to hold the bottle and loosen the stopper again. He struggled to get it to the correct position. This was definitely a skill he didn't yet have. He cursed himself for not practicing with one before he came. He knocked the mask with the bottom of the bottle and Cameron caught it just before it went over the edge of the table and onto the floor.

"Think nice thoughts Mister Andrews," Cameron said reassuringly. He could tell Spen was enduring a moment of panic. Yvonne glanced briefly at her husband with an expression of concern. It said 'was Spen making a hash of this?' Eventually a fine stream of chloroform dribbled out of the bottle and onto the mask. Everyone could smell it. It even gave them a little light relief from the necrosis. Spen looked down at the man's eyes. They were already closed but a trickle of a tear had started to roll into his sideburn before reaching his ear. The man was actually crying (silently) with fear.

"This is life-saving surgery Mr. Andrews, you'll live a long and happy life after today sir," said Spen confidently. He didn't really know what to say, and thought he probably was lying, but hoped it was what the poor man needed to hear. Spen looked up for reassurance but instead saw Yvonne bend down to collect the gardeners spray off the floor.

"Close your eyes, Mr. Andrews, that's it, sweet dreams." Cameron put his hand palm down on the patient's chest. He lifted it off as he breathed in and lowered it when he exhaled. This was a sign to Spen. He read it well and lifted the mask slightly as Andrews breathed out. "Maybe a little more Doctor?" said Cameron softly to Spen. Spen gave the mask two more drops and looked up at the real doctor. Cameron nodded that he should add another one. He did, then another nod, another drop. "One every thirty seconds Doctor Robinson, to keep the mask moist," said Cameron softly.

Yvonne had put the sprayer on top of the side bench next to a towel then lifted up the man's dressing gown. She began washing and wiping the man's painful blackened leg, but he made no complaint. She patted it dry with the towel and stopped to look at her husband. "How are you feeling Mister Andrews?" asked Cameron. The patient made some kind of incomprehensible murmur, so Cameron nodded to his wife, who put down the towel and reached for a small three-legged stool unseen by Spen until then. She put it by the side of the bench on the left side and lifted his pink left leg off the table and placed his good foot on the stool tying the lower leg to the side of the table somewhere with a strip of bandage. This allowed plenty of sawing room either side of his right leg. Spen smiled at how well Yvonne and Dr. Cameron worked together. She was very efficient, almost reading the mind of her husband.

Spen put down the bottle between drops and felt the carotid artery in the neck of his patient, it was slow but regular. But wait, it just missed a beat. No, it restarted and was pumping away nicely again. "He just missed a beat, but I think he's fine," said Spen. Cameron was impressed that young Robinson had shown initiative in feeling the man's pulse so early in the operation without being instructed.

"You're doing fine too Spen," he said with a smile.

"Thank you sir, I'm happier now I've got to grips with the one handed bottle and stopper."

"Just takes a bit of practice, that's all." Yvonne added her smile of reassurance too. She had given the spray to Cameron and found another clean dressing. He sprayed, she wiped. "Five percent phenol," he said, presumably for Spen's benefit. "Have you had any talks on asepsis Spen?" he asked.

"Not yet sir." Yvonne threw the wipes into the now empty wash basin and handed Cameron a brass handled surgical knife. The sort that might be used to slice tomatoes. Next Cameron leant close to Spen and lifted one of Mr. Andrew's eyelids, being careful not to breath in as he did so.

"Is there anyone home?" he asked, which amused both Spen and Yvonne.

"He always asks that, he thinks he's funny Spencely," said Yvonne with a grin. She was at the extreme end of the table, and as Cameron returned from the top, she lifted the leg and Cameron slid the slender knife under it just below the knee. He pressed it upwards and pulled it back towards himself. Spen felt a little queasy when he saw just how easily the sharp knife cut through the flesh. Spen was also surprised at how little blood there was; he was expecting it to come spurting out. He was absolutely fascinated. Cameron worked quickly drawing the knife repeatedly up and round the sides of the calf muscle. Over the other side too, very deftly. This man was good, thought Spen. He was gripped.

Cameron glanced to the head. "One drop every thirty seconds Spen if you please, go by the clock on the wall. Spen suddenly remembered why he was there as he glanced up to the clock. It was a quarter before eleven. Where had the time gone, he wondered? Spen took Cameron's words to be a small admonishment that he should concentrate on his own job and not be distracted, or even transfixed, by what was going on in front of him. He could quite easily see why surgeons were regularly using a second doctor to apply the anaesthetic dosing.

The skin was peeled back, and further cuts of flesh were made to start filleting the muscles and tendons from the knee joint. Yvonne reached behind him to take a tiny length of looped catgut off the side table. She then looked into the open end of the wound towards Spen and pulled on what he assumed to be the end of an artery or vein which needed sealing. Spen noticed there were another four loops of catgut prepared. He looked over Mr. Andrews portly figure straight into the face of the lovely Mrs. Cameron. She was incredibly beautiful, even with her hair tied back in a bun under a nurse's bonnet. She grabbed an artery and pulled it slightly towards the foot, he slid the loop off the tweezers and onto the end of the artery, pulling it tight and sealing off the vessel. This happened twice more. They made a good team. They looked at each other and Spen knew that they would both be looking up the table to him next. He quickly looked down at the face of his patient obviously concentrating on his part of the deal, well, that was the impression he hoped he was giving. The truth was that he was actually managing quite well, or so he thought. Lifting and lowering the mask gently. Dropping on the clear fluid, checking the pulse rate occasionally, watching the chest rise and fall steadily.

The patient groaned. Was he waking up? Spen was shocked into giving two more drops immediately despite not long since having given him the previous one. Cameron nodded that he should perhaps add another. This was, after all, a sizeable patient. But a lot more than two drops came out of the bottle. Spen wondered if Cameron had seen his mistake. He lifted the mask after a few seconds to reduce the concentration of the chloroform being inhaled by the patient. He didn't groan again. Spen decided to give a drop every twenty-five seconds, perhaps every twenty seconds. Sometimes the drops looked bigger, they could be thirty second drops. Yvonne caught his eye and placed another bottle of chloroform next to the patient's head at the top of the table. Spen looked at the bottle in his hand and yes, it was nearly empty. He nodded his thanks. She smiled in return as Cameron went to the sink to wash the blood off his hands before the next step.

Cameron bent down to the wooden box bringing out a carpenter's tenon saw. Yvonne moved around to the opposite side of the table to her husband. She grabbed Mr's Andrew's bloodied lower leg with both hands, one either side of the gaping bone. Cameron placed the saw blade on the first bone, inched it up towards the flesh and began sawing. They heard a laugh come from the large operating theatre along the corridor. Davies and 'The Assistant' must have been in full swing with their pantomime dissection. The first bone was quickly through and the next one separated even quicker. Yvonne took away the black skinned leg and as she did noticed for the first time that there was no big toe on the foot. Poor Mr. Andrews must have been suffering for some years with this complaint of blockage in the circulation. She placed it in a narrow box covering it with a few bloody rags. Meanwhile Cameron was adjusting something in the open wound and returning the previously folded back skin. Yvonne wiped the table of some of its gore and brought a small tray upon which were more cat-gut threads, a cloth and a fine needle. He applied another small squirt from the garden spray then seemed to trim back some more of the skin, after which he began stitching the wound closed. Yvonne brought a fine brass syringe from the side table. "One ounce morphine still?" she asked.

"Yes, said Cameron, "At least until he wakes up and starts complaining.

We may need to give him more at..." he looked up at the clock, "about three." At that Yvonne pushed up Mr. Andrew's red satin dressing gown to reveal a fold of his excessive buttock and injected the morphine into the muscle of his gluteus maximus. A little more application of the garden spray and then a neat bandaging of the stub by Yvonne.

"Do I stop yet Doctor? Asked Spen.
"Start reducing but give us another ten minutes to clear up before waking him please. 'Don't really want him to come round and see blood and guts everywhere." Yes, that made sense realised Spen. He wondered next about where the man might recover and how he would get there. He suddenly realised too that his embryonic doctor's bag back at 2A was a long way short of what he would need as a surgeon. He would need his own 'Yvonne' for a start; John and Andrew didn't really fit that bill. He also realised that his left hand was getting cramp from holding the mask in the same way for over an hour.

He observed how Cameron and Yvonne were just as busy after the operation as during it. They pottered around cleaning up and clearing away. They cleaned themselves and their instruments after cleaning any signs of blood from the floor, table, sink, patient and themselves. They then sprayed their knives and saw, replacing them in the velvet lined toolchest on the floor. Yvonne untied the left leg from the table's side and removed the three-legged stool to its original position. "That's enough then Spen, let's bring him round," said Cameron opening the door and letting in the sound of another laugh from down the corridor. He went through and somehow caused fresh cold air to blow into the building. Spen presumed he'd opened the rear door through which they'd tried to enter earlier that morning. Unfortunately, not a lot of the fresh air came into their operating room. "Are you Mr. Andrew's footmen?" asked Dr. Cameron of two unseen gentlemen in the corridor. "This way please," he said returning through the small door into the operating room. "Did you bring the chair?" Following Cameron were two very smart looking wigged footmen wearing full livery.

"No sir, but it is ready at the Hall sir."

"Not a lot of damned use there I fear," said Cameron with a tut. I'll see if I can lay my hands on one. Having seen their master lying on the table with only his left leg issuing from the lower hem of his dressing gown, one of the footmen hurried to the sink whereupon, he threw up.

Cameron bumped in through the door pulling a wheeled chair behind him. The four men heaved the groaning Mr. Andrews off the table and into it. Spen wondered for a moment if it would take his weight. "Is his cart outside?" enquired Cameron, wondering if that too might still be at the home of Mr. Andrews, (It was). "You'll need help with him onto it.

"We have brought back the coach sir, Mr. Andrews doesn't travel on a cart," said the more senior of the footmen haughtily. Spen observed Cameron's frustration, but said nothing. Outside in the street it soon became obvious why Cameron had given instructions to send a cart rather than a coach. It looked a little like the second pantomime of the day as the four of them tried to lift a sizeable, though barely conscious Mr. Andrews up and into a very springy carriage, through its narrow door and onto one of its straight-backed seats. One of the footmen's wigs was knocked onto the floor and the other was nudged to a jaunty angle which was even funnier. Spen glanced up to see Mrs. Cameron on the pavement lift her hand to her mouth to stifle a giggle. This amused Spen and he struggled to maintain his composure too. The footman sitting next to Mr. Andrews momentarily let go and he flopped over from the vertical knocking the man's wig askew for a second time. All the way through this charade, the coachman sat atop the rig and looked implacably forward, unconcerned by the struggle below him.

As Spen stepped down from the carriage the pavement was suddenly full of his peers leaving the house after the dissection. They all noticed him and rightly assumed, by his rolled-up shirt sleeves, that he had been part of some proper medical procedure that morning. They all recognised Dr. Cameron too and wondered why Robinson had become some sort of 'chosen one.'

Two elderly gentlemen came out of the house with the others and greeted Cameron; he obviously knew them, and they stopped to pass the time of day with him. Spen didn't recognise either of them, but when Yvonne came up to talk to him, he instantly forgot all about them. "You did well this morning Spencely, you will make a fine doctor," she said with a smile. He loved the way she spoke, and smiled, and moved. Cameron was a very lucky man, he thought. She was still in the nurse's frock but had removed her bloodstained apron before going out onto the street. She'd also let her hair down having removed her bonnet. She peeped into the coach and checked briefly on Mr. Andrews and the two footmen holding him upright. She looked down at the bandage and checked it for blood stains. The wound looked to have sealed quite well, it seemed. "We shall visit the house tonight to change dressing and check up on him," she said to the footman who seemed to be in charge. She then nodded to the driver and the coach clattered off along the cobbled street and headed to Mr. Andrew's baronial hall.

Spen stood and hovered a little, wanting to have a final word with Dr. Cameron. He picked up some of what Cameron was saying to the two gentlemen as he turned round to face him. The doctor held out his arm towards Spen. "Robinson, come and meet Messers Laggan and Lubnaig, some colleagues of mine." Spen walked briskly across to the three gentlemen and joined their group. Cameron introduced him as having been his 'stand in' anaesthiologist that morning for the unfortunate Mr. Andrews.

"Did the patient wake up alright?" asked one in a jolly tone.

"Yes, the old buffer's doing fine," added Cameron before Spen could speak for himself.

"Yes, we find that any fool can put people to sleep with chloroform, the real skill is in being able to wake the patient up again afterwards with no impairment of brain function," said Spen in his new-found confidence. The four of them laughed together briefly before Cameron excused himself and went back into the house with Yvonne.

142

"Tell me Doctor Robinson, how long..." But Spen felt a genuine need to be honest with these two gentlemen who looked as if they were men of real standing in the community.

"I'm sorry, sir, but I'm not a doctor, not yet anyway, I'm at the university, still undertaking my training."

"That would be the reason for your youthful appearance then Robinson, but you are a medical man I trust?"

Then the second, rather shorter and more serious gentleman added, "Of course he is, Cameron has just told us that he was the anaesthiologist at this morning's operation on Andrews. You don't look a day over fifteen." This sounded less like an amusing line and a little more like an insult. The first man spoke again.

"We are having a gathering and we'd like you to attend, if you could make it?" Spen didn't have any qualms or suspicion, not at that point anyway, as the gentlemen simply seemed to want a demonstration by someone who knew what they were doing with Chloroform. They wanted him to attend and show them all the powers of anaesthesia. It would be the following Wednesday evening, at their Club, The Wellesley. Would ten pounds cover his expenses? Spen was amazed how quickly he'd gone from humble cash tight student to 'Would ten pounds be enough' territory. What else could he say but, "Yes, I'd be glad to help gentlemen. Wednesday, at..?"

"Eight should be fine," said the talkative man. They shook hands, but the second man simply turned away and walked off. Cameron re-appeared carrying the 'tool box' and his bag, Yvonne was behind him holding a carpet bag which was packed to bulging point. They stopped, Cameron dropped his bags and reached for his wallet. But Spen spoke first.

"No sir, I won't hear of it, I should be paying you for the experience, which by the way was a most useful one sir. Thank you."

"Not even a pound Spencely?" he asked.

"No sir, I insist. The pleasure was all mine. Thank you."

"Well, next time my usual man lets me down I'll come knocking on your door. Thank you for your help Old Man. By the way, what did Lub and Lag want you for?" asked Cameron in a somewhat suspicious tone. "Oh, they've asked me to help at a gathering, some sort of a display for gentleman at their club."

"Hmm," said Cameron suspiciously, "Be polite and don't get too involved, stand your ground if the need arises." He shook Spen's hand and began walking across the road with his shapely wife. Spen hoped that one day he would be in a position like Doctor Cameron; money, wealth, respect, and an adorable wife. Spen watched them go and wondered what Cameron had meant by not getting too involved with Mr. Lubnaig and Mr. Laggan. What did he mean by 'Stand your ground?' Maybe he would find out at 'The Wellesley on Wednesday at Eight.'

Later John told him that he was foolish to refuse the offer of money from Cameron. "He was obviously making a fortune out of his wealthy clients." But Andrew, for once agreed with Spen, that it was better to show a little graciousness at being given an opportunity, not only to witness the great man's talent first-hand, but also to be offered the privilege of taking part."

Chapter 9 – The Wellesley

Sunday was a lazy day, no work, no lessons and no exams on their near horizons. Andrew lain in his bed and looked at Doyle's drawing of Mary-Ann hanging on their wall. Let's take a walk down the towpath shall we? "Let's go and see the Slateford aqueduct over the Waters of Leith." No-one had any better ideas, so they rose, breakfasted and walked Westwards out of the city.

They walked and talked of girls and futures and hopes and dreams. Andrew liked girls, but they didn't seem to like him, John thought it was maybe his dancing English Midlands accent that was putting them off. John himself had never really had anything to do with girls in Shetland. They were all mad there, he was convinced of it. He liked the upper crust ones in Edinburgh though, the ones who spoke well and were somehow more gentrified. Andrew said that it was perhaps because Edinburgh girls weren't bent double against the wind all of the time, with a silver line running across the leeward side of their face from their noses to their ears. John asked Andrew when he'd been to Shetland as he obviously seemed to know the girls there rather well? Andrew replied that he was there when John was last in Walsall.

They reached the warehouses at the Lochrin basin and turned West along the towpath. They had to stand aside occasionally to let the odd horse with its guiding lad past. One or two horses were guiding themselves as their bargees stood on the back of their ship smoking a pipe or sipping tea. The day was very summery, and it reminded Spen of home, and of course Emily. She wasn't as pretty, or indeed as shapely as the lovely Yvonne, but he loved her. He wondered if he would be an acceptable suitor once he was qualified and had a practice of his own.

He asked his friends where they might practice medicine when they'd completed their training? The discussion alternated around the pros and cons of a country practice working for the commoners, or a city practice, for the wealthy. Andrew pointed out that most of the poorest of the nation were in the cities too these days and they needed doctors just as much if not more so than the cossetted rich. Spen said how the hospitals and infirmaries had also started employing full time doctors. A very reliable income that would be.

The Slateford aqueduct was an impressive sight though they seemed to be on it even before they'd realised. It was very high above the valley but was somehow starting to show its age now that the new railway crossing had been built next to it. It looked a little forlorn and forgotten, overtaken by the modern way of doing things. They clambered down the steep bank to take a look at the arches from below. The three of them stayed at river level for some time watching an industrious dipper going in and out of the shallower sections of the brown water. It re-appeared and flew back downstream and again began walking up against the current.

They climbed back up the grassy bank and reached canal level just as a small boy led a plodding horse past them. They stood and watched its following barge floating serenely by. Its cargo was one of wooden baulks of golden timber; each about six inches square in section and sixteen to twenty feet long. "Just like the ones we produce on the estate," said Spen. And, just as he said it, he realized, they weren't just similar, but probably identical. He wondered if they *were* from the Forbes sawmill. The bargee had his back to them but slowly twisted round to look at them as the boat went by. He stared at them, they stared back. John looked again at the timber laying in the hold of the barge. He couldn't read what was printed on the wood as it was mostly sheeted over, but it looked a lot like 'Perkins of Falkirk.'

"Perkins of Falkirk," said Spen, "recognise the name?"

"No," said Andrew, "should we?" And Spen went on to remind them of the night they chased the man (probably a bargee) from The Spurtle to the wharf...

"And you were laid low from behind?" said John.

"Yes, that night. Do either of you remember seeing wood on the wharf like that wood on the boat?"

"Yeah, there might have been some timber on the quayside." Said John.

"Do you remember what it said John?" continued Spen.

"It was pitch black Spen!" exclaimed Andrew. "There was some printing along it, but heaven knows what it was."

"It said 'Perkins of Falkirk, just like the timbers on that boat." Spen didn't really know where his reasoning was taking him, but his instinct told him that this 'coincidence' was suspicious. "I don't see why?" said John.

John reasoned that the boat was only going at walking pace so he suggested they followed it back to Edinburgh; after all, the barge could hardly turn off suddenly down a blind alley and lose them.

So they strolled along steadily, at a pace slightly slower than they would have preferred. That way they didn't get too close, a hundred yards away felt about right. They intended to follow it back all the way to the Hopetoun basin if necessary. They stopped briefly at the Harrison Park bridge to buy three pies off a pie seller; they were starting to feel famished as it was late afternoon by then. But they soon caught up with the boat again. The bargee glanced back occasionally and must have known he was being tailed.

"It's Sunday, so probably no lumpers at the wharf. It'll be unloaded tomorrow," suggested John.

"When we're in lectures" added Spen. "Let's catch up and have a word anyway," said Andrew.

They put on a spurt and calculated that they would catch the boat about the same time as it reached that warehouse with the timber along its outside wall, if indeed that was where it was headed. "Of course, timber that size will need a lifting derrick or a good number of men to handle it ashore." Offered Andrew, thinking out loud. The thought of there being a gang of dockers (always up for a brawl) waiting for them made them slow their pace a little.

They stood at a distance as the horse stopped but the barge continued on slightly. Another man came out of the boat's cabin and walked along the side deck to haul in the towline which the lad had unhitched from the horse. The man on the tiller swung it over and the boat grazed past a tiny landing, whereupon the second man stepped off with the rope in one hand and a bargepole in the other. No matter what Spen, Andrew and John might have thought of these ruffians, they certainly knew how to manhandle a barge without too much effort.

They walked forward, determined to play it softly-softly, though making sure that if the bargee fled, then they wouldn't lose him. As they got within range the man on the steering platform of the barge ignored them. "Good afternoon gentlemen," said Spen. But the bargee just turned towards him and nodded without saying anything. The second and third men finished securing the mooring lines and came back along the yard to stand near to the young men. Spen continued, "Where have you come from?" he asked hoping it would be received favourably. The bargee pointed to the timber and said slowly "Falkirk". He looked at the printing on the wood as he spoke. "Do you know where the wood originated?" he asked, but the reply came from one of the two on the wharf-side who'd come to help land the barge. "Acorns, that's generally how they start," said one of them with a smarmy grin. The other two laughed. "Not these," said Spen sternly, "they're Scots Pine not Oak."

"I only do the transport," said the man still on the barge. After an uncomfortable moment of impasse one of the men asked, "Anything else we can help you gentlemen with?" There wasn't. Spen could hardly accuse the men of stealing the wood from the Forbes estate. He had no proof. But at that moment he decided to visit Mr. Perkin's woodyard in

Falkirk next time he was home.

The two men still stood in front of them, threateningly. "Well, thank you for your time then gentlemen," said Spen beginning to move forward and past the two other bargees. But one sidestepped to block his way forward. At this the man on the barge quickly stepped off it and moved behind the three students.

"Private property" said the man standing in Spen's way. His mood was becoming uglier. It was obvious to everyone that if they wanted to go further up along the side of the canal, then they were going to have to fight. The decisive turning point in the standoff was when one of the two men on the bank allowed a short but solid iron bar to slide out of his sleeve down into his hand. "Probably this way is quicker Spen" suggested Andrew, and the three turned to retrace their steps away from the wharf and warehouses.

They discussed what the bargees could be up to and Spen shared the history of the Forbes sawmill and of Mathew Carter the old estate manager being sacked and leaving under a cloud. Spen could never think anything but good things about Mr. Carter. But maybe that was just one of life's lessons in how you can never truly know people.

They looked back as they left, and saw the men obviously laughing at them. "Revenge is a dish, best served cold," said John.

On the way back to their lodgings Spen shared more on the Matthew Carter story, how he was a lifelong loyal employee but had been sacked by Sir William, who he thought was his friend. Carter was obviously still bitter at the injustice. Spen recounted Carter's last words to him, which were that "Not all of your enemies come from in front of you." He wondered where he was now and if he was happy. "Who's the Estate Manager now Spen?" asked Andrew. And Spen explained about Charles Richardson-Eames. How no-one liked him and even his wife Lady Mary was having a difficult time with him.

Then Andrew, who was always the wise one of the group asked a very pertinent question: "Given that Mr. Nasty is now in the post, you don't suppose that he had anything to do with the removal of your friend Spen?" It was certainly an interesting viewpoint.

"He has rather taken over the estate and lord's it over everyone and everything," said Spen thoughtfully. He spoke again of the estate being rather run down with some of the cottages looking like they needed repairing but had been left unattended. Meanwhile the 'Residence' seemed to have extensions and refurbishment lavished upon it.

"You've spoken of this before Spen, I think it's a ghost of yours that needs exercising," said John. Andrew added that exercise would only make his ghost fitter, he meant exorcising.

The talk turned to the subject of the Wellesley Wednesday and how Spen would need his own supply of Chloroform and a mask. John was unsure of the commercial wisdom of the three clubbing together to buy a bottle and mask only for Spen to use it all up making money for himself. They agreed to lend Spen the money and for him to repay them once he'd performed his magic on Wednesday evening.

* * *

Wednesday came and was a hectic day of slicing and staining specimens for slide preparation in the Histology Lab. Hence they were quite tired when they arrived at the Wellesley just before Eight. John and Andrew went over the road into an altogether less salubrious establishment called the Tattershall Castle to await his return.

Spen was quite nervous as he carried his Gladstone bag up the steps to the grandiose front door of The Wellesley. The large door was opened to him before he could knock on it, and a smart young gentleman in an evening suit greeted him and led him along a warmly lit corridor. On the floor was a thick shag carpet and the walls were lined with expensive flocked coverings. The man knocked on a door and opened it, standing aside to allow Spen through. Once inside Spen immediately felt under-dressed. Three elderly gentlemen were standing there, brandy glass in hand, talking to a young lady. She was giggling as they amused and charmed her. She held a half pint glass of ale, which was three-quarters gone. It was Betsy from Doctor Choudhury's hypnosis lecture. Spen expected a lot more gentlemen to be at the demonstration than just the three of them. Maybe more would be coming. "Ah, Robinson, you found us."

"Yes sir, will there be more?" replied Spen.

"More?" asked Laggan, or was this one Lubnaig? "...more what? No, only the one," (meaning Betsy), he said, not really understanding the question.

"More gentlemen attending the demonstration sir?" asked Spen quietly.

Before Laggan could reply, the third man, the one he didn't recognise, butted in with "No, they couldn't make it." Spen thought it must have been a very expensive evening just to show three gentlemen the benefit of anaesthesia. Spen was uneasy but consoled himself with the thought that at least one of these gentlemen, perhaps all of them might need surgery and wanted to see anaesthesia in action before undergoing it themselves.

Laggan palmed two five-pound notes into his hand when Betsy had her back turned; one of the others was filling her glass asking if she would like anything stronger. "I presume our subject for the evening is..." asked Spen nodding towards the lovely Betsy.

Lubnaig was rather dismissive in his reply, "Yes indeed, I would have thought that was reasonable obvious Robinson." As Lubnaig had been a little haughty with him, he simply excused himself from his company and walked no more than three steps over to Betsy and the taller gentleman.

"Betsy, isn't it?" enquired Spen.

"This is Doctor Robinson Betsy my dear, our anaesthiologist," said the stranger with no introduction of himself. Betsy looked at him, held out her hand and dipped in a small curtsey.

"Pleased to make your acquaintance sir." She said politely, not recognising him.

"May I have a quick word?" he said, pulling her gently by the arm away from the others. The three men grouped together and looked suspiciously at them both. They went quiet in an attempt to overhear what Spen was saying to her.

"Are you accepting of this anaesthetic Miss Betsy?" he asked her. She was. "And you are being paid for your time and your acquiescence?"

"My what sir." Maybe it wasn't a word which was used much in the slums of Edinburgh.

"Are you fine with me putting you to sleep Betsy? With Chloroform."

"Yes sir. I think so. Won't hurt, will it?" Spen looked up over Betsy's hat at the other three gentlemen. Having heard a 'yes sir' a couple of times they had become less concerned that their *demonstration* wasn't going awry.

"And may I ask how much they are paying you Betsy?" he asked quietly. She leant forward and her eyes opened wide.

"Ten sir, I have it already," she said patting her pocket. She could barely contain her excitement. Spen was very surprised indeed at the amount too. These men must be made of money, "What, ten pounds?" asked Spen softly.

"Ah way... "she said with a big smile. "Shillin's sir." Yes, that made more sense, Spen concluded; no-one ever got as preposterously rich as these gentlemen by giving their money away. He asked her to take off her hat. She reached up and slid out a sizeable hat pin and lifted off the large hat, obviously her best one. It was decorated with two flowers one of which was starting to wilt. Spen realised that it was a real one. "Hair down sir?" she asked. The other three had stopped talking and started to watch them "That won't be necessary."

"Yes, yes, hair down..." said one of the gentlemen, a little too enthusiastically. Spen wondered why he had an opinion on the subject which he felt he'd needed to express.

As Spen moved the chaise longue away from the wall and Betsy removed her jacket. One of the old men went to help her off with it. As he did so, Spen looked up at the other two gentlemen who were watching her. He thought they might possibly have been leering at her curvy figure. Neither of them offered to help him move the furniture. "Please take a seat Miss," requested Spen gesturing to the couch with an open hand. "Please lay down with your head this way and your ankles over the headrest at the end please if you will," instructed Spen with a calm authority.

"Don't you think the head would be better resting on the *head* end Robinson?" said one of the gentlemen.

"Not really" replied Spen, "I need her chin high and her airway patent; if her legs are higher that will help blood flow to the head as her blood-pressure lowers too," he said fully expecting that to be enough explanation for the gentlemen, he was the doctor after all.

"This way miss," said one of the gentlemen and he began man-handling Betsy into the direction opposite to that which Spen had requested. Though it did look a comfortable and a much more natural position on the long seat.

"But you see, her chin is on her chest now, that won't do at all," said Spen, but before he could persuade Betsy to lay in the opposite direction as he wished, the same old gentleman had his arm under her armpit and was heavying her up saying,

"Move your pretty little bottom slightly higher my dear." Betsy obeyed and her head slumped backwards over the padded end of the couch in a pose which made her stare up at the ceiling. At least there her airway would be clear.

"Are you comfortable Betsy, may I call you Besty?" said the first man, and looked up to Spen and nodded.

Spen wasn't at all happy with the way his concerns as a medical professional were being ignored. He also wasn't happy that the old man had started to manhandle the poor woman and refer to her 'pretty little bottom' in such an inappropriate manner. He wasn't keen to continue but realised that he'd already been paid, as had the girl, so perhaps they should just get on with it, get it over and done, then go home.

The three men stood in a row as Spen lifted a plush padded footstool and placed it at the head of the chaise longue. He sat down on it and slid his bag next to him. He unbuckled it with one hand and at the same time asked Betsy if she was happy for him to continue. "Yes, sir, I'm fine, you just do your bit and I'll do mine. He looked at her inverted face and saw her wink at him. He was unsure if that was an attempt to flirt with him or just a knowing wink that she would fall asleep as they all intended. At that point he was even less convinced by the power of Choudhury's hypnosis. (The last demonstration at which Betsy had *performed*).

He put the mask on her small face, no whiskers this time to get in the way, he thought. He pulled out the dropper bottle and deftly managed to hold up the stopper just a little. The practice back at 2A had paid off. This time he looked much more like he knew what he was doing. The chloroform trickled onto the muslin and spread out "You'll feel a little dizzy Betsy, a bit like you've had too much to drink," said Spen softly.

"Ooh, I know that feeling well sir," she said with a giggle. Her eyes flashed open again as she said it. He looked over the mask at Betsy's chest slowly rising and falling. The two middle buttons were tilting towards each other as the garment flexed slightly with the motion. He looked up and noticed that two of the old gentlemen were looking at her chest moving too. "A small trickle to moisten the mask initially, to put the patient asleep, then one further drop every forty to fifty seconds as this patient is quite dainty. You are quite dainty Betsy, aren't you?" said Spen, not really as a question. But from beneath the mask Betsy muttered something incomprehensible.

Spen replaced the stopper firmly and put down the bottle. He reached round to the open side of the couch and held Betsy's forearm vertically with her elbow on the couch. "Would you hold your arm there for me Betsy please?" He let go and the arm flopped straight over.

"Good Lord" exclaimed one of the gentlemen softly. "Is that it? Is that all it takes?

"Between three and five minutes to put the patient to sleep, that's all, it's a very powerful drug," said Spen, hopefully as a warning to the men that they should take it most seriously and not treat it with disregard. "And how long will she be asleep for?" asked one of the gentlemen. Another picked up her arm and held it in the same position he'd witnessed Spen place it. He let go and it flopped over a second time. Another man lifted up the same arm and just let go of it, and sure enough, it fell limply back onto the plush quilted velvet couch. They seemed to be amusing themselves. "And if the, erm, surgeon needs longer than ten minutes?" Spen took up the bottle from the floor again and applied another single drop.

"Then a further drop is applied at the requisite interval, and she will stay asleep for as long as needed," he said looking up to the three whiskered faces. One of the men stepped forward a little and, most inappropriately put his hand on the woman's blouse and moved it slightly as if to feel its texture. As he did so he glanced round at another man who immediately looked to Spen to see if he was noticing. He was. Spen noticed their expressions as the men glanced at each other. Previously Spen had only *suspected* that their motives for anaesthetising a young woman weren't entirely wholesome, but at that instant he became rather convinced of it. He decided that that would be enough of a demonstration for the night. He stood up after replacing the mask and bottle into his bag. He bent down again to replace the footstool back to where it had been originally in the room, then he stepped away from the patient, willing to try and bamboozle his way through any questions which might come from the men next. No questions came.

"Well, that was most informative Doctor, thank you for coming," said one as he put his arm to Spen's back and began urging him towards the door.

But Spen stood firm and said, "It is my duty to stay until the patient is fully recovered sir."

"Do you expect complications Robinson?" asked one of the other two.

"No sir, I just consider it my professional duty."

The third man handed Spen his bag from off the floor saying, "We'll look after her Robinson, we'll take up no more of your time."

And the first gentleman again added "Thank you for coming, it's been most informative."

Spen really wasn't happy about being ushered out of the room in such a forceful manner, but the three wealthy gentlemen were obviously used to getting their own way in life. He managed a last look at Betsy over his shoulder as he left and was at least satisfied that she was breathing steadily and would probably wake up soon.

He skipped down the steps of The Wellesley club and across the road to the Tattershall Castle. Andrew and John had seen his approach and ordered him a tankard of Ale. "What's the matter with you Spen?" asked a concerned Andrew. It was Spen's expression which had given away his mood as he entered the bar. Spen noticed that a pair of young lovers were leaving a table by the front window and Spen urged the other two to move across to it and sit there.

"We need a view of the Wellesley. I need to talk to Betsy when she comes out," he blurted to them.

"Is there anywhere you ever go where there aren't women falling at your feet Spencely Robinson?" asked John. "Betsy, it was Betsy from Choudhury's lecture on hypnosis. I put her to sleep. She must have thought that the same rules applied..." he couldn't get the words out quick enough.

"Spen, calm down, go from the beginning. What rules applied?" said Andrew calmly.

"Betsy, she thought that she was going to have to pretend to go to sleep, just like we all suspected she'd done in the Hypnosis lecture."

"You mean she wasn't asleep?" asked John innocently.

"Of course not, everyone could see that," said Andrew.

"Well, it worked for me," said John again.

"Yes, everyone noticed that too," said Spen with a smile. "Anyway," he continued "There were only three elderly gents in the room, and it wasn't really a demonstration at all. I reckon I've been used to drug a poor woman purely for the amusement of some old men with more money than manners."

"So what happened?" asked a concerned Andrew.

He continued; "I put our Betsy to sleep and as soon as she was out, I was packed off, out the door. I have no idea what's going on in there."

"Hmm, aiding and abetting rape, I wonder how many years that would get you?" said John, thinking he was being amusing. Spen was forced to recount every detail of the evening until Andrew (who was looking out the window) saw a woman walk swiftly down the side of the Wellesley and onto the street. He cut in saying "Is that her?" Spen leapt to his feet and rushed out of the pub. He narrowly avoided being struck by a Hansom as he darted across to talk to Betsy. John and Andrew remained seated and watched the whole show from the pub window.

"Betsy, are you alright?" he asked as he caught up with her.

"No thanks to you, call yourself a doctor? I didn't know where I was." She exclaimed nearly in tears.

"Sorry, Bets, they threw me out as soon as you were asleep, I wanted to stay but they wouldn't let me. I've been waiting for you, to make sure you were alright." He looked down at her jacket as they walked past a gaslight. Spen could tell that her blouse had been buttoned up speedily as one of the button-holes had been missed. He remembered that they were the buttons he'd seen tilting as he watched her breathe earlier in the evening. They definitely hadn't been buttoned up irregularly then.

But she didn't want to talk much, perhaps through embarrassment. All she offered was "I came too with mi skirts above mi knees and some whiskers in mi face, horrible it was. Bad breath and all that. Ma hatpin came in very handy though, I don't mind telling you."

"Good for you Betsy. But you're alright now eh?" he asked, though she certainly seemed to be fine by the speed she was walking.

"Aye, no thanks to you though..." she scorned. He stopped walking and apologised again as she disappeared into the darkness.

Back in the Tattershall Castle John asked if he'd been paid as expected?

"Yes, no bother at all," was his reply.

"Cohh, what easy money, why don't I ever get offers like that?" he said looking into his beer.

"Well, I shan't be doing it again, I assure you" concluded Spen.

Chapter 10 – The Frank Discussion

As Spen's train pulled into Falkirk station he spotted a petite figure dressed tightly in black on the Edinburgh bound platform. He looked at her hourglass form as his train squealed to a halt. It may have been her shape, or perhaps the style of hat, but she reminded him of the beautiful secretary who'd dealt with his Scholarship papers and money at Brader's Solicitors in Edinburgh. As he stood up to leave the compartment he looked again. In fact, he thought it could easily have been her. Moira Beaty, that was her name (how could he forget?) But he nearly jumped out of his wits as a steam engine thundered past his window and its following train blocked his view of the woman.

Having stepped out of the carriage, he stood on the platform for a moment waiting for the two trains to leave in their opposite directions. As the second one, the Edinburgh train, pulled away it revealed an empty platform apart from an elderly couple having just arrived from Glasgow or perhaps Kirkintilloch. 'Obviously' Spen thought to himself, 'she was waiting on the platform to catch that train to Edinburgh.' That's what people did in railway stations. He'd like to say that he'd thought no more of Miss Beaty on his long walk home, but actually, he did. Not least, he tried to imagine what business she might have in Falkirk.

He managed to hitch a ride on one of the returning timber wagons the last mile or so onto the Stannet-Forbes estate. He was probably distracted by the thoughts of the perfect miss Beaty to realise that the wagon he was riding on was heading back from Falkirk to the Forbes own sawmill. If he'd have been paying attention, he might have realised that it shouldn't have been: they only exported wood from their local canal jetty, a short half mile journey from the mill. And it all went to Glasgow.

His mother Dorothy hugged him for a little longer, even than she had hugged him at Christmas. And wanted to look at him, while he stood there in the evening light. She beckoned a neighbour over and invited her to come and look at her fine son too. My, my, wasn't he growing up fast? Spen tried to point out to the gloating women that he had indeed grown up, in fact he had done so a number of years back. But the neighbour told him that, as Dorothy's youngest, he would always be her baby. Though pointing out that he was also her eldest son too, didn't seem to counter her reasoning.

The following morning Spen got a similar prodigal son type greeting from Emily too. She had missed him so much that she nearly squeezed him to death too. Had he missed her? He supposed he had. "Emily, do you think you could get me an audience with your father please?" he asked rather formally. Though a little crestfallen, she replied, "No need, let's go now, I think he's at home. He'll be glad to see you, probably could do with some cheering up." From the look on her face, he realised that he had flipped the conversation maybe a little too quickly away from how much she'd missed him and onto his next topic. So he stopped and looked at her. "Yes, I've missed you, a lot, Emily." She smiled broadly and seemed to have any possible fears regarding Spen's diminishing interest in her, allayed. But he didn't want to go to the Hall right then, in his scuffs, he wanted to dress up a little and present himself as a serious gentleman.

Less than an hour and a half after Emily and Spen had parted for Lunch that morning, a footman on a trap drew up outside Dorothy's cottage. He was wearing full livery, though no wig, Sir William couldn't bring himself to force his footmen to wear wigs too.

All the neighbours came out of their cottages to watch and poke a little ribald fun at the young man as he dismounted from, and nearly fell off, the trap. The horse even seemed to join in the fun as it jerked the small carriage forward when he stood in front of its wheel. Spen appeared at the door behind his mother and recognised the man as the young Mr. Clarke, the new starter at the Hall. He'd been engaged after the staff numbers had been thinned out when some were asked to work for Charles and lady Mary.

Clarke composed himself, straightened his collar and marched towards Dorothy. Spen Squeezed himself out of the doorway which was being partly blocked by his mother. Clarke stopped, placed his feet together in front of Dorothy and bowed slightly from the waist. Spen strode forward holding out his right hand and said "Mr. Clarke isn't it, how are you?" Clarke couldn't stay impervious to such a warm greeting and broke into a smile that nearly became a laugh. He'd never been spoken to in such a friendly manner before. Never in uniform certainly and, from what he could remember, nor at any other time either. Once the two had greeted each other, somehow as old friends might, Mr. Clarke took out an embossed envelope from an inside pocket and asked cheekily, "I don't suppose you have a silver platter which I could borrow for a moment please, so that I might present you with this?" he said offering the envelope to Spen. "Well, we have, but unfortunately it's in town, we're having it polished this week," laughed Dorothy. Clarke, Spen and all the neighbours joined in the joke.

"Would you be collecting ours too please when you go?" offered another,

"Aye, and ours if you would ne mind?"

They all felt it was good of Clarke to infer that Spencely Robinson, one of their own, was worthy of being handed his mail on a silver platter, just as Sir William would be.

Spen thumbed open the envelope and pulled out the matching note paper. It read 'The presence of Mr. S Robinson is humbly requested by Sir William Stannet-Forbes, Fifth Earl of Calendar, At The Hall, at a time that is convenient, preferably this afternoon, or whenever you can make it dear chap.' Spen smiled at the beautiful way the simple sentence went from grand formality to simple friendliness in the space of just a few words. He handed the letter to his mother, then looked at Mr. Clarke. But Mr. Clarke spoke first, he obviously knew the purpose of the communication, "What time shall I collect you sir?"

"Give me a minute Mr. Clarke and I'll return with you now if that's alright?" said Spen as he turned to rush back into the house. "Mother, have we a lemonade for Mr. Clarke please?"

"Yes, your Pomposity," she said with a genteel curtsey. "We do know how to treat guests out here in the wilds too you know." Spen rushed back out of the door, kissed his mother on the cheek and rushed in again.

Within a few minutes Spen and Clarke were bouncing along the track and onto the drive which led up to the Big House. They exchanged meaningless small-talk but little else. Clarke would have liked time to talk more seriously with Spen, but realised he had neither the time nor intellect, nor even the social position, to interact meaningfully with Spen. After all he was nearly a doctor.

Emily kissed him on the cheek as she met him at the doorway of the grand entrance hall. "Father's waiting for you, I think he's in the library." They walked through the high-ceilinged house, which was as beautiful and ornate as it had always been. At the tall solid door to the library she stopped, turned, and smiled at him. He knocked and went in.

Spen didn't know how he was going to begin broaching his topic to the laird, so he opted to say nothing for a moment and instead took a deep breath. The Laird stood erect, holding an open book and was staring into it. He finished his sentence and looked up at the approaching Spen. After putting the book down gently on the table he walked towards him and stretched out his hand with a welcoming smile. "Thank you for seeing me sir" said Spen smiling back. "Always a pleasure master Robinson, now, tell me, how the dickens are you?" Ah, niceties first obviously. "I'm well sir thank you, very well indeed. And you sir, how are you keeping?" At this, Sir William stood for a moment and stared briefly at the floor. "I remember the first time you asked me that Spencely, in here, at that very spot," he said pointing to the square of parquet flooring upon which Spen stood. Spen immediately wished that he'd polished his shoes this morning. "I think you were probably seven, can't have been more, looking at a book on dandelions as I recall. You asked me how my mother was." They both smiled again at the innocence of childhood.

"Did I sir, I can't remember, though I do recall having some of my happiest days in this room, as I was growing up."

"I'm honoured to have been the provider of your delight dear chap," he said wistfully. Spen noticed that he hadn't answered the question of how he was, though people tend not to; it's not really a question so much as something to say as a greeting. Spen also noticed that The Laird hadn't referred to him this time as 'dear boy,' but as 'dear chap.' That had felt good, as it was some sort of acceptance into adulthood by a man for whom he held the deepest respect. He might even say 'love for' in a parental sort of way. "Shall we stand for the next bit, or sit?"

"Perhaps we should sit sir," said Spen looking towards the two chairs arrayed at either side of the table. Spen rightly guessed at the Laird wanting, perhaps needing to sit for a moment as his back was quite old and might be aching.

Sir William pulled out a chair and asked, "And tell me, how is the course going Spencely?"

"Oh sir... it's what I was made for. Each day brings a new revelation of wonder on how the human body works, how it repairs itself, how it grows and develops and how I can have a hand in helping it do so, helping people. It's marvellous, I never knew there existed such fulfilment for one human being." He'd started to giggle as he spoke, but then stopped suddenly, realising that The Laird might just have been looking for another 'Yes sir, fine thank you.' But he could see by Sir William's expression that the old chap was taking pure delight in Spen's innocent enthusiasm for life.

Then there was a moment of stillness, and it was obvious to both that they should get down to the business of why Spen had asked to see him. But just as Spen took another large lungful of air, to calm his nerves, the door swung open, and Mr. Bateman came in with a large silver tray upon which were all the paraphernalia for afternoon tea. Neither talked and both watched the sober Mr. Bateman stride over with the tray and put it on the table next to the book in front of them. "Shall I pour sir?" he asked his master. "No, thank you Bateman, we can manage." Bateman looked up from the tray and saw Spen smiling at him. "You're looking well Mister Bateman," said Spen. Bateman smiled back at him, nodded, turned to the Laird, nodded again, then turned and went.

Once the butler had pulled the door closed behind him, Sir William turned to pour the tea and said, "Good heavens, I do believe he smiled." But Spen knew that this thin veil of animosity didn't begin to hide the lifelong unspoken agreement that these two men had to look after one another. "Milk?" asked Sir William.

"Yes, please sir. Sir, it's a difficult topic, and I hope you won't think me impertinent by my broaching it." He reached forward to take the porcelain cup and saucer off The Laird.

"Well, I doubt I will, but be assured, I'll let you know if I do."

"It's regarding your Sawmill sir."

"Sawmill!" blurted Sir William, "Good Lord, I thought you were going to ask me for Emily's hand in marriage!" The two laughed out loud, then Spen thought he might be being a little insulting that proposing marriage to his daughter should be laughable. Oh, he thought, he hoped not, 'calm down' he told himself, don't dwell, move on.

"Sir, I believe that you export your sawn timber to Glasgow, via the local estate wharf..." he didn't wait for the answer as he thought that might appear to be too inquisitive into Sir William's business. "Why I ask sir, is because I believe I have seen some of the Stannet-Forbes estate wood on the quayside in Edinburgh sir."

"Really?" said Sir William in a non-committal sort of way.

"Yes sir, but, more to the point, the baulks have 'Perkins of Falkirk' stencilled along their length. Yet I'm convinced it has come from your yard here on the estate sir."

"And what gives you such an impression, may I ask?" he said. Again, he was un-emotional.

"They're between six and eight inches, square section, sawn by a circular saw of large diameter, not a reciprocating saw, and they're between fourteen and eighteen feet long. Scots Pine sir." The Laird looked pensive and said nothing. Spen tried to reinforce his case a little. "Emily told me that you export all of your timber to Glasgow via the Stannet-Forbes own canal wharf sir."

"Yes, quite so... I'm sure the Forbes sawmill isn't the only sawmill in the area which produces that type of wood in that size," said Sir William, but though that might have been technically true, he also suspected that young Mr. Robinson was right. "Spencely, it is possible that Perkins may have bought the timber from our agents in Glasgow, added their name along the length and sold it on to a buyer in Edinburgh." Though he said it, he didn't believe this was likely as the cost of a barge trailing three days West to Glasgow, unloading, storing, re-loading and floating along for another three and a half days East again would make the wood over-priced. "Yes sir, it is possible..." said Spen accepting the Laird's point.

"But as we both know, it's highly unlikely," added Sir William. He looked down at the table, and after a thoughtful moment he continued "You do know why I finished Mr. Matthew Carter Spencely?"

"I don't sir, not for a fact, but I have my suspicions."

"It was because I found him cheating me in the period after the sawmill had the new engine installed. I found that there were more wagons going out, some indeed to Mr. Perkins at Falkirk, than we had received payment for. I saw the wagons going out and I checked the ledger of sales with my own eyes." At this point the Laird had to stop talking and began coughing slightly. He brought out a large kerchief from his side pocket and coughed into it several times. The coughing became more vigorous, so he poured milk from milk jug on the tray into his empty teacup and swigged it back. That helped. Spen noticed at that moment how much the Laird had aged even more than the others on the estate whilst he'd been away.

"Are you alright sir?" he asked wondering if he should do something or call someone. But Sir William waved that notion away and took the kerchief away from his mouth a second time. As he did so Spen was shocked to see blood on the white kerchief. Not just a small drop or two, but quite a smear.

He took a moment before speaking again. "I feel I should tell you that Matthew Carter swore that he knew nothing of the extra wagons of timber not following the usual route from our wharf to Glasgow. All I knew was that I was being cheated and Mr. Carter was the Estate Manager to whom I had entrusted my affairs."

"But you suspect now perhaps that he was innocent?" ventured Spen, hoping that he'd read Sir William correctly.

"Indeed, I dread the thought of me having made a terrible mistake and of having been unfair to the man in the extreme. Why Spencely, do you have any evidence on the matter?"

But Spen could only add fuel to the fire of injustice that Sir William had inflicted upon his estate manager. "No sir, I'm afraid I haven't, but I can tell you of the time Mr. Carter discovered that something underhand was happening; I was at the sawmill one evening and I remember being surprised to find the engine still working. Mr. Carter rode up and he seemed genuinely surprised too sir. He enquired of the men as to why they were still working late and was told of their extra instructions that had come from Mr. Richardson Eames sir." Sir William closed his eyes and sat back in a moment of grim realisation.

"Oh dear," said Sir William, "that falls in with what I know or, rather what I was told of that event years ago." Spen shuffled a little closer to

the table and listened carefully to the candid words of the Earl of
Callander. He recalled how he knew that straight after that incident,
Carter had gone to see Charles to report the matter, but Charles had
told Sir William the visit was instigated by Charles himself, not by Mr.
Carter. Charles told him that he'd challenged Carter over the issue and
had accused Carter of deceiving the estate out of many hundreds of
pounds each year. "Charles then came to me and explained, asking me
to dispense with Mr. Carter's services, which I did. It all seemed so
disappointing and unexpected, but the solution then was so obvious."

"And it was Mr. Richardson Eames who told you about the deceit sir?"

"Yes, I'm afraid it was. I checked the story as best I could at the time, I
followed a cart of wood to Perkins' yard, I looked in the ledger, no entry,
it was obvious I was being cheated. I remember feeling indebted to
Charles at the time, for flushing out the bad apple."

"But got the wrong apple perhaps sir.?"

"I fear I may have done Spencely, I fear I may have done." Spen
realised that the only mistake Carter had made was to tell Charles and
not Sir William directly. But before he could suggest it Sir William
coughed weakly another twice before staring at the book on the desk in
front of him. Spen thought he shouldn't press Sir William on the topic
for another minute or two. But impatience and a need to bring the
whole story to the surface made him push Sir William just that little
further.

"Sir, forgive me, but I came here today to alert you to the possibility
that you are somehow being cheated still. The wood, on Edinburgh's
quayside from 'Perkins' supposedly."

"Still being cheated eh? Even with poor Mr. Carter gone a number of
years now." He coughed again. Spen had never noticed how much the
Laird had coughed before. Spen wasn't much of a doctor yet but he
could notice when a patient needed rest. So, he decided he should take
his leave. As he stood up to excuse himself and go, there was a double
knock at the library door and it immediately swung open. Again Mr.
Bateman strode in purposefully. Obviously he was there to collect the

tea tray. Sir William stood up too as he approached and Spen naturally presumed he was standing to shake hands good-bye. Instead, he palmed something from his pocket to Mr. Bateman. Something which Bateman silently took without a word, glance or even surprise. He put it straight in his own pocket. It had come out of the same pocket into which Sir William had put his bloodstained kerchief. Spen glanced at the Laird's pocket, it bulged no longer. But Mr. Bateman's pocket did though, just a little. The butler picked up the tray from the table, took a step back, boughed slightly to Sir William, then turned and left.

"Sir, with your permission, and perhaps a day's loan of a pony, I'd like to make some enquiries of my own." Sir William lifted his eyebrows at Spen for perhaps a little more information. "At the sawmill sir, and then perhaps at Falkirk." He turned and headed for the door. But he stopped and spun back to The Earl, "One final thing sir; How could Matthew Carter have proven his innocence sir?" Sir William thought for a moment then soulfully admitted, "No, I don't suppose he could."

"Good day sir, thank you for seeing me."

Chapter 11 – Perkins' Yard

The following day Spen returned to The Big House and went round the back, through the courtyard and into the stable tack room. A young lad whom Spen didn't recognise was polishing a saddle over a beam. When he first heard Spen, he jumped up and stood to attention. Then, once he realised that the visitor was not who he thought it was he relaxed a little. But he didn't recognise Spen, the well-dressed stranger. "Oh, sorry sir, I thought you were someone else." Spen was just about to introduce himself when a man who's voice he recognised came into the room behind him. "Well, well, what a fine looking gentleman you turned out to be. Tell me, didn't you used to be that grubby little urchin Spencely Robinson?" Spen turned round with a broad smile. "Indeed I did Mr. MacDougal, and I'm amazed you're still alive, you must be at least a hundred and fifty years old if not more..." The two held onto each other for a moment.

Mr. MacDougal told Spen that The Old Man (meaning The Laird) had instructed him to loan a horse to Spencely Robinson so he'd fetched him the wildest, unbroken, most skittish stallion he could find. They laughed again. MacDougal lifted a small saddle off a bar and walked through to a stable. Spen followed him in. The horse was barely tall enough to push her head over the stable door. "Hmm," said Spen, "looks vicious. Did you nay have a smaller one?"

"We save the bigger ones, the real ones, for work, hunting, or people who know what they're doing on a horse. Anyway, last time I set eyes on you, you were only eleven."

"Well I didn't expect a Clydesdale, Mr. Mac, but neither did I expect to be dragging my feet along the ground as I rode along either." As MacDougal strapped up the saddle and lowered the stirrups, Spen put the bridle over the horse's head and the bit into her mouth. "I'll be here when you get back. And if it's got dark, I'll go scouring the ditches and hedges for ye."

* * *

Spen ventured a canter over the sheep fields, through the stream and along the edge of the Thirty Acre wood until he got to the sawmill. It was working as usual. No wagons were there but the store racks in the stacking shed looked quite empty, as if a load had just departed. The high-pitched squeal of the sawblade severing bark from heart was replaced by the thrumming of the engine as another big log was flipped and reversed ready for a second pass. The bark lengths were still thrown one way by a man on each end ready to be shortened into firewood. Spen was disappointed not to see some small boy come and collect it ready for taking out to folks on the estate. He thought back and remembered his own industriousness.

He talked at length with Mr. Barnes, still the lead hand, and, though at first he was quite reticent to discuss any detail of the shipments, he had to admit that he wasn't at all comfortable with Mr. Richardson-Eames' continual request to tell no-one about their business. He used the excuse that if other businesses could find their suppliers and buyers then the sawmill could be commercially usurped. Mr. Barnes didn't really know what that meant. But he did reveal that one of the weekly Perkins' wagons (there were generally three) had left earlier that same morning ago and would be nearly at Falkirk by now.

He thanked Mr. Barnes, and with a wry smile asked him not to tell Charles about their conversation. He then kicked the horse into a trot.

Spen didn't expect to see the 'Perkins of Falkirk' woodyard to be so high up on the South side of the town. He'd forgotten how much above sea level the canal had climbed to just west of the town through those horrendously slow eleven locks from the Forth and Clyde Navigation.

Nor did he expect to see a woodyard to look so much like a prison. There was a high perimeter fence with a full height double gate into it. As he approached, a man magically came out and noisily unchained the gates to let him in, a most unusual occurrence. Then he realised, that the man was unchaining the gates to let an empty cart out, not to let him in, of course.

He watched the empty wagon trundle past him and nodded to the driver, whom he didn't recognise. The smell from the wagon was unmistakeably of freshly sawn timber. The wagon itself was also typical of the type used to transport wood having a flat deck with no side walls and three solid cross-beams upon which the logs sat. The coiled ropes thrown loosely on the top confirmed his conclusion.

Spen realised he was taking a bit of a risk entering the yard before the man could swing the second gate closed. He greeted him with a nod and a confident "Good mornin' te ya," in an attempt to allay his suspicions, even though he didn't feel at all confident. He only hoped that he could get out of the place in a hurry should things turn a little difficult. It was starting to feel as if he was entering a den of vipers.

The yard was flat, large and unkempt. The canal edge ran for approximately fifty yards in a hard stoned straight line along one edge of it, enough for four barges side on; there were two berthed there. A short line of buildings went along its other side with fencing before and a large high shed after them, probably a storehouse. Some piles of cargo lay grouped together in the yard; many sacks, probably lime, two large piles of coal, and a great many baulks of timber, some stencilled with the words 'Perkins of Falkirk, some unmarked. Two barrels stood forlornly on end next to the coal, obviously nothing valuable, not brandy, because they weren't in the shed.

At the door of one of the single-story grey-washed buildings hung a sign saying 'office.' There Spen dismounted with as much aplomb as he could muster and looked around. At the far end of the quayside one of the barges was being loaded with the timber. There were three men and a derrick operator working there. Spen could see no sign of a sawmill, nor hear one; no tall brick chimney belching smoke from a boiler fire, no rhythmic chugging of a steam engine nor intermittent scream from an angry sawblade. He wondered how he was going to find out more about the double dealings without getting himself beaten up, or even killed. He continued to take in his surroundings. Down the side of the office building was a narrow passageway which led through the perimeter fence, and presumably, into the street. There was a pedestrian sized door through which Spen presumed the workers came into the yard each morning.

He wondered if he should try buying some wood from the yard. But that would just net him a lot of wood and no information. Maybe he should come straight out and ask how he was getting the wood from the Stannet-Forbes sawmill without paying for it. They'd be unlikely to tell him and at the very least might throw him in the canal.

An oldish but tough looking man came out from the office building and stood before him as he'd dismounted the horse. Spen nodded to him as he looked about him for something upon which to secure the reigns. Spen looked to the man, but he gave him no hint of where he might secure his horse. Spen thought he should take the initiative. "I've come from the Forbes Estate and I'm looking for Mister Perkins." Spen purposely left off the 'please,' though it didn't come naturally to do so.

"I'm Perkins, please state your business young fella." As Spen looked at Perkins he noticed that behind him, at the end of the block of single storey buildings was a lone window with some bars on it. None of the other windows had the bars. It looked out of place.

Spen took a moment, then went out on the biggest scariest limb of his life. "I bring a message from the Forbes' Estate Manager."

"Do you now? And the message is?" growled Perkins, showing not a hint of interest.

"He asked me to tell you that things have changed suddenly..." but Spen's voice had started to quiver a little.

"Yes...?" said Perkins moving a little closer to Spen. He continued and tried to sound convincing.

"He says there'll be no more wood from the estate and you're to pay me now the amount owing."

But Perkins didn't seem to be surprised by the request. His low deep voice was still calm and devoid of feeling, "It's odd that he didn't tell me this news himself. Most odd," said the crusty old man. He stared threateningly up into Spen's eyes. Spen waffled a little and looked over his shoulder at the large perimeter gates now locked firmly shut. Spen continued to shoot from the hip, but he felt his shot falling rather short.

"He only came to the decision yesterday, something bad has happened."

"But Charles Ponsonby-Smallpiece was only here... this morning. Funny 'e never mentioned it." Oh dear, that was a bit of a check-mate statement. The situation had suddenly turned sour as he thought it might, and he'd need a lot more than clever words to extricate himself now. Perkins twisted around and whistled a quick single note to the three men doing the timber loading further along the water's edge. One of them noticed and beckoned the others. Spen realised that the one man in front of him would be easier to fight on his own, before the others added an extra layer of difficulty. But as Spen turned back to Perkins from looking up the quay, Perkins' fist was well on its way to meet heavily with his mouth. He didn't see it in time to reel back out of the way and he took the full force on his lips and gums. The horse too was shocked and pulled on the reigns still in Spen's right hand. Another thump was coming his way again, but this time he was fast enough to see it and managed to jinx out of the way. He gave Perkins a left hook with his only free hand, but it didn't seem to have much effect. Matthew Carter's words came back to him, 'stay calm, think, don't get angry.' He had a sudden realisation. It was obvious, how stupid he was.

When Perkins came at him again, he lashed the loose ends of the reigns into his face and it obviously stung. Perkins had a cut below his eye but as he tried looking at Spen to show his bravado Spen lashed him again having lengthened the amount of the leather strap emanating from his hand. He added a further left hook again for good measure, and Perkins swayed before going down.

He realised he only had seconds before the three stevedores and the derrick operator would be upon him, so he moved swiftly to the blind side of his horse and leapt up onto it. Before he'd had chance to get his feet into the stirrups, he kicked the horse and charged the remaining ten yards or so into the group of three men running towards him. But the horse wasn't confident at charging straight at people who were running straight at her, and she reared up. Spen clung on as the horse tried to tip him off its rear. One of the men, on the canal side had to dodge violently out of the way of the hooves and wobbled precariously at the water's edge. He's not sure how, but he managed to give the man's chest a kick to help him to topple backwards into the canal. 'Lucky he hadn't found those stirrups quickly' he thought. He galloped along the quayside towards the lifting derrick towards the fourth man, again thinking that men on their own would be easier to defeat than all together in a group. A sort of divide and conquer tactic. The man lumbered towards him but only swung one arm, his right. He carried his left in a sling as if it was broken. Ah, that's why he was operating the derrick and not doing the manual labour. Spen decided to just gallop past him but the end of the yard had a fence which blocked it off right up to the waters' edge. No way out. He circled round the man with the gammy arm, and they looked at each other quite closely. They'd met before. It was Spen who was the one who broke that arm. Suddenly the man knew it too. Oh dear, when Spen was captured, he could no doubt expect to have his arm broken in retribution, painfully. Better not get captured then, he thought. The horse was his only hope.

As he galloped back up the quay he took stock. Perkins was on his feet but bleeding heavily and being tended to by one of the men. As he looked, Perkins was pushing away the help and gesticulating towards Spen. One was in the canal and was being helped by another to climb out. It all looked a bit of a farse, but Spen knew that as he approached a second time the man doing the rescuing would be re-directed to help bring Spen to heal. He knew he needed an advantage. Luckily, he spotted two shovels leant against the sacks of lime. He pulled the horse over towards them and grabbed one of them as he went past. He could at least take another one of them out before they could grab the horse's bridle and bring it to a halt. He kicked the horse into another gallop though both the horse and he were becoming breathless. He whirled the shovel round and charged the group as if he was in some high-class polo match. But as he went through them a second time, they all managed to dodge out of the way. One of the men, who he also had a feeling he recognised from that same night, sneered at him obviously expecting that the challenge was only going to end in their favour. Then it would be their turn to have some fun.

As he went past the end of the office, he spotted the pedestrian gate opening inwards and someone coming through. Oh, great, fresh reinforcements. So he turned the horse quickly towards the narrow passageway and yelled "Hold the gate!" He leant forward and down along the top of the horse and let go of the shovel. He held the horse around her neck and kicked onwards despite the poor animal already continuing as best it could. The lintel of the doorframe brushed along Spen's back painfully, but they were out, and still alive. What relief. The nanny in the road walking her two charges was somewhat surprised to see a man on horseback coming out of the gate marked 'Workers Entrance.' Spen went to dough his hat to her as he said, "Good day madam," but his hat was gone, lost in the melee.

Once out, he suddenly realised that his lip was throbbing. As he touched it he could tell that it was swollen. It stung too. For some reason John suddenly came to mind with 'Doctor, my lip hurts when I touch it. John would say. 'Well stop touching it then.' He smiled as he thought, but smiling only caused the lip to sting again.

As he walked the horse back home along the road out of Falkirk he 'took stock.' He realised that the medical training had taught him to appraise situations; firstly, to bring to mind all that he had learnt from the event, then to consider what that meant, and perhaps what the consequences of his future actions might be. Firstly, though Perkins hadn't confirmed or denied that the wood was coming from the Forbes estate, he considered it a safe bet, that it was. Spen had only brought a message from the estate manager and hadn't mentioned Richardson-Eames by name, yet Perkins obviously knew who he was dealing with. In fact 'Ponsonby-Smallpiece' seemed somehow appropriate, amusing even. Therefore, secondly, Charles was obviously the orchestrator of the deceit; Everything else seemed to pale into insignificance after those two facts. Though, the third fact that Perkins didn't have a sawmill was a bit of a surprise. He must be just a simple dealer, a merchant, not just a dealer in wood, but in coal and lime too. He wondered what else he might be dealing in.

And those two ruffians in the yard, the ones he thought he recognised; well, they certainly looked like they knew him. He was sure he'd seen them attacking that young girl, trying to abduct her on the late night in Edinburgh. It was very dark back then though, so he couldn't be sure. Why would they do that? Ha, unless Perkins was dealing in people too. No, that was just too ridiculous a thought to be taken seriously. But *someone* must be supplying fresh corpses, and it was quietly accepted by everyone that they couldn't all be legitimate. Was Perkins the type to do that? Hmm, most certainly he was. And might his staff be complicit, if that was so? Yes, absolutely, they all seemed to be very loyal to him back in the yard, and as rough as a badger's rear end.

But this surely was Spen allowing his mind to run wild and free. He was making ridiculous assumptions. But then he remembered the evening with Professor Davies, after that long walk to track him down. Davies had told them of his suspicions that many of the corpses were 'illegally sourced,' he'd told them that women's bodies get a higher price. And corpses of more than a few days old were worthless as everyone was repelled by the stink. He'd mentioned how Rotuida had to give a whole audience their money back once because of it. He only made that mistake once. And how could he be selling tickets for next weekend's dissection, and the weekend after that, and even the weekend after that? How could he guarantee to have corpses available? Surely it was impossible to have such a regular supply.

Well, it was a girl those two men were trying to abduct that night in the city. And they hadn't coshed her to keep her quiet, no they were trying to take her alive, and undamaged. Alive so that she'd keep longer, fresher perhaps? Spen shuddered at the thought. But undeniably, he now knew that those two men (the abductors), worked for Perkins.

He tried to put the thoughts out of his mind as they were just fantasy. But Mary-Ann, she was a woman too, of that there was no doubt. Yes, the dissection theatre was full – of men, that morning. No problem selling tickets there. Davies' reasoning made sense, Spen knew it from first-hand experience. His mind was abuzz with criminal possibilities.

Spen mounted the horse again and sat up straight, his rear end was really aching now, though not throbbing quite as much as his lip was. He felt it again, there was some dried blood and a lot of swelling. "Cold compress," he said out loud. But it was one thing to know what the treatment for an ailment was, and quite another having it to hand. He looked straight ahead and tried to block out the pain from his backside and his mouth.

A picture came into his mind, it was of the barred window to the room at the end of the yard's offices. Why would anyone need to protect the contents of a room from a yard which was itself already fenced off? Maybe that was where Perkins kept all his money? But wouldn't it be safer at home under a mattress? At least there it would be out of the way of the untrustworthy bargees. Perhaps the bars weren't for blocking entry, so much as preventing exit? Spen didn't dare let himself think of the obvious use to which such a prison cell might be put.

Chapter 12 – An Unfortunate Event

Spen was the last man back to the room at 2A and John and Andrew were talking in heated tones about whether women should be allowed to take a degree in medicine. Or a degree in anything for that matter. Andrew's strong Christian influences led him to believe that a woman's place was in the home. God had made women with certain softer body parts which He obviously intended were to form them into home makers, breeders of families, bringers up of Children. It was obvious. There was no point in displacing a man from the course only for her to become qualified, then meet the man of her dreams, marry and settle down to have a family. Never actually practicing as a doctor. In doing so, he said that she would merely waste all that learning. Sure, women had a place in medicine, in nursing certainly, in midwifery probably, but as physicians, probably not.

Unsurprisingly, John took the polar opposite view. He said that women had as much right to a degree (in anything) as the next man (woman), and there was nothing fundamentally different about lady doctors to men doctors. Well, the doctoring part of them anyway. All this tosh about women looking at naked men's bodies and swooning, was simply chauvinism gone mad. Why didn't men doctors lose all control of their passions when they looking upon a naked female patient in the same manner? "Spen, what do you think?"

At the time he was busy unpacking his case but stopped to give the matter some consideration. "I agree," he said. But with whom? He told them if a woman displaced a man from a position on the course, then it was because she was a brighter candidate. If there weren't enough places for all of the candidates who were worthy (despite gender) then that was the fault of the universities. It could hardly be the fault of all womankind. Andrew had to agree. Spen also asked, if women were 'good enough' to be nurses and midwives then what was the sudden mysterious shortcoming holding them back from being a doctor?

Anyway, why were they even considering the argument, women had already been accepted into the universities. It surely would only be a matter of time before they were doing degrees in History or, heaven help us, in Mathematics. It went by the term "progress in action" and that, dear chaps, was an immoveable fact, cast in stone forever. John pointed out to Spen that stone can't be 'cast.'

What had brought the topic up was the undercurrent of disquiet around the seven lady students who had been accepted onto the medical degree course at the university last year (1869) but were being charged higher fees than the male students. This was deemed necessary because they were having to be taught separately to the men. But Spen and John couldn't understand why they were having to be taught in separate lessons, why couldn't they just join the men's lectures and tutorials? Andrew couldn't offer an answer either and he was fed up arguing over the point. John said that was because he knew he had a week argument.

* * *

A few mornings later a note was left in Room 32's letterbox in the entrance hall. It was sealed in a light brown coloured vellum envelope and looked rather upper crust. 'Dr. S. Robinson' it said rather grandly on the front. Spen opened it as his two friends (rather rudely) looked over his shoulder and read the short note. "Oh," he said, "it's an offer of more work, they want me to drug some poor unsuspecting female so they can have some more fun."

"And that's a problem Spencely? Look at the amount they're offering you to do it. Ten quid!" said John. When Spen told them that he wouldn't be taking the job and they could find themselves another desperately poor unwitting student to fulfil the post, John immediately said he'd do it. "What!" said Andrew "weren't you the one who was arguing that women were the equal of men and should be treated as such?"

"Yeah, but ten quid was ten quid!" Perhaps John's father's money hadn't made it all the way down from Shetland so early in the term and he was struggling for money. He would need to borrow the mask and dropper bottle from Spen in order to do the job. Yes, the one which they'd not gone thirds on, the one which Spen had bought with his own money. John said he would make it up to him somehow.

So, reluctantly, despite the fact that John had never drugged anyone to sleep before with Chloroform, he wrote back to Messrs Laggan and Lubnaig at their bank and told them that, although he himself was unavailable he would be sending someone in his stead. Much coaching went on in their room on the delicacies of applying Chloroform, though Andrew continually refused to be put to sleep by John or Spen.

By the time the evening of the event came, John looked to be the consummate professional; handling the bottle in the one hand and deftly lifting the stopper between his first two fingers to allow just enough of the clear pleasant-smelling liquid out in a trickle or dropping flow. His other hand held the mask, with the little finger hooked under the chin as he'd been shown. He practiced watching the chest rise and fall, as it rose the mask went down onto the victim's, sorry, he meant the patient's face. As the chest fell, he lifted off the mask to allow expelled air out through the gap rather than back through the mask again. Spen had told him that he should go in the finest clothes he had, and he was to maintain a bearing of professional confidence, and not get flustered. Oh, and don't have too much to drink, as it will be free.

When the night came Andrew and Spen insisted on waiting across the road in the Tattershall Castle again. Although John said that he didn't need such close support, they'd told him that they were there for the support of the patient, not the doctor.

Spen and Andrew were being pressured to buy more drink as they sat there in the window seat. The barman said that they weren't there to sip like genteel old ladies taking up time in the best seats in the house. They reluctantly asked for two more halves.

John was taking his time across the road; it was at least half an hour past when they expected him to re-appear. Then, as Andrew glanced out the window and across to the Wellesley a young gentleman in servant's garb came out speedily, skipped down the steps and ran off. No-one chased him. Andrew asked Spen if he thought John might have forgotten that they were there waiting for him and had slipped out the back of the building un-noticed and gone home. He was probably asleep in bed by then and they were there, as promised, politely waiting and sipping beer which they didn't want. They watched a hansom cab trot by, but it didn't stop. They agreed to give it another ten minutes but couldn't agree what they should do when the ten minutes were up.

Reluctantly they quaffed the last half inch of warm beer in their tankards and stood up to leave. Spen wobbled a little as he did so. They were the last but two to leave, and the barman said to them to please call again when they'd got less time, but they thought he was just being snidey. They stood there outside the 'Castle for a moment giving the Wellesley one last lingering look, hoping that John was alright in there. They heard the clatter of wheels on cobbles, but much slower this time, and no horse's hooves. A small man hurried out of the darkness and walked straight up the steps into the gentlemen's club. He was greeted at the door by a man unseen by Spen and Andrew until that point. He went in. Next a cart came bouncing out of the shadows and into view. One man pulled, another pushed. The puller strode up the steps and had to knock on the door to have it opened, but he wasn't allowed in. Some suited figure inside spoke to him as he stood there looking up. Spen wondered if he harboured some burning jealousy of inequality in his soul. Neither Spen nor Andrew could hear what was being said in the darkened doorway. The man came down the steps again and the door closed. They started the cart moving and one of the men looked across the road towards them. He must have said something quietly to the other man behind him, because he then looked across too. Spen knew they'd been spotted and would need to move on. As they did so they witnessed the two abruptly turn the cart down the side of the large building towards the rear entrance and disappear again into the blackness.

"This doesn't look good," said Andrew in a soft but worried tone. Spen responded with, "An odd time of the day to make a delivery, don't you think Andrew?" As Spen lead the way slowly across the street he answered Andrew's unspoken question, "The cart had a tea chest on it, and by the looks of the way it was bouncing around over those cobbles, it was empty. Maybe they were not delivering, but perhaps collecting instead?"

The awful realisation that something had gone terribly wrong that evening at the Wellesley, dawned on Spen and Andrew. And poor John was there in the thick of it. Spen shuddered to think that the late-night visitation by the men with the handcart was to collect a body in that tea chest. His next obvious question was, 'who was the victim?' Was it the drugged girl, or worse, was it John himself? He dared not share that thought with Andrew, it was obviously his over-active imagination running wild again.

The two of them stood there in the darkness for a moment, saying nothing. Then a figure came out of the Wellesley and bounded down the steps in two leaps and ran across the road towards the Tattershall Castle. He was carrying a Gladstone bag. It could only be John. "Thank the Good Lord for that," murmured Andrew. Spen too breathed a sigh of relief but used the air to whistle their friend and attract his attention to their presence in the shadows. John looked round but didn't see them.

"John!" shouted Andrew, and with that he came trotting towards them.

"Let's move, quickly," he said as he walked straight past them.

"What happened?" asked Andrew though he could see John was upset and wanting to put as much distance between himself and the Wellesley as possible.

As they moved with a walk so hurried that it was nearly a trot, John uttered "She's dead."

Andrew flashed a horrified look at Spen just as they passed a gaslight. "You mean you've killed her?" asked Spen in as calm a way as such a question could be asked. But John stopped.

"No, it wasn't me, I didn't kill her, she was perfectly fine when I left her."

He began to move again but Spen grabbed his sleeve and stopped him. "John, this is serious, you must tell us what happened."

So John stood for a second, collected his thoughts, and began recounting the whole evening. How it had started quite amicably, respectfully even. He told of how he'd spoken to the girl, 'Clara,' a nice girl, though Clara probably wasn't her real name. He'd put her to sleep, and the five gentlemen were quite pleased with him. Then the oldest man, a banker with whiskers, had taken him through into the barroom of the club and given him a very large glass of a silky Speyside malt and talked of the prospect of more work for him. It was going so well, until about twenty minutes later when one of the other four, the youngest one, had burst in and asked for the doctor. I'd actually forgotten that I was a doctor at that moment until the man came charging up and urged me to join him back in their private room again. The poor lassie was white, limp, not breathin', just lying there on the couch with her blouse torn open. I tried blowing on her, I called for fresh air, smelling salts, I shook her, she just had no pulse. "But she was fine when I left her, I promise you."

Andrew made a good point when he thoughtfully asked, "Where was your bag all the time you were being *entertained* in the bar?" John struggled to remember the details but eventually explained that it must have been in the room with the girl, as he definitely hadn't taken it to the bar. At that moment Spen bent down to the bag and took it off his friend. He crossed the street into the loom of a gas lamp, put it down on the pavement and opened it. He reached in but couldn't find the Chloroform. There were only two bottles, and both were nearly empty. He pulled them out one at once and held them up to the light. The first one was dark and looked black in the dull glow. It was the iodine. But the other had clear liquid and it had Chloroform etched on the glass, sure enough it smelt heavily of chloroform too. There was barely an inch left. "Heavens above John, how much did you give her?" asked Andrew. But John snatched the bottle from Spen's hand and held it up in disbelief. "Hell's teeth, not *that* much."

But before they could work out what had happened, Spen said that he wanted to do something. He realised that the men with the hand cart and the tea chest obviously had been called to come and collect the body from the Wellesley club. They would need to take it away to somewhere and Spen wanted to know where. "You can do what you like, I'm going home," said a frightened John. But when Andrew pointed out that they'd probably be heading for the canal basins and Spen would need support. John reluctantly agreed to go with them. After all, they'd waited all evening for him.

They hurried back towards The Wellesley just in time to catch sight of the two men manhandling the cart down the side of the building and out into the street. From the way they were pushing it, the load on the cart definitely looked a little heavier than it had done earlier. The three young men followed at a discrete distance and dodged between the shadows in an attempt to avoid being noticed. But the journey wasn't as lengthy as any of them were expecting in the end. Although initially they seemed to be heading for the canal, they turned off and headed across to Graham Street. "Yes, that made sense. It was that assistant fellow who the old men had sent for when the situation had turned sour," John told them. Hadn't he mentioned that bit? Ah, that would be the young man racing out of the Wellesley and off into the night; the one who looked like he was being chased but wasn't. And, therefore, the first man back into the Club was that chap, 'The Assistant,' the one who'd helped Professor Davies. What was his name, it sounded Greek?

Andrew closed his eyes, recalled from the deepest recesses of his mind and spoke slowly..." Voithos Rotuida or similar."

"Yeah, he wanted five pounds off us as a fee."

That's not bad thought Andrew, until it became obvious that it was five pounds off each of them. "Thirty pounds!" he exclaimed and was immediately 'shushed' by the other two.

"Only twenty-five actually," said John, "I paid the man nothing."

"And they were happy with that?" asked Andrew.

"Not really, though the posh gents were fine with it when the 'Assistant' told us all that as I'd decided not to pay, he would make sure the blame for the girl's death was laid at my door." So, suddenly, the three of them were all in bother. Deep bother.

They followed the cart at a distance through the narrow Herriot Place passageway then left into Keir Street and along to its junction into Graham Street. There, they witnessed it going down the side of the grand house. It followed the same route which they themselves had taken when they had gone to help Cameron with the leg amputation. That's what the hand cart was there for. Yes, and the tea-chests; they were nothing to do with disposing of household waste but were for shifting and storing bodies. It all became clearer when they thought more darkly. Hence the barrels of formaldehyde too. What a grand business, The Assistant was being paid to remove bodies and then being paid again to supply those same bodies to the University. Or charging students to view whilst being cut open in a dissection. Even the parts were sold as a side-line. "That's how he can afford a house like that one," said Spen looking across the street to the grand Georgian building taking up most of the West corner.

John was a bag of nerves on the walk back to the boarding house, he desperately wanted to sleep, but was shaking with fear over the prospect of him being accused of murder, and moreover, not being able to prove himself innocent. Worst of all, he may not even *be* innocent. He could have murdered the lovely Clara and would spend the rest of his life at the end of a rope in some prison yard.

In the morning they were nearly at the point of going to the nearest police station and pre-empting the police coming knocking on the door of room 32 at No. 2A Candlemakers Row. They played the various parts of the imaginary interview. Andrew went first, "Mr. MacFarlane, you say that you have murdered a young Lady, who's name is …?" he didn't really know. "…and why did you murder said unknown victim?" He didn't mean to, it was a mistake, but was asked to do so and was even paid to do so by five men who stood there and watched him do it, unwittingly." And when we interview these witnesses, if we can find them, will they be able to corroborate your story?" No. "Where is the body now sir?"
He wasn't sure but suspected it to be "Inside a big house in Graham Street."
"'avin' been transported there in a tea chest on a 'and cart by persons hunknown and himpossible to find hor hidentify," added Spen for good measure. Did they honestly think it would still be there when the police went to search the building?
Andrew joined the levity with, "Oh yes sir, we find lots of unknown young ladies being murdered but only in the more salubrious parts of the city, by rich old gentlemen, who do it all the time simply for their own entertainment. Oh yes, they come in here every week wanting us to lock 'em up and throw away the key sir." Andrew's voice had started to sound like that of a music hall comedian. John had to admit, the officer would laugh him back out onto the street, should he walk into a police station and try and accuse five of the city's leading lights with such an implausible story.

They went to their lessons instead.

Chapter 13 – His Real Father?

Spen showed up at the time and place which he and Mr. Smith had agreed to meet before the summer break. Spen had told him clearly that he was going back to stay with his mother for the five weeks of the holiday and wouldn't be able to meet him during that time. Maybe Smith had forgotten what he'd said, maybe he'd been over to the pub where they'd met, a couple of times and because Spen wasn't there to meet him had given up on his free beer and food evenings. If the spoilt young social philosopher with his fancy clothes didn't want to waste his money further, then so be it. Spen hoped not, but it didn't look like he was going to turn up this time.

As Spen had the evening to himself he thought he might take a walk down to the canal basin and seek out the stable where Smith worked. All was quiet, the day's work complete, everyone relaxing, or in the pubs, or as one chap was doing, just fishing on the canal-side. Spen Strolled up and greeted him with a casual "Fine evening." The man was quite friendly in his response and he and Spen passed a few moments of small-talk before he ventured the question "Do you know if there's a stable here-abouts to keep the barge horses safe overnight?"
"Aye, ya mean Robson's stable. The man continued talking in half words which he formed quite badly but he pointed and flapped his arms about as he spoke. Spen got the impression that the yard was further along, on the north bank, which became the west bank as the canal turned Northwards at the Lochrin branch. He thought that was what the fisherman had said, though he couldn't be too sure. But he'd called it Robson's stable. He was looking for a stable where Mr. Smith worked. Perhaps Smith worked for Robson. Maybe it was a different stable. Or had he called it Robson's stable because that's how he knew the man whom Spen knew as Smith? Spen knew that his prospective father used a number of aliases after all. And another possibility, one which would fit very nicely with Spen's theories was that the fisherman hadn't even said Robson, but Robinson. His diction was indeed very poor. That

would add weight to Spen's theory that Smith truly was his father. Of course, another much simpler explanation was that his name was Robson Smith. That might be the simplest explanation. Occam's razor after all. Then Spen's clinical mind reminded him that Occam's razor was not about the most likely explanation, but about the one making fewest assumptions. And assuming that he had referred to the stable as Robinson's was a very large assumption indeed. He decided he take a stroll and see for himself.

He crossed over at the footbridge and went along the cindered towpath. Soon he spotted an old wooden shed down to the left with the world's smallest field next to it. Just a patch of grass really. But a horse was standing there watching him. From the shed came the noise of a horse whinnying. This had to be the place. Spen walked down a short bank away from the canal, then up to the front of the building. It had a half height door typical of stables. He looked in. Two horses looked back at him from their individual stables. Another one on the opposite side just stood there unimpressed by his sudden appearance. In the quiet Spen could hear someone steadily brushing an animal's coat. "Mr. Smith?" Spen said softly. The brushing stopped and a pair of eyes appeared through the gloom from behind the far horse. "Ye found me then..." said Smith. When Spen replied with, "You're working late," Smith simply told him that he wasn't working, just being with his friends.

Spen had found the man again, the one who he was convinced was his father, but suddenly he felt bereft of conversation. Maybe it was the stable that did that to people. Maybe, it was just time to come clean. "May we talk, Mister Smith?" Smith slowly came out of the stall and shut the half gate gently behind him "I thought we were doing," he said. Spen turned to go outside again, and Mr. Smith followed him into the light. "Robson's Stable they said."
   "Like I said, I go by a number of names, it's easier that way."
   "But why 'Robson' Mister Smith?" asked Spen in a soft tone to match the moment.
   "Robinson, it's a name I used to go by once. I was happy then." Spen was happy that his theorizing was turning out to be true. But not so happy that his father had reached such a low point and didn't seem to have much of a life.

"Mister Smith, I've asked you about your life and you have been good enough to share much about it. But you haven't asked me about mine sir."

"Well, you're a gentleman sir, you would consider it an impertinence if I were to ask you about your life…"

So Spen launched into his next sentence and watched Smith's expression closely. "I was born in eighteen forty-nine on the Stannet-Forbes Estate to a wonderful mother called Dorothy." Spen was expecting a reaction from Smith at that point, but none came. He just stared straight ahead, though Spen strongly suspected that the older man had gone deep within himself. Spen continued, "My father left before I was born, and I was brought up by my mother." He stopped again to see if Smith would have any input, perhaps some questions. Eventually, it came.

"How is your mother boy?"

"Dorothy sir, she's well, thank you."

"That's good, that's good …married again?"

"No sir, always single, ever since you left"

"It must have been tough for her." But Spen ignored the statement, he needed his father to justify his terrible action.

"Father, why did you leave?" At this Smith stopped staring blankly ahead and turned to look at Spen. "I believe you left even before I was born, you never even held me in your arms." Spen had decided he no longer wanted to use the respectful term 'sir' at the end of his sentence. But what came next, he could never have foreseen.

"I was Adam, living in the Garden of Eden. A true paradise. We had enough to eat, enough to share. We lived in paradise itself. The only thing we didn't have was a child. We didn't have you." All manner of thoughts flooded into Spen's mind about pulling the family back together again and trying to remake that garden of paradise, but he was cut off by Smith's account. "We tried for years, five years, from the moment the ring was on her finger. We knew that she'd have to give up her job as governess, but we would have gone through the fires of hades itself to have our own child." A tear had started to form. "I can't be your father young sir."

But Spen started clutching at straws; "It just takes time; some folks get pregnant only after years and years of trying."

"My second wife Mable, she never had children either, well, none fathered by me leastways." That was another big revelation and one which rather seemed to prove his point that Smith truly couldn't be Spen's father.

"She already had children when you married her sir? Perhaps she didn't want any more..."

"Oh no, she would have had the full regiment, loved kids did Mable. I heard she had another two by her third husband."

Well, that would seem to bring Spen's theorising to a dead end. The two strolled back along the canal towpath a little as Smith, funny how Spen still thought of the man as Smith, told him that he had spent the last twenty one years regretting his decision to leave his mother. When Dorothy became pregnant he knew that the baby had been fathered by someone else, probably by someone in the big house, or at least someone on the estate. The Laird was the obvious choice, though he always seemed to Spen to be a gentleman who was much too honourable to have had an extramarital affair. He was also in love with Lady Sarah. Perhaps his father might be Matt Carter, he hadn't always been the estate manager. After all, he'd been the only man to ever give him a hug, had even called him 'son' once.

Mr. Bateman, another single man with influence. Now Bateman had always looked upon Spen with favour, like a son almost. Could it be him? Or perhaps it was just a passionate fling with one of the footmen or grooms, gardeners. Perhaps it wasn't even consental, perhaps his mother was raped. Heaven forbid that that should have happened. Perhaps Dorothy had engineered the pregnancy hoping that her husband would think the child was his and bring it up as his own. Spen felt weepy. As they sat together on a log Smith put his arm affectionately round Spen's shoulder and said gently. "Sorry son, but I'm ney your father."

That was it then. Spen was a little sorry that Smith wasn't his real father. He seemed to have grown used to the idea since that first meeting in the hypnosis lecture by Doctor Choudhury. Spen reached into his pocket to hand Smith some cash, but Smith waved it away. "Let me buy you a meal then, and a beer," he said nodding his head towards a hostelry.

A man carrying a rod and a wicker basket walked past them on the towpath. "Ye found him then eh?" It was the man who was fishing earlier.

They sat outside at a bench table and had a grand plate of stew and dumplings with neaps and tatties, plus a very large tankard of ale. They both felt it was a bit of a last supper together. Unsurprisingly, conversation was a little stilted after the earlier life changing revelations. Perhaps Spen should just have given him money and left earlier.

For something to say Spen asked Smith about the business on the canal but again got little by way of conversation. Smith seemed hungry, he'd probably not eaten all day. It was obvious to Spen that Smith found himself unable to stay with an unfaithful wife all those years ago, and Spen wondered what he would have done in Smith's shoes.

Across the other side of the canal, though much further along, a small horse drawn cart rolled up and the two men on it jumped down. They walked onto a small jetty which barely made it two yards out past the bulrushes and into the canal proper. Smith turned round to see what had caught Spen's eye. "One off, one on," he said as he forced in another large forkful of dumplings and swede. Spen looked questioningly at him. "You'll see," he said looking over his shoulder again. "...here it comes." Sure enough, there was a horse in the distance plodding towards them, and at the other end of its long rope was a narrowboat set well down in the water. Spen thought that it was an unusual place to discharge or load cargo, though isolated jetties were not unknown; generally it happened at farms or villages, or major road crossings. This place looked like it had been chosen because it was quiet, yes, quiet was indeed the word. Spen was intrigued to see the two men skilfully lift the barrel off the small cart using a glorified stretcher; a lifting frame with a pair of handles at each side. They carried it out to a point just short of the base of the little landing. Spen thought it a bit odd that a barrel shouldn't be rolled along, well, like a barrel, but he suspected that if the lid didn't fit very well then it would need to be kept upright or else lose all its contents through seepage.

Smith had obviously finished his ale and was sat waiting patiently for

Spen to offer him another. He caught the bar tender's eye as he collected glasses in the last of the evening sun. Spen didn't want another as he still had a half left. He must have been too engrossed in the canal goings-on to concentrate on eating and drinking. But he did want to stay at least long enough to see this barge collect its cargo of one barrel.

As the narrowboat neared the small jetty the men heaved up the barrel in its frame and slowly walked it to the end. They'd obviously timed their walk to reach the end of the jetty just as the boat was in a position for them to keep walking straight onto it. Spen couldn't see what happened next but within thirty seconds the same two men, with what looked like the same barrel came staggering back off the boat and along the jetty towards the cart. This second barrel looked heavy too.

Spen initially thought one must be full and the other empty, but by the way the two men were heaving, they were both full. "Hmmm, obviously the wrong sort of brandy," said Spen whimsically, but he noticed Smith was watching the horse, not the men.
"Not really," he said, "ya wouldnay want to drink what was in those barrels," he said without even looking up.

Spen glanced back down the canal to see the two men look to each other, then both bob down to get their shoulders under the handles of the frame. Together they heaved upwards to lift it high, then staggered either side of the cart to land the barrel solidly on it. The horse took up the slack and the boat continued its way towards them and into Edinburgh's rough quarter. The men with the cart and barrel also came towards them on the opposite bank but turned off before reaching them. They too were headed towards the city, but the rather more salubrious part.

Then, much to Spen's surprise, Smith ventured a little more information. "McLoughlin reckons he heard someone say it was an illicit trade in somethin' very odd. He couldn't imagine who on earth would want to buy whatever was in those barrels."
"McLoughlin?" prompted Spen.
"Aye ya man fishin' earlier, sits on the bank all day drownin' worrams, see's everythin'." The barman put another tankard of ale in front of

Smith, and he took a long swig. Spen hoped that by not saying anything he might elucidate a little more. He did: "Ah think he talks tosh but Mac reckons that one barrel regularly goes to Glasgow and another regularly comes back to Edinburgh."

"Why on earth would he think such a thing?" It did seem like and awful waste of energy and resources. Spen tried hard to imagine what Glasgow might produce that Edinburgh needed, and a similar commodity that Edinburgh had which Glasgow wanted so much?

"Mac reckons he met a man once who claims he was going to have a peep in one of the barrels late one night, just in case it *was* brandy. But he didn't know what he'd found because he'd never seen him alive again after that night. Fol'win' week got a stoved-in heed." Smith and McLaughlin sure seemed to mix with some rough types.

Smith shovelled in his last mouthful, swigged his last and stood up abruptly. "Thank you very much, for your fine and gracious hospitality Mister Robinson, I'm sorry to be the bearer of bad news, but I'm not your father, though I can tell you that I wish you were my son. Ah don't suppose I'll be seeing ye again." And he held his hand out across the table. "Please give Dot my best, tell her I'm sorry for all the hurt I caused her. Perhaps tell her I'm deed or been gone te Australia or somethin' like that." Spen had no intention of lying to his mother but could see why Smith couldn't bring himself to try again and rake up the past. Perfection could never be regained; it was a paradise he'd given up. They shook hands.

Chapter 14 – Riot and Bankruptcy

Spen had lost interest in talking to Mr. Smith, not because he no longer wanted to talk about his past, he did, but because he found his present crowding in a little. There were to be examinations in November and every one of them must be passed. So once more the three room-mates knuckled down to serious study and hence committed themselves to drinking and frolicking a lot less. They'd randomly ask questions of each other like 'where does the Hemi-Azygos vein go from and to? Then they'd compete to find the answer the quickest, though that race was often won by the person who happened to be nearest to Gray's Anatomy. Where was the Fossa Ovalis? That was an easy one, it was in the heart, between the two Atria in the Atrial Septum. But what caused it to close, and at what age, and how many adults still had it patent? None of them had seen an actual hole in the heart on the anatomy slab and they made a mental note to look out for one next time they had a heart in front of them. Providing of course that they were allowed to slice into it. Did cows and sheep have a Fossa Ovalis too? They presumed so, but not even 'Grays' would tell them that.

It seemed that each week they would hear a story of some-one else leaving the medicine course. Simply not being able to cope was never one of the reasons actually mentioned, but they suspected it happened quite often. Other reasons also abounded; illness was a popular one, but family bereavement leading to a lack of financial support also figured. Spen wondered if the day would ever come when bright children, though from poor families, could ever hope to qualify as a doctor. He sincerely hoped so, but that day looked to be a long way off. It all made him think about his own situation. Who *was* paying for his training? He'd quietly held the assumption for a long time, that his father who'd left home before he was born, had possibly been transported to Australia and perhaps somehow made a fortune there in the gold rush. He'd assumed that he was anonymously supporting his son as some sort of recompense for leaving. But Mr. Smith had never made a fortune. It certainly wasn't him who had been supporting him, of that he was convinced.

Spencely often wrote to his mother about the course and his friends and the professors and the funny things that happened to them at the social events which they attended. Though he never mentioned anything about Mr. Smith and the long talks which they'd. Smith didn't seem to want to meet Dorothy again, and from what he knew she had no burning ambition to rekindle and re-float her emotional shipwreck with him. So he just didn't tell her. He'd also left off any information regarding Mary-Ann's murder and the whole train of intrigue that had followed in the wake of that.

He also thought it best not to tell his mother about one of his dear friends, with whom he shared a room, having possibly though inadvertently murdered a poor unsuspecting young woman. She probably wouldn't understand. After all, young men away at university get up to all sorts of things and it's generally nothing to worry about.

But he told Emily everything. She was interested in Spen's life. Every aspect of it, and for all her high breeding and rich status she was actually very jealous. The best she could ever hope for was to join him one day in Edinburgh society and meet his new friends. Surprisingly, she wasn't too interested in hearing about the famous Edinburgh Seven; the seven young ladies who were going to be the first in Britain to qualify as doctors. No, she just wanted him to be happy in his chosen career and for her to be by his side.

He told her about Mr. Smith, how he'd met him as an object of study in a Hypnosis lecture and how he had discovered that the man had been his mother's husband once, though not his own father. He implored Emily not to mention that bit to his mother. He even shared with her more details of the Perkins woodyard and what he'd said to her father on his last visit home. Because he knew there was no love lost between herself and her brother-in-law Charles Richardson-Eames, he felt he could tell her how he knew that Charles was cheating her father. Indeed, cheating the whole family, by selling wood to Perkins and pocketing the money. He may have inferred that Perkins was also involved in other underhand dealings, but he had no proof as yet. He knew that as he explained these things to Emily then the very notion of explaining them out loud might clarify the truth, or at least perhaps reveal the next step he should pursue in his investigations.

Emily's letters by return sounded a little boring at the side of his. Spen's stories of murderous intrigue on the one hand and saving lives on the other, made her latest book or the health of her parlourmaid sound very tame. However, the one repeated topic was most definitely her concern over her father's health. Sir William had taken to his bed through ill health more than once since the summer. He would always brush off her and Catherine's pleas for more information about his complaint, and about what they might do for his benefit. He told them that simply seeing their smiling faces was all the tonic he needed. Though she knew deep down that he obviously needed something a lot more efficacious. Sometimes he wondered around the house like a sunken-eyed ghost, looking very pale and wan. He didn't seem to sleep very well either. Visitors had stopped coming to the house and she thought Lady Sarah was missing her social life as Father no longer had the energy for it.

Spen knew better than to attempt a diagnosis on the skimpiest of evidence coming via a letter, but that didn't stop him from doing it anyway. His first thought was of the pale face and the vacant ghostly demeanour. He was probably taking opium; therefore, he must be in pain. But no outward signs of injury, probably internal then. He wasn't limping and didn't have a fever. This made Spen lean heavily towards cancer. Ah yes, that took him back to the summer, in the library. He'd had a coughing fit and brought up blood. Then he'd surreptitiously palmed the kerchief to Bateman who had done the honourable thing and hidden it without mention or attention. Lung Cancer then? Of course there could be other ailments giving similar symptoms and requiring similar medication. But Spen would have to guess, if pushed; 'Lung Cancer.' Oh dear, he felt for his life-long role-model, his guiding light, his mentor.

He wondered how long Sir William might have, six months perhaps, but that was a real guess in the dark. There was no cure. But then Spen's thoughts naturally gravitated towards the Stannet-Forbes Estate and what would happen to it and all the staff once the Earl was dead. Undoubtedly it would be left to the girls and therefore Mr. Richardson Eames would have absolute control, as Mary was the eldest and the only one to be married. Maybe Emily would want to get off the Estate once it was being run by the horrible Charles. But what of Lady Sarah, and how would Lady Catherine cope? Charles would certainly prevent her from seeing her dear-heart Lottie. Maybe she would run away too. Then Charles would be left with the big prize all to himself. Oh dear indeed, Spen slumped down on the wooden seat by the microscope as he read the letter. Charles had won. Lady Sarah would doubtless not live much longer after her husband, and Charles would probably make her life a misery in her final years.

"Chin up Buddy, it can't be that bad," said the ever-cheerful Andrew. But it could be, and it was. Maybe not yet, but it was coming. The end was nigh. At least Spen realised he had his training and would be a doctor. He could look after Emily and her mother, perhaps even Lady Catherine at a push. But he couldn't see anything good coming from the letter he had just read.

The next letter from Emily Spen even dreaded to open. After the usual lovey dovey, girly beginning, yes yes, I love you too Emily, please get on with it; she'd heard Father and Charles arguing in the 'Morning Room. That in itself wasn't too unusual these days, but what was surprising was what Mr. Bateman had done. Although he hadn't been summoned, he hurried through the dining room (where they were seated) and just barged straight into the 'Morning Room without a knock or a 'bye your leave.' She thought Bateman just wanted to make Charles aware that he had witnessed him being rude and disrespectful to the Laird. A very large sin in Mr. Bateman's book. 'Oh,' thought Spen as he read that part, 'that was the end of poor Mr. Bateman's career as soon as Sir William died.

The whole issue of The Stannet-Forbes Estate being turned upside down rather pervaded his next month or two's studies. But he tried hard to put it out of his mind and concentrate on the job in hand. They also had no time to pursue their investigations into the undercover dealings in bodies and body parts, and its possible connections to murderers and abductors.

But time and tide wait for no man, or woman, as it turned out, and November the eighteenth, Eighteen Seventy arrived with plenty of warning but an insufficiency of preparation. The Anatomy exam would be in the Surgeons' Hall at ten AM. And would last two and a half hours. All first- and second-year students must attend.

John seemed to have a bit of an inkling about what might happen on that day. He told Spen and Andrew of the ill feeling that had been brewing towards the seven women on the medical course. He strongly suspected that it was being stoked by some members of the medical school staff themselves, but he couldn't explain why. Was it chauvinism or just mere tradition? The situation wasn't helped when Spen pointed out that *tradition* was simply another term for 'peer pressure from dead people.' John laughed.

The area on Southbridge in front of the Surgeon's Hall was very busy indeed. There was a lot of noise too, from what seemed to be hundreds of onlookers. There could be no more than a hundred and twenty medical students, so who were all the rest? Many were obviously students but not on the medicine course, perhaps history, or law. A large portion of the crowd were hurling abuse, a smaller number were hurling actual mud and even rotten veg. Unfortunately, there had been much horse drawn traffic along Southbridge too that day and the usual evidence left by the horses was also being flung. It was aimed at a small party slightly behind them. They were in black with their heads down. They were also heading for the entry gate, hurrying as best they could through a crowd that somehow didn't want to let them through. Sure enough, it was the ladies' group of medical students.

Spen and John got to within a few feet of the entrance gate but the crowd there seemed to have stopped moving altogether. The ladies were gaining on them from behind and they too were starting to catch small missiles of rubbish and horse dung on them. Not as much as the poor women had received though, for they were now well anointed. Spen was utterly ashamed of his fellow students who he judged to be acting in a totally unacceptable manner. Even Andrew thought it totally deplorable. He looked over his shoulder and saw the worried face of Miss Edith Pechey. Indeed, she looked a little more than worried. Terrified would be a better description. Sophia Jex-Blake looked up and shouted for 'the gate to be opened if you please.' She wasn't shouting at anyone in particular, but as Spen looked forward again he could see that the gate into the yard had been slammed shut. There were many students already inside the yard so it must have been open only a few moments earlier. Someone had witnessed the group of ladies approaching and had unlatched the open gate and forced it closed. Could this action really be going on at Edinburgh Medical School in eighteen seventy he asked himself?

He'd had enough. He put his arm around the shoulder of John and shouted at him "To the gate". They put down their heads and strained forwards as a pair of fullbacks from Rugby might have done. They forced their way the six feet or so to the black iron railings of the gate. It was already being attended to by a grey coated old man who appeared to be trying to unfasten and open it again. They watched him and as the iron bar lifted from the hasp Spen and John leant heavily against it, forcing it slightly open. One man inside the yard was knocked over and they had to hold position for a moment to prevent trapping his foot under the gate as it swung open. A gracious act thought Spen amid all this unkindness. But the man leapt to his feet and immediately put his shoulder against the gate again to try and force it closed. His cheek was pressed against the bars not six inches from Spen's head. He wondered if he could punch the man through the gate without breaking his fist on an iron bar as he did so, so went for the lesser option of poking him in the eye with his knuckle instead. It had the desired effect and the resistance reduced in an instance.

Once the gate was open a torrent of bodies came through. Spen and Andrew were surprised just how many were there for the exam, and who actually wanted to be inside the Hall. Things calmed a little after that. Once away from the crowd something rather nearer the quiet reverence of an exam room was regained. They were a little late in starting, but not ten minutes into the exam proper there was a rattle of a doorknob behind them then the sound of excited voices again. Spen looked across the room to the group of women sat together. He saw the young Edith slump her head down so low that it very nearly rested on the exam paper. She looked exhausted. Spen felt for her, for all seven of them. Why did so many people not want these seven human beings to have the same opportunities that they themselves were enjoying? It was selfish intolerance gone mad.

Sure enough, laughter was followed by lots of chattering, even by some of the students who were taking the exam. Then the noise of one or two chair legs being forced back over the floor as some rose to their feet. Spen could hardly believe his eyes, but an adult sheep was trotting up between the lines of desks. Two of the cloaked masters were trying to urge and guide it back the way it had come. The poor thing looked frightened stiff. Almost in confirmation of its fear the sheep defecated on the parquet flooring. More laughter emanated from the back door into the hall. Spen looked about him and noticed that a number of students sitting the exam were grinning too. Spen was still disgusted and ashamed, not at the sheep, but at his fellow students who could orchestrate such a riot.

Sanity was returned as the sheep was herded (if it's possible to herd a single sheep) back the way it had come. Once more heads bowed in concentration. Before Spen had chance to finish the last question to his satisfaction the large wall clock ticked onto twelve forty-three and an invigilator shouted to 'stop writing.' Spen sat back in his chair and wondered what tomfoolery might await them on the trip home. Spen and Andrew started drifting across the hall as everyone milled about aimlessly after the exam. More talk was about what would happen next than about exam questions on anatomy.

He headed for Edith as she seemed to be the most approachable of the women's group. He asked her "May I, and my friends, join you on your walk out Miss?" Edith smiled with gratitude, at least it wasn't the *whole* world who were against them. But before she could give a response an Irish voice spoke from behind him saying, "That won't be necessary, thanks Robinson, we've got this." A dozen or so, mainly Irish students had formed an ad hoc band of vigilantes ready to protect the seven ladies on their way back to their lodgings.

In the following days the Irishmen were as good as their word and were apparently escorting the ladies to and from classes every day, whether they wanted it or not.

Spen wrote at length to both Emily and his mother about how the world was changing, and at such a speed. He hoped that one day, if he had daughters of his own, that they would have the same opportunities as his sons (if he had sons). Emily didn't so much read the bit about new opportunities as the world changed, just the bit that said Spen wanting daughters and sons one day. Spen's mother read his letter and simply worried about the prospects of her son being injured in some brutal city riot.

* * *

After one of the lectures a chap approached Spencely head on and asked if he might have a word. He knew the man as another student, probably a year above him, but on the Law course rather than Medicine. They walked around the magnificent columned square inside the Stone built Old College and the young man asked him if he knew anyone called Richardson-Eames? "Yes, he's my dear friend's brother-in-law," replied Spen innocently. At this Spen noticed the man's eyes widen slightly. "Why did you want to know?" But instead of answering he simply asked how he could find him. He sounded slightly suspicious. What did he know about him? Again, Spen offered the little bit of information that he had on Charles: He was from Surrey as his family had land, or an estate or something down there. But Spen stopped, looked straight at the man whose name was Friedman, and told him that he had no desire to benefit Mr. Richardson-Eames in any way at all.

"In that case, you and I should really talk. Seven tonight, come to my rooms, they're in James Court, above the Jolly Judge, off The High Street, you know; The Mile."

Spen wasn't too enamoured at being given instructions to appear at the lodgings of a fellow student in such a manner, but he decided to go along anyway. He presumed 'The Mile' must refer to the Royal Mile up to the Castle. Folks had been dropping the term 'High Street' lately. An expensive area to lodge, probably the most desirable in all of Edinburgh, if you didn't mind bagpipes and canon shot that is. But then Friedman had also said 'my rooms', plural, as if he had a suite of rooms rather than just one, even one he'd share with two others. Hmm, interesting.

That evening Spen walked up the short but steep climb through Grassmarket and up towards Saint Giles Cathedral. Then up the *Mile* a little until James Court went down to his Right. It certainly didn't look much from the outside but inside it was a different story. Young Mr. Friedman's family obviously had money, not only were his clothes top quality, but his rooms were furnished in some exotic style which Spen imagined to be from Nice or Monaco, not that Spen had ever been there, or was even likely to go. But the place had an air of true quality, an *Ambiance*, didn't they call it? Most unlike anywhere else he knew in Edinburgh. Did it even top Professor Cameron's place? He thought it probably did.

Friedman was happy just to be known as Friedman, none of this first name sissy nonsense. Spen knew the sort, public school, old money, naked cold showers after rugger, probably landed gentry. Though Spen initially had his guard up, he slowly warmed to Friedman. He explained to Spen that he had a friend who had heard him talking at a gathering, perhaps a party, he'd forgotten exactly where, but that was unimportant now. Spen had mentioned how he was somewhat disgruntled with Emily's brother-in-law who was one of the Richardson-Eames clan. "Claims to have land in Surrey, does he? Tell me, have you ever seen it Robinson? Have you ever been there?" Spen had to admit, he hadn't. "And may I ask, do you know anyone who has seen it? Anyone you would trust that is?" This was all very interesting, though a little uncomfortable. Friedman initially made Spen feel like he was in a witness box and was being cross examined, but when he realised the effect this was having on poor Spen, he changed tack, and became less confrontational. Friedman told of his father's firm of lawyers in Guildford, which was in Surrey, having liquidated the estate of the Richardson-Eames family. Spen showed his surprise at the news, but when he heard that this had happened a dozen or more years ago, Spen became flabbergasted.

Of course, all of the information exchange went totally against patient confidentiality, or whatever the lawyer's equivalent was, yes, client confidentiality, that was it. But technically, Old Charles Oscar Richardson-Eames was Friedman's father's client so, what Friedman had to say now about Charles the younger wasn't a transgression, merely gossip, so it was alright. But the bit about his father needing to track down old Charlies' son Charles was really important. So important that Spen could make some useful cash out of the deal. He was now owing a lot of money in Surrey and Friedman senior would be paid again handsomely if he could only track Charles (junior) down and extract the money owing. Old man Richardson-Eames had died a few years ago in a paupers' cottage in a Guildford suburb somewhere. So the debts were down to his son to repay, if only he could be found. Friedman didn't know for sure, but Charles junior had either gambled away, or mis-invested money on the railways and had given his father's estate as surety, so confident was he of his own future success. Even liquidating the estate wasn't enough to cover the debts, and there was still a small fortune left owing.

"So, Charles junior had basically ruined his own father?"

"Correct, but also his mother, sister, and two younger brothers with him." At this point Spen laid his cards on the table and told Friedman about the way he'd never really trusted, or even liked Charles Richardson-Eames. Friedman complimented Spen on being a good judge of character. However, Charles had married the eldest daughter of the fifth Earl of Callander and when the old man died, which, from a medical perspective looked rather imminent, he would probably inherit the lot. To have it all then sequestrated to pay the debts of such a foolish blackguard as Charles Pitiful-Richardson-Eames, seemed all too horrible to contemplate. Spen wondered if his honesty had snookered the future happiness of Lady Sarah and her three daughters. He asked Friedman what he should do to prevent this fate worse than death from happening. "Get Legal advice, probably put the estate into a trust, maybe put the only beneficiaries as the other two daughters and cut Charles' wife out of the deal altogether, but it had to be done before Sir

William's death. And he had to be in full charge of his faculties when he changed his will.

Spen immediately considered the deleterious effect on Sir William's health if he were to be told that his son-in-law was a liar, a cheat and a wastrel. What a mess this was all turning out to be. Should he go back to Falkirk to try and break the news to Sir William as soon as possible or simply write? He certainly couldn't stand by and do nothing. As it was Monday, he decided to write, that would be quicker than waiting until next weekend. The old man might not want to hear the news, but he would have to.

It was late when he got back to his room in Candlemakers Row. He sat down and began writing to Emily. He found that writing to Emily and setting all his facts and thoughts down on paper helped to clarify his mind and order his reasoning. Sure, this letter was going to have to be an epic one: The Surgeon's Hall Riot and now Friedman's revelation over her brother-in-law Charles. Oh, and could he have an urgent meeting with her father this weekend please?

It took him a full ninety minutes to set it all down and when he'd finally got it finished John and Andrew were snoring like tops. He had decided that as well as writing, the proper thing to do was to go back to Falkirk next Friday evening after lessons, he must speak with Sir William again.

On Tuesday, after dinner Spen had a stroll down to the canal basin to clear his mind again. He had a lot going on in his head. As he regularly did, he brought all the things to mind that he was grateful for and happy about. It was a good exercise and usually made him feel better. But it was a bit of a boring exercise too as the things which made him happy were generally the same things which made him happy last time: Family, friends, health, born in a free land, in a time when he wasn't required to go and fight for his queen and country. Enough food in his belly, shelter, warmth. His loved ones weren't in any danger. At least he presumed they were safe.

When he arrived at the stable where Mr. Smith worked there was no-one there, nor any horses. Spen supposed that with no horses to look after then there'd be no point in being at the stable. He swung the half door of the stable open and shouted in. There was no answer. In the gloom he nearly stepped in a large pile of horse droppings. Obviously, Smith hadn't been there for a while. The horse which had left him that particular message had gone too. Spen went back out into the last of the evening light and looked up and down the towpath. A large grey stood a short distance away patiently blocking the towpath and awaiting its next instructions. Instructions which probably wouldn't come until tomorrow. Everywhere was quiet.

"Where's ya man Smithy?" came a surprise question from behind him. Spen swung round quickly to see an old man carrying a large wicker basket and two halves of a fishing rod.

"Mister McLoughlin isn't it?" The man nodded, suspicious that Spen should remember his name. "I would have thought you might have known the answer to that one," said Spen in a friendly tone, adding a slight diffusing smile too. Mac said how he'd 'ne sin Smithy fe a couple o' days evn though there wiz still plenty o' work fe him ti dee.' He nodded towards the Grey further along the path. Spen had to admit that he was surprised to find that Mr. Smith had gone. Though when he recalled their last parting he had said 'don't suppose I'll see you again.' Spen had assumed he was talking about Spen having lost interest in their meetings once he knew he wasn't Spen's father. But now it seemed quite possible that Mr. Smith was planning to leave and that was why he wouldn't be seeing him again.

"Mister Mac, may I ask you something?" Mac wasn't usually addressed as *mister* anything. But he knew people who had polite manners very often had spare cash too. And Mac remembered that Smithy, or Robbo, as he knew him used to tap money out of this fellow.

"Am pressumin' there'll be a drink in it?" Spen smiled again at Mac's total lack of subtlety. He reached in his pocket and brought out a florin.

"What dya wint te know sir?" So Spen asked about the strange comings and goings on the barges, particularly Mac's ideas on the trade in body parts.

McLoughlin reckoned that people murdered in Edinburgh were less likely to be recognised in Glasgow, and vice was versa too. But that wasn't his best bit of news. He had another theory. One of the narrowboats had a slightly longer cabin! Aha! Mac stared at Spen expecting a look of amazement. Spen looked blankly back and asked Mac to go on a little and fill in some of the gaping chasm in his understanding. Dead bodies had a certain price but live ones, well they were a different kettle of strawberries altogether. Spen thought he was following, at least the gist. Out of date bodies had to go to the rat's nest once they'd 'gone off' and got smelly. But a good way to keep them fresh was to keep them alive.

"And the long cabin?" prompted Spen. The long cabin was only long on the outside. On the inside it was a little shorter. Mac believed there to be a secret space inside where live bodies were transported between the two cities. "You mean prisoners Mister Mac?" That's exactly what he believed. He'd listened to the screams late on a Friday night. Not like the usual drunk husbands coming home and beating their wives. No, these screams were different, doleful, dying screams. Every Friday, usually two o clock in a morning. In the dead of night, so to speak. He smiled at his own joke. Spen was horrified. Mac had never had anyone listen quite so attentively to his ramblings before. He was glad of the audience, especially one who gave him two bob for his valuable information.

So, just to clarify, there was a trade in dead bodies, carried in barrels of preservative, between the cities, and there was a different trade in live bodies, murdered late on Friday nights "Aye, te give them time to cool before they were sliced up by the university gentlemen." Spen presumed the gentlemen he referred to were people like Davies who did the extra-mural teaching of Anatomy on Saturday mornings. Spen asked Mac what the name of this vessel was? But Mac seemed to need a little addition to his 'drink' fund to aid his poor memory. Spen reached for another coin and threw it to Mac. "Pink Thistle," aye that was it. And it was always this one boat? He couldn't swear to that, but he thought so. Spen asked if that was another attempt to extract more cash from him, but no, Mac said not, he genuinely couldn't be sure, cross his heart and hope to die. And how did he know all this? Well, his home was a valve house as he called it, on the side of the canal, he nodded towards a tiny stone building only feet away, in the gloom.

Spen's mind was spinning with what he'd learned. He wondered if it was all just a ruse, an entertaining story which he'd been sold for three shillings. What he did know was that neither the medical faculty nor the extra mural anatomy classes could ever get enough corpses. And that story of 'Daft Jamie' being recognised on the table by so many people had meant that it was an un-sustainable business to murder the residents of Edinburgh for dissection in Edinburgh. It had brought about the end of Burke and Hare and would do the same for anyone else who was stupid enough or greedy enough to try it. But the canal, and the railway line had given the 'business people' a means to exchange the bodies between cities and increase the level of anonymity.

To continue that same possible business model, why not take bodies from Falkirk and Kirkintilloch along the way? Why not indeed? He thought back to the yard at Falkirk, Perkins' yard. Gee, he hoped he would never have to meet that man Perkins again. He looked back and realised how he might have ended up in one of those barrels himself, or even in the dreaded secret cabin on the Pink Thistle.

This was starting to make sense. Oh, how dense he had been. Perkins' yard actually had two barrels standing there in broad daylight in the yard. Perkins' Yard might be some sort of collection point or a marshalling yard for bodies. Yes, any man who was happy to be involved in the large-scale theft of wood from the Stannet Forbes estate was probably the sort of person likely to buy and sell bodies too. Why not just steal them off the streets and sell them too? You could pick and choose who you took then. Obviously, you'd go for women, the younger the better. More lucrative that way. This was all falling into place. Those two villains from the Yard at Falkirk, they were bargees, they had been the ones trying to abduct that waif in the street at Edinburgh. She would fit the bill very nicely. And no doubt would also fit nicely in the secret Cabin of the 'Thistle. Spen's heart skipped a beat when he remembered that night. She had been so close to death. How stupid he'd been.

It all made sense to Spen, he thought he could see the whole picture. But what was he going to do about it? Tonight? Nothing. He was going to go home and get some rest.

Chapter 15 – The Scented Letter

The morning dawned grey and windy and Spen and the boys had an early start. They had a talk by some visiting Alumnus on dosing, the prospect didn't sound gripping. As Spen skipped down from the last step into the entrance hallway he noticed there was a letter in his pigeon-hole. It was another one from Emily, her handwriting was unmistakeable, and the quality of the envelope was of the very best. He imagined Emily sitting at her father's writing bureau with her long billowing dress tucked in beneath it. He realised that the letter must have been sent just before she could have received the last letter from him; the one telling all about Freidman and his revelation regarding the trouble Charles was in, and therefore possibly the whole family. They must have crossed in the post. But the rain had started plopping onto the stone pavement outside, so he pushed the envelope into his inside pocket promising to read it later. Spen suspected this was the end of a fine autumn and the start of another real raw Scottish winter.

The lecture on dosing was as dull as they expected but Spen tried to make copious notes with links between illnesses, the size of the patient, grains or ounces of the drugs, ministered over how many days, etc. At the end of the talk the visitor said that they needn't try and remember all of this as he'd written a book on dosing and he would let them have a signed copy for the price of an unsigned one. An offer most students found easy to resist. Most felt cheated that they'd all sat through a sales pitch masquerading as a lecture.

Spen's mind was on his impending visit home at the weekend and how he should break the news to Sir William about his worthless and deceitful son-in-law. Hopefully he'd already have an inkling. His mind drifted along to Charles getting in with Perkins and that wood business. Charles must know that Spen had been to see Perkins and would probably be challenging him to a dual with muskets or whatever public-school boys used to settle their differences with these days. No, it wouldn't be muskets, pistols perhaps, yes, that's what he meant. Or they might try slapping each other to death with a leather gauntlet?

Then a thought struck him. He wondered if Charles knew about Perkins' body trade. That was a whole new world of horror. Surely not. But why not? And if he did, then what would that mean? But that was a question too far for now, and he chose not to think about it. Oh, how he longed for the simplicity of his childhood. The world was so much purer then.

Lunch in the refectory, more lectures in the afternoon. This learning took some keeping up with. There was an awful lot of it. No wonder people fell by the wayside. There were illnesses to discuss, deadlines to meet, case studies to document, ward rounds at the Infirmary to witness. And it seemed they all had to be done at once, or at least fitted into a timescale which couldn't be relaxed or stretched any further than it already had been. The day flew by, they always seemed to.

On the rather slower walk home, he noticed the rain had stopped and it caused him to remember Em's letter. He pulled it from his pocket and held it to his face. They were always scented with Emily's Eau de Cologne. Instantly she was with him. It sounded like it had been written in a different world than the one he was living in. He longed for those simple times again. The long walks in the fields holding Emily's hand, her warm soft embraces, those simple uncomplicated days on the Estate. Where had they gone, and what had he got himself into?

He looked down at the writing again. She did have a beautiful hand, not quite copper plate, but it did have an elegant sweep to it. "Going to see Perkin..." it said. 'WHAT!' he hadn't read that part before. How had he missed that? He stopped in his tracks and read through that last paragraph again. 'It reported how she was jolly-well going to visit Mr. Perkins at Falkirk and sort him out. She believed Mr. Perkins' deceitfulness was one of the reasons for Father being so poorly. But she wasn't going to tell her father that she was going, as she didn't want to cause him any upset. Actually, she wasn't going to tell anyone. She merely wanted to resolve the problem amicably and was sure Mr. Perkins would listen to reason.' Spen looked at the letter again. The first two sheets were written on one side only. The last sheet had the usually loving sign off with kisses and promises but then overleaf was this Postscript of her intended actions. That's why he hadn't seen it before. He hadn't turned over the last page. How stupid he was. This was serious. What did she think she was playing at? Poor Emily lived in a world where honour and reason were unwavering ground rules for everyone. She must be mad. He had to stop her. But how? He read the letter again to see if he could glean a hint about when she intended to visit Perkins. It just told of how Father was upset by the matter with Perkin's woodyard in Falkirk and it was causing his illness to get worse. Charles had said he would sort the problem, but father had set a man called Barnes to count wagons of wood each day and Father had counted the number of payments. They still didn't match. Yes, yes, he knew all that. But when was Emily going to visit Perkins?

Spen knew that Perkins wouldn't be changed by anything Emily could say or do. But surely, he wouldn't hurt her, would he? Heaven forbid. Of course, he would just laugh in her face and send her on her way. Wouldn't he? Spen strongly suspected that he was trying to convince himself that Emily would be alright. But deep within him, he knew the strong possibility that she might not be. Oh, he knew that she wouldn't be. She was a delicate damsel fly futtering straight into a vicious poisonous web of death and deceit. He imagined his beautiful Emily would be suffocated by brutes then her body crammed into a barrel. This was just too horrible to contemplate.

Perhaps he should return home to Falkirk right there and then. Or should he send one of those Telegraph things to warn her against going. Obviously, simply writing a letter wouldn't do, not quick enough by half. But he'd never sent a telegraph before. He'd heard of how there were companies who would somehow take a message from a receiving station and then transport it by horse rider, or perhaps even by one of those 'high wheelers' out to find the intended recipient. Oh, it was all too complicated for his fuddled brain at that moment. Andrew had a phrase for times like these. He referred to them as having a head full of broken biscuits. Quaint, but never truer than now.

He'd started to trot along the pavement towards his lodgings. What exactly was he going to do? He formulated a plan as he went. He'd best go in the morning. He'd just have to catch up with his studies later. He'd go first thing. He mentally counted up the money he had in various pockets. There'd be nothing for his mother on such an unprepared visit as this, but if she was there with him at that point what would she tell him to do? GO! So long as he had enough for the train fare to Falkirk, that's all he needed.

He turned the corner into Candlemaker Row and got the shock of his life; a bowler hatted gentleman who looked the image of Mr. Bateman was going through the front door of 2A. What a coincidence that someone should look so much like Sir William's butler, he thought. Spen hurried over the road and skipped in through the open door. The old gentleman had gone steadily up the first flight and was turning round to face back towards him for the second. Heavens above, it *was* him. "Mr. Bateman, how good to see you." But Bateman didn't look well, though not so much unwell, as troubled.

"Ah, Master Robinson..." began Bateman somewhat out of breath, "I'm glad to finally meet up with you." Spen took the old man's bag with one hand and began helping him up the stairs with the other.

"Are you alright sir? What do you mean 'finally meet up'?" Bateman stopped halfway up the third flight of stairs. He couldn't breathe and talk at the same time.

"I arrived at two thirteen and I've been trying to find you ever since."

"But what's wrong sir, It's wonderful to see you, of course, but I suspect this is not a social visit? Is Sir William alright?" But Bateman insisted on getting into the privacy of Spen's quarters before saying any more. Once inside the top floor room he was a little taken aback to see three beds in there and even a fully clothed body lain supine upon one of them. Andrew was reading but leapt up from his bed when Spen brought Mr. Bateman into the room and introduced him as Sir William's butler.

Even without being invited Bateman slumped into the seating position on Andrew's bed with a little wave of an apology as he did so. Spen quickly told Bateman that he could say anything in front of the third gentleman as he had Spen's full trust and confidence. Bateman began with a big lungful of air. "Everything has turned a little sour since last you left Master Robinson," he stopped to breathe again.

Spen spoke as Bateman gulped air, "Is the Laird well sir, please tell me he hasn't died Mister Bateman,"

"No, no, sir, he's quite well. Well... he's not well exactly, but he hasn't died, no." Spen didn't speak, but simply gesticulated a small prompt at Bateman to get to the point. But instead of Speaking immediately Bateman took another breath.

"Mother, is she alright?" Spen couldn't stop himself. But then it was Bateman's turn to gesticulate for Spen to stop talking so that he might tell him.

"As far as I know sir, she's well, why, has she been ill?" At this Spen was nearly tearing his hair out with frustrated impatience. But with a magnificent application of self-control, he said nothing and simply waited for Bateman to speak again. "It's Lady Emily sir, she's gone missing. Please tell me you know where she is and that she's here, safe with you?"

"I wish I could Mister Bateman, but I don't know where she is." Bateman was again wearing his look of pained disappointment.

"Oh dear, you mean she hasn't come here to Edinburgh to be with you sir. The family thought that she'd been pining a little lately." At this Andrew elbowed Spen in the ribs with a smirk suggesting Spen had an admirer.

Spen pulled out his letter from Emily again and sat down next to Bateman on the bed. Andrew stood and wondered if he should go and continue his lie down on someone else's bed, as it all seemed to have become a little crowded lately. Mr. Bateman recognised the envelope and the hand immediately. "No sir, she says that she was going to meet Mr. Perkins at his wharfage in Falkirk."

"Does it say when sir?" countered Bateman.

But at this point Andrew had a concerned question of his own. "When did she go missing Mister Bateman?" He reported that she was last seen on her own in the middle of Tuesday afternoon. Bowes the groom had harnessed Jess to the trap at her request. "And was she driving it herself?" continued Andrew.

"Yes sir, I believe so," said Bateman, finally breathing a little more easily. Spen glanced at his friend with a quizzical look.

Andrew went on. "If she was on her own, doesn't it suggest that she was going to make the visit in Falkirk and then return home? If she intended boarding a train to Edinburgh wouldn't she need a second driver to return the rig to the estate?" What brilliant thinking.

"So, we know that she went to see Perkins at Falkirk yesterday, Tuesday, and she didn't come home last night. So, Perkins has got her," gasped Spen, which was a bit of a jump to a conclusion. This was only the beginning of his worst nightmare.

As they rushed down the stairs Spen asked Andrew for any spare cash he had on him. He would need money at Waverley for the day's last train to Falkirk for himself and Mr. Bateman." He had no time now to go to his bank. "What about me?" asked Andrew inferring that *he'd* need a ticket too. But Spen gave him some different instructions. As they stood outside the door to the lodgings waiting for Mr. Bateman to arrive at ground level, Spen explained his worst fears. He told Andrew that Emily was likely to be in a barred cell on the wharf at Falkirk, Perkins Yard to be exact. But at some point, he knew not when, she would be killed, probably suffocated and put in a barrel, possibly with formaldehyde, maybe not, and put on a train or barge to Edinburgh, possibly Glasgow. He needed Andrew, and hopefully John, if he ever turned up, to go to the Lochrin basin, maybe Hopetoun, and await the arrival of a narrow boat called the 'Pink Thistle,' though there could be other vessels involved. It might just have Emily aboard. "So basically, you haven't got a clue then," encouraged Andrew.

The boat was likely to arrive before Friday night. Heaven forbid that her poor body should be in a barrel by then, but if she was alive, then she might just be held prisoner aboard the boat somewhere; perhaps a secret compartment in the living quarters, Oh, this was all too much. "God willing she'll be alive" added Andrew as some kind of heavenly insurance policy. "She's unlikely to get to the basin tonight Andrew, probably late tomorrow, if I know anything."

"We'll not risk it, we'll go tonight." At this Mr. Bateman came out through the door of the lodging house. He walked straight between them and out onto the street. A Hansom cab was struggling up the steep slope of the Candlemaker's and Mr. Bateman purposefully walked straight in front of the horse, causing it to halt abruptly with a snort from its nostrils. He walked down the side of the carriage, looked inside it and then up at the driver high on the rear of the shiny black cabin.

"To Waverley station as quick as you like my good man." Spen had started to explain the situation to John who had casually strolled up, but Bateman yelled at him from the cab and commanded that he get in.

"You explain to him Andrew," said Spen as he too went in front of the horse and bounced up through the open door. Even before he'd hit the seat next to Mr. Bateman the horse had been whipped into action and they were clattering their way along George the Fourth Bridge, straight across Lawnmarket onto the short Bank Street. Spen and Bateman were initially concerned that the man on top didn't know where he was going or at worst was simply taking them for a ride. He took them left, down the hill of North Bank and a tight right at the bottom to go back along Market Street. Spen was sure the right wheel of the carriage left the ground in the turn as it pattered over the cobbles, but it turned out that the driver knew exactly what he was doing. Rather than taking them to the front of Waverley station, halfway across Waverley Bridge the carriage veered again sharply right and went down a long slope which neither passenger knew existed. He neatly brought them to a halt in the cab rank at the level of the railway lines. He dropped them virtually outside the ticket office. Spen was pleased at the man's help and hence gave him rather too much of a tip. Bateman was unimpressed by Spen's lack of thrift but even more so by the cabby's lack of change.

Tickets were easy enough to purchase, at least when they finally got to the front of the queue and could speak to the sedate man behind the glass. But then the wait for the train was interminable. Forty-five minutes was an age when someone's life was in danger. Spen's stomach had gurgled earlier in the cab and he worried that it could be heard above the noise of the iron tyres over Edinburgh's cobbles. So he strolled across to the pie seller and bought two pies, Mutton and Mushroom. Though Bateman professed himself to be unable to eat at a time such as this he did manage to force it all down. They both remembered the time when they first came to Edinburgh together and Mr. Bateman had bought them pies then. Weren't they mutton and mushroom too? Spen realised that, although it was probably less than two years ago, they both seemed so much younger then than now. Rather quicker on his feet in Mr. Bateman's case, somewhat more gullible in Spen's. Certainly more innocent. Though he realised that this opinion might be a little biased.

Spen was relieved more than pleased when their train finally came into the station. They clambered aboard and found a vacant compartment. They sat there urging the train to begin moving again. Once in the

privacy of a compartment Spen tried to offer Mr. Bateman a little
warning regarding the type of men they might be dealing with at the
yard in Falkirk. They would probably be violent so he wasn't to do
anything which might lead him into being hurt or injured. Did he
understand? Mr. Bateman heard him well enough, but didn't speak or
nod any acquiescence. Spen was a little worried at what Mr. Bateman
might be thinking.

 The sky was pitch black when the train drew up at Falkirk High an hour
or so after leaving Edinburgh. Spen worried that the walk up the hill to
the canal might be too much for the old man but in the end, they just
took it steadily and arrived without overstressing Mr. Bateman's heart.

 The outside fencing to the yard was just how he remembered it. But it
somehow looked even more sinister in the dark. The front wall of the
office was cold stone only breached by that single red wooden door that
he'd ridden Jess the horse through. No wonder he'd caught his back
going under that lintel, the doorway looked tiny. No-one was about but
as their eyes got used to the gloom they could see two narrowboats
moored at the canal's edge within the bounds of the wharf. No lights
blinked anywhere. Spen tried the red door and looked above it. He
could just make out the word 'Entrance.' Mr. Bateman was breathing
heavily and was looking up and down the wall to try and spot a way in,
or simply to look for people. It must only have been in the eighth hour
after noon but the black sky and the unlit area made it feel like the
middle of the night. Bateman tried the doorknob too. He twisted the
handle and gave the door a good nudge with his shoulder. Neither
spoke. Mr. Bateman carefully observed which side of the door had the
hinges. He took a step back, reached out with his arm to push Spen
away a little, or was it to steady himself, and stood on one foot whilst
raising the other; quite high for an old man, Spen was impressed. He
quickly shunted the his foot against the edge of the door. It flexed a
little but sprung back immediately. They both looked around them to
see if the noise had awakened any dead from the nearby graveyard.

Bateman moved a little further from the gate, leant back as if to counterbalance the weight of his raised leg again and lunged forwards kicking the door much harder the second time. Something cracked and splintered. Spen hoped it wasn't Mr. Bateman's leg. But deftly, before Spen could persuade him to move out of the way and let him have a go, Bateman had hopped onto the other foot and given yet another kick with his other leg. Another crack, then Spen moved in quickly to barge the door open with his shoulder. A second attempt, and they were through. But then what? After all that noise it seemed a little incongruous to be taking dainty steps to lessen the noise of their footfall.

One of the narrow boats was just perceptibly swaying as if someone was moving around inside it. They froze and watched it for a moment. But the hatch didn't slide open as they had expected it to. Spen heard a slight grunt from close behind him, though Mr. Bateman was away to his right. In the fleeting moment it took for Spen to realize that the grunt was of the type made just as someone took a swipe with an axe, or cricket bat, he instinctively dodged to one side and ducked sharply. A sharp piece of two by two caught him on the shoulder but thankfully missed his head. He stood upright and swiftly punched into the darkness hoping that his attacker might be the surprise recipient. He connected with something though he had no idea where or who he'd hit. He then followed the imagined line of travel of the wood until his hand met up with it. He grabbed at it and felt a large splinter enter the base of his thumb. Somehow, he caught site of a silhouette against a reflected light in the water and lashed out a second time at the man, then a third. and another. The man went down with a grunt. Spen gave the figure a kick more to find out his exact location than to hurt him. He fell to his knees on top of him and grabbed his wrists, pinning him to the ground.

"Where's Emily?" spat Spen into the man's face.
But he spat back "Go an' boil ya heed"

"Alright that's enough, I'm sure we can talk about this like grown gentlemen." What Spen initially thought was Mr. Bateman's voice turned out to be that of Perkins, the yard owner. He brushed past them and found the door to the office. He must have pulled a key from his pocket, and the door squeaked open. He walked through into the pitch blackness expecting the others to follow him. But Spen stopped and waited for the light of a candle before going into who knows what danger. Safer that way. Perkins went into an office which contained a large solid desk and sat grandly behind it. This was obviously his domain. Spen initially stayed near the door, the only one in the room, again he thought, that was the wise thing to do. But Mr. Bateman was behind him and Spen gallantly moved forward to make room for him to enter. The fourth man followed Bateman, and his face showed signs of being thumped. Mr. Bateman had to continue into the room another step so Spen shuffled in even further from the safety of the door. By this time Spen was furthest into the room with three people between him and the room's only exit.

"Now then, an unusual time to call for business but Perkins is always open to the right trade. How can I..." but he stopped short, just as he looked up and recognised Spen. Spen was pretending not to listen and held his arm up closely to the light from the candle. He looked at the light brown splinter sticking out of his hand. "You again" growled Perkins in a slightly lower tone. "The boy who managed to cut off my supply of cheap wood." Spen pulled at the splinter. His hand stung, and then bled a little.

"The girl, we just want the girl," said a resigned Spen. He would have just taken her away at that point, but he suspected that the opportunity wasn't going to come any time soon.

"I don't know what you mean," said Perkins. At this point another figure, a much bigger man came through the door and stood there assessing the situation and taking stock. He held another short length of two by two. Spen suspected there might be other men coming, and

Perkins was simply spinning them along until they had gathered to block their way out of the room. Doubtless they would be beaten to a pulp in due course.

Spen felt foolish, a total amateur pitched in against a professional, nay, a champion team of murderers. What did he think he was doing wandering along there in the dead of night, even worse bringing old Mr. Bateman with him too? So, with his last ounce of bravado he made an attempt to tough it out. "Emily Stannet-Forbes, give her to us and we'll just leave," he said as forcibly as he could.

"And I'm supposed to be grateful for such a kind offer am I?" said Perkins calmly. The big man by the door smirked. "I don't think you gentlemen understand," continued Perkins as he casually leant back and put his hands on his head. He stretched out his legs under the table. "You don't understand at all." He was just about to set his pair of two-legged rottweilers on them when Mr. Bateman surprisingly lifted his left hand out of his coat pocket and held it up in a manner suggesting 'halt.'

"If I may be permitted…" He turned to look at Spen who half smiled wondering what Bateman was going to say that could radically alter the proceedings in their favour. Then he glanced to Perkins behind the desk, who waved a hand in a 'please continue' gesture, obviously considering Mr. Bateman as a cute irrelevance. "Oh, Mr. Robinson and I understand only too well, but I think it's you gentlemen who are labouring under a misconception. Is there no way we can persuade you to release Lady Emily into our care?"

"Pretty Please," toyed Perkins.

"Pretty please," said Bateman. And oddly added "last chance."

"What? What do you mean Last Chance you old fool?" Spen could see that Perkins was tiring of this game and he was about to give the order for their demise. Again, Bateman added a bizarre phrase, the meaning of which only he seemed to know "Beaumont and Adams couldn't persuade you to release dear Emily then Mister Perkins." Spen did think that Beaumont and Adams sounded like a firm of aging solicitors. Not a lot of use here and now, he thought.

But at that moment when they were all stood round wondering what to do next, Bateman withdrew his other hand, his right, out of his other coat pocket. In it he was holding what looked to Spen like a modern army pistol, a service revolver, as some were calling them. The two rottweilers by the door took half a step back and one of them let out a little expletive. Even Spen would admit to having moved back a little at that point too. "When I said 'Last Chance,' I meant last chance." Then the loudest bang any of them had ever heard shook the place. The top of the ornate desk suddenly had a hole, quite a large one, in the middle of its top surface. Shards of wooden splinters lined the jagged edges of the hole. The blotter and a paper also had a huge hole in them. Spen wondered how far the bullet had gone, indeed where it had gone. But he had a clue when he saw Perkins lunge forward in agony and grip his leg under the table.

Bateman flicked the gun left to the big man with the piece of wood, who immediately dropped it to the floor even before being told. "Have you gleaned understanding now gentlemen? Or would you like a little more persuasion?" The two men by the door put up their hands and the smaller one volunteered, "She's nay here. She left earlier."

"How?" prompted Bateman.

"On the boat" squirmed the man again.

"Which boat?" asked Spen thinking he already knew the answer.

But after a couple of glances towards the man writhing behind the desk Mr. Bateman shouted, "The gentleman asked which Boat?" and as he spoke he raised the revolver towards the man's leg and straightened his arm in preparation for a second shot.

"Thistle, she's aboard the Pink Thistle," he blurted. The poor man couldn't get the words out quick enough.

"And they're heading for where?" asked Spen.

"Edinburgh, she's still alive. Don't shoot, I've git five kids ti feed."

"Outside all of you" said the man with the gun, still very much in charge. Spen couldn't resist a smile as he followed on behind this aging Butler. He suddenly understood slightly better the relationship which Mr. Bateman and Sir William enjoyed. Bateman was quite happy to commit murder if he had to, to save one of Sir Williams daughters. What a dark horse Mr. Bateman was. "Not you," Bateman said to Perkins as they left, even though Perkins couldn't possibly have made any attempt to raise himself from the chair.

Perkins began pleading, "But I could bleed to death here" he said in tortured half words.

"Yes. Or you may die of lead poisoning," added Bateman.

Spen couldn't resist this little piece of theatrical revenge and added "My money's on blood poisoning, what with all those fragments of desk in there."

Bateman was on fire and thinking very clearly. It was just like the old days. "Where's Lady Emily's Pony and Trap?" he demanded of the two bargees. All that filled Spen's mind was Emily aboard the Pink Thistle heading for a rendezvous with suffocation and dissection.

"Trap's in that shed, the pony's in that field." Said the smaller man.

"Right," said Bateman. "You two on that boat and don't make a sound. If you come out I'll shoot you both." The two thugs obediently went to the narrowboat, hopped aboard and swiftly disappeared inside it. Bateman leant towards Spen in the dark and whispered, "I'm really rather enjoying this Mister Robinson." The two exchanged a smile in the dark even though neither of them could see the other man properly. Bateman continued, "Sir, may I suggest you take the horse and my gun and go along the towpath until you find the boat and rescue your maiden fair sir."

"But what about you Mr. Bateman? What will you do here?" But Bateman assured him that he was in no danger, even without his hand-gun, and he might take a little stroll into town and report the event to the police. Then perhaps spend the night at his sister's house. He'd not seen her for some time and she "...won't mind an unexpected visit sir."

Spen simply couldn't get over just how calm and collected Mr. Bateman was being after facing down murderers and villains. He acted like disabling a murderer by shooting him in the leg was the most natural thing in the world to do. Indeed, an everyday occurrence. Spen smiled when he heard Bateman talk about visiting his sister next and perhaps taking tea. Ha.

But Spen was brought back to his senses once back in the street and under the dim glow of a gas lamp. Bateman pressed the gun into his hand. "Six bullets, one gone. Hold those three fingers and your thumb tightly around the grip. Squeeze the trigger, that's this one, gently with your forefinger. Safety catch here, that's off. On." He deftly clicked something with his thumb. "And don't point it at anyone unless you intend to harm them. Good luck sir.

"Wait, show me the safety catch thing again please sir?"

Bateman took the gun again and flicked the safety catch deftly with the end of his thumb. "Fire. Safe. Oh, I think that's the right way. I'm sure you'll get used to it sir, you're a bright chap." But Spen hardly had time to be aghast at Mr. Bateman's suggestion that he would get used to using a gun. "Good day to you sir," said Bateman doffing his bowler hat and sedately walking off down into Falkirk. "Good luck."

Now, where was that horse.

Jess the horse still hadn't grown any bigger, but at least she did recognise Spen in the darkness. Probably his smell. On the one hand such a low horse was easier to get onto without stirrups. Though on the downside she wasn't easy to control without a bridle, bit, or reins either.

After Perkins yard Spen quickly led the horse back onto the towpath going East towards Edinburgh. It was still very dark indeed and Spen really wasn't sure of the wisdom of trotting a horse so close to the side of a canal in the dark. Get the footing wrong and they could quite easily both end up in the water.

But after only two hundred yards or so the canal took a sharp right bend and disappeared into a hole in the side of a hill. The horse stopped abruptly; it wasn't keen. Spen slid down off the horse (which wasn't far) and wondered if horses could see better than humans in poor light, a bit like cats or owls could. He inched forwards through the dark waving one arm around feeling for the stonework of the tunnel's entrance, leading Jess with the other. He'd heard about this tunnel called Falkirk tunnel. It had been reputedly built by William Burke, or was it William Hare. Whichever one it was, he presumed he'd had some help. Wasn't it caused to be built by one of Sir William's forbears who allegedly didn't want to have his view spoiled by narrow boats gliding serenely across the landscape?

It took forever to get through, it must have been close to seven hundred yards long. He spent the whole time talking to Jess and feeling for the side of the tunnel wall. The only sounds were Jess's hooves, his own voice and the occasional plop of water from the roof down into the canal.

Once through, Spen was surprised to find how much he could see now that he'd been released from the tunnel's extra blackness. Maybe a few stars had come out. He threw himself onto Jess's back again and she gayly trotted off down the canal once more. The difficult bits were overhanging branches and he spent a lot of his time laying prone and holding Jess round her neck; a position with which he was becoming quite familiar. Only once or twice did he get a painful branch on the head or nearly lose one of his eyes to a low hanging twig. They trotted on for an hour, perhaps more. It was nearly forty miles to Edinburgh so Spen reckoned that at three miles an hour the boat wouldn't have gone far before stopping for the night. Spen surmised that if it really was smuggling bodies then they'd probably stop in the middle of nowhere.

Sure enough, through the gloom he thought he could discern the black bulbous mass of a narrowboat's stern. "Woah Jess," he said softly to his new friend. They waited. No lights, no sounds. Then Jess spotted the other horse. She snorted and began walking forward to go and meet it. "Woah, Jess, Woah," insisted Spen softly, but Jess could smell the other horse and was keen to make friends.

Spen slid off the horse and began tiptoeing along the path. He stared hard through the darkness at the painted name on the boat. He felt down at the heavy weight in his pocket. Mr. Bateman's gun was still there. He put his hand in and found the comforting feel of its solid handle. He was very careful to avoid pulling the trigger and risk shooting his leg off. The boat's name was 'Rose' something, and as if to confirm there was a painting of a rose. That was disappointing, yet a relief at the same time.

Spen turned back towards the horse, but then looked again further along the canal. There was another, perhaps even two more boats, in front of the Rose Something, moored up on the canal side. So much for his theory of The Thistle finding a remote spot. He continued his silent stroll. The next boat wasn't the one he was looking for either, as it had no superstructure at all, nor even a steering position. It had no name, and Spen quickly ruled it out as being the second barge of a pair. It was full of coal and sat low in the water. He walked a little further. The night air was cold and it was a little breezy. He froze, as up ahead he spotted what he imagined to be a man peeing into the hedge. The man stood there and gave a little wobble, probably through inebriation. Was he just walking back home from some alehouse, or was he one of the bargees? It must be closing time by now. Maybe even midnight.

Spen was really unsure of how to approach this. He knew that there would probably be more than one man aboard the boat. From the little he knew of narrowboats they had a single entrance to the world's smallest living space at the rear, so any secret space would probably be accessible only from inside the cabin. Probably. He reckoned that if McLoughlin the fisherman was right, and he'd seemed to be right about everything so far, that's where he'd find Emily. Unless the boat carried a barrel. He tried to put that thought out of his mind immediately.

He waited for the man to finish what he was doing and leave. He half expected him to come towards him and continue his walk home along the tow path. But he walked straight towards the bank, up a short gang plank and stepped aboard the boat. He opened the companionway hatch and a warm orange glow lit him as he descended into the welcoming cabin. Spen heard a voice, a low but angry voice; something about closing the door and keeping the warmth in, perhaps. Spen moved forwards again slightly. All became still again. He picked out the name painted on the stern of the boat. He couldn't be sure, but it resembled enough of the words 'Pink Thistle' for his heart to miss a beat. In fact, he was suddenly terrified.

If he were to just start shooting people and Emily turned up at home the next day then Spencely Robinson would be hung for murder, bringing shame on his mother and a painful and sorry end to a short but great life. However, if Emily was in the secret compartment in that cabin somewhere, then his way to her was barred by two ruffians who would doubtless object to him just wandering through their living quarters and rescuing her. Hmm.

Spen walked forwards a little more considering how best to approach this. At the front of the cabin was a sheer wall which separated the cabin from the boat's load bay, which was also piled high with coal. But wait, wasn't that a barrel thrown on there too? Spen's heart sank. Was he too late? Maybe that's where Emily was? The thought was too horrible to contemplate, but it did serve to crystallise Spen's fears into action. He suddenly forced himself to take courage, though he still hadn't got a plan. He decided that if Emily's body was in the barrel then he would just shoot the crew of the boat anyway. But, he must act on the premise that she was still alive. Still in the secret compartment. Somewhere.

It was possible that only inches away from him now, behind the metal plate of the cabin was Emily, his love. That's what he had to believe. Almost without thinking he knocked on the steel plate and shouted "Emily!" quite loudly. There was a cross between a murmur and a scream from within. He couldn't tell if it was Emily, but it was certainly someone. A girl.

That was all the information he needed to go in and start shooting, even murdering, certainly causing mayhem. But suddenly the hatch slid open, and a figure appeared. He looked forward at Spen before his feet had even hit dry land. He came running at Spen and leapt onto him holding him in a bearhug and forcing him to the ground. He was big, and very strong. Spen tussled and tried to free his arms to start hitting the man and fighting back. Spen moved his head quickly to dodge a punch from the oaf and his fist hit the hard packed mud of the towpath. But another punch from his other hand caught Spen full in the jaw and knocked him almost senseless. Spen was torn between fending off the relentless tirade of punches or trying to reach for the gun.

Through the gloom he could just about make out a second man exiting the cabin. This would surely seal his fate, unless he could get his hand on that gun. Another blow struck him, and he felt a tooth loosen. Only one or two more like that and he would be unconscious. The brute sat on his stomach and was putting such an effort into his swipes that his knees were taking it in turns to come slightly off the floor. Spen somehow found the opening to his coat pocket. He flailed with his left hand trying to fend off the punches to keep himself conscious long enough to use the gun effectively. He managed to poke the man in his eye, which seemed to buy him a little time. Without trying to even remove the gun from his pointed he pointed it upwards slightly and pulled at the trigger. Nothing. He pulled again. The only thing that happened next was a painful swipe to Spen's left eye from the brute's right fist. Lessened by the resistance of Spen's arm, but still incredibly painful. He was probably cut. Just as he felt that his soul was preparing to leave his body, Bateman's voice came back to him; 'Fire. Safe.' He felt for the safety catch with his thumb. Oh, why hadn't he practiced reaching for the damned thing? He usually did practice these things. He realised the brute had stopped hitting him. Maybe he was too tired to carry on. Perhaps he thought Spen was unconscious already. Spen had indeed stopped moving, though he was concentrating on feeling for the little switch on the side of the gun. He felt it click. He moved the gun up again to point it into the man's groin. Even before he'd pulled hard on the trigger there was a very loud bang and the gun jumped violently in his hand. The brute raised his arm to give Spen another whack with his fist but then the most unusual thing happened. His arm seemed to flop down in the darkness, and this was quickly followed by his body slumping from the waist. His head contacted Spen's head heavily as if he'd meant to butt him. His stubbly chin tried to graze Spen's cheek as it hit the ground.

Spen pushed at the dead weight of the man in an attempt to extricate himself from underneath him. As he pulled his hand out of his pocket it was soaked momentarily in a warm squirt of Blood. There was the smell of what he presumed to be burnt gunpowder, mixed in with stale beery breath of the oaf, and maybe a little coal-fire smoke from the canal-boat's chimney.

"Davey, are ya'arright? Speak ti mi Davey." The second bargee surely wouldn't be stupid enough to try and strike Spen after he'd just witnessed him shoot his colleague. But these men were murderers, and as Spen struggled to his feet the man bending over his injured friend stood up and looked threateningly at him. "Have you shot Davey?" Spen thought that was rather a stupid question given the loud bang and the slumped figure on the towpath, presumably with blood leaking out of him somewhere. His mind started to race again, and he wondered if he and Mr. Bateman would be hung side by side. But as the second smaller man began moving forwards towards him, he reached again for the gun in his pocket. He struggled to pull it out as there was now a rather large hole in the front of his packet and it seemed to hinder the process. But he'd got the gun out just in time and the man stopped in his tracks. Obviously, the light was sufficient for him to see that he was going to be next.

The two of them looked down at Davey. He was slumped in an uncomfortable looking heap and motionless. "I only want your prisoner," said Spen hoping the man wouldn't be stupid enough to attack him too. The man thought for a moment, obviously weighing up his limited options. He decided not to try pointlessly attacking the man with the gun and instead knelt down quickly and attempted to tend to his friend. "Davey, are ya' right mate?" he asked again forlornly. But Davey didn't answer.

"How many are onboard?" asked Spen regaining his wits. But the man ignored him. Spen's eye really stung, and he wobbled his tooth with his tongue. He pushed past them and went to the stern of the vessel. He stepped onto the steering platform and was quite surprised how little it moved under his weight. He held the gun in front of him as he felt for the edges of the companionway steps with his foot. He descended slowly, quietly into the dim orange light of the cabin expecting that at any moment someone else might surprise him from underneath the coach-roof. No-one did. He continued his descent. It was a very crowded interior. A small table with two hands of playing cards, a lamp and two glasses on it. One empty. A small sausage sandwich had a squirl of steam coming up from it and disappearing into the breeze from the open hatchway. There was a tiny bed one side with a heavily used grubby quilt covering it. He presumed a seat was on the other side. Round to his left the warmth from a stove made its presence felt. But where was Emily? There was no door at the front of the cabin as he'd expected. His future prospects of avoiding the hangman's noose didn't look good at that point. Particularly if the injured man outside on the towpath didn't survive. In that moment Spen was nearly at the point of returning to the man and stemming the bleeding, but instead he shouted again, "Emily, it's Spen." He hoped more than anything in the world to hear Emily's voice shout back saying that she was alright. But it wasn't Emily's voice he heard behind the panel. "Help!" shouted someone weakly. "Where are you?" said Spen quite loudly. But after a short pause the weak voice said. "Ah don't know." It definitely wasn't Emily's voice, but at least if it was someone and his shooting, perhaps even the murdering of the brute outside might be justified. "How do I find you?" he asked, which, on reflection was a rather pointless question. He put the gun back in his pocket, then wondered if the safety catch was still off. He gently put his hand back inside the pocket and gingerly pulled out the gun into the light. There was no hint engraved on the gun as to which was 'Safe' and which was 'Fire.' He clicked the safety catch forwards and squeezed the trigger slightly. The hammer started to move back slightly. He released the trigger and clicked the catch back. He squeezed the trigger again slowly pointing the gun at the side of the cabin, just in case it should go off. The trigger was stiff, and the hammer didn't move. He was assured that the safety catch was 'on.' Should he consider what the second man was doing now? He may have gone to the other occupied narrowboat to garner help. Huh, what help would anyone be against a man with a gun?

"Where are you?" he said again, looking all around him hoping that something might give away the position of a doorway or hatch. There was nothing. He reasoned that the secret cabin had to be on the forward end of the compartment. After all, the boat was so narrow. But there was only a double row of a simple bookshelf one side then shelves to the other with some tins, packets of food and a little collection of crockery. Behind him was the tapering end of the narrowboat, with the rudder pivot going up to the tiller on the deck. No, she could only be behind that forward bulkhead. He sat on the bed for a moment and looked again. Wait a minute. Bookshelf? Why would two oafs who were most probably illiterate, have books? Spen grabbed at the spine of one of the books. It didn't move. Maybe it was jammed in. The next one to it didn't move either. None of them did. They weren't books at all, just their spines cleverly assembled to look like a full bookshelf.

"Are ya still there?" came the voice. "Please hurry." Spen grabbed at the picture of Eilean Donan Castle propped on the shelf above the books, but it didn't move either, it was fastened to the shelf. The whole panel was a hoax. Now, how did it open? The girl must be behind there, somehow. Spen pressed on the shelf's edge and observed it flex. He moved along the shelf to the right and pressed again. It flexed again, but much less the second time. That must be the end where the hatchway was hinged. Or possibly fastened. He moved left again. And felt and observed and pressed until he found a vertical shoot-bolt cleverly hidden behind three real books. The scheme was brilliantly thought through. Spen worked the shoot-bolt left and right easing it up until it could be with-drawn. The door pinged open slightly and he only had to pull back a couple of blankets and part of the horsehair mattress on the bunk to allow the small door to swing fully open. A young girl's face looked out at him and made him jump. She looked filthy and half dead. She gasped for air as Spen forced the door open wide. She held one arm up to him and he tried to help her as she heaved herself up with the other one. Her hands were the temperature of ice. "No air," she gasped.

"Just you, or are there others in there?" he asked as he helped haul her scrawny cold body up and onto the bunk. He realised that the secret cabin was very deep and totally devoid of any creature comforts.

He grabbed one of the candles from the table and brought it near the tiny doorway. He peered inside before the stale air made the flame flicker and go out. The young girl scrambled past him grabbed one of the blankets and moved towards the companionway and the cold night air. It certainly was cold, but it was fresh and clean. "How many of you?" he asked the girl. She looked round nervously, probably checking if he was going to beat her or not, "'wis three, but Ar think one's deed."

He lit the candle again from the other one on the table and leant towards the hatch again. The candle dimmed as it came near but he kept it high and didn't push it into the blackness before the air had chance to circulate a little.

He pressed his head through the hatch and brought the candle through the hole slowly enough to keep it lit. He could see two more bodies crowded into the black space which couldn't have been more than two foot long, front to back. The vertical sides were obviously the inside surface of the hull, cold and wet to the touch. A little water sloshed over the keel plate and reflected the candle back up to him. Both bodies were slumped against the cold iron plates, they must have been freezing too. Neither bodies were moving. One wore a dark smock and no shoes, The other wore a large flouncy dress, quite bright coloured, like the sort Emily would... He scrambled into the hatch but then realised going in head first was a sure-fire way to fall straight onto the iron keel of the boat. He pulled himself out again and turned round lowering himself backwards into the chest deep hole. "Emily, Emily," he said softly hoping it was the other body who was the dead one. His feet touched some stretched out legs and he carefully danced over them like a mother hawk in a nest full of chicks. He reached back through the hatch for the candle and carefully brought it in. He bobbed down in front of Emily. She was stony cold. He found her wrist and felt carefully for a pulse. Yes, that must be it. Or perhaps he was kidding himself. He felt her neck for the carotid pulse. Yes, definitely, it was there, he wasn't deluding himself. She truly was still alive. Though close to asphyxiation and very definitely hypothermic.

He pulled her towards him away from the freezing cold steel hull and clasped his hands behind her back. It took him a long time to get Emily anything like stood on her feet. Her legs wouldn't lock straight, and it was difficult to move their two bodies in such a confined space.

Finally he got her head and one shoulder through the tiny hatchway and over the bunk in the cabin. He bobbed down and put his arms around her legs and heaved upwards with all his strength. Finally, in a most ungentlemanly manoeuvre he got behind her and squatted a little, as far as he could before his knees touched the back of the secret cabin and his own rear end was pressed against the front of it. He put his shoulder as best he could against Lady Emily's bottom and clamped her legs with both arms again. She was up and mainly out. She'd started to regain consciousness and murmured a couple of syllables. Spen didn't know what.

He bobbed down and felt for the limbs of the other figure in there with him. He found a thin but rather stiff forearm. As he lifted it to search for a radial pulse it felt very heavy and there was a crack from the shoulder. Before he'd confirmed that there was no pulse, he knew from the rigor that she had been dead for near to twelve hours. Nothing to be done there. He crossed himself in some sort of honouring salute to a life lost in such horrible circumstances. Even he wasn't sure why he did it, it just seemed appropriate.

He struggled out through the hatch and onto Emily's frame. He'd almost forgotten about the young girl who was first out, but there was no sign of her now. Charitably, he thought she might just be outside gasping at the fresh air, but he knew it was more likely that she would have just riffled through the pockets of the unconscious man on the towpath, and then run off.

There was enough light in the cabin for him to land a kiss on Emily's cold cheek. "I love you," he said softly. He took off his coat and threw it over her. He looked to the stove and saw an air vent, and a door which he opened. He even managed to throw on a couple of lumps of coal from the bucket. At least on a barge transporting coal there was never a need for the cabin to go cold. Small blessings. He lit more candles and placed them around the cabin before looking out through to hatch and scanning round at the scene. Still very dark out there, but quiet too. The only identifiable sign of life was the body still slumped on the towpath. Sign of Life? He hoped he was still alive. Perhaps now he should go and attend to the bleeding of the bargee. Instead, he decided to slide close the hatch and try and preserve some heat inside the cabin. The cabin which contained the love of his life. Over the next three or perhaps four hours he lain next to this woman and resolved to make her his bride. He'd always said that he wanted to be with Emily for always, but he never believed it in quite the same way as he did at that moment.

He lain there next to her, holding her close trying to make as much surface contact with her as he could. That way, he hoped she would warm up from his transferred body heat. He was wide awake. Even though he had been awake for hours and been through so much. All he could think of was Emily. He found a kettle half full of water and poured some into a pot mug. He urged Emily to drink. She was probably dehydrated as well as everything else. He supposed the whole aim of the captivity was to get the bodies to expire without damage. Hypothermia, dehydration, hypoxia. All went in favour of the murderers and reduced the need for a final suffocation. At the very least it would reduce the victim's resistance to it.

She spoke in murmurs. Occasionally her arm pulled him close. He presumed she was conscious now, but asleep, he wasn't sure. She must have been through so much. How dare they try and hurt his Emily. His beautiful, perfect Emily. But then, as if to bring him back to the world's imperfections a slight smell of decay wafted out of the open hatch of the secret cabin. He remembered the poor creature still in there. Nothing to be done for her, a life cut short far too early. The pitch and toss of fate was so unfair, but the only right response was to accept graciously the hand that it deals, and try and improve things for yourself, your loved ones and everyone else too. He felt very emotional. His hatred for the organisation of murderers and suppliers of bodies for the dissection classes fell to a new depth. They were doing exactly the opposite of improving the lot for their fellow man. They were an abscess on society. Yet, he realised that he had personally benefitted from their business. He'd attended, even paid for, those dissection classes. Did that make him culpable? Oh, this was all too much philosophising so late in the day. Or was it so early in the day now? He presumed it would be light soon. He swung the door of the secret compartment closed again with a small apology to the body still in there.

Emily sat up slowly but stiffly and looked at him. "How did you find me?" she asked. "That's a story for another day my sweet, I'm just so glad that I did."

"And Little Laura, is she alright?" Ha, typical Emily, always concerned for others.

"She went outside, I think to get some fresh air, probably halfway to Edinburgh by now. Never mind her, how are you feeling Em?" She liked it when he called her 'Em,' he was the only person ever to call her by that name.

"Cold. I need a bath."

They heard a noise outside. "Ahoy the Pink Thistle. Is there anyone aboard?" Spen thought that anyone shouting such a formal introduction would hardly be a threat. It was Two constables from Falkirk, accompanied by none other than Mr. Bateman.

Chapter 16 – A Death in the Family

Back at the Estate everyone was very relieved to see the three of them arrive back safely in the police cart, but then all quickly became horrified at their shocking appearance. Particularly Spen's bruised and battered face, to say nothing of the worryingly large bullet hole in his pocket. Emily looked like a street urchin with her dress torn and her face filthy. Mr. Bateman looked like he'd not slept for ages, which he hadn't.

All was hurriedly told and then, after bathing Spen was given one of the guest rooms and the three heroes had a much-deserved rest. There was a flurry of action around the house with fires to stoke higher, meals to be prepared, Dorothy to be sent for... much of it un-organised without the calm guiding effect of Mr. Bateman. Bateman had also taken to his bed for an attempt at rest, but it wasn't long before he arose from his quarters and took control of the house once more. His next major concern was the health of The Laird. It seemed that Sir William had not risen from his bed for some days and had finally stopped eating altogether. He was obviously going through a rough patch in his illness.

Charles appeared and attempted to take over but somehow was largely ignored by everyone. He forbade Spen to see Sir William, a command which was immediately over-ruled by Lady Sarah. She thought a visit would be a treat for her husband, might even perk him up a little.

Spen was shocked to see Sir William; his face was grey and his eyes sunken, his spectacles slightly askew. The old man was half asleep when he went in but opened his eyes and even managed a slight smile. Spen sat on the bed and held an available hand. Was this truly the tall stout figure of moral fortitude and wisdom whom he'd looked up to all his life? Spen didn't really know what to say. "How are you feeling sir?" didn't really suffice.

Spen put out of his mind any thoughts of broaching the difficult topic of Charles' debts and hence the need for Sir William to take professional advice. Discussing cutting Lady Mary out of her inheritance to save the estate from Charles' creditors was not for this moment. Surely that time would come within the next day or so.

"You found her then," said Sir William as he struggled for breath.
"Yes, I found her sir. She's safe."
"A true relief to us both." His voice was getting a little croaky. He tried another smile. But this was somehow a knowing smile.
"Sir... You know I love your daughter. I've always loved her."
"Really, which one?" At this Spen couldn't stop himself letting out a little laugh. Not because the Laird didn't know it was Emily he'd always loved, but because he still retained his sense of humour, even at a time like this. A time when he was standing in front of death's black door, waiting for it to creak open.

Spen looked down at the crisp white linen sheets. And took a long slow breath. "Sir, I think we both know that I've always loved Emily, and, if circumstances had been different, If I'd been born a gentleman, then I could have married her and spent my whole life making her happy. But that's not how things are." Spen looked up at the Laird, who'd closed his eyes but was obviously still listening. He went on "But even so, given all the imperfections of our different status, I wondered, with all my heart, if you could ever bring yourself to agree to me marrying her sir. Please?"

He looked at Sir William again. The old man groaned, not at what Spen had said, but more as an agonal snore. That's what he hoped anyway. Did he really just hope that Sir William's breathing was agonal? A sign of impending death?

Spen felt his hand being squeezed a little. He'd forgotten that they were still clasped on to each other. The Laird made a real effort to breathe in. "I've loved you" he began, and took another breath, "like a son." Another slow breath. Was the answer going to be yes... or no? "But, very very unfortunately, I cannot agree to such a req..." Spen was disappointed afresh, but this simple confirmation of the thing he had always known was a new train crash to his soul. He was again beaten into the ground by his own low-born status, unable to change it. In that instant he resolved to be Emily's secret lover, for the rest of her life. If she wanted him of course.

Spen looked into the face of the Laird. It was indeed very grey and very poorly. At that moment he wondered at the wisdom of delaying broaching the subject of Charles and the massive debts he had. But to tell Sir William about it now would just make it sound like sour grapes. He wondered if the old man perhaps already knew, or even if he'd acted upon that letter he'd written to Emily. It was only a day or two ago, and the Laird had been in no state to discuss anything with solicitors. Also, Spen realised that Emily must have left to 'sort out' Perkins before even receiving his letter about Charles.

The prospect of Sir William dying and leaving Charles to first inherit, then immediately losing the estate was too horrifying for words. At a stroke all his loved ones would be made homeless, all he'd worked for gone. He looked at Sir William and said nothing. He must be asleep; his face wasn't moving. The pulse in his temple which Spen had always been drawn to, was no longer jumping. Spen lowered his gaze slowly to the old man's crumpled night gown. It had stopped moving too. He loosened his grip from the old man's hand and felt for a radial pulse. He couldn't find one. He moved his finger around and loosened his grip slightly thinking he might be stopping the pulse through his own tight nervous grip. Nothing. He felt for a pulse in his neck. There was nothing there either. "Sir...Sir... can you hear me sir?" A rather foolish question really, as the old man's soul had obviously just left his body. He realised that he was looking at just another empty shell on Earth's long beach. Spen gently leant forward and kissed the old man on the forehead, "Goodnight sir, thank you for everything."

Then, quietly, as if to not waken Sir William he slowly rose to his feet. He faced the old gentleman squarely, took a small step backwards and bowed from the waist. He was astonished to discover at that point Mr. Bateman was at his shoulder, also bowing at the same time. Neither man spoke for a moment. Then, without lifting his gaze from Sir William, Spen uttered, "Best man I ever knew."

Bateman turned slowly towards Spen and said softly, "Best man I ever knew too sir." The two smiled a comforting smile at each other before Bateman continued, "If you want to break the sad news to the others sir, I'll just attend to his Lordship for a moment."

Spen thought that it was fitting and right for these two great friends to have a final moment with each other, so he left.

He collected his thoughts as he slowly descended the stairs. That was the first death he'd witnessed. He wondered if Mr. Bateman had been present at the moment Sir William had said no to the marriage of him and Emily too. It crossed his mind that he should maybe just tell everyone that Sir William had agreed to the union. Who would know? As he stepped off the bottom step Emily came to him. By the look on his face, she knew that something grave had happened. She suspected the worst but said nothing. Spen took her hand and asked, Where's Lady Sarah?"

"She's in the 'Drawing Room reading," she answered without asking the obvious question.

"Em, please fetch Lady Catherine and meet us in there would you?" Without question she let go of his hand and went off to fetch her sister. He went to the oak paneled door and knocked twice and went in. The new chamber maid carrying a coal scuttle on the far side of the room caught his eye and he nodded his head sideways towards the door at her. He'd hoped that she might take a hint and leave, but maybe his hint was a bit too subtle. "Miss, could you leave that for a moment please?" She set down the scuttle by the hearth and glanced at his puffy eyes in horror, before curtseying properly towards Lady Sarah and leaving. She had to wait to let Catherine and Emily come through the door before leaving and carefully pulling the door closed behind her.

Neither Emily nor Catherine sat. Lady Sarah stayed seated but looked up from her book expectantly and took off her reading glasses. "Lady Sarah, Lady Catherine, Lady Emily," he began, as this was a time for sincerity and formality, "I'm afraid to have to give you the sad news but Sir William died a few moments ago." A tear trickled down his cheek. He thought how this was totally the wrong way round as he should be the stoic one and tears should be the ladies' domain.

"Are you sure Spencely?" asked Lady Sarah softly.

"Good heavens mother, he's a damned doctor, he should know."

"I'm not quite a doctor Miss Catherine, not yet, but yes, I am sure ladies. You have my sincere condolences."

"Oh hell!" said Catherine. Things had been bad enough for her and Lottie under the protective guidance of Sir William, but she knew things would be unbearable for her once the sadistically closed-minded Charles was in charge. Her life had just changed forever, and not for the better. "Someone needs to inform Mary. I suppose I should go immediately."

Chapter 17 – Revelation

In the intervening week Spen wondered if he should return to Edinburgh but he decided in the end to just write letters of explanation to his lecturers and tutors telling them why he was unable to attend. He wrote too to John and Andrew telling them of the adventure of rescuing his beloved from the ruffians and how he'd shot one of the murderers, though not before taking a beating and losing a tooth. He had a formal interview with a police inspector and wrote down a lengthy statement explaining everything he'd done. The inspector could see from the state of his face that he probably was telling the truth. Mr. Bateman too was talked to, but was his usual matter of fact honest self. Forthright and unemotional.

He walked again with Emily though they had to be well wrapped up against the cold winter wind and the occasional flurry of snow. She told him that Mr. Bateman had let it be known to her mother that he had no wish to stay on and serve Mr. Charles Richardson-Eames and hence would retire, to somewhere, though he knew not where at that time.

Spen's own mother Dorothy seemed to take the death of the Laird quite badly but to every cloud there was a silver lining, and she got to spend some more golden moments with her precious son. When Lady Emily visited, Spen would sit and observe the interaction between her and his mother. Though a generation apart they could have been sisters. They giggled a lot together. He wondered sometimes if Emily enjoyed his mother's company more than his own. But he wouldn't change a thing.

Up at the big house Emily reported that Charles was making far more visits than needed. He'd suddenly taken an interest in the place. But although he was strutting around the rooms snapping orders to folks who needed no direction to do the tasks which they had always done, he had graciously allowed Bateman and lady Sarah to make the funeral arrangements, so long as he was informed and kept abreast of everything. Emily would joke that Charles was climbing to new depths of pomposity and ascending to new lows of self-importance. She knew things would change once the estate was run by him. Spen ruefully thought that it wasn't just a little change that was coming, but massive change, shocking change. Change that might probably make all the family peasants.

Dorothy spent sleepless nights worrying what would befall her. She was in her mid-fifties and it had been many years since she'd worked in the capacity of Governess. Who would want her now? She had to admit that she was probably not going to be allowed to stay on in her free house on the Stannet-Forbes estate, not once Charles was in charge. Would the place even still be known as the Stannet-Forbes estate? Heaven forbid that it should become the 'Richardson-Eames' estate.

Spen had heard that one of the footmen at the hall and a worker at the sawmill were leaving though no-one could say if they were leaving of their own volition, or if they had been forced to go. Perhaps they could see into the future and somehow knew what was coming. Perhaps they would have been going anyway, even if the Laird hadn't died. Who knows? Bit of a coincidence though, thought Spen, and such an unusual time to leave in mid-winter.

On the rare occasion that week that Spen did visit the hall Charles had once cornered him and pointedly asked if he had a home to go to? Spen resisted the temptation to reply in similar vein of 'yes, have you?' But for the sake of peace in the 'Big House' he took the insult on the chin, and simply promised himself that when Charles finally evicted his mother from the estate he would just come and find Charles and hit him, good and hard. The thought made him smile. But for the interim, he'd stay quiet. Mr. Bateman largely stayed clear of Charles and even ignored him in front of one of the footmen once as he instructed Bateman to stoke the fire and not just appoint someone else to do it. Charles was fuming to be affronted in such a way. The footman made the mistake of letting his internal amusement show on his face which meant Charles became incandescent with rage. He stormed off and slammed the door behind him. The footman regained his composure and carefully threw more coal on the fire with the tongs. That's what he had arrived to do anyway.

When the day came for the funeral, there were a lot of carriages for a lot of dignitaries and many society folk. Spen stood at the side of the drive next to his mother, along with all of the other estate workers. They stood there in the drizzle for a good fifteen minutes even before the carriages started filing past them. As the hearse came along the long line of farm workers, sawmill workers, staff, artisans and peasants, all of the gentlemen removed their hats and held them to their chests. Spen was glad that it was raining. He didn't know if he was crying, but if he was then the rain would hide it nicely.

The four large black horses bedecked in their fine black plumes pulled the glass sided hearse. It was followed by a gleaming black carriage with Ladies Sarah, Mary, Catherine and Emily in it. Charles was next in an open Landau with an ill-fitting and somewhat hastily arranged black canopy over it. Spen wondered if the stable workers had done that on purpose just badly enough to try and humiliate Charles but without making it too obvious. It made him smile though.

After that was a line of carriages, and assorted jigs, traps and horse riders. The more senior estate workers were quietly murmuring who was who to each other as they went by. Spen noticed that Mr. Bateman hadn't been invited, Nor Lady Catherine's friend Lottie. The rumour was that Lady Mary had insisted on going in the first carriage with her

mother and her two sisters, rather than accompanying her husband
Charles in his carriage. Ooh, thought Spen, Charles wouldn't like her
disloyalty displayed in public like that. As the last horse pulled the last
trap by them, Dorothy quietly said to those about her "Our house is
nearest, and the kettle's on." But Spen's eye was caught by the lady sat
in the back of the last Trap. He knew the trap to be that of the Estate,
indeed he himself had ridden in it many a time. But the elegant young
woman riding in the back seemed to notice him too. He recognised her
as Miss Beaty, from the Edinburgh Solicitors Brader and Sons. No-one
could ever forget such a face as hers, nor her perfect almost angelic
shape. She had leant forward and spoken to the driver, at which point
the pony halted. She looked directly at him. He looked about him to
confirm in his mind that it was indeed himself that Miss Beaty was
looking at. She simply patted the seat next to her with her hand and
waited. Spen knew what she was signalling for him to do, but he hadn't
been invited to the funeral. He trotted forward anyway to talk to her
and to explain that he couldn't come with her. The workers with whom
he'd been stood, stopped and turned to watch this minor subject for
future gossip. When he explained that he had no invitation, Miss Beaty
simply replied, "I'm inviting you Mister Robinson."

In a flash he was sat across from the young woman and the pony jolted
the trap into action again. He sat on the left, she on the Right. He was at
the back, she at the front. This way their knees had no chance of
touching. Furthermore, sitting next to her would have meant that their
buttocks or thighs might meet as they bounced along together, and that
would never do. Obviously, sitting in the diagonally opposite seat meant
that the trap was more evenly balanced too. Obviously.

By way of conversation, Spen said that he had very briefly witnessed a
woman who looked just like her standing on Falkirk station catching a
train to Edinburgh. About four weeks ago. She neither confirmed nor
denied that it was her, so Spen asked if she had a twin sister, which
made her smile a little. She had no sisters, only two rather good for

nothing brothers. Spen was drawn by the dimples in her cheeks when she smiled. It made him just want to make her smile even more. He knew she was married, and that he also was betrothed, in his mind at least, so this wasn't flirting, no, it was quite safe.

She told him that her father and Sir William had served together in some War of Retribution in Afghanistan and had been lucky to escape with their lives. They'd been friends ever since eighteen forty-two. Her father Basil had taken over her Grandfather Sir Callum's law business and the Earl had used her father as Solicitor in all business and private interests ever since. But why had she stopped to pick Spen up? She told him that it was only right and proper that he should be at the funeral, and that all would be made plain in due course.

He sat at the back of the cold stone church next to Miss Beaty and the two of them shivered near the ill-fitting door. The minister did nothing to make their time more bearable, droning on much longer than necessary in a volume which most couldn't hear. The draught was really having a field day with everyone's damp clothing.

Afterwards the coffin was lowered into the hole and few except Lady Sarah and the daughters stood around for longer than a few minutes. A veritable jam of carriages went on outside the church and Spen had to explain to Miss Beaty, technically *Mrs*. Beaty, how one's right of way was only dependent upon one's social status, Earl's carriages gave way to those of the Lords, no matter that it forced some horse drawn carriages to have to back up unnecessarily. Spen and Mrs Beaty watched the melee and stayed out of the rain under the shelter of the church's litch-gate. After which, they simply walked out to the trap, got on and set off. They soon caught up with the train of carriages which were heading back to the hall. As their driver turned in under the archway at the entrance to the Stannet Forbes estate Spen began thanking Mrs. Beaty for the privilege of her company and for allowing him to attend the auspicious funeral of his dear mentor. As he tapped the driver on the shoulder to halt and let him out Clarke turned round and smiled at Spen. "Just Here Doctor Robinson sir?" All that way and he'd never even noticed who it was that was driving them.

But Mrs Beaty butted in with, "No, no, keep going please. To the house." Clarke duly obeyed the lady.

If Spen thought that Charles might have been a little angry at him for attending the funeral, then he was on the puce side of livid when he was delivered to the front door of the hall. And all this just as Charles was greeting as many big-wigs as he could creep round, kissing the ladies' hands and walking them into the shelter of the entry hall. Presumably, Spen was merely ignored rather than berated so as not to cause a scene. So, he patiently joined the footmen carrying away damp coats and bringing warm tea. He saw a need, so he filled it. As he did so, some oaf bumped into him from behind and spat into his ear, "You're no longer wanted here." Of course, it could only be Charles. But Spen tried to explain that he had been formally, if only verbally, invited to join them. He took tea to Mrs. Beaty, but no sooner had she taken hold of the saucer than Charles removed it forcibly from her and suggested that she drink a hot toddy with him instead. Warm her up from the inside out. He said it in a somewhat lascivious fashion, which wasn't at all appropriate, nor welcome. He handed the tea back to Spen without looking at him.

He was just about to move off when Mrs. Beaty smiled at Charles and said, "No thank you Mister Eames, I'm on duty." She turned back to Spen and held out her hand for the saucer a second time. Charles was seething inside as Spen had seemingly got the better of him once again without even trying. "Would you excuse me Mr. Robinson. Please stay for the reading of the will as I may need you." Spen was touched that she should ask him for his help and imagined that he would be useful in simply finding all of the faces which she only knew as names on a list.

Spen asked Clarke to check that there was no-one in the library, and if there was, to kindly ask them to vacate as soon as possible please. He observed Mrs Beaty going to Lady Sarah on a settee, whisper something in her ear, then move across to find Emily. She did the same with her, then had another small conversation which resulted in Emily pointing across to her sister Mary. The same thing happened, and two or three more times to various people. Interestingly, Bateman was one she spoke to though Charles didn't seem to be. Not that Charles noticed. Charles himself was occupied entertaining a small group of his friends who were trying to remain dignified and retain decorum for such a 'delicate' occasion. Many people in the room saw Charles go to the whisky decanter and slop another hefty draft of it into his glass, though much of it went onto the French polished sideboard top.

"May I have everyone's attention please, just for a moment. The reading of the will, will take place in two minutes in the library. Only those who need to be present should join us please," announced the petite Mrs Beaty in a more powerful voice than should be expected from such a petite frame.

"No, no, no, will-will indeed, there'll be plenty of time for that, let's stay and have a drink first," shouted Charles thinking he was being funny. Only his three friends laughed in sympathy, everyone else was slightly embarrassed.

"But I have another appointment sir," said Mrs. Beaty wondering what she should do next.

But despite Charles' embarrassing protestations at 'what could be more important than this,' Lady Sarah had arisen from her seat and had started gliding towards the library.

As she went past Mrs Beaty, she said to her, "This way my dear." Some of the guests followed. Others were left somewhat bewildered as to what they should do next.

As she got close to the wall Mrs Beaty stopped and looked around at those following. For the second time that day she caught Spen's eye and with the slightest of eye widening and a barely perceptible nod she bade him to come and join them. As he moved forwards the other large door from the entrance hall opened and John and Andrew were shown into the room. They were soaking wet. But Spen had no time to greet them properly but did have time to rather rudely shout to Clarke across the room and ask him to look after their needs please.

At the door to the library Spen and Mr. Bateman fought over who should hold open the door for whom and hence be last one into the room. But Bateman had spent a lifetime being the last one in and it was a habit, nay a duty, which he wasn't going to break now that the Laird had died. Even so he did have to playfully, though rather forcefully push Spen in the small of his back to get him through first. Spen couldn't resist a smile at his own trifling with this grand old gentleman.

The ladies were all seated around the central table, Charles was slumped in a chair which he'd noisily dragged across from the corner. Spen and Mr, Bateman stood together side by side. Other gentlemen aged between forty and eighty also stood around. Before Mrs. Beaty even had chance to clear her throat Charles noisily asked, "What the hell is he doing here?" He was pointing to Mr. Bateman. "Sir, the lady asked that I should..." but Charles cut Mr. Bateman off with more rudeness, "Not you. Him," he said, pointing to Bateman once more. Spen Stepped forward from behind Mr. Bateman and turned to the crowd with, "I think he's referring to me."

"Too bladdy true I'm referring to you..."

But then it was Mrs. Beaty's turn to butt in. Not noisily or aggressively, she simply said, "Because I asked him to attend Mister Eames."

"It's sir, I think you'll find, not just Mister Eames to you, and anyway, who the hell *are* you. You're only a woman." He truly was becoming obnoxious. One or two of the other elderly gentlemen tutted. Spen wondered if the time for his parting shot of a punch on Charles' nose might be drawing very near. Mrs. Beaty, must have been ruffled, but she didn't show it. She simply took control again and everyone gladly gave her their full attention.

"Yes, sir, thank you for pointing that out. Despite being only a woman, I'm here representing the Edinburgh Solicitors firm of C. Brader and Sons. Firstly, may I offer you all my sincerest condolences. I met Sir William on a number of occasions and always found him to be a true gentleman. Always polite, always gracious..." but again, there was a rude interruption from the chair.

"Yes, we all know he was a good egg, get on with it." One or two of those present secretly rolled their eyes at Charles the chump. They all waited for her to continue

"...Unfortunately not all men are even gentlemen, let alone true gentlemen." This brought a little supressed laughter as it was obvious that she was openly making fun of Charles. But he knew he could do little about it as he was desperate to hear the announcement that meant he took over the estate. "So, to the reading."

"Finally," groaned Charles.

She took hold of a long slender envelope previously unnoticed by everyone on the table in front of her and deftly pulled open the flap. She reached in and pulled out the will. After carefully unfolding it and opening it to the first page she cleared her throat once more. Charles jumped to his feet and blurted, "Oh, for heaven's sake give me it here."

"How rude," said one old gentleman standing to. Bateman and Spen both moved forward to cut off Charles before he could reach the solicitor.

But everyone was made to jump when Lady Sarah yelled, "Sit down this minute Charles, and don't say another word. Kindly remember where you are and what this is all about!" And then in a much more reserved tone, "I do beg your pardon Miss Beaty, please continue."

Mrs Beaty began again, "This is the last will and testament of Lord William Spencely Stannet-Forbes." Spen never knew that Sir William had a middle name of Spencely. What a coincidence he thought. "I, being of sound mind do hereby bequeath, for perpetuity, to my dear friend, wise counsellor, confidante, mentor and loyal servant Mister

Harris Algernon Bateman the sum of one thousand pounds…" There was a gasp, "What!" exclaimed Charles, but no-one moved their gaze from Mrs. Beatty. "…per year. This sum is not negotiable and if ever the turnover and profits of the estate be insufficient to afford this expense then land or property is to be sold to provide it. This for each year of the whole of his life and the life of his wife, should ever any poor woman be lucky enough to wear his ring, heaven help her." Mrs. Beaty herself joined all the others in the room (bar one) as she also couldn't resist a smile at this. There was a giddy round of laughter, and a few looks at Mr. Bateman. Spen simply put his hand to Mr. Bateman's shoulder and gave it a gentle pat. The Laird was making everyone smile even after he'd gone. Well, nearly everyone.

"A thousand pounds! That's a king's ransom," shouted Charles.

But Lady Sarah again turned towards him, and this time simply said. "He's dead Charles, he can't hear you."

Mrs. Beaty continued, "and furthermore, lifelong rent-free accommodation in whichever cottage on the estate that he should desire."

There followed a lengthy description of hunting rifles bequeathed to friends which they were delighted to receive. Long case clocks and small monetary gifts to members of the household, and some distant relatives etc. Trinkets to friends, first editions from the library to be given to societies and universities. Spen thought that he had obviously been invited along to receive something which Sir William had imagined he'd be pleased to receive. He was touched that Sir William had thought of him in such a way, He was excited to see what it would be.

Mrs Beaty took a sip from a glass of water, and said, "and now for the estate and the family." Everyone leant in a little to catch every utterance of this, the main topic. Oh dear, thought Spen, he got nothing, that was a little disappointing. "The estate land, properties, businesses, all my shares, options and interests in other companies, I leave…" She paused slightly as if waiting for a roll of drums. "…to my only son..." a much bigger gasp of breath went around the room. The Laird had a son? Who knew? Spen looked at Lady Sarah, who seemed unmoved, she obviously knew. Spen turned to face Mr. Bateman, but he was still stoically looking to his front and waiting on Mrs. Beaty's next words. He couldn't really tell if Bateman knew that the Laird had a son. Charles was on his feet with his head in his hands.

Moira Beaty simply added, "Mister Spencely Robinson," then looked straight at him. Everyone else in the room looked at him too. All except Charles that is, he simply shrieked "What! My worst nightmare," and he slumped back into his chair. He then turned to the diminutive solicitor and demanded, "Then why am I here for God's sake?" Her answer was a masterpiece of eloquent revenge, "Yes Mister Eames, indeed, why are you here? All these good people were *invited* to join me. I know, I invited them."

"No, no, no, this cannot be" he appealed. Then his head once more was cupped in his hands.

But Mrs Beaty was only too delighted to continue. "But with great privilege, goes great responsibility, and so I also bequeath and encumber you to take on the responsibility of managing the estate and running it in such a way that will support my dear heart Sarah and our three gifts from heaven, Mary, Catherine and Emily..." Spen's mouth had fallen open and he felt a sudden need to sit down as his legs had begun to weaken. He suddenly had a head full of broken biscuits again. Yes. His mother would be safe in her cottage. Mr. Bateman wouldn't have to leave. But, and it was indeed the biggest 'but' that ever was. Of course, that was why Sir William refused Spen permission to marry Lady Emily. Because they were half sister and brother. Oh, it all fell into place. Not malice, or class difference at all. So simple when he knew why. Obvious. But this meant they could always walk the fields and be together, every day. But they could never marry, never have a family of their own. The broken biscuits crumbled a little more.

Spen suddenly realised that everyone in the room was clapping, and they were clapping their congratulations at him. The small crowd were facing him, and everyone was smiling. Mr. Bateman stopped clapping and put an arm to Spen's back, giving it a gentle pat of congratulations. Spen leant sideways a little towards him and whispered, "Please don't leave."

The four ladies had risen from their seats and were moving across to him. He wondered how they had taken the news. He still didn't really know how he'd taken the news himself. Emily was first to him but instead of going for any politeness she grabbed him bodily and said nothing. She squeezed him in a bear hug and held onto him for a long time. He looked over her shoulder at Lady Sarah, he doubted that she would be giving him a bear hug too, well, not anytime soon as Lady Emily was still holding onto him. But when Em finally let him go, Lady Sarah did indeed give him an embrace, gently, briefly, but an embrace of genuine relief, acceptance, friendship and sincerity. Spen realised that Lady Sarah's emotions must also feel like they were being poshed repeatedly in a dolly tub, He knew he wasn't her son, and she suddenly didn't have a bloodline.

Catherine was next. He held out his hand for her to shake, and she pushed straight past it and went in for the full bear hug again. Most undignified. She even went one extra over Emily and kissed him on the cheek at least seven times in quick succession, finishing with "Hello Brother, can I invite Lottie to stay for the weekend?"
Spen leant away from her, looked her straight in the eye and told her, "That's entirely up to you dear sister, for me she can stay as long as she likes." Catherine lunged at him again. She didn't dare speak incase she broke into sobs of joy. Spen got the impression she was rather grateful.

Lady Mary was next to congratulate him. A simple handshake, but a warm smile and a polite 'congratulations.' Spen realised that her emotions must be everywhere too; she was no longer going to be the lady of the estate. But then she couldn't show her true feelings as her husband was standing there in the same room, watching them. It was clear to everyone where Charles' emotions lay; disappointment, anger and frustration couldn't begin to cover it.

As some of the old gentlemen moved forward towards him, Spen turned to look at Charles. He was still there, hissing venom. "Ha, hail the new Laird, Mister Spencely Bladdy Robinson. But aren't we all forgetting something?" he shouted. One or two looked to Mrs. Beaty, but she simply waved at him to continue, as she knew she had covered everything. The onlookers silently turned to him. "It means that Mister Bladdy Robinson here and the lovely Lady Emily are now blood relatives and hence cannot be married. Ha!" He finished his sentence with a sneering laugh and another gulp of whisky as what he saw to be a fitting though final verbal knife in the ribs. It was clear that some of those in the room weren't even aware of the possibility of Spen and Lady Emily being married. Unfortunately, this fact had also not sunk home to Emily at that point and she let out a small whimper. Again, she moved to Spen and gave him a hug. Another murmur went around the room, before Lady Sarah took another turn to speak.

"Once again Charles, your vindictive nastiness even surpasses your lack of knowledge." Everyone had a blank expression wondering what Lady Sarah was referring to. Catherine asked "Mother, please explain yourself." So, Lady Sarah slowly, and deliberately, turned to face Emily. She moved forwards and took both of her hands in both of hers. "I hoped never to have to tell you this Emily, indeed I hoped never to have to tell anyone."

"Tell me what mother, that I'm not your daughter?"

"You *are* my daughter dear, yes. It's just that Sir William is not your true father." Poor Emily looked for a moment like she had been mortally wounded. The gathering was holding their collective breath. Everyone was in a stunned silence. "Then who is?" she asked from teary eyes. "Who is my father mother?"

"That's unimportant, but what it means is that you can marry young

Spencely here, heaven help him!" blurted Catherine. The smile suddenly returned to Emily's face. She turned swiftly round to face Spen again. But he was gone somehow. She looked down and found him on one knee looking up at her. He reached for her hand, took it from Lady Sarah's with a quiet, "May I borrow that a moment please Lady Sarah?" he asked, "Emily, my love, will you marry me please?" She bobbed down so the two of them were eye to eye. She smiled broadly and slowly began to nod. She reached for his other hand and raised them both urging him back onto his feet. "Spencely Robinson, I've waited for this moment all my life. And now it's here, I just want it to last. Just a little longer." But lady Catherine was almost hopping with excitement. "You might want it to last but we can't wait a second more! Will you Marry him Emily?" Emily turned from Catherine to look back into Spen's eyes. "Yes, it's yes, Oh absolutely yes. I can't wait a moment longer to be your wife forever." They hugged and another spontaneous round of applause broke out. Almost un-noticed a door slammed in the background.

END

Epilogue

Spencely and Emily were married the following Spring.

Spen managed to persuade Mr. Bateman to stay on and manage the household; he didn't take much persuading as that had always been his life's ambition. Bateman made sure Sir William's family were well looked after and his staff well treated. He chose not to move into an estate cottage as there wasn't one available at the time, so he remained in his quarter's downstairs in the Big House. He did however take half a day off per week to visit his sister in Falkirk.

Charles Richardson Eames left the estate and Lady Mary's life the day after that reading of the Will. Oddly, though it came as no surprise to Lady Mary, her chambermaid Elizabeth McFael, also disappeared on the same day as Charles. Lady Mary, and indeed most of the staff suspected Charles had been 'carrying on' in the shadows with another woman, she only shared her suspicions regarding Miss McFael and Charles after they had left; she thought they were having an affair even before she and him were married. Elizabeth had been the only one to volunteer to go and work at The Residence. At the time everyone thought that she'd wanted to go there out of duty to Lady Mary. No, it was to be near Charles, it seems. But only weeks after she'd left, a footman mentioned that she was back living with her aging parents in Stenhousemuir.

Catherine began her best years. Lottie all but moved in with her into the big house and they rode and read and walked and laughed together every day. Catherine's hatred for Charles became even deeper when Lottie revealed to her the time when Charles physically attacked her threatening to show her what she was missing by not having a *real* man

256

to satisfy her. What Charles had somehow unfortunately forgotten, was that Lottie was from Glasgow. It took him a week to recover. Charles never attacked her a second time.

Mary decided not to seek out a second attempt at marriage as the first one had ended so disastrously. She became Lady Sarah's companion, and they read together and hosted ladies meetings encouraging education, as well as needlework and handicrafts generally. Within a year the ornamental garden had taken on an altogether more exotic character.

Spen became the sixth Earl of Callander, but he never shared the title with his friends, though he believed John and Andrew must have worked it out for themselves. Emily moved to Edinburgh to be with her new husband and the two bought a simple town house in which to live until Spen could qualify as a doctor. It also gave them time to decide what they were going to do with the Stannet-Forbes Estate. Spen employed C Brader's grand-daughter Mrs Moira Beaty to find Mr Matthew Carter. Spen went to visit him and asked him to return to the estate and take up managing it again. Lady Mary graciously moved out of The Residence and back into her old room in the Big House to make room for him. Matthew Carter had come home. The two never boxed on the lawn together again. Mr. Carter considered himself too old, he was happy to settle for listening with intrigue to Spen's stories of the time when he rescued a waif from some ruffians, or fought his way out of Perkin's yard using the skills Carter had taught him. I suppose both Mr. Carter and Mr. Bateman liked to think of themselves as having had some positive fatherly influence on Spen's formative years.

Spen asked Mrs. Beaty to try and find Mr. Smith, or Robinson, but there were too many other pseudonyms and 'nom-de plumes' for him to be tracked down successfully.

Neither Spen nor Bateman were prosecuted for the two men shot when the business of the body trade was successfully foiled. The police were happy to take the credit for the detection and wrote off the injuries as collateral damage in their investigation. Dissections became slightly more expensive for the Edinburgh students as bodies became harder to source.

All seven ladies of the 'Edinburgh Seven' eventually qualified as doctors, though not without a lot of un-necessary chauvinism and angst put in their path. The world became a better place once they had succeeded.

Needless to say, Spen gladly spent a sizeable sum on renovating the cottages for the estate workers but perhaps he spent a little more on Dorothy's than the others. She didn't want to move out and into something more befitting the new Laird's mother, especially once the draughts were sealed, the roof was fixed, and that new range was installed. She'd never had the need before to open a window in the middle of winter due to the warmth in the parlour.

Regarding Emily having a different father, it seems that after the stress of family life, with a demanding two-year-old (Mary) and another on the way (Catherine), Lady Sarah found that she was always tired, worn out even, nerves always frayed. Her husband Sir William was away a lot trying to improve and expand the estate businesses; after all, so many peoples' livelihoods depended on them. Things even got a little worse when the baby came along. No one cares to remember who the gentleman was who showed an interest in Sarah at that time. Some suspected the gardener Mr. Carter, but no-one spoke of it. Whoever he was, he became the father of the third child a couple of years later. However it happened, Sarah and Sir William's marriage certainly went through a rough patch. Perhaps her affair was why the Laird felt that he too was allowed to progress his affections for the talented and vivacious new Governess Dorothy Robinson. She came to the House every day, always smiling, always witty. They had a number of wonderful and passionate evenings together before they both were racked with guilt and ceased the affair. In this life there is no perfection to be had, and Lady Sarah and Sir William started to consider what they did have in each other rather than what they didn't. It was more than anyone had a right to expect. So, they re-committed themselves to each other and that's how they stayed, in sickness and in health, until death finally parted them.

As Dorothy had always suspected, it was The Laird himself who paid for Spencely's education through the Edinburgh Medical School. It was after all, the least he could do for his son.

Cast

Spencely Robinson (Spen) The only child of Dorothy. Lives with her in an estate cottage. Respectful, bright, hard working.

Dorothy Spen's mother, once Governess to Mary and Catherine but then she started a family of her own and moved out of the big house and into an estate cottage.

Lord William Stannet - Forbes 5th Earl of Callander. A scholar and businessman. Owns the estate which has farms, woods and a limestone quarry. Owns shares in coal mines. Married to Lady Sarah.

Lady Sarah, Lady of the House, mother to three girls. A dutiful wife. A little aloof, distant, interested in society and its trappings.

Lady Mary Eldest of Sir William's three daughters, slowly turning into their mother.

Lady Catherine A happy child, but a troubled adolescent. Happier once she had found herself.

Lady Emily Happy, friendly. Trusting, a tad plump. Somewhat innocent.

Harris Algernon Bateman Sir William's loyal Butler. Stoic though a little dour.

Charles Richardson-Eames Up from Surrey. A cheat, poor but well presented. Well bred. Oxford educated but failed his classics degree. Dis-owned by his family. Not much known about his past.

Lottie Catherine's very dear lady friend. Glaswegian. Full of character. Good for Catherine.

John McFarlane, Spen's roommate is agnostic and up for anything. Shetlander, a skilled practical man.

Andrew Lewis, Spen's other roommate. Christian to the core. Cautious, Caring, Charitable. A thinker.

Clarke Friendly footman. Takes a shine to Spen.

Matthew Carter Estate manager to Sir William Forbes. Diligent, Bright. A bachelor.

Miss Campbell, Spen's school teacher. Overstretched, not really in the right job.

Miss Fowler Present governess to the Laird's three daughters.

Mags A schoolgirl friend of Spen. Stood to protect Spen from Eric in a fight.

Eric School bully

Barnes Top dog at the sawmill.

Harry The Lancastrian who stayed at the sawmill to help run the boiler and engine.

Mrs. Moffatt Spen's Edinburgh landlady.

Mr. Perkins, The yard owner in Falkirk who is illicitly receiving wood from the estate.

Elizabeth McFael Lady Mary's chambermaid.

Moira Beaty of Messrs C. Brader and Sons on Rutland Court. The real worker at the Law firm. Slim, trim, professional, bright, a cool cucumber.

Little Laura The young lassie in the secret cabin with Emily. She ran off after Spen released them.

Dr Arthur Cameron A professor and surgeon. Worldly wise and friendly.

Yvonne Cameron Professor's Cameron's beautiful French wife. A trained nurse.

Smithy Groom for the horses drawing the barges. Lives by the canal. Known sometimes as 'Robbo'

McLoughlin An angler, friend of Smithy. See's everything taking place on the canal.

Mary-Ann Probably a prostitute. Always looking to make a shilling.

Betsey Young bonny woman who makes a living any way she can, Is seeking a husband of standing.

Professor Davies A bachelor. Professor of Anatomy. Missed his vocation; should have been on the stage.

Voithos Rotuida. The Assistant. Appears to aid and serve the professors in the dissection classes but all the time is orchestrating an illegal operation making himself lots of money. (Voithos is Greek for *Assistant*. Rotuida, spelt backwards Adiutor is Latin for *Assistant*). The man was actually born in Wigan to Doris and Roy Entwistle

ABOUT THE AUTHOR

I am happily married and have been for longer than Yvonne cares to remember. We have two beautiful daughters, both grown, flown and married. I am the happiest and most blessed amongst men: Any that were, are, or will be.

I have been an industrial draughtsman for all of my working life. Though it had its moments I generally did it only as a means of putting bread on my family's table. Hence I sought my fulfilment in my personal life; I bought a yacht, learned to fly, made films, taught myself animation, rode my bike to Budapest, I even did wedding photography for a while. Though I'd always enjoyed writing, I'd never had a subject for a book before. Then something rather life changing happened; in June 2015 I had a heart attack on a coast-to-coast bike ride. I underwent triple bypass surgery and overnight gained a fascination with Medicine. What were the surgical techniques used on me, the anaesthetics, the pain relief medication, the aseptic and antiseptic treatments? They all must have been discovered by someone and developed somewhere. Medical history is a fascinating subject and came to a sharp focus back in the late nineteenth century, an ideal time in which to set great stories.

So writing is my next interest, and I hope it will remain so for many years to come.

Don Stark

Printed in Great Britain
by Amazon